After Hours

BOARDROOM TEMPTATION

ABBY GREEN

CAT SCHIELD

CHRISTY McKELLEN

MILLS & BOON

AFTER HOURS: BOARDROOM TEMPTATION © 2021 by Harlequin Books S.A.

RUTHLESS GREEK BOSS, SECRETARY MISTRESS
© 2009 by Abby Green
Australian Copyright 2009
New Zealand Copyright 2009
First Published 2009
Fifth Australian Paperback Edition 2021
ISBN 978 1 867 23980 2

A MERGER BY MARRIAGE
© 2014 by Catherine Schield
Australian Copyright 2014
New Zealand Copyright 2014
First Published 2014
Third Australian Paperback Edition 2021
ISBN 978 1 867 23980 2

UNLOCKING HER BOSS'S HEART
© 2016 by Christy McKellen
Australian Copyright 2016
New Zealand Copyright 2016
First Published 2016
Second Australian Paperback Edition 2021
ISBN 978 1 867 23980 2

Published by
Mills & Boon
An imprint of Harlequin Enterprises (Australia) Pty Limited (ABN 47 001 180 918), a subsidiary of HarperCollins Publishers Australia Pty Limited (ABN 36 009 913 517)
Level 13, 201 Elizabeth Street
SYDNEY NSW 2000
AUSTRALIA

MIX
Paper from responsible sources
FSC www.fsc.org FSC® C001695

Printed and bound in Australia by McPherson's Printing Group

CONTENTS

Ruthless Greek Boss, Secretary Mistress

Abby Green

Abby Green got hooked on Mills & Boon® romances while still in her teens, when she stumbled across one belonging to her grandmother in the west of Ireland. After many years of reading them voraciously, she sat down one day and gave it a go herself. Happily, after a few failed attempts, Mills & Boon bought her first manuscript.

Abby works freelance in the film and TV industry, but thankfully the four a.m. starts and the stresses of dealing with recalcitrant actors are becoming more and more infrequent, leaving her more time to write!

She loves to hear from readers, and you can contact her through her website at www.abby-green.com. She lives and works in Dublin.

CHAPTER ONE

'YOU'RE THE COLDEST man I ever met. If you have a heart it's made of stone. You're cruel and contemptible. I *hate* you.' The woman's strident voice quivered dangerously on the last word and came through the heavy oak door with effortless ease.

There was silence, and then the ominously low rumble of a man's voice. Short, sharp, succinct. Lucy could imagine only too well the glacial look that was most likely accompanying those indistinct words. She sighed as she heard the woman splutter indignantly, but then she was off again, her voice rising so high now that Lucy feared for the crystal decanter on the drinks board nearby. While Lucy was new to these scenes first-hand, she had to reflect that the rumours she'd heard over the past two years hadn't been a myth after all. The voice was drawing her attention back to the present moment.

'Don't think that you can seduce your way back into my bed after treating me like this!'

Lucy had just enough time for a cynical smile as she reflected that if her new boss was to so much as arch an eyebrow this woman would undoubtedly be back in his bed in a heartbeat before the door was suddenly flung open. She looked studiously at her computer screen, trying to sink down in her seat and be as unobtrusive as possible.

Being unobtrusive was her trademark: it was what had got her this coveted job, along with her impeccable credentials and references. There was a lull, a pseudo-calm in the middle of the storm. Lucy didn't look up, but could visualise the woman standing dramatically on the threshold of the palatial office. Tall, sleek and blonde. Stunningly beautiful, from the top of her shiny head to the tip of her expensively manicured toes, evident through the peepholes of a pair of sky-high heels. She was reputedly one of the most alluring women in the world, but apparently hadn't managed to hold his attention for longer than a few weeks.

'Needless to say you won't be hearing from me again.'

The door slammed shut with such violence that Lucy winced. He wouldn't appreciate that. Even though Lucy had only been working for him for two months she already knew that he hated scenes. A cloud of noxious perfume lingered in the wake of the tall woman's exit. She hadn't even glanced Lucy's way.

Lucy breathed a sigh of relief and then heard a loud thump, as if a fist was connecting with a hard surface. She counted to ten, and on the count of ten the door opened. She looked up and willed any emotion or reaction from her face. Her boss stood there, filling the frame easily. Veritable sparks of energy crackled from his body.

Aristotle Levakis, CEO of Levakis Enterprises which encompassed all aspects of a dizzyingly successful global imports and exports business.

Tall, broad-shouldered, lean hipped. Every hard-muscled, dark olive-skinned inch of him adding up to a—currently bristling—Greek alpha male in his potent and virile prime.

His distinctive light green eyes skewered Lucy to the spot, almost as if the last ten minutes had been *her* fault. Instantly she felt breathless; her heart hammered. She hated that she was aware of him. But the best part of two years spent viewing him from a distance, along with every other ogling female in his thousand-employee-strong company, had done little to help diminish the devastating impact of working in such close proximity to him. A memory surfaced and familiar heat flooded her. If only she *had* been kept at a safe distance he might not be having this effect on her now—but there had been that moment in a lift, almost a year ago… Lucy ruthlessly crushed that memory stone-dead. Now was *not* the time.

But, much to her chagrin and dismay, she couldn't halt her reaction. It was something about the way he'd obviously just raked a hand through his unruly ink-black hair, leaving it even more dishevelled, and the way his jaw was so defined and hard it looked as if it was hewn from granite. His cheekbones and that full lower lip softened the hard edges, giving him the look of a master of sensuality—which by all accounts he was. Yet dark brows drawn together over those deep-set, amazing eyes took away any lingering pretty edges.

'Lucy,' he rapped out, distaste for the recent dramatics etched all over his handsome face. 'Get in here. *Now.*'

Lucy blinked and landed back to earth with a bump. What was she doing? Sitting here mentally listing her boss's attributes as if he wasn't standing there looking at her as if he wanted to throttle someone. Caught short, which she never was, she scrambled up somewhat inelegantly from her chair and walked towards him, but then, to add insult to injury, she dropped her pad and pen from suddenly nerveless fingers. She bent down to pick them up, cursing herself in her head, *and* cursing the fact that her skirt was too tight when it resisted her movement. She'd put it in the wrong wash and it had shrunk about two sizes; with no time to shop for a replacement it had had to do, but now she was terrified it might split at the seams. The thought of that made her go hot all over.

If Aristotle Levakis so much as guessed for a second that he had any effect on her she'd be out on her ear and replaced so fast her head would be spinning. She didn't have to remind herself that was exactly what had happened to his last two unfortunate assistants.

Speed had been of the essence as his in-house head-hunters had scrambled to find the next best person. Lucy had since discovered that Levakis Enterprises was involved in a top secret series of merger meetings, and the luxury of extending the search to outside the company hadn't been an option.

As luck would have had it, Lucy's boss, Levakis' senior legal counsel, had retired the very day of the last unfortunate PA's demise. Lucy had been vetted and promoted within twenty-four hours to the most terrifying and yet exciting position of her career so far: Levakis' personal secretary, heading up a team of five junior administrative assistants, not to mention staff in Athens and New York.

When she straightened up, taking care to breathe in, all this raced through her brain and she felt thoroughly flustered. She pushed her glasses higher on her nose and felt her cheeks grow even hotter. Aristotle moved back to let her precede him into his office, and she caught the look of exasperation that crossed his face as he articulated her own thoughts out loud with narrowed eyes,

'What is wrong with you today?'

She burned inside with humiliation at her lack of control. She was no better than the swooning legions of girls who gathered in the kitchens on each floor of this impressive London headquarters to eulogise over his mythical sexual prowess and inestimable wealth.

'Nothing,' Lucy muttered, and called on every bit of training she had to regain her composure. When she heard him shut his door behind them and follow her in she closed her eyes for a split second and took deep breaths. She chastised herself roundly. This job was so important; the sharp increase in wages meant that she was finally able to take care of her mother properly.

She couldn't jeopardise all that now by turning into a bumbling, stumbling, mooning idiot—no matter how gorgeous her boss happened to be. A voice mocked her inwardly. It wasn't as if she even *wanted* a man like him to notice her. She *had to* control these wayward thoughts. They disturbed her more than she cared to admit, making her think of long-buried memories of her childhood.

It should be easy enough to do after witnessing that last little scene. Evidently Aristotle Levakis went for quivering, highly strung thoroughbreds, all lean and sleek with good bloodlines. Lucy Proctor was more along the lines of a…a placid cart horse, and her bloodline was considerably less blue than he was used to. More of a murky brown.

She watched as Levakis came back around the other side of his desk and gestured impatiently for her to sit down and take notes, not even glancing her way. Lucy willed her heartbeat to slow down and sat, legs tucked under the chair demurely, pen poised over a blank sheet of paper, and prayed that her skirt wouldn't split open.

Aristotle Levakis stood behind his desk, hands deep in the pockets of his trousers, and looked at the demurely bent head of his new assistant. It was most irritating to be faced with the fact that Augustine Archer had forced him to reject her by demanding more of a commitment than he was prepared to give right now. To any woman.

His assistant shifted in her seat minutely, making Ari's eyes narrow on her. That ripple of awareness ran through him *again*. It was faint, elusive, yet irritatingly insistent, and had been ever since she'd walked into his office two months before in a primly structured suit.

An uncomfortable suspicion made him tense inwardly; was it this *awareness* that had had an effect on the lessening and ultimate annihilation of his desire for Augustine Archer? Her shrieked words still vibrated in the air, but at that moment Aristotle would be hard pushed to bring her image to mind. Immediately as he realised the import of what he was thinking he rejected the notion as utterly absurd.

Lucy Proctor, his relatively new assistant, was as far removed from his habitual choice of lover as could be humanly possible. He couldn't believe he was even giving a second of his time to this subject, or putting those two words *Lucy* and *lover* in the same sentence, but almost against his will his eyes flicked down from shiny, albeit non-descript dark brown hair to where her knees were tight together, legs tucked under the chair.

His almost contemptuous regard stopped for a moment to take in what could only be described as wantonly voluptuous thighs encased far too snugly in the confines of a pencil skirt. Irritation prickled stronger. He would have to have a word with the head of Human Resources and tell her to pass on a discreet message about the code of dress he expected from his assistant. And yet his expert eye hadn't missed the surprisingly small waist, cinched in by a belt. That realisation stung him.

He tried to reassert his self-control. She was big…all over… His eyes flicked back up to the line of more than generous breasts under her silk shirt. And yet, prompted a little rogue voice, she looked as firm as a succulent peach. And her face… that was something he realised now he hadn't really given much time to study, seeing her only as someone employed to do his bidding, but now, much to his chagrin, his gaze wanted to stop and linger. Look properly. Take in the surprisingly graceful curve of a well-defined cheekbone. Aristotle's blood was starting to heat up; with a kind of desperation he noted that she wore glasses, as if that might have the effect of a cold douche on his suddenly raging hormones.

It didn't. He battled with his libido but it seemed determined to confound him, and he wondered what on earth was precipitating this reaction when Lucy had worked for his company for two years already. He'd only met her intermittently in that time, as she'd worked for his legal counsel, and she certainly hadn't had any discernible effect on him then. But now she was his assistant, and a welcome relief after dealing with a succession of simpering, moon-eyed idiots.

With that in mind, he called on all his powers of logic to explain the bizarre anomaly of his physical reaction, and finally felt some equanimity return: he was a red-blooded male, he was bound to respond arbitrarily to some women, even only passably attractive ones.

Except this wasn't the first time: he uncomfortably recalled one morning when he'd stepped into the staff elevator, because his own private one had been closed for repairs. Someone had run to stop the doors closing and launched themselves into the lift with such force that they'd careened into him. He'd felt every contour and curve of a very lush female body plastered against his for a second. It had been Lucy.

The memory seared him now. She'd been as curvaceous as something brought to life from a painting by Rubens, and the minute she'd walked into his office to interview for this job he'd remembered that moment in annoyingly vivid detail. Right now all he could think about was how she'd felt pressed against him. Especially when compared to the more sparingly built Augustine Archers of this world.

Lucy Proctor had shown no hint of remembering the moment in the lift, though, and Aristotle certainly wasn't going to admit to such a chink in his own legendary control. But when she sat in front of him now, the vision of her thighs straining against that too-tight skirt on the periphery of his vision, he could feel his body responding to her with a strength that disturbed him—a strength almost beyond his control…

The object of his uncharacteristic pondering looked up then quizzically, clearly wondering why he wasn't saying anything. Irrational rage rushed through him. He wasn't used to being rendered speechless like this. But in that moment, as if to compound every other revelation, he noticed she had the most unusually coloured eyes: a dark slaty grey that was almost blue, framed with the longest blackest lashes. Her mouth opened, as if to speak, and entirely against his will his eyes moved down. He'd not noticed until now that she had a sizeable gap between her front teeth. It was all at once innocent and unbelievably erotic.

Shocking and out of nowhere Aristotle had a sudden vision of those lips wrapped around a part of his anatomy, those almond-shaped eyes looking up into his as she— Lust exploded into his brain and turned everything red.

Lucy looked up at her boss and her mouth went dry. Her pulse, which had finally started slowing down, picked up pace again and she could feel herself grow hot. He was looking at her with such intensity that for a moment she thought— Instantly she shut down those rogue thoughts, and as if she'd imagined it the lines in his face tightened. He was positively glowering at her. Inwardly she quivered, outwardly she clung onto her poise and acknowledged that it was no wonder his adversaries hadn't ever got the better of him.

'Sir?' she said, thankful that her voice sounded cool and calm, unruffled.

He kept glowering at her for another long moment, and Lucy felt inexplicably as if some sort of battle of wills she was unaware of was going on.

Eventually he bit out, 'I think you can start calling me Aristotle.'

His voice sounded rough. She guessed it must be the remnants of his anger at the recent scene, but even so Lucy's belly quivered. She knew some close colleagues called him Aristotle, and she'd heard the beautiful blonde requesting breathily to speak to *'Ari'* when she'd phoned before the dramatics this morning, but the thought of addressing this man by his first name was having a seismic effect on her whole body.

'Very well,' she finally managed to get out. But couldn't bring herself to actually say it.

Aristotle sat down as if he hadn't just invited her to call him something far more intimate than *Sir*, or *Mr Levakis*, and proceeded to dictate with such lightning speed that it took all of Lucy's wits and concentration to keep up. In truth she was glad of the distraction, but by the time he was done her head was ringing.

He dismissed her with a brusque flick of his hand, his head already buried in some paperwork, and Lucy stood up. She was at the door when she heard a curt, 'Oh, and see to it, please, that Augustine Archer is sent something…'

Lucy turned around, and the look of dark cynicism she saw on Levakis' face made her draw in a breath.

'…*suitable*.'

Lucy looked at him, nonplussed for a moment. Her previous boss had never made such a request. Did he mean…?

As if he could read her mind, Aristotle said ascerbically, 'That's exactly what I mean. I don't care who you call, just make sure it's expensive, anything but a ring, and send it over with a note. I'll e-mail you the address.'

Lucy's hand was clutching the door, and she didn't know why this feeling of something like disappointment was curling through her. Anyone with half a brain cell would have been able to tell her this was exactly how a man like him operated. And wasn't it confirmation of another rumour about him? How well he compensated his lovers? But still…he wasn't even taking the time to compose a note himself.

She forced herself to sound non-committal. 'How would you like the note to read?'

He shrugged one broad shoulder and smiled sardonically, cruelly. 'Make it up. What kind of platitude would *you* like to hear from a man who has just dumped you?' His mouth twisted even more. 'I think it's safe to say that someone like Ms Archer will throw away the card and move straight to the main prize, so I wouldn't worry about it too much. Just keep it as impersonal as possible.'

Shock at his cold words impacted Lucy right in her belly. Her face must have given something away, because Aristotle lounged back in his chair and looked at her with a dangerous gleam in those fascinating green eyes.

'You don't approve of my methods?'

Lucy could feel a tide of heat climb up from her chest. She alternately shook and nodded her head, and some garbled words came out. 'Not at all…' She realised what she'd said and groaned inwardly when she saw a flash of something dark cross his face. She could not let her own personal opinion of his behaviour jeopardise this job. Too much now depended on her wages.

She gestured clumsily. 'I mean, I have no problem doing as you suggest. Your methods…are your methods. It's not for me to judge.'

He sat up and raised a brow, and Lucy wondered dismally how on earth they had got onto this. She wanted to be back outside, with a wall and door between them, catching her breath and restoring her equilibrium, not discussing how best to let his mistress down.

But he said, 'So you admit there is something to judge, then?'

Lucy shook her head, drowning in heat now. 'No—look, I'm sorry, I'm not being very articulate. I'll do as you ask and make sure that the accompanying note is appropriate.' She added hurriedly, 'I can show it to you before I send it…?'

He shook his head and his face became impassive, hard. Lucy stood there for another moment, not sure what to do and then he bit out,

'That'll be all.'

Stung, and more than mortified, Lucy mumbled something incoherent and fled, shutting the door behind her. Amidst the embarrassment, anger surged—why was she surprised or, worse, disappointed? She'd seen this kind of behaviour from men all her life.

But still, what an *absolute*— She halted her racing thoughts as she sat behind her desk and fought to steady her breathing and hammering heart. The last five minutes was the closest she'd come to a personal discussion with her new boss. She should have just bowed her head and walked out. She cursed her expressive face. Her mother had always told her it would get her into trouble. And hadn't it just? Her inherent distaste for his coldly generous dismissive treatment of his ex-mistress hadn't been well hidden enough. But the truth was it had tapped into a deeply buried pain, a very familiar pain. She'd witnessed the other side of someone on the receiving end of that treatment. Over and over again.

Lucy shuddered inwardly when she woke her computer from sleep and struggled to concentrate on work. Aristotle's cynical view of how Ms Archer would receive his gift was no doubt spot-on; hadn't she witnessed her own mother reduced to that level after years of similar treatment? Although Augustine Archer didn't strike her as the kind of woman who had to survive on hand-outs. No, this was a different league. Lucy's soft mouth tightened as bile rose from her belly. That kind of so-called *main prize* would have been just the kind of thing her mother would have used to pay for Lucy's school uniform for another year—the sort of thing that had financed their lives.

Lucy forced her anger down. She had to think of her boss purely in professional terms. What he did or how he acted personally was none of her business. She didn't have to like him; she just had to work for him.

Thank goodness she'd forged a different path. She would never be beholden to any man or, worse, held in his sexual or financial thrall. She'd worked too hard and her mother had sacrificed too much to make sure she avoided exactly that scenario. Just as her computer screen came back to life and she saw her bespectacled face momentarily reflected on the dark surface she felt unmitigated relief that she need never fear the kind of attention her mother and women like Augustine Archer courted. She was safe from all of that.

Aristotle watched the closed door for an inordinate amount of time. Heat still coursed through his body—heat that confounded him and every effort he made to try and dampen it. All he could see in his mind's eye was the sway of that well-rounded bottom as she'd stopped by the door, and how he'd blurted out the first thing that had come into his head, as if he'd had to stop her, not let her leave.

He flung himself back in his seat and raked a hand through unruly hair, unusually diverted from work. He cursed the fact again that he'd had to let Augustine go at this point in negotiations. He briefly considered wooing her back, but his fists clenched in rejection of that idea. He would never debase himself by grovelling to a woman—not for *anything.*

He considered the request he'd just made of Lucy; he'd always made the call to a jewellers himself before, and would instruct them to compose a suitably impersonal note. Usually it wasn't even a note—just his name. A clear indication that whatever he and the particular woman had shared was over and she shouldn't come calling again. And invariably they knew not to. Few were as impertinent as Augustine Archer, confronting him directly. His mouth twisted in recognition of the fact that as he got older and remained single he represented some kind of irresistible challenge to those women.

He diverted his thoughts from an area he didn't want to investigate: that of having to contemplate giving up his freedom, which he knew would be inevitable at some stage. The future was unavoidable. He would have to find a suitable wife and produce an heir, purely to protect all that he was now putting in place from the greedy clutches of others.

The prospect evoked no more emotion in him than mild uninterest and irritation. He'd long ago learnt the lesson of what marriage really meant—at the age of five, when his father had introduced Helen Savakis as his new stepmother and she'd quickly shown him the cold hatred she had for a son who wasn't her own. Whatever dim and distant memories Ari might have had of his mother, who'd died when he was four, and a halcyon time that might never have existed except in some childish fanciful memory bank, had long been quashed and buried.

The fact that those nebulous memories rose to haunt him in dreams so vivid that he sometimes woke in tears was a shameful weakness he'd always been determined to ignore. It was one reason he'd never spent a full night with a woman.

As if drawn by a magnet his thoughts again went to his assistant, who was fast assuming a place in his imagination that he did not welcome. Why had he felt goaded into saying all he just had? And then been surprised by the blatant look of distaste on her face—annoyed by it? And he had not left it at that but engaged her in a dialogue about it. As if he even cared what her opinion of him was! He was aware of a niggling desire that he'd wanted to see her somehow…rattled. Since she'd been working for him she'd always seemed to fade into the background, barely noticeable.

But he *was* noticing her and she *had* just reacted, her cheeks flushing prettily. He frowned at that. Since when had he started thinking of her as pretty? And since when had he been interested in *pretty*?

And, not only that, what on earth had compelled him to tell her to call him Aristotle when he'd always preferred his PAs to call him Mr Levakis? It was something in the way she'd looked up at him and said *sir*.

In a bid to restore some order to his life, which seemed to be morphing out of all recognition, he rang through to Lucy and gave her the name and number of the latest English socialite who had been chasing him, instructing her to set up a date for that evening. He ignored the way even her voice seemed to send a frisson of reaction straight to his groin. With that done he felt some semblance of calm wash over him. Life would return to normal. He would forget all about this bizarre obsession with his secretary's far too provocatively well-built body and concentrate on the merger.

* * *

The following morning, when Lucy was walking the short distance from her bus stop to work, she still burned with mortification. In her hand she carried a small overnight bag which held a change of clothes and some evening wear. She'd taken a call from the head of Human Resources the day before and been informed stoutly that she needed to think a little more thoroughly about the way she dressed, and that it might be a good idea to have a change of clothes in the office at all times to cover for emergencies. Like too-tight skirts, she thought churlishly. The fact that Levakis had gone over her head and asked someone to speak to her made her skin crawl with humiliation—not to mention the fact that he'd obviously noticed her bursting out of that skirt.

With getting her mother settled in her new home she simply hadn't had time since she'd started working for him to kit herself out with a new wardrobe, despite being given a generous allowance to do so. It had been full-on from day one.

Luckily last night had been late-night shopping, and Levakis had left relatively early for the date Lucy had set up for him. Her belly clenched at the thought of that. The woman she'd rung hadn't been in the slightest bit fazed that Aristotle himself hadn't bothered to call, and of course she'd been free at a moment's notice. A wave of disgust washed through Lucy and she pushed it down along with bitter memories. She didn't care what he did or who he did it with. A voice mocked her inwardly: who was *she* to judge anyway?

Just at that moment the heavens opened from a slate-grey sky and Lucy yelped as torrential rain poured down, comprehensively drenching her in seconds. *No*! She ran across the road towards the refuge of the huge gleaming Levakis building, her mind filled with the fact that they had an important meeting to attend in less than an hour on the other side of London.

Aristotle strode through the reception area, raking a hand through rain-wet hair, and mentally cursed the inclement English weather which had momentarily darkened the enormous glass atrium. He stepped into his own private lift—no possibility of a lush, curvaceous body colliding with his today—and stabbed at the button to whisk him all the way to the top of the building, irritated beyond belief to be thinking of that *again*. Was he actually hoping for it? he asked himself derisively.

His starkly handsome face was reflected back to him in the steel surface of the door, but he didn't see that as the lift zoomed skyward. No, what he saw and what he relived was the fact that last night he'd taken a beautiful *available* woman on a date and she had done nothing for him. His mouth twisted. It hadn't been for lack of trying on her part, or even on his, which had been a novel sensation.

In a bid not to be dictated to by his malfunctioning hormones, he'd escorted Arabella—*or had it been Mirabella*?—up to her apartment, but had realised with sickening inevitability that nothing would be happening. With her, anyway. He'd been rendered impotent from the waist down. She'd become petulant and increasingly desperate, seeing correctly that she hadn't managed to snare Aristotle's interest, and he'd had to extricate himself with more diplomacy than a head of state during peace negotiations.

So now, as he strode out of his lift and towards his main office, he was thoroughly disgruntled. Ignoring the assistants sitting meekly at their desks in the ante-room that preceded his and Lucy's offices, he opened the door and took a breath, preparing to fire a series of commands at the woman who had been the singular cause of his unsatisfying night.

But the office was empty.

He had the most curious sensation of his belly hollowing out before he heard movement coming from the door which led into the bathroom just off their offices. While he had a private bathroom too, this more communal bathroom had a shower and a dressing room, which Aristotle availed himself of whenever he was required to go straight to a function from work.

Closing the main door quietly behind him, without really

being aware of what he was doing, he walked silently into the office. He heard a muffled curse and then something drop.

Feeling like a voyeur, and not liking it, he halted by the door which lay slightly ajar. Through the crack he saw Lucy, and when his eyes registered what he was seeing his whole body locked, every muscle taut. Unable to move, all he could do was take in the sight with widening eyes. Lucy's wet hair hung in long dark tendrils over luminously pale shoulders. She was bending over to pull trousers up over long, surprisingly slender legs. Her legs led upwards to those shapely thighs, which curved out to a lushly rounded bottom encased in some kind of black lace and silk concoction.

She wriggled her bottom and her hips as she pulled the trousers up fully, and then twisted towards Aristotle to tie the fastening at the side. Heat engulfed him. His blood hummed and his heart picked up an unsteady beat. Facing him as she did, both hands to one side, her perfectly formed breasts were enticingly pushed together and towards him with unknowing and unbelievably erotic appeal. Her bra looked hardly adequate to contain the generous mounds of alabaster flesh—he wondered dimly if any of her clothes fitted properly. And who would have known that she'd have such exotic tastes in undergarments underneath that prim exterior? Arousal soared.

Another muffled curse came as an even longer tendril of dark hair swung over her shoulder and clung wetly to the slope of one unashamedly voluptuous breast. Aristotle's gaze moved up with supreme difficulty, and he saw that gap in her front teeth as she bit her lip, a hectic flush across her cheeks.

As if entranced by a siren song, he couldn't move. His gaze slid down again and took in that small waist, which he'd only noted yesterday, and her belly, which was sucked in to help with the obstinate fastening. It was soft but gently contoured, as if she fought some kind of battle to keep her body in check but it was determined to thwart her efforts and retain its inherently seductive softness. Her hips flared out generously from that waist with such hourglass perfection Aristotle felt momentarily dizzy.

Abruptly she moved, having at last managed to fasten her trousers, and straightened. Her belly was still sucked in, pushing her breasts out even more as she reached for something else which Aristotle could see was a shirt.

His brain wouldn't function. He couldn't move. All he could see was Lucy and her half-naked body, that long dark hair clinging provocatively to her skin like wet skeins of silk.

That thing that he called *awareness* had just exploded into full-on lust.

Lucy yanked the tag off her new shirt and pulled it on impatiently, all fingers and thumbs on the buttons of the slippery grey silk material. She'd never have gone for something like this normally, but after being hauled over the coals the day before she'd known that she had no choice but to buy the kind of uniform that someone like Aristotle Levakis would expect—and that meant expense, and things like silk as opposed to cotton. She breathed out thankfully. At least she'd had that change of clothes. No way could she have faced him this morning looking like the drowned rat she'd been just moments before.

With the shirt finally closed she tucked it in hurriedly and desperately listened out for a heavy footfall or the door opening. She knew he was due in any minute—he was more punctual than any boss she'd ever known. That had to be the reason her heart was thumping so hard: the fear of being caught like this. She raked a brush through her hair, wincing as it caught on the still-damp strands, and quickly twisted it up into a chignon of sorts. It would have to do.

Slipping her feet into flat shoes, she stuck her glasses back on, gathered up her wet things, looked up—and stopped breathing. In the crack of the open door her boss was just standing there, looking at her.

CHAPTER TWO

How long had he been standing there? The words barely impinged on Lucy's consciousness. She was too full of raging heat, embarrassment, and something more disturbing.

On some self-protective level she refused to believe he had seen her yanking her clothes on with all the grace of a baby elephant. He wasn't moving. He looked slightly shell-shocked, and mortification rushed through Lucy. She managed to move and opened the door fully, gabbling something she hoped was coherent to fill the awful silence.

'I got caught in the rain shower. I was just changing.'

She stepped out and past Aristotle, who turned to follow her with his eyes as she retreated to the safe zone behind her desk, not even sure why she needed to feel safe.

When she could bring herself to look at him, she registered that his hair was damp, his suit slightly wet. She met his eyes, and in that instant something passed between them, something electric and elemental, and Lucy knew that he *had* seen her dressing—even though stubbornly she still refused to believe it. She recoiled from the uncomfortable awareness deep within her. It scared the life out of her.

Still babbling, she said, 'Looks like you got caught too. Do you want to change before we go? I've instructed Julian to have the car downstairs in fifteen minutes, and I can have your suit sent out to be cleaned.'

Aristotle, seemingly completely unconcerned about the meeting or changing his clothes, lounged back against the doorjamb and crossed his arms. His gaze swept down over Lucy's outfit and she cringed, wondering if she'd left a tag on somewhere. She fought the urge to check herself.

He just continued to look at her with that disturbing intensity before saying, 'Tell me, did you wear that skirt yesterday on purpose? Aware of how provocative it was?'

Shock, disbelief and cold horror slammed into Lucy. Her mouth opened for a moment but nothing emerged. She couldn't articulate, but finally managed a strangled, 'Of *course* not. I would never be so…' Words failed her again and she closed her mouth helplessly.

Aristotle could see injured pride straighten her spine, the shock on her face. He had the absurd impulse to apologise, but couldn't help remembering the way she'd looked so wantonly luscious in it, straining against the material. He could imagine inching it up over those pale quivering thighs as she stood with her back against him, how the full globes of her bottom would press into him as he pushed her forward over his desk, reaching down between them to hitch her skirt higher and free his own— *What the hell was wrong with him?* His mind never deviated to lurid sexual fantasies with so little provocation.

He stood away from the door abruptly and curtly informed Lucy to make sure she had all the necessary papers and documents required for the meeting ready. He then went into the dressing room and breathed deep, as if he could inhale some common sense. But instead an evocatively feminine scent teased his nostrils and brought the last few minutes vividly back. Along with his libido.

With a growl of intense irritation Aristotle yanked a clean suit from the well-stocked wardrobe and stripped off to step into the shower, turning it onto cold. It did little to help.

* * *

Lucy flinched minutely and scowled at her computer when she heard the phone being slammed down in her boss's office. He'd just taken a call from his half-brother in Athens, and while he never seemed to welcome those calls he usually acted with more restraint than that. She shook her head. He'd been in a foul humour for two weeks now. *Ever since that morning.* Heat still crawled over her skin when she thought of the way he'd lounged against the door and looked at her, and mentioned that skirt. *He believed she might have worn it like that on purpose.*

And yet since then he had proceeded to treat her either as if a) he couldn't bring himself even to mention her name, or b) as if he might turn to stone if he so much as looked at her for longer than two seconds.

Lucy had to assure herself that nothing *had* happened, and if anything this was just a normal working relationship. Aristotle was famous for his brusque, no-nonsense approach. What had she expected? Warm and fuzzy? She shifted in her seat uncomfortably, the fact was she did feel inordinately *warm*—especially when he was around. She also felt constantly on edge, as if a kind of prickly heat lay just under the surface of her skin. She felt achy and jittery, but no symptoms of a flu or a cold had developed, so she couldn't put it down to that. She was beginning to despair of ever having any sense of equilibrium again. At times like this she longed for the uncomplicated working relationship she'd had with her last boss. Her mouth quirked wryly. But then, he had been nearing seventy, well past retirement age, and had a huge typically Greek family.

Lucy nearly shot out of her chair when she heard a coolly drawled, 'Something funny on the internet today?'

She quickly pressed a key so that her blank document disappeared, and took a breath before looking up, steeling herself. She had to steel herself a lot around this man. She smiled brightly, but it faded when she saw something dark cross his face.

'No… I was just…going over the latest mail from the Parnassus Corporation.'

She mentally crossed her fingers and breathed a sigh of relief, because that was exactly what she *had* been doing—*before* she'd been looking at a blank document for minutes on end like some moon-eyed idiot.

Aristotle emerged from his office and prowled towards Lucy. Her blood-rate shot up.

'Liar,' he said softly.

Her back straightened. 'Excuse me?'

He came to her desk and rested on his hands over it, looming over her. She fought against shrinking back as his eyes bored into hers. It was making her dizzy after days of only the most cursory eye contact.

He arched one slashing dark brow. 'If that's the case, tell me what Parnassus proposes we do in the final stages of sealing the merger?'

Lucy looked up, spellbound. As if from a long way away her more rational and professional self, the one that wasn't melting into a puddle in her chair, came back. Miraculously, information came into her brain, and she clung onto it like a life-raft.

Unable to break eye contact, and feeling as if her voice had been dipped in rust, Lucy said, 'He…he suggests that the final stages take place in Athens, as that's where the two companies originated one hundred years ago. He thinks it should be there that the merger is finally revealed. He wants it to be a triumphant homecoming to the country he and his family fled from when he was young, and for Athens to be the symbolic and actual birthplace of the greatest merger in Greek shipping and industrial history.'

Silence lengthened and tautened between them. Electric awareness quivered in the air until finally Aristotle just said quietly, 'Good. And I presume you have everything in order for you to travel to Athens for three weeks?'

Lucy just blinked stupidly for a moment as numerous things

impacted her brain. Primarily the fact that she hadn't actually considered the fact that *of course* she'd be expected to go to Athens too, in little over a week from now.

All she could say was, 'Yes, I do,' when in actual fact for some reason—even though it had been talked about for weeks—she'd never considered for a moment that she'd be accompanying Aristotle on such a prestigious engagement.

Her lack of foresight mocked her; of course it had to be her, no one else had had access to all the vital and top secret information—information so secret that she'd had to sign a contract the day she'd been hired, forbidding her to divulge any information to anyone. If she committed such an offence it could see her being fired on the spot, and certainly ruined for any future employment within these circles…

The full enormity of the size of this merger and the importance of the man in front of her started to sink in very belatedly. Mortifyingly, Lucy knew that a large part of her distraction had to do with finding herself working for someone who had reached into a secret part of her and shaken her up so much that she had to spend an inordinate amount of time just denying it to herself. Even now, as he still loomed over her, she denied it to herself.

She reassured herself desperately that she was just reacting to Aristotle Levakis' undeniable charisma, like any other red-blooded human being.

With that in mind she took a sheaf of papers that needed filing off her desk and stood up, clutching them to her chest. It was a blatant attempt to put some distance between them. Aristotle straightened too, and with arms folded surveyed her closely. That treacherous heat pooled within her again, but now she knew what it was she could deflect her own reaction to it.

She hitched up her chin. 'Was there anything else?'

He shook his head slowly and a lazy smile curved his lips. Lucy felt like clinging onto something.

'No, that's all for now.' He turned to go back to his office, but just when Lucy was about to let out a sigh of relief he turned back. With his forearm resting high on the doorjamb, drawing her eye to his long and hard muscled body, he said, 'Don't forget we have that engagement tonight. Be ready to leave at six-thirty. I'll get dressed in my office; you can use the dressing room.'

He disappeared into his own office then, shutting the door behind him, and Lucy all but sagged onto the floor in a heap. She *had* forgotten all about the function they were to attend that night. She cursed herself as she sank down heavily into her chair. What was wrong with her? Forgetting the function, not realising she would have to go to Athens… Her brain was turning to mush. And in this job that was not a luxury she could afford.

How could she have forgotten that terse conversation just days ago, when he'd said to her with a grimace on his face, 'You're going to have to come to the Black and White Ball with me.'

Lucy's belly had clenched. She'd expected that she might have to accompany her boss to some functions, but with Aristotle's extremely healthy social life she hadn't considered it would become a reality so soon. And did he have to look so reluctant at the prospect?

She'd ignored the ridiculous feeling of hurt and asked hopefully, 'But surely there must be someone else…' *anyone else* '…you could call?'

After all, as she'd restrained herself from pointing out, last-minute dates were not something he shied away from. He'd had more than a few since the Honourable Augustine Archer and then the even more Honourable Mirabella Ashton, each one well-documented in the press that gloried in his playboy exploits. And yet the morning after each date he'd appeared taciturn and as irritable as she'd ever seen him.

He'd curtly instructed her to send each night's delectation a disgustingly expensive bunch of flowers. Lucy had cynically assumed that none of the women were performing well enough to hold his interest and merit a piece of jewellery.

It was then that she'd realised that she hadn't arranged a date for him in at least a week. The thought had unsettled her more than she'd liked to admit.

He'd looked at her with narrowed eyes. 'As I am currently partnerless, not that it's any of your business, I've decided that *you* will accompany me. Do you have a problem with that?'

Feeling sick, Lucy had shaken her head rapidly. She had to stop reacting to this man and provoking him. 'No. Not at all. I'll put it in the diary now.'

Lucy came back to the present moment. She was still holding the sheaf of papers clutched to her chest like some kind of shield. She looked at the open diary beside her and there in stark letters was written *'Black and White Ball, Park Lane Hotel. Seven p.m.'* The thought of spending any more time than was absolutely necessary with this man was causing nothing short of sheer panic inside her.

She put down the papers and picked up the phone to make a call to the home where her mother was resident. She asked them to pass on the message that she wouldn't be able to visit that evening.

The matron on the other end said gently, 'I'll pass on the message, Lucy love, but you do know that it won't make any difference, don't you?'

Lucy felt very alone all of a sudden. She swallowed back the ever-present guilt, pain and grief, and nodded even though the other woman couldn't see her. Her voice was thick with emotion. 'I know…but I'd appreciate it all the same, if you don't mind.'

Lucy could hear Aristotle moving around in his own office as she changed in the dressing room. This was a formal event, so she had to wear a long dress, and the one she looked at now in the mirror was perfectly respectable—if completely boring. It was black, which meant it was slimming, and it had a high neck which covered her breasts adequately. Anything that did that was fine with her. And anyway, she told herself stoutly, she wasn't dressing to impress, she was dressing to accompany her boss in a work capacity.

She left her hair up and put on some make-up: mascara and a little blusher. Then, slipping her feet into a pair of plain black high heels, she picked up her weekend bag stuffed with her work clothes and took a deep breath before walking out, feeling ridiculously nervous and hating herself for it.

That breath hitched in her throat and her brain stopped functioning when she saw Aristotle emerge from his own office, resplendent in a traditional tuxedo. The black made him look even darker, and very dangerous. Lucy fought back the wave of awareness, her hands gripping her bag.

He looked up from adjusting his cufflinks then, and the snowy perfection of his shirt made the green of his eyes pop out. He ran quick eyes over Lucy, making her squirm inwardly before quirking a brow and saying mockingly, 'Well, if you're trying to fade into the background it's already working.'

Lucy swallowed past a dry throat. 'I'm your assistant, not your date.'

More's the pity, Aristotle surprised himself with thinking as he took her in, just a few feet away. Although not in that dress. It was basically a sack: a black sack covering her from neck to toe. It might as well have been a burkha for all he could see of her body, and he knew with a hunger that had been growing day by day and minute by minute that he very much wanted to see her body showcased in something much more revealing and *tight.* Like that skirt which had assumed mythic proportions in his fantasies. He beat back an intense surge of desire, in spite of the awful dress, and noted the hectic flush on her cheeks, the wary glitter of her eyes.

She was intriguing him more and more—not only with her luscious curves, but in the way she reacted to him, his spikily quick responses. Every expression was an open book as it crossed her face. She wasn't afraid of him, and that was heady in itself. That she didn't approve of him was glaringly obvious, and it was a novel sensation to have that from a woman.

Aristotle was looking at her far too assessingly. Lucy's belly quivered in response and she told herself sternly that she *wasn't* responding to him; she was just responding to the charisma of the man.

But then he strolled towards her nonchalantly and she had to fight the urge to turn tail and run. He walked around her as if inspecting a horse, and she turned around, unable to bear the thought of him looking at her too-large bottom. She cursed her genes again and felt acutely self-conscious. Why couldn't she be a slim, petite little thing like her mother?

Her voice was high and defensive. 'Is there something wrong? This dress fits perfectly well. It's not too tight, if that's what you're afraid of.' She wouldn't be making *that* mistake again.

Aristotle's eyes flicked to hers. They glittered with something dark and indefinable.

'The dress is fine. For an old lady.'

Lucy sucked in a shocked breath. She'd spent a small fortune from her allowance on this dress. But before she could say anything he was gesturing to her head.

'It's too late to do anything about the dress, but leave down your hair. You look like you're going to work.'

His normally accentless voice had lapsed into something unmistakably Greek, and it resonated within Lucy. Her mind blanked and her hand went up instinctively in a protective gesture. Her hair was part of her armour, she suddenly realised. No way could she take it down. She might as well just strip off the dress and stand in front of him in her underwear. Treacherous heat licked through her again, making a mockery of her attempts to rationalise it. She shook her head dumbly.

His eyes held hers and he just said quietly, 'Take it down Lucy.' It was so utterly shocking to be standing in front of her boss and have him speak to her like this, that Lucy found herself obeying him. With extreme reluctance she took out the pins from the back. She could feel her hair loosen and fall with annoying and heavily layered predictability around her shoulders and down her back.

Aristotle fisted his hands in his trouser pockets to stop them reaching out to feel the texture of that heavy silky mass of hair. It was darker than he'd originally thought, and luxuriously unruly, reaching down as far as her shoulderblades. He had an image of her reclining back on a sumptuous divan, tendrils of that glorious hair over her shoulders and trailing over her the tops of her bare— *Get a grip, man*! With a supreme effort of will Aristotle reined himself in and said gutturally, 'That's better. *Now* you look as if you're ready for a function. Let's go.'

With an easy and automatic courtesy which surprised Lucy, and she wasn't sure why that was, he took her case from her white-knuckle grip and led the way out of the office. She stumbled as she followed his graceful stride down the corridor to his private lift. She had a moment of dithering, stupidly wondering if she should take the staff lift just a few feet further down, but as if reading her mind *again* Aristotle flicked her an impatient glance and she stepped in.

It was only when they were ensconced in the lift that the memory of the last time she'd shared such a space with him came back in all its glory.

She couldn't help her reaction flowering. Too much had happened since then. Now she stood there, with her hair down, feeling as exposed as if he'd just run his hands over her naked flesh—especially when she recalled his look from moments ago, a look that had to have been some projection of her own awful, twisted feelings. The tall man beside her oozed with sexual heat. She could smell him and feel him. Suddenly she had the strangest sensation of holding something huge back… Wanton images hovered tantalisingly on the periphery of her mind and threatened to burst through, mocking her for a control that was beginning to feel very shaky.

Lucy gritted her jaw and looked resolutely up at the display as the lift seemed to inch downwards, willing it with every fibre of her being to go faster.

The effort it took to stay apart from Lucy in that lift, amidst a rush of memories of how she had felt pressed against him, which once again stunned him with their vividness, washed away Aristotle's last resistance where this woman was concerned. He'd never experienced this level of sexual awareness before, and in truth frustration was a novel sensation when he was so used to getting what he wanted, when he wanted. He didn't stop to question his decision or his motives for a second.

It was quite simple. He had to have this woman in his bed—and as a soon as possible. He would sleep with her. Then she would lose her allure and this bizarre spell she held over him would be broken. In three months he could let her go. Or less, if he got bored. According to her contract he could terminate employment with due notice; she, however, could not walk away unless she wanted to seriously sabotage her career. Because of the top secret nature of the merger she was tied to Levakis Enterprises until the whole thing became public.

Work, which he'd always strictly compartmentalised as separate from pleasure, would become pleasure—*his* pleasure. And Lucy's too. He wanted her with him every inch of the way as he took her again and again to sate this burning ache. Somehow instinctively he knew that one night would not be enough, and it made him uncomfortable to acknowledge it.

Nevertheless, as the lift descended the final few floors, a fizz of anticipation ran through Aristotle's veins and he felt truly alive for the first time in a long time. Even thoughts of the merger were receding into a background place. A dim and distant alarm bell sounded at the back of his mind, but he was too fired up to notice or dwell on it.

The lift juddered softly to a stop and the doors swished open. He stood back and gestured for Lucy to precede him, looking at her carefully as she did so. She was avoiding his eye with all the finesse of a guilty-looking six-year-old caught with her hand in the cookie jar.

She stumbled slightly stepping out of the lift, and Aristotle took her bare silky smooth arm just above the elbow. The frisson of pleasure that went through him nearly made him sway. He could feel the swell of her breast tease his fingers and a primal instinct to possess this woman coursed through him. The fact that she held herself so rigidly at his side didn't put him off. She was as unmistakably his as—for now—he was hers.

A colleague of Aristotle's had just walked away. Lucy watched him go with a feeling of mounting terror. She did not want to be alone with her boss.

They were standing side by side under the seductively soft lighting of the main ballroom in the exclusive London hotel when she heard his drawling query, 'You don't need your glasses? Or are you wearing contacts?'

She nearly choked on her sparkling water and lowered the drink carefully, realising without even making a reflex gesture to check that she had indeed forgotten her glasses. She could picture them right now, sitting on the vanity cabinet in the dressing room of the office. She flushed guiltily and sent a quick, fleeting look to Aristotle. Standing here in this milieu, with his tall, hard body just inches away, was making her nervous. It made her so nervous, in fact, that she didn't stop the truth from spilling out.

'They aren't prescription glasses.'

She saw him frown from the corner of her eyes. 'So why do you wear them?'

He sounded aghast, and Lucy had no doubt that he could not understand why any woman would knowingly want to make herself any less attractive than she already was. A sense of extreme vulnerability washed through her.

She shrugged minutely and avoided his eye. 'I started wearing them when I was looking for work after college.' She squirmed inwardly. How could she explain to this man that she'd grown sick and tired of prospective bosses ogling her sizeable assets rather than her CV? A memory made her shiver with distaste: her first boss, whispering lasciviously on more than one occasion that he liked *big girls*.

Ever since then Lucy had made sure to be covered up at all times, hair pulled back and glasses firmly on. Yet, uncomfortably, she had to acknowledge that she'd found working with Aristotle Levakis something of a relief in that she knew there was no way on this earth a man like him would look twice at her. That assertion suddenly seemed shaky.

As if to compound the feeling, from the corner of her eye she could see Aristotle turn subtly, so that he had his back to the room full of people. She even saw one person in the act of approaching falter and turn away, as if he'd sent off some silent signal she couldn't see. She couldn't resist sending him another quick look. He had an expression on his face that caught and held her, and she couldn't look away.

His eyes flicked down to her breasts—in exactly the way she'd seen men do all her life, ever since she'd developed out of all proportion in her early teens. But instead of her usual feeling of disgust and invasion, to her shame and horror she could feel herself respond. Her breasts grew heavy, their tips tight and hard. For a cataclysmic moment she actually felt the novel desire to know what it would feel like to have this man touch them. Shock at the sheer physicality of her reaction made her feel clammy.

Aristotle's eyes glittered. A whisper of a smile hovered around his mouth and then he said, 'And did it work?'

Shame and chagrin rushed through Lucy. Was she really so weak? With one look this man was felling all her careful defences like a bowling ball sending skittles flying.

Her voice sounded strangled. 'I found that, yes, it did work.' *Until now.*

Lucy felt like a trapped insect, flat on its back and helpless in the face of a looming predator. Determined to negate her disturbing reaction, she looked away and said crisply, 'Plenty of people wear glasses for cosmetic reasons. I would have thought that you'd approve.'

His voice was curt. 'Your CV and your work ethic speak for themselves, Lucy. You don't need to bolster your image by making it more businesslike.'

Too-tight skirts, yes. Glasses, no. Aristotle swallowed a growl of irritation at his wayward mind.

Lucy looked back. She was more than surprised at his easy commendation of her ability. So far it was only the fact that she hadn't been let go that had given her any indication of how well she was doing her job. She had to fight the urge to cross her hands defensively over her chest, but that was ridiculous. He wouldn't be looking at her like that. He'd just been making a point.

She inclined her head and said, 'Fine. I won't wear them.' She bit back the reflex to say *sir*. The last thing she needed now was for him to repeat his request to call him Aristotle. What she did need was for this evening to be over as soon as possible and to have a whole two days away from this man, to get her head together and clear again. Especially when the prospect of spending three weeks in Athens with him loomed on the horizon like a threatening stormcloud.

A few hours later Lucy breathed a sigh of relief when the car drew to a smooth halt outside her apartment block in south London. She'd tried to insist on taking a cab from the hotel, but Aristotle wouldn't listen. Then she'd tried to insist that he be dropped home first, but again he'd been adamant.

She reached for the door on her side and looked back to say a crisp goodnight. Her ability to speak left her. Aristotle was lounging in the far corner like a huge, dark avenging angel. A surge of panic gripped her and she felt blindly for the door handle, all but scrambling in her haste to get out and away. But just as she opened the door, extending one leg out of the car, the awful sound of ripping material made her heart stop. An ominously cold breeze whistled across the tops of her thighs.

She looked down and her jaw dropped when she saw a huge rip extending down the side of her dress from mid-thigh to hem. Only peripherally was she aware that it must have snagged on something. Her white thighs gleamed up at her in the gloom.

As all this was impacting on her brain, she heard a coolly sardonic, 'You don't seem to have much luck with clothes, do you?'

The sensation of wanting the ground to open up and swallow her whole had never seemed more strong than at that moment. She heard Aristotle say something unintelligible to his driver and then he got out. Lucy couldn't move. She was terrified that if she did something else would rip and her entire dress might fall off. But then Aristotle was standing there, looking down at her with a mocking smile and extending a hand.

With the utmost reluctance she put her hand in his and felt the world tilt crazily as he pulled her up. With her other hand she scrabbled to hold her dress together. Her face felt as red as a traffic light. Aristotle now had a light grip on her arm, and Lucy noticed that he held her bag in his other hand.

That, and the way he was looking at her now, made her feel extremely threatened. *It was the way he'd been looking at her that morning in the office.*

She felt jittery and stiff all at once, and tried to get her arm back.

'It must have caught on something. I'll be fine from here. You must be impatient to get home.'

But Aristotle ignored her and easily steered them towards the path, not letting go for a second. Lucy's blood was starting to fizzle and hum in her veins. She tried again while keeping a desperate clasp on her ruined dress. 'Really, Mr Levakis, my door is just here.'

She even dug her heels in, but he called back to the driver, 'That's all, Julian. You can go. I'll get a cab from here.'

'You're sure, sir?' The driver's surprise was evident in his voice.

'Yes. Goodnight, Julian.'

And with that, before Lucy could formulate a word or acknowledge the escalation of pure mind-numbing panic in her breast, she was being led to her door and Aristotle was looking down at her with his trademark impatience.

'Your keys?'

Lucy spluttered. The driver was pulling away from the kerb, making her even more panicked. 'Mr Levakis, *really*, you don't have to do this. Please. Thank you for the lift, but you shouldn't have let Julian go. You'll never get a cab from here…'

He looked down at her, those green eyes utterly mesmerising. 'I thought I told you to call me Aristotle. Now, your keys? Please.'

Much like earlier, when he'd told her to take down her hair, Lucy found herself obeying. She knew on some dim, rational level that it was just shock. She awkwardly dug her keys out of her handbag, while trying not to let the dress gape open, and watched wordlessly when Aristotle took them and opened the door, leading them into the foyer and to the lift. He looked at her again with a quirked brow and Lucy said faintly, 'Sixth floor.'

As the lift lurched skyward Lucy felt somehow as though she must be dreaming. She'd wake any moment and it would be Monday morning and everything would be back to normal. But then the lift bell pinged loudly and Aristotle, *her boss*, was looking at her again expectantly. She had no choice but to step out and walk to her door a few feet away.

Her brain was refusing to function coherently. She simply could not start to pose the question, even to herself, as to what he was doing here. She turned at her door with a very strong need to make sure she went through it alone and this man stayed outside.

She held out her hand for her keys, which he still held. She couldn't look him in the eye. The bright fluorescence of the lighting was too unforgiving and harsh. Although she knew that it wouldn't dent his appeal.

'Thank you for seeing me safely in.'

'You're not in yet.'

With more panic than genuine irritation Lucy sent him a fulminating glance and grabbed her keys. She opened the door with a hand that was none too steady. She could have wept with relief when the door swung open. She turned back and pasted on a smile.

'There—see? All safe. Now, if you just take a right when you go out, the main road is about a hundred yards up the street. You should be able to get a cab from there.'

CHAPTER THREE

ARISTOTLE LEANED NONCHALANTLY against the wall, hands in the pockets of his trousers. At some stage since they'd left the hotel in town he'd undone his bow tie, and it hung rakishly open along with the top buttons of his shirt. Dark whorls of hair were visible, and Lucy felt weak with shock again at his bizarre behaviour. Belatedly she wondered if he might be drunk and she looked at him suspiciously. But then she recalled that, like her, he'd barely touched alcohol all evening. So if he wasn't drunk… Her belly fluttered ominously.

'I thought you said I'd never get a cab from there? Would you let me wander the mean streets of south London alone and defenceless? I can call a cab from your apartment…and I could murder a coffee…'

This man and the word *defenceless* did not belong in the same sentence. He smiled and her world tipped alarmingly for a second. Lucy had to swallow her retort, along with the stomach-churning realisation that she was being subjected to her boss's teasing and charming side. She heard the lift jerking into life again. More people arriving home from a night out. Suddenly she was terrified that it might be her very bubbly but very nosy neighbour Miranda. She could just imagine trying to explain this: a gorgeous, lounging six-foot-four Greek tycoon in their mildew stained hallway. Her dress was suddenly the least of her worries.

'OK, fine. I'll call you a cab and get you a coffee.'

Lucy walked in and stood back to let Aristotle through. Immediately the air seemed to be sucked out of the room and replaced with his sheer dynamism. Lucy closed her door just as she heard the very drunken-sounding laughter of her neighbour and gave a sigh of relief.

As Aristotle started to prowl around her humble sitting room Lucy spied a lacy bra hanging over the chair nearest the kitchen. She dived for it while he was turned away and hurriedly balled it up. Aristotle turned round and Lucy's belly spasmed.

'Coffee,' she babbled. 'I'll get the coffee on.'

She turned and fled into the small kitchen off the sitting room and stuffed the bra into a cupboard, taking out coffee and setting the kettle to boil. She kept looking surreptitiously into the sitting room. Aristotle was still prowling around. Except now he'd taken off his jacket, and she could see the broad line of his back tapering down into an impossibly lean waist. Her gaze followed the line down over taut buttocks and long, long legs…

The shrill, piercing scream of the kettle made her jump, and she winced when drops of boiling water splashed on clumsy hands. She gathered her dress together and walked back into the sitting room, noticing that Aristotle had put on some lights. Their glow of warmth lent an intimacy to the scene that raised her blood pressure. She had the vague thought of going to get changed out of the dress, but couldn't contemplate the idea of removing a stitch of clothing while he was anywhere near. She noticed then that he was studying a photo in his hand, with a slight frown between those black brows. Lucy was terrified he might recognise the woman in the picture. She handed him the coffee, forcing him to put the picture down and take the cup.

He just gestured with his head. 'Who is that? You and your mother?'

Lucy looked down at the photo in the frame and fought the

urge to snatch it out of sight. It was a favourite one of her and her mum, taken in Paris when Lucy had been about twelve. They were wrapped up against the cold, their faces close together, but even from the picture you could tell that Lucy hadn't taken after her mother's delicate red-haired beauty. She'd already been taller than her mother by then.

She nervously adjusted it slightly and replied, 'Yes,' clearly not inviting any more questions.

Aristotle looked at Lucy. She was as nervous and skittish as a foal—avoiding his eye, her hand in a white-knuckle grip on that dress. That was what had pushed him over the edge. Seeing those soft pale thighs exposed to his gaze, one long leg already out of the car. It had taken every ounce of restraint not to reach out and run his hand up the soft inner skin of one gloriously lush thigh.

Especially after an evening that had been a form of torture, trying to focus on work while she'd stood beside him. Following her out of the car and up to this apartment had felt as necessary as breathing. But now he forced himself to take a step back, sensing her extreme nervousness.

She gestured jerkily to a seat. 'Please, sit down while you have your coffee. I'll call a cab. It may take a while to come at this hour.'

Aristotle sat down on a springy couch under the window and watched as Lucy went to the phone on the other side of the room and made the call, turning her back firmly to him. He tried to bank down the intense surge of desire even her back was igniting within him and thought back to the function.

She'd been a surprisingly pleasurable and easy date, offering intelligently insightful comments on more than one person, showing snippets of dry humour. At one point she'd caught him off-guard entirely, when she'd seamlessly switched to accentless and fluent French. He'd become accustomed to people *saying* they were multi-lingual and meaning they had the basics, like hello and goodbye. Something dark lodged in his chest. He'd also been inordinately aware of the keen male interest she'd generated and how seemingly oblivious she'd been to it. He wasn't used to that.

Fighting the sudden surge of something very primal, he let his eyes drift down over her body and long legs; a vivid image exploded into his head of the moment her dress had split. He wondered how those legs might feel wrapped around his waist as he thrust deeper and deeper into her slick heat. Arousal was immediate and uncomfortable. He shifted on the seat, and even the evident relief in Lucy's voice when she got through to the cab company did little to dampen it.

When Lucy put the phone down, she could finally turn and look her boss in the eye. Escape was imminent. She just had to make some small talk. 'Ten minutes for the cab.' She sat down gratefully in the chair beside the phone, relief making her feel weak. She was still clutching the torn dress over her legs, hanging on to it like a lifeline.

Aristotle leant forward and put down his coffee cup. He had an intense gleam in his green eyes. 'We're going to be spending a lot of time together in Athens.' He looked around her apartment, and then back to her. 'I thought this might be a good opportunity to get to know each other a little better.'

Something treacherously like disappointment rushed through Lucy, but everything within her rejected it. Had she been so blind? Had she truly suspected for a moment that Aristotle had been rushing her up here to try and make love to her? She felt very brittle all of a sudden.

'Of course. I mean, I could…' She racked her brain. Evidently she had to find some way of giving some information to Aristotle, so he didn't feel as if he had to follow her up to her apartment to talk to her. 'I could fill out a questionnaire…?'

He arched a brow.

'A personal questionnaire…if you want to get to know more…about my history.' A leaden weight made her feel heavy inside.

She'd become an expert at putting a glamorous spin on her life with her mother. On her history. Glossing over the reality.

But Aristotle was shaking his head and standing up, coming towards her. He came and stood right in front of her, and Lucy realised that she was in a very vulnerable position, her eye level at his crotch. She stood too, so suddenly that she swayed, and Aristotle put out his hands to steady her. They were on her waist. Immediately it was an invasion of her space—especially when she was so self-conscious about her body.

With one hand she tried to knock him away but his hands were immovable. Her other hand was still clinging onto her dress with a death grip. She looked at him and her brain felt hot, fuzzy. He was too close. She could smell his fresh citrusy scent, mixed in with something much more male, elemental. All she could see were his eyes; all she could feel were those hands, like a brand on her body.

He was talking. She tried to concentrate on his words.

'…more along the lines of this…'

And then, as realisation exploded inside her, Aristotle's head was coming down, closer and closer. Everything went dark as his mouth covered hers, warm and firm and so exotic that she couldn't move.

It was so shocking that Lucy continued standing there like a statue. Through her mind ran the comforting words, *You won't feel anything. You're cold inside. You're not your mother. You don't react to this. You don't crave men...sex... You've proved this to yourself...*

But, as if disconnected from her mind, a radiating heat was taking over, spreading upwards from a very secret part of her. A core she'd never acknowledged before. A core that had never been touched.

Aristotle was pulling her closer. Those big hands were still around her waist, spanning it now, fingers digging into soft, yielding flesh. He was warm and firm, and as he brought her flush against his body she realised just how hard he was. How tall, and how strong. He was huge, and she had the distinct impression for the first time in her life of being…somehow delicate. No one had ever made her feel like that.

He moved one of his hands upwards from her waist, skimming close to her breast which tingled in reaction, the peak tightening almost painfully. But then he speared that hand through her hair, around the back of her head, angling her towards him more. She was aware of the rush of disappointment that his hand hadn't lingered, cupped the weight of her breast.

His mouth was insistent, but something inside Lucy was like ice amidst the heat, still protecting her from fully feeling. It was a wall of defence she'd erected over a long time…and yet even as she thought that she suddenly visualised that defence crumbling.

As sensation got stronger, igniting an alien urgency, panic surged. Aristotle could have no idea of what was happening inside her, how cataclysmic her reaction was, but at that moment he took his head away and looked down into her wide eyes. Somewhere Lucy was dimly aware that she wasn't pushing him away…which she could. But she felt so heavy, so deliciously lethargic, and she couldn't think when he was so close and looking deep into her eyes like this.

He said gutturally, 'Lucy… I can feel you holding back. You're shaking with it.'

And then she became aware that she *was* shaking—like a leaf, all over. Reality exploded around her. She was in her boss's arms and he was kissing her! The feelings rippling through her were intense to the point of overwhelming her completely, more intoxicating than anything she'd ever experienced, or thought she could experience. With that thought sanity tried to break through: she didn't respond to kissing in this way. And yet… she was.

Aristotle chose that moment to kiss her again, and Lucy was caught between two worlds, defenceless and vulnerable, conflicting desires whirling in her head, making her dizzy. Making her weak against this far too seductive attack on her senses. One hand was curled against Aristotle's chest, and as his mouth moved over hers once again her fingers unfurled, like the petals of a flower opening to the sun. When his tongue traced along the seam of her tightly closed mouth the sensation made her open her lips minutely, some dark and distant part of her wanting this, wanting to experience this, and Aristotle took immediate advantage, opening her mouth, forcing her to accept him. And to respond.

When his tongue-tip touched hers it set off a chain reaction in her body. Suddenly she was *feeling* for the first time, and it was too strong to resist—like a flash-flood carrying her downstream. She moved closer to Aristotle's body and felt his growl of approval. His tongue stabbed deep, exploring and coaxing hers to touch and taste. The hand at her waist brought her even closer, and the evidence of his arousal pressing into her soft belly elicited a deep craving feeling not of disgust, but of desire to experience *union*.

Her fingers tangled in surprisingly silky hair; she could feel her back arch wantonly towards him. He shaped the indent of her waist and hips and Lucy didn't feel self-conscious, she felt exultant. When his hands moved to cup her buttocks and pull her even tighter into the cradle of his lap her breath caught.

Aristotle tore his mouth away and looked down at her. Their bodies were still plastered together. Their breath came swift and uneven, and he didn't take his eyes off hers as he reached one hand down between them and found where her hand was still tightly clenched over the rent sides of the dress. He loosened her fingers and, helpless, Lucy could only look deep into his glittering eyes as she felt the dress fall apart and his hand smooth up over her thigh, then between her legs, climbing higher and higher.

He was looking at her. His eyes were on her…studying her. While his hand—

'You're so beautiful. Why do you hide yourself away, Lucy?'

It wasn't his hand climbing to such an intimate place but his words that broke her out of her sensual stasis: *so beautiful...*

She wasn't beautiful. She'd heard those words a million times before. Not directed at her—never at her. But at someone else. Someone who had craved them; someone who had spent her life being defined by men's opinion of her.

The shock of everything suddenly hit her, and made Lucy jerk back violently, knocking his hand away and pulling her dress together again. She had the mortifying image in her head of wantonly pressing as close as she could, and the shame of her reaction to that made her feel nauseous. Between her legs she throbbed and tingled.

Her voice was shaking and thin, too high. 'This is completely inappropriate. I'm your *assistant*.'

Aristotle's face was uncharacteristically flushed. 'You're also the one woman I can't stop thinking about and wanting. And it's a bit late to put on the injured virgin act.'

He raked a hand through his hair in frustration, leaving it gorgeously unruly.

Lucy shook her head in rejection of that, trying to ignore the way her mouth felt so full and plump. She felt anything but virginal right now. In a few seconds he'd managed to blast to smithereens the knowledge that she'd comforted herself with ever since she *had* lost her virginity: she was frigid.

'No. I'm your assistant. This is not possible.' More shame rushed through her as she said, 'If you think I gave you some indication that I might welcome...' She couldn't even say it. 'You're just...bored or something. You can't possibly—'

'Can't I?' he interrupted harshly. He stood with hands fisted at his sides and glowered at her. 'I saw you changing the other morning and I felt like a schoolboy watching a naked woman for the first time. No woman has ever reduced me to that. And you want me too, Lucy. You've just shown me that.'

Embarrassment washed through her in a wave of heat. He *had* seen her. She'd known it...but to hear him confirm it nearly made her mind short-circuit. And along with the embarrassment came another feeling, one of illicit pleasure, when she remembered seeing his face. She shook her head again, even fiercer this time, both hands clutching the dress.

Just at that moment the phone rang shrilly. Lucy jumped. She was starting to shake; reaction was setting in. 'That's the taxi. Get out right now.' When he didn't move she said, *'Please.'*

Aristotle finally strode over to pick up his coat and, flinging it over one shoulder, he walked to the door. He looked back at her for a long moment, hugely imposing and dark in her plain little apartment. Men like him weren't meant for scenes like this, she thought.

The phone had stopped, but now started again.

'I'll see you on Monday, Lucy. This isn't over—not by a long shot.'

And then he was gone. Lucy stood stock still and could barely breathe. When the phone impacted upon her consciousness again she went over and picked it up. 'He's on his way down,' she said.

When she was certain he had gone, Lucy undressed and had a steaming hot shower, thinking perhaps it might eradicate the painfully intense feelings Aristotle had aroused in her when he'd touched her and looked at her. She dressed in her oldest and comfiest pyjamas and made herself a hot chocolate, dislodging the bra she'd hurriedly hidden as she did so from the cupboard. Heat rose upwards again, but she resolutely ignored it and went into the sitting room and sank onto the couch, cradling the hot cup in cold hands.

She reached up and took down the photo of her and her mother and tears filled her eyes as emotion surged upwards. She felt incredibly raw after what had just happened.

Her mother had been diagnosed with early onset Alzheimer's two years ago. It had come on the back of her growing ever more forgetful and irritable, prone to mood swings and dramatics. It had been so unlike her usually sanguine mother that Lucy had insisted she go to be checked out by a doctor. They'd run some tests, and as soon as a diagnosis had been made her mother's condition had worsened by the day—almost as if naming it had allowed it to take hold completely.

At first Lucy had been able to look after her in their small townhouse near Holland Park, but when she'd come home one day to find her mother wailing inconsolably in a flooded kitchen, with all the gas rings of the cooker on and alight and no idea how or why she'd done it, Lucy had known she couldn't fight it on her own any more.

She'd started with home help—the cost of which had rapidly eaten up all their savings. Her mother had never worried about money too much beyond making sure Lucy was provided for, and there had invariably been a new rich lover more than happy to provide. However, in recent years Lucy's mother had been coming to terms with the harsh realities of aging in a world where youth and beauty were a more potent draw to powerful men. The protection of rich lovers had all but disappeared.

Lucy's mouth compressed as her finger ran over her mother's image in the picture. She supposed in the nineteenth century her mother might have been considered one of the most famous courtesans of her time. But in this lifetime she'd been a famous and much sought after burlesque dancer—a true artist. Lucy's mouth tightened even more; her mother had simply got used to the attention of very rich, very powerful men.

She'd craved the control she'd had over them—her ability to reduce them to ardent lovers, desperate to please her in any way they could. Her allure and beauty had been legendary. Her powerful lovers had funded their lives, and unwittingly helped put Lucy through the best schools all over the world. She couldn't denigrate her mother's memory now by judging her over where that money had come from. Her mother had simply used all the tools at her disposal to survive.

Her father had been one of those men. When he'd found out

Maxine was pregnant and refusing to give up her baby, he'd paid some maintenance but hadn't wanted anything to do with Lucy. When Lucy was sixteen he'd died, and maintenance had stopped abruptly—because of course he hadn't told his family about her.

What had upset Lucy more than anything else was the lack of confidence and self-esteem her mother had suffered that only she, as her daughter, had been privy to. While on the one hand her mother had been in control, using those men as they used her, on another, much more vulnerable level she had craved their affection and approval. She'd used her beauty to enthral her lovers, but she'd been broken in two every time they'd walked away, leaving behind nothing but costly gems, clothes—*things*.

It had been shortly after finding her mother so distraught in the flooded kitchen that Lucy had discovered the house they'd lived in—a generous present from another lover—had never been signed over to her mother, despite assurances at the time. The man was a prominent politician who'd just died. Lucy's mother's solicitor had advised that Lucy should not contest ownership of the house when the family had discovered its existence, as obviously they had no idea of their father's secret affair. The family had debts to clear on the death of their father, and Lucy had had no option but to let the house go. The precariousness of their situation had forged within Lucy a deep desire for order and her own financial independence.

About a year ago they'd moved into her current small apartment. Lucy had still hoped that home help would be enough, but the cost of it had barely left her with enough to buy food at the end of each week. Her job at Levakis Enterprises was the only thing that kept them afloat. And now with her increase in wages, it was the only thing giving her mum the opportunity to have decent care.

Lucy stared unseeingly down at the picture, and suddenly an image broke through—Aristotle standing right here in this room, holding her close, his hand between her legs. She could remember the way she'd throbbed and burned for that hand to go even higher, to where she ached. *To where she still ached.* Lucy shifted so violently in reaction that the picture fell from her lap to the wooden floor and the glass smashed in the frame. With a cry of dismay she put down her cup and picked it up carefully. As she did so, something hard solidified in her chest.

She knew exactly how to handle this situation, how to handle Aristotle Levakis and make sure everything returned to normal. She couldn't contemplate how her decision would impact her mother just yet. All she knew was that she had to protect herself—because she'd never felt under such threat in her life. She would make sure her mother was safe and cared for. *She would.* She just couldn't do it like this.

On Monday morning, early, Ari stood at the window of his huge office, with its commanding view out over the city of London and all its impressive spires and rooftops. From the moment he'd been placed in charge of Levakis Enterprises at the age of twenty-seven, on the death of his father five years previously, he'd moved the power centre of the business here to London, his adopted home.

He'd told himself it was for strategic reasons, and certainly the business had thrived and grown exponentially since he'd moved it here, but it was also a very distinct gesture from him to his family, to say *he* was in control, not them. They'd shunned him enough over the years. No way was he going to play happy families back in Athens. And while he had left the original office there, which his half-brother now oversaw, they all knew that it was just a symbolic front for the business. Ari controlled its beating heart, and it lay here, under the grey and rain-soaked skies of London.

But today his main focus was not on business; it was on something much more personal and closer to home. On something so exquisitely feminine and alluring that he didn't know how he'd managed to control himself for the past weekend and not go back to that small dingy apartment, knock down the door and take Lucy hard and fast, before she could draw up that *faux* injured virgin response again. He could still feel the imprint of every womanly curve as he'd held her close to his body. She'd been more lusciously voluptuous than any fantasy he could have had.

His hands were clenched to fists deep in his pockets now, and his jaw was gritted hard against the unwelcome surging of desire. His assistant was causing him frustration of the most strategic kind.

She wanted him. And he couldn't understand where her reticence came from. No woman was reticent with him; he saw, he desired, he took. It was quite simple and always had been. An alien and uncomfortable feeling nagged him as he acknowledged the dominant feeling he'd had the other night. He'd felt *ruthless* as he'd coaxed and cajoled a response from Lucy. When she'd finally capitulated, even for that brief moment, it had been a sweeter conquest than any victory he could remember. He didn't usually associate ruthlessness with women—that was reserved for business—and the fact that such a base emotion was spilling over into his personal life was—

Ari heard a noise come from the outer office—Lucy's office—and his body tensed with a frisson of anticipation, all previous thoughts scattered to the winds.

He wanted Lucy Proctor and she would pay for making him desire her by giving herself up to him, wholly and without reservation, until he was sated and could move back into the circles in which he belonged. He vowed this now, as he heard a sharp knock on his door, and waited for a moment before turning around, schooling his features and saying with quiet, yet forceful emphasis, 'Come.'

Lucy took a deep breath outside the heavy oak door. As soon as she heard that deeply autocratic *'Come'* her nerves jangled and her heart started racing. Just before she opened the door, her hand clammy and slippy on the round knob, she prayed that the make-up she'd put on that morning would hide the dark circles under her eyes. She hadn't slept a wink all weekend.

Steeling herself like never before, she opened the door and stepped in. Aristotle was standing with his hands in his pockets and his back to the huge window. Waves of virile masculinity seemed to radiate from him and Lucy's throat went dry. For an awful second her mind seemed to go blank and be replaced with nothing but heat…but as her hand clenched on the envelope she gave an inward sigh of relief and reminded herself that she'd soon be out of this man's disturbing orbit.

She walked further into the office and tried to ignore the way Aristotle's narrowed gaze on her was making her even more nervous. She came to a halt just a few feet from the desk.

She cleared her throat. 'Sir, I…' Heat washed into her face. 'That is… Aristotle…' She stopped. She was already a gibbering wreck.

'I thought I told you there was no need for you to wear your glasses.'

Lucy's hand went reflexively to touch the sturdy frames. She cursed herself for having told him she didn't need them, and bristled at his high-handed manner. The sharp edge of the envelope reassured her.

'Well, I feel more comfortable wearing them. The fact is that—'

'Well, I don't.' He was curt, abrupt. 'You work for *me*, and I don't want to see them again. And you can also stop tying your hair back as if you're doing some kind of religious penance.'

Lucy gasped. She could feel the colour washing out of her face, only to be swiftly replaced by mortified heat.

Knowing that she had nothing to lose, she didn't curb her tongue, but her voice when it came was slightly strangled. 'Is there anything else you'd like to comment on while you're at it?'

Aristotle leaned back against the window and negligently crossed one ankle over the other, crossed his arms over that formidable chest. His eyes took on a slumberous quality that made Lucy's breath falter and a tight coil of sensation burn down low in her belly.

'Have you thrown out that skirt yet?'

Lucy's hands clenched. She didn't feel the edges of the envelope any more, or remember what she was here to do. Right now she was being subjected to the lazy appraisal of a man who, she told herself, was just like every other man who had traipsed in and out of her mother's life. The fact that her predominant emotion wasn't the anger she'd expected made her feel very vulnerable.

'It's none of your business where that blasted skirt is. You can rest assured that you won't have to be subjected to seeing me wear it again, because I'm here to—'

'That's a pity.'

Lucy's mouth was still open on the unfinished part of her sentence. She blinked as his words sank in. She shook her head. She had to have misheard. Distracted, and hating herself for it, she asked, 'What did you say?'

He stood then, and even though he didn't come towards her she took a step back.

'I said, that's a pity. You'd be surprised how much of my mental energy that skirt has been taking up. I think I may have been too hasty in my judgement of it.'

Lucy shook her head again and could feel herself trembling inwardly. She felt as if she were in some twilight zone. What about the Augustine Archers of the world, impeccably groomed to within an inch of their skinny designer lives? Surely he couldn't really mean that he preferred…? Her mind shut down at that, but the words slipped out and she watched herself as if from a distance as she said faintly, 'But…it was just a high street skirt that shrank in the wash. I didn't have time to get a new one. You thought it was inappropriate enough to have me taken to task for it.'

'That was a mistake.' His eyes flicked down over her body,

and Lucy's flesh tingled as if he'd touched her. Even though she wore perfectly fitting and respectable trousers, a high-necked shirt and a jacket, she felt undressed.

When his eyes rose to meet hers again she registered the dangerous gleam in their depths. The bubble of unreality burst. Self-preservation was back. The envelope. She held it out now, with a none too steady hand.

Aristotle looked from her face down to it and then back up. He arched an enquiring brow.

Lucy stammered, 'It's—it's my letter…of resignation.'

Ari's hands clenched. Something surged through his body—a primal need not to let this woman go. No way was she walking out of here. That ruthless feeling was back.

He shook his head. 'No, it's not.'

'Yes, it is,' Lucy replied automatically, a little perplexed.

'No. It's not.'

Anger started to lick upwards as it dawned on Lucy that this wasn't going to be the quick result she'd hoped for.

'Yes, Mr Levakis, it is. Please accept my resignation with the grace with which it's tendered.' She held out the envelope further. 'I am not available for…extra services outside work, and your behaviour the other night was not acceptable.'

Lucy's eyes had turned to a dark slate-grey and they were flashing. There was a resolute tilt to her chin. Ari marvelled that he hadn't noticed it before now, but this woman had passion oozing from every pore of her tightly held body. She had backbone. Far from fading into the background, as he'd so misguidedly believed her to have done from day one, she'd been there under his nose the whole time. He could see now that her appeal had been working on him subliminally, bringing him to the point he had now reached: the point of no return, unless this woman was with him.

Ari moved around the desk and perched on the edge, arms still folded. When he saw Lucy's eyes flick betrayingly down to his thighs he smiled inwardly, and smiled even more when he saw a flush stain her cheeks. *How* had he ever though of her as plain or unassuming? He ignored her outstretched hand and the white envelope.

Lucy refused to show how intimidated she was by moving back, but she wanted to—desperately. Her breath was coming in shallow bursts. She felt as if she wanted to reach up and undo the top button of her blouse.

Aristotle cocked his head and asked enquiringly, with a small frown, 'Now, exactly what part of the other night would you say was not acceptable?' He answered himself. 'The part where I escorted you safely to your door? Or perhaps the part where I accepted the coffee you made me?'

Lucy's other hand balled into a fist and she bit out, 'You know exactly what I'm talking about.'

His face cleared, the frown disappeared and he said, 'Ah! You mean the part where I proved just how mutual our attraction is?'

CHAPTER FOUR

LUCY FLUSHED EVEN HOTTER, mortified heat drenching her in an upward sweep. Much to her utter humiliation she knew it wasn't *all* mortification. Some of it was pure…*thrill*. This man was doing nothing short of creating a nuclear reaction within her, comprehensively threatening everything she'd protected herself with for years.

She dropped her outstretched hand without even realising what she was doing and shook her head, finally taking a step back, pretending she wasn't as affected as she was as if her life depended on it.

'You mean the part where you mauled me? That wasn't mutual attraction.'

Immediately he tensed, and his eyes flashed dangerously. Lucy swallowed. She knew she'd just said the worst thing possible. Most bosses in this situation would sense the potential danger of having a sexual harassment suit landed against them and back off. But Aristotle Levakis was not most bosses, and Lucy guessed belatedly that no woman, *ever*, had accused him of mauling them. Certainly her dreams over the weekend hadn't been of someone mauling her—quite the opposite, in fact.

Aristotle stood to his full height, power and pure sexual charisma bouncing off him in affronted waves. He arched a brow, his arms still folded tightly across his chest, the biceps of his arms bunching even through the material of his silk shirt.

'*Mauled*?' he repeated softly, dangerously.

Lucy swallowed again, her throat suddenly as dry as parchment. She nodded, but felt herself curling up inside with humiliation.

Aristotle came and stood very close Lucy had to tip her head back and look up. She clenched her jaw. He was looking down at her with an expressionless face, those light green eyes glittering. Dark slashes of colour highlighted his cheekbones. He was livid, she recognised, and a flutter of fear came low in her belly, along with another flutter of something much more dangerous.

He started to walk around her. Lucy held herself rigid.

From behind her she heard him say, 'When I put my hands on your waist you didn't stop me or push me away.'

'I—' She began, but stopped as the memory of his hands on her waist speared through her. How his fingers had dug into her soft flesh. How she'd wanted them to dig harder.

'Then, when I kissed you, you also didn't pull away.' His voice was low and sultry. 'I know when a woman is enjoying being kissed, *moro mou*, believe me.'

He was still behind her, and Lucy was finding it increasingly difficult to concentrate. His voice was so hypnotic, resonating with something that pulled on her insides and left her weak.

'I… I…didn't like it.'

'Liar.' It came so softly from close behind her head that she jumped minutely, her skin breaking into goosebumps.

He moved to her side. Lucy fought against closing her eyes and wondered dimly why she just didn't walk away, but she knew on some level that she was afraid if she moved she might fall down. She stayed rigid.

'You did like it…when my tongue touched yours…when you let me explore the sweetness of that mouth. Did I tell you that I'm fascinated by the gap in your teeth? Right now all I want to do is kiss you again until you're so boneless in my arms that all I'd have to do is carry you to the couch over there…'

Lucy's breath had stopped. Her brain had certainly stopped functioning. The couch was in her peripheral vision, and Aristotle was right in front of her again. For a big man, he moved as silently as a panther.

She closed her eyes in a childish gesture to block him out, but quickly realised what a mistake that was when he continued, 'I'd lay you down and remove those glasses and let your hair out of its tight confinement…'

At that moment Lucy's head throbbed unmercifully, as if in league with him.

'Then I'd start to undo your buttons, one by one, but I probably wouldn't be able to resist kissing you again, coaxing you to bite down on me too, so you could feel how I might taste.'

The sensation of what it might be like to bite into the sensual curve of his lower lip was shockingly vivid. Lucy was starting to quiver badly now. Her eyes still closed tight, she felt hot and flushed all over, and between her legs… Her mind seized.

'Stop…' she said threadily. 'Please…'

'But you see you wouldn't want me to stop, as your shirt fell apart, baring those gorgeous breasts to my gaze… Is the lace of your bra chafing you now, Lucy? Are your nipples tight and tingling? Aching for my touch? Aching for my mouth? I would take those peaks and suck them into my mouth, hard, until they're aroused to the point of pain. And then I'd cover your body with mine, so that you could feel how turned-on I am. *Even right now* I'd lift up your leg and let my hand slide over the silk of your stocking, all the way to the soft pale flesh of your thigh. You'd be moaning softly, willing my hand even higher, to that secret place between your legs where you're aching for me to find the silk of your pants drenched with desire. You'd beg for me to slide them aside so that I could feel for myself—'

'Stop!' Lucy's eyes flew open and in an instant she was jerking away—only realising at the last second that he wasn't even holding her. He held up his hands to prove the point. Her breath was coming in short, shallow gasps, her breasts felt heavy, their tips tight and tingling, exactly as he'd described, and between her legs seemed to burn a molten pool of something dangerous and unwelcome… It was that that had finally woken her out of this awful, *delicious* dream.

But it wasn't delicious—it *wasn't*, she told herself desperately as she looked anywhere but at Aristotle. She felt disorientated, dizzy, as if she could almost believe she *had* been on that couch. Her upper lip felt moist. Her hands clenched and she realised that she no longer held the envelope. In that instant she saw that it was in one of his hands and he was ripping it in two.

She put out a hand. 'Wait! What are you doing?'

Lucy also realised, along with everything else in that moment, that contrary to her own state of near collapse Aristotle looked cool, calm and collected—a million miles away from the man who had been just whispering in her ear how *aroused* he was. She was a quivering wreck and he hadn't even touched her.

His cool voice cut through her like a knife as she watched him turn on his heel and walk back around his desk. 'I'm putting this letter of resignation where it belongs—in the bin.' And he promptly did just that.

Lucy was a mess, still reeling from the way his voice and words had affected her, and how utterly unaffected he clearly was. He was sitting behind his desk now, for all the world as if nothing had just happened, and as if he was waiting for her to sit and take notes.

'Mr Levakis—'

His voice was curt. 'We've been through this before. I told you to call me Aristotle. I don't want to tell you again.'

Lucy all but exploded. 'I am resigning. There is nothing you can do or say to stop me. I will not stay and be subjected to the kind of treatment you just…just subjected me to.'

Aristotle was looking down, flicking through papers, and he said easily, 'Lucy, I didn't even have to touch you to turn you on, so when the time comes and I do touch you for real can you imagine how good it's going to be? Why would you deny yourself that?'

For a million and one good reasons! Lucy saw red spots dance before her eyes. His words had impacted upon her so deep, and in a place so visceral, she nearly screamed with frustration. But she swallowed it down and said, as coolly and calmly as she could, 'It's clear that your arrogance is clouding your ability to assimilate this information. Perhaps it'll become more clear once I've gone. I can send you another copy of my resignation. Good day, Mr Levakis.'

She turned on her heel and was almost at the door when she heard him, deadly soft. 'If you walk through that door, Lucy Proctor, you'll be hearing from my lawyers within the hour.'

Lucy stopped in her tracks, her hand still in the act of reaching for the doorknob. She turned around slowly and saw that hard green gaze spearing her on the spot. Her stomach felt as if she was in freefall off a huge cliff.

'What are you talking about?' But dread was already trickling through her as her professional brain went into overdrive and she had a sickening memory of signing that other contract along with the one for her job. She really hadn't thought this through with her usual clear rationality at all.

'Well, for a start, you're obliged to give me at least four weeks' notice, as per your standard work contract, and if you leave before the merger is completed you'll be sued. It's quite simple.'

And utterly devastating... Lucy realised with mounting horror.

He sat back in his chair. 'We leave for Athens in a week. You know far too much, and have been privy to all the top secret discussions. Quite apart from that, if you left now you'd be leaving me without an assistant for the most important joining between two Greek companies in years. That is something I will not allow to happen. If it means I have to threaten you with legal action to get you to stay then so be it. I won't hesitate to use the full force of my power.'

He sat forward then, and he had never looked so intimidating. 'Lucy, I don't think I need to tell you that your career would be comprehensively ruined if you insist on leaving. You could be crippled financially for years.'

Lucy wasn't sure how she remained standing. She'd known all this—she'd *known*. She'd been smart enough to read the fine print of both contracts, and at the time it had given her a sense of security to know that Levakis wouldn't be able to turn around and get rid of her at a moment's notice. It was what had given her the confidence to put her mum in that home—the confidence to go to the bank and take out a loan which would assure her mother's place in that home for at least a year. Lucy had known that as long as she could keep up the payments everything would be secure for the short term, and hopefully for the long-term future.

But now…if she walked out of here and incurred Aristotle Levakis' wrath she'd be kissing all that goodbye. She could well imagine the loan from the bank being called in. Losing her job would quickly mean that she'd have no source of income with which to pay for her mum's accommodation. She'd be back to square one, becoming the primary carer, and without a job that would be impossible.

She said now, in a small voice, 'You would do that…' It wasn't a question.

'Without a doubt,' he answered grimly. 'This merger and this company are too important to me. They are everything.'

So what am, I then? Lucy wondered a little wildly. Just a convenient plaything because you happen to be bored with all the usual sycophants?

He stood again then, but Lucy was in too much shock and distress to move as he came closer, hands in his pockets. He looked smug. He knew he had her effectively trapped. Suddenly she longed to have no responsibilities, so she could just disappear. But she did, and she couldn't.

He stopped a few feet away and looked at her. Her world had been reduced to this room, this man and those eyes. And that voice.

'Lucy, I don't want to be ruthless about this, and I certainly don't relish the thought of taking action against you. I want the merger, yes, and I'll do whatever I need to to protect it and make it happen. But I also want *you*, and I will do whatever I need to in order to make that happen too.'

Lucy shook her head dumbly, even now fighting. It made something in Aristotle's eyes flash dangerously. She had thought that someone like him would give up when faced with obstinate resistance, although that assertion was now fast losing ground. She had to acknowledge that he'd most likely rarely, if ever, faced resistance from any woman.

'You've made it quite clear that it is impossible for me to leave.'

That was the understatement of the year. Her conscience mocked her. She should have realised all this at the weekend, but he'd had her head in such a tizzy all she'd been able to think of was getting away from him. She realised now that if she had thought it through she could have done her best to keep him at arm's length for the duration of the merger and *then* given her notice—instead of these dramatics, which were so unlike her.

'I'll stay for the merger and then I'll be giving you my notice.'

She would just have to worry about her mother when that happened. She hated the fact that she wasn't strong enough to try and stay and resist this man indefinitely.

Aristotle just looked at her for a long, heated moment. Lucy saw a muscle throb in his temple and it made her insides quiver like jelly. He reached out a hand and cupped her jaw. Shock and instant heat paralysed her at his touch.

'Say what you want, Lucy, if it makes you feel better, but know this: we *will* be lovers. It's as inevitable as the inclement

English weather. There's something raw and singularly powerful between us and I've no intention of letting you go—either in the boardroom or in the bedroom.'

Lucy swallowed painfully. His hand still cupped her jaw, his thumb moving lazily against the sensitive skin under her chin. One thing was certain: if, in some parallel universe, she actually gave in to this man, she had no doubt that far from being given the luxury of giving notice *he'd* be the one saying goodbye—and so fast that her head would be spinning. Something like four weeks' notice would be reduced to a mocking sham of a professional nicety.

She hated the fact that it was the thought of *that* right now that made her feel more vulnerable than even the prospect of the battle to come. One other thing was sure: with every bone and last breath in her body she would resist the seduction of this man. Yet, she had to ask herself inwardly, for someone who prided herself on being frigid, why did it suddenly seem like such an uphill struggle?

A week later.

Lucy sat opposite Aristotle on his private jet as it winged its way to Athens from a stormy London. She could almost believe for a moment that she'd imagined what had happened in his office last week, when he'd declared so implacably that he was determined to have her in his bed.

Since that day when she'd been so firmly put back in her place, her letter of resignation torn up, Aristotle had been utterly consumed with business and preparations for the merger. They'd worked late into the night almost every night, and she'd been in the office most mornings as the cleaners were still finishing up. She'd never been so tired, yet so contentedly exhausted. Despite her trepidation at the undercurrents flowing under the surface, professionally speaking she'd never worked at such a heady pace, nor been entrusted with so much responsibility. The sense of pitting her wits against Aristotle and keeping up with him was exhilarating. She blocked out the snide voice that mocked her with the assertion that *work* was the only exhilarating thing.

Thankfully she hadn't had time for much more than falling into bed, snatching some food, and getting up again. The weekend had been a blur of last-minute visits to the office, packing, and a bittersweet visit to her mum, before she'd been collected by Aristotle's driver that Sunday afternoon. The visit to her mother had been bittersweet because she'd had one of her brief lucid moments, recognising Lucy as soon she'd walked into the private room at the home.

'Lucy, darling!'

Lucy had had to swallow back a lump as she'd watched her still beautifully elegant mother rise out of her chair by the window to greet her with her usual warm and tactile affection. Lucy had missed it so much. On Maxine's good days, and obviously this was one, she took care of her appearance. On her bad days Lucy would come in and, if not for the care of the attentive staff, her mother could look as unkempt as a bag lady. It made her heart ache with sadness as her mother had always been so fastidious about her looks.

Lucy had been careful not to let the emotion overwhelm her; these moments of lucidity were growing further and further apart, and she'd have her mother with her for only ten minutes before the inevitable decline came. The sentences would stop and falter, her eyes grow opaque, until finally she'd come to look at Lucy with a completely blank expression and say, 'I'm sorry, dear, who are you?'

It broke Lucy's heart to know that there was no point in even trying to explain where she was going, or that she was going to be out of the country for a few weeks. At least she could give thanks for the sterling round-the-clock care she could now afford. It made her attempt to resign from her job seem all the more childishly impetuous now. How could she jeopardise her mother's security? And yet how could she keep working for Aristotle once this merger was completed?

'Lucy.'

Lucy's head jerked round from where she'd been looking out of the window at the sea far below. Aristotle must have called her a couple of times; she could hear impatience lacing his voice. He was looking at her sternly, and at that moment Lucy realised how little space was between them—just a small table. Even as she thought that she felt Aristotle flex a leg and it brushed hers. She froze, all that heat and awareness rushing back, mocking her for believing it might have disappeared under a pile of work.

'I'm sorry. I was just thinking about something.'

He quirked a brow. 'Something more interesting than me? Or this merger? Not possible, surely.'

Lucy froze even more, she couldn't handle Aristotle when he was being like this…flirty. Yet with a steel edge. She couldn't imagine him ever being truly light, free and easy. Smiling. He was too driven, intense.

She smiled brittlely, determined that he shouldn't see his effect. 'Of course not. How could I?'

At that moment the steward arrived to serve them lunch. Lucy automatically went to clear the table and her hands brushed against Aristotle's. She flinched back but tried to mask her reaction, a flush rising up over her chest. It would appear their tenuous 'work truce' had ended. Tension was a tight cord between them.

Lucy studied her food, a delicious-looking Greek salad and fresh crusty bread.

'Would you like some wine?'

She looked up to automatically shake her head. Wine on a plane with this man was a recipe for disaster.

'Some water will be fine, thanks.'

She watched as Aristotle's lean dark hand elegantly poured himself wine, and then water for her. She muttered thanks and took a deep gulp, hoping it might dampen the flames that were licking inside her.

They ate companionably in silence. It was one of the things that perplexed her about this man. They had moments like this when she could almost imagine that they might be *friends*. She'd noticed in general that he didn't feel the need to fill silences with inane chatter, and neither did she. It surprised her to find that in common. In all honesty, if it wasn't for the great hulking elephant in the room, Lucy had to admit that so far she'd enjoyed working for Aristotle and admired his work ethic.

She was finishing her final mouthful of salad when she sensed him leaning back in his chair. She could feel the brush of his leg against hers again and fought not to move it aside. She was aware of his regard and it made her self-conscious.

'You really don't approve of me, Lucy, do you?'

She looked up, surprised. It was the last thing she would have imagined hearing him say. She gulped and wiped her mouth with a napkin, a flare of guilt assailing her.

'I… I don't think one way or the other. I'm here as your assistant, not to form a personal opinion.' She wondered wildly what had brought this on.

He folded his arms across his chest, supremely at ease.

'I've seen those little looks you dart at me—those little looks that have me all summed up. And when I asked you to send a gift to Augustine Archer, you most certainly didn't approve of that.'

Lucy was so tense now she thought she might crack. 'Like I said before…it's not my place to judge—'

'And yet you do,' he inserted silkily.

Lucy's face flamed. Yes, she did. She had him wrapped up, parcelled and boxed as being exactly like the men she'd seen court her mother, and no matter how she'd seen him treat women, the inherently unfair judgement of that made her feel unaccountably guilty all of a sudden.

It goaded her into saying, 'All right. Fine. I don't think it was particularly professional of you to ask me to send a parting gift to your mistress. It's not my business, it made me uncomfortable, and I felt that it crossed the boundaries.' *Not to mention that it made me feel angry and disappointed too.* But Lucy held her tongue. She couldn't go that far, and those revelations made her feel far too vulnerable.

She felt as prim as a mother superior, and couldn't look Aristotle in the eye, sure he had to be laughing his head off at her.

'You're right. I won't ask you to do that again.'

She looked at him in shock. His face wasn't creased in hilarity, it was stone cold sober.

'To be honest, Lucy, I did it to get a reaction out of you… and you gave it to me.'

She frowned and shook her head minutely. 'But why?'

He shrugged one broad shoulder nonchalantly, not at all put out to be discussing this, his gaze on hers not wavering for a second. 'Because I sensed something about you, under the surface…' His gaze dropped to where she could feel her breasts rising and falling with her breath. He looked back up and her heart stopped. 'And I suddenly realised that you were causing me an inordinate amount of…frustration.' His mouth tightened. 'I blamed you for the fact that it had become necessary to say goodbye to a perfectly good mistress.'

His words caused little short of an explosion of reaction within Lucy. She tried desperately to block it out—the realisation that even then—Her brain froze at that implication. Her hands clenched tight on the table and she hid them on her lap.

'Look, Aristotle…' She knew she was all but begging. 'I've already told you, I'm not interested in anything…like that. Really, I'm not. If I've given you that impression I'm really sorry.'

His eyes flashed and he leaned forward, hands on the table, starkly brown against the surface. 'Don't patronise me. You give me that impression every time you look at me. It's there right now. You're desperately aware of where my leg is—how close it is to yours under this table—'

'Stop it,' Lucy all but cried out. 'Don't do that words thing again.' She wouldn't be able to handle it.

Triumph lit Aristotle's eyes. 'See? You want me, Lucy. I can smell it from here. But don't worry. I'm not some lecherous boss who is going to force you into some compromising position. You'll come to me. It's just a matter of time before we see how long you can hold out against it.'

Between Lucy's thighs she felt indecently damp. She coloured even more hotly. Could he really smell that? Did desire have a smell? And since when had she admitted it *was* desire and not just sheer banal human reaction? The thought made her squirm, but also made her feel weak and achy. She scrambled out of her seat. She had to get away.

As she pushed past his chair he snaked out a hand and caught her wrist. She looked down, and he was looking right up at her, trapping her. She watched as he took her wrist and brought it to his mouth. He pressed his lips against the sensitive skin on the underside. And then she felt his tongue flick out to taste her there, right against her pulse. With a strangled cry that spoke more of desire than disgust, she yanked her hand away and ran, aiming for the toilet at the back, his mocking chuckle following her all the way. Any complacency she'd felt in the past week was blown sky-high to smithereens. He'd just been biding his time.

She locked herself in with shaking hands and looked at herself in the small, unforgiving mirror. She had to fatally and finally accept the knowledge that she desired this man. It wasn't just his indisputable charisma, it was *him*. And his effect on *her*. She wanted him with a hunger that she'd always intellectualised as something she'd never experience. Except now she was. And it was ten million times worse than anything she could have ever imagined.

This was nothing short of catastrophic when she'd happily devoted herself to a life that had promised to offer up only the sort of passion she could handle. Safe, staid, unexciting. She hadn't committed herself to being celibate—she did hope to one day meet someone and settle down, perhaps even have children—but at no point had she ever hoped for the kind of fulfilment that was a deep throbbing ache within her right now.

She'd unconsciously left her hair loose, and now she bundled it up again, tight, digging out some hairpins from her pocket to hold it in place. Then she searched for and found the comforting frames of her glasses. She'd kept them close by but hadn't worn them all week, as she'd been genuinely afraid of what Aristotle might do, but now she needed to send him a message once and for all. Lucy Proctor was not available and not interested. And never would be. If she told herself that enough, she might actually believe it.

Even though Aristotle might be laughing at Lucy's reaction, his body most certainly wasn't laughing. His body had never felt so serious and intent on one thing: carnal satisfaction, and with that woman. He burned from head to toe with it. The past week had been pure torture. They'd worked in such close proximity that it had taken all of his strength and will-power not to sweep aside the paperwork, throw her across his desk and take her there and then.

The only thing holding him back—apart from the very real need to prepare for the merger, and it irked him that that hadn't been enough—had been Lucy's own reaction. Any other woman, knowing that he desired her would have happily laid herself bare for his delectation. But not Lucy. She'd avoided his eye—she'd avoided *him* at all costs. She'd scurried out every night and been there quietly, studiously working every morning. Buttoned up and covered up to within an inch of her life in shapeless boxy suits.

It inflamed him and perplexed him. He'd genuinely never had to deal with this before. But what it was doing was raising the stakes, and raising his blood pressure. He was too proud to force her, even though he knew she wasn't far from tipping over the edge, but damned if he'd do it.

No, she would come to him, just as he'd declared. When she was weak with longing and stir crazy with desire she'd come to him, and this build-up would finally explode in a blaze of mutual satisfaction. He heard the bathroom door click open behind him and shifted in his seat to ease the constriction of his trousers. He picked up some work papers resignedly and it chafed—because he was not a man used to *resigning* himself to things.

For now, though, he'd use work to drown out his clamouring pulse. He would not let her see the roiling waves of frustration that gripped him and tossed him like a tiny boat in a thundering storm. When she came and sat down opposite him, and that sensual womanly smell that was so at odds with her prim appearance teased his nostrils and made his arousal even more acute, he almost groaned.

He looked up for a second. Predictably, she was looking down, immersed in papers. He saw what she'd done to her hair and the firmly reinstated glasses. He felt a surge of adrenalin and thought to himself, *Fine, if that's the way you want it.*

He pulled out his laptop and fired off a curt but informative e-mail to his assistant in Athens, instructing her to have everything ready by the time they landed in two hours. For someone with his wealth and resources, what he'd just asked for shouldn't be hard to pull off, and as he sat back he realised with a jolt that once again he felt more alive than he'd done in months.

The fact that the merger was once again relegated to second place raised just the dimmest clanging bell in his consciousness.

CHAPTER FIVE

A FEW HOURS LATER, Lucy sat on the bed of a palatial suite in one of the most expensive hotels in Athens. She'd never seen such opulence and luxury in her life. Everyone here seemed to talk in hushed tones. She'd even found herself almost whispering *thank you* to the concierge who'd shown her to her room.

Her mouth quirked dryly. Needless to say, the manager himself had shown Aristotle to *his* room. She'd seen that they were more or less next door to each other, he in the Royal Suite and she in a smaller adjoining one, although she had no intention of using the interconnecting door that had been pointed out to her. She was already far too close to her boss for comfort.

Feeling antsy, she got up and wandered about the room for a bit, looking out of the window, taking in the view of Syntagma Square and its elegant lines and trees. She hadn't expected Athens to be so…elegant. She'd seen the Acropolis in the distance and felt a lurch of joy; even though she'd travelled extensively due to her peripatetic childhood, she never tired of seeing famous monuments.

Her thoughts went inward. She hadn't failed to notice that the closer they'd got to Athens, the more tense Aristotle had grown—until by the time they'd been walking through the airport, his hand tight on her elbow, he'd been positively radioactive. She knew it had nothing to do with her. She suspected it had something to do with the way that, whenever he had to deal with his stepmother or half-brother, he always seemed to go inwards and become monosyllabic. Clearly there was no love lost between him and his family or his ancestral home, and it made Lucy wonder about that—before she realised what she was doing and put a halt to her wayward thoughts.

She checked her watch. They were due to have informal drinks with Parnassus and his team in one hour and she had to wash and change, but there was still no sign of her luggage. Lucy called down to Reception, and what the girl said made her frown.

'I'm sorry? You say my clothes are here? But I'm still waiting for my case.'

The hotel receptionist's tone was smooth, as if she was used to dealing with recalcitrant hotel guests. 'I think if you check your wardrobe, Miss Proctor you'll find everything hanging up and ready for your use. The chest of drawers is also full.'

Lucy thanked her faintly and put the phone down. She knew that Aristotle's wealth could just about do anything, but surely it couldn't magically conjure up her suitcase, unpack and store all her clothes without her even noticing? With a snaking feeling of *something* slithering down her spine, Lucy threw open the ornate door of the wardrobe in the corner and gasped.

It was full, heaving with a myriad assortment of every piece of clothing any one woman could possibly hope for. Day-wear, casual wear, evening-wear. Lucy flicked past dresses and suits and trousers and shirts and wraps and capes, feeling more and more dizzy as she did so. All sorts of shoes were lined up below the hanging clothes.

She backed away from the wardrobe with something like horror in her chest, and went to open the drawers of the chest beside the wardrobe. She pulled out T-shirts, shorts, casual trousers, capri pants… They all fell from nerveless fingers. There was thousands of euros' worth of clothes in front of her and not one stitch was hers. A deeply scooped-neck T-shirt fell from her hands and she looked at it and shuddered at the thought of how much cleavage *that* would expose. Suddenly realisation struck. *Aristotle.*

Without thinking, galvanised by pure anger, she marched over to that adjoining door between their rooms and yanked it open. To her surprise his own door was already open, leading into a room that made her own opulent one look like a prefab.

He strolled out at that moment from what she presumed must be his bedroom, naked except for a small towel around lean hips. All Lucy could see was a magnificently bronzed muscled chest, a light smattering of dark hair and long, long muscled legs. His hair was wet and slicked back, making him look somehow more approachable, vulnerable.

Seeing him like this completely scrambled her brain and defused her anger.

'I…' She realised she was breathing hard.

He stopped and looked at her enquiringly, and then she watched him lift his wrist to look at the heavy platinum watch.

'A little longer than I thought it might take, but still…not bad.'

It took a few precious seconds for what he said to sink in. He'd planned this. He'd orchestrated this and had been waiting for her to react exactly as she had. Sheer fury and impotence rushed through Lucy in a wave so strong she shook.

'Where is my case, please?'

Aristotle folded his arms and that was worse—because where his shirt might have hidden those biceps, now she could see them in all their olive-skinned, bunched glory. Lord, but he was beautiful, and her body was reacting like the Road Runner, seeing his mate in the distance.

'Your case is somewhere safe. I've taken the liberty of removing the items I think you'll need, like your toiletries. I didn't want to presume to know what products you like to use.'

'Yet you can presume to know what clothes I may like and my size?' Her voice fairly crackled with ice.

His gaze drifted down over her body, and she cursed herself for inciting him. His eyes met hers again and he drawled, 'I think you'll find that everything…fits.'

She cursed him under her breath. She wouldn't be surprised to find them all a size too small, and if they were…

But he wasn't finished. 'I also decided that from what I've seen you're more than capable of choosing your own underwear. You'll find the items I've taken out there, in that bag.'

He gestured to a table nearby, where one of the hotel bags was sitting, a lacy bra strap dangling provocatively from the top. Blind rage and humiliation at the thought he'd handled her intimate clothes, and at remembering that he'd seen her changing, almost made Lucy stumble as she stalked over to get it. But in that instant she vowed she would not react as he was expecting her to. She would not give him the satisfaction.

So she merely walked back to the door, turned and, avoiding his eye, said grimly, 'I'll see you in the lobby in forty-five minutes.'

'I'm looking forward to it, Lucy.'

It took an awful lot of restraint not to slam both interconnecting doors as Lucy went back into her own room, but under a steaming hot shower minutes later she vented her anger with no holds barred.

Some forty-five minutes later Lucy paced in the lobby and ineffectually tried to pull the dress down again. It felt indecently short, even though it came to just above her knees. She hated the fact that otherwise it fitted like a glove. And she'd never worn shoes with heels so spiky they looked like a lethal weapon, but it had been them or flat shoes, and even *she* had enough fashion pride not to make a complete fool of herself. She also hated the fact that they made her feel somehow…powerful. She couldn't say the word *sexy*. Her brain seized at the mere nebulous thought.

Aristotle watched Lucy from behind a plant for a moment, feeling curiously protective—and something else: surprised at her obvious reluctance to embrace her innate sexiness, especially when she oozed such voluptuous femininity. She'd chosen one of the least revealing dresses, but even that made his blood boil over with lust.

It had a high neck but, unlike her other sack of a dress, this one was cut to define a woman's body, to hug and emphasise its curves. When she turned to the side he had to draw in a breath. Her breasts were so beautifully shaped and enticingly full that he noticed more than one man falter as he saw her.

That galvanised Aristotle to move. Possessiveness was an alien emotion, but it was coursing through him now as he took in the way the dress drew the eye to those stupendously long and slender legs, a discreet slit showcasing their shapeliness. And those shoes…

Lucy turned away abruptly. She'd noticed a man nearly tripping over himself as he'd seen her and she flushed with mortification. He probably thought she was a call girl. She felt like one. This was ridiculous. She was going to demand her own things back—

Suddenly Aristotle was right in front of her and, as was becoming annoyingly familiar, her brain emptied of all rational thought. He was dressed in a black suit, white shirt and royal blue tie. It somehow made his eyes pop out, even though they were a dark slumberous green. But weren't they normally light green? As Lucy was wondering this, as if it had become the most important question in the universe, Aristotle moved so fast that she didn't even notice until he'd whipped her glasses off her face and removed the pins from her hair.

'Hey!' she cried out, too late, only to see him calmly snap her glasses in two and feel the heavy fall of her hair around her shoulders. He took her by the arm and marched her out towards the entrance, handing her broken glasses and hairpins to an unsurprised-looking doorman, who took them obsequiously, clearly not fazed by such behaviour. It made Lucy even madder. Those glasses had been her last bastion of defence and he'd merely ripped it away, like removing a toy from a cranky child.

She barely noticed the pleasantly warm early evening air caressing her skin between the hotel and the luxury car. When they were ensconced in the back, Aristotle curtly ordered the driver to put up the privacy partition, which he duly did. Lucy's mouth was opening and closing ineffectually, steam practically coming out of her ears as Aristotle rounded on her, blocking out any daylight coming through the tinted windows. Absurdly, in that split second Lucy thought how unbearably intimate it seemed to make the space.

'Enough,' he growled out, and before she knew which end was up Aristotle had reached out, hauled her into his chest and his mouth was over hers. He was kissing her as if his life depended on it, one arm like steel across her back, one hand in her hair, clasping her head. There was no hesitation. Lust exploded in a blaze of heat.

All of Lucy's reflex denials melted away in a flame of desire so profound and deep that she couldn't question it. All she knew was that Aristotle's mouth was on hers, his tongue stabbing deep, with ruthless precision, and she was *craving* it. Her breasts were crushed against his chest, her hands trapped against those hard contours, and the beat of his heart was an unsteady tattoo that made her own beat faster.

She forced her hands free to twine them around Aristotle's neck, fingers pushing upwards into the thick, silky hair that brushed his collar. He groaned deep in his throat, their mouths not parting for a moment, lost in a dark, lustrous world of tasting and touching, of sensation heaping on top of sensation so acutely delicious that when Lucy felt herself being lowered back onto the seat behind her, and Aristotle coming over her, she too gave a deep moan of approval.

All she knew was here and now. Sanity had ceased to exist. The outside world? Gone.

This was her world, and this man was the only thing in it. His huge hard body crushed hers to the seat beneath her, but her arms were free and she explored and spread them under his jacket to feel the latent strength of his broad shoulders.

His mouth left hers to blaze a trail of hot kisses along her jaw and down her throat, where he nipped gently and then sucked, making her squirm as an arrow of pure lust shot to her groin, making her wet.

As if he'd read her mind, she felt his hand encircle her ankle and start to travel up her leg. He breathed into her mouth, 'Remember what I said the other day?'

Words couldn't impinge upon her mind in this drenching of desire. Lucy couldn't function. She was finding it hard to open her eyes, finding it hard to breathe as she looked up and drowned in dark green oceans. She didn't recognise the man above her. The expression on his face was so raw and elemental. All she knew was that he looked exactly how she felt. Her breasts were tight and aching, tips chafing against the confining bra and dress. And slowly, so slowly, his hand was climbing with relentless precision, until its heat was wrapped around her upper thigh, where her sheer stockings ended. His fingers spread wide to encompass as much as he could touch. Any second now they'd be on her bare skin. She stopped breathing in earnest.

'Please…' Was that voice hers? Who was she anyway? She was suffering from temporary amnesia. Somewhere distant, where a bell was ringing, she felt something wanting to intrude, but more than that she wanted *this*. It felt so right and so necessary. Too right to question.

'Please… *Ari…*'

With a muffled groan of something that sounded Greek and almost painful, he lowered his head, took her mouth again. Their tongues connected feverishly just as his hand hovered and tantalised at the tender place of her soft inner thigh, on the edge of her silk pants. Lucy tore her mouth away and arched herself towards him, gripping his shoulders. She could feel the heavy stabbing weight of his erection against her leg and she moved experimentally, exulting in his answering growl of unmistakable torture.

And then he was *there*, fingers pushing aside the barrier of her pants to slide into hot slickness, where she ached most. She sucked in a breath, shocked eyes opening wide. She looked up and his fingers began to move, finding the secret spot and pressing it, flicking it. Blood roared into Lucy's head, drowning out everything but the clamour for satisfaction which was coming towards her like the mirage of an oasis in the desert.

And then suddenly, as quickly as this insanity had taken over, it was gone. Aristotle was taking away his hand, moving back, his features harsh and unbearably tight. Cold seeped into Lucy as she realised where she was. She was supine on the back seat of a car, her legs spread, and her boss had just been—

Oh God.

She also realised what Aristotle had realised way before her: they had stopped, obviously at their destination, and the driver was patiently knocking on the privacy window. They hadn't heard him because—

Oh God.

More shame and mortification and self-disgust than she could ever remember feeling coursed through Lucy in a tidal wave of heat so intense she felt feverish. She scrambled to sit up, hands shaking as she pulled her dress down to cover her thighs.

A large brown hand came over hers, and she had to stop herself flinching back.

'OK?'

The huskily asked question surprised her. *It was almost as if he really cared.* But she couldn't look at him, just nodded jerkily, a curtain of hair hiding her face from view. She could give thanks for once that it was down. She didn't think she could ever look at him ever again. In the split seconds they had as they gathered themselves and she heard Aristotle—*Ari*—speak to the driver, Lucy tried to assimilate what had just happened.

The fact that she'd all but drowned in an instantaneous pool of lust in his arms was evident enough. She'd deal with that in a darkened room on her own later. But it was the fact that it had happened without hesitation, with not even a flicker of rejection or desire to draw back. Was it simply because after weeks of denying this to herself, weeks of this desire building and building, the merest touch had sent her up in flames and she'd been unable to draw up even the flimsiest of defences? She'd turned into a complete wanton.

When Aristotle climbed out of the car, and Lucy readied herself to step out too, she realised that any vulnerability she'd felt before had paled into pathetic insignificance. The truth swirled sickeningly in her breast. She truly was her mother's daughter, and that knowledge jeered her for all her efforts to deny it for so long.

There was no going back now, not after that little performance, and she quaked when she saw the huge looming shape materialise on the other side of the door. That everything she feared most lay outside that door right now was obvious, and also the fact that she'd just kissed goodbye to any pretence of a defence she might dream up to excuse her behaviour. The door opened abruptly and Lucy was compelled to step out, taking the hand that was offered and forcing down the frisson of electricity at even that innocuous touch. She felt as though the entire world had changed, and suddenly her place in it.

It was while they were standing alone for a moment, in the luxurious salon of the palatial Parnassus villa on the outskirts of Athens, that Lucy felt Aristotle turn towards her. She closed her eyes momentarily and pleaded silently, *Please don't look at me...please don't say anything.* But since when were her prayers answered? She opened her eyes and gritted her jaw.

Aristotle looked down at Lucy and felt completely out of his depth. He still couldn't quite believe what had happened in the back of his car. He'd never, *ever* been so consumed with lust like that—that he'd laid a woman down in the back seat and all but made love to her there and then. When he thought of it now, of how close he'd been to unzipping his fly—his hand clenched around his drink and he had to force it to unclench.

Lucy hadn't looked at him since she'd stepped out of the car and he couldn't blame her. What was it he'd said? That he wouldn't be a lecherous boss? And then within seconds of getting into an enclosed space… But she'd been so responsive, dammit. Like his most potent dream, his hottest fantasy. She'd been hot, willing, passionate…*wet* for him. His body tightened again. She'd shown him the woman she was hiding under all that primness.

It was hard to equate the woman who'd paled at seeing her bra strap hanging out of a bag earlier to the woman who'd almost come apart in his arms less than a couple of hours ago.

'Lucy?'

He could see her grit her jaw, and it was only then that he noticed the faint pink mark on her neck. Shock coursed through him—and self-disgust. He'd given her a love bite? The last time he'd given a woman a love bite it had been a *girl*, and in a boarding school in England, probably at the age of thirteen. All of a sudden Aristotle felt anger for what this woman was reducing him to.

He took her arm and tried to ignore the way her skin felt, tried to ignore the way he wanted to caress it, tried to ignore the way she looked almost green.

'Lucy, look at me.'

With the utmost reluctance Lucy turned her head and looked up, willing her reaction far down. She even pasted a smile on her face. 'Yes?'

Aristotle looked angry. 'Lucy…' He sighed with exasperation and ran his other hand through his hair, leaving it to flop back in such sexy disarray that Lucy felt her knees tremble.

'I had no intention of kissing you like that, and I'm sorry. It shouldn't have happened—'

'No, it shouldn't.'

His eyes narrowed dangerously. He turned so that the room was blocked out and it was just the two of them facing each other.

'That's not what I meant. I was going to say it shouldn't have happened *like that.*'

'Well, it shouldn't have happened at all.'

Aristotle's brow went up. Lucy hated that brow.

'Are you going to try and tell me that you didn't like it? Or that I was mauling you again? What was it you called me? *Ari*?'

'Stop it,' Lucy hissed, a crimson tide washing into her face when she remembered that passionate entreaty, how easily it had fallen from her lips. 'Of course I'm not going to say…that. But it shouldn't have happened, and it's not going to happen again.'

Aristotle moved closer, and Lucy realised that she couldn't move back as there was a plant behind her. His heat and that innately musky scent came and wrapped itself around her, binding her into the memory of what had happened, making longing rush through her. And she hated it.

Aristotle's face was a harsh mask of self-recrimination as he said, 'It *will* be happening again, Lucy—just not in the back seat of a car. Somewhere infinitely more comfortable, where we won't be constricted by space and hampered by clothes.'

Just then someone approached, and Aristotle smoothly turned to deal with the newcomer, stunning Lucy with his ability to morph from intensely demanding alpha male to urbane businessman. And for the rest of the evening, as she accompanied him around the room, meeting and greeting the people involved in the Parnassus side of the merger, she could almost be forgiven for thinking she'd imagined the whole thing.

While they were in Athens Lucy was to be Aristotle's executive assistant. She'd met Martha, his Greek PA, a pleasant older lady who she'd spoken to on the phone before. She met them at the hotel earlier. *She* was going to deal with the day-to-day office stuff. Martha wasn't aware of the merger. In fact none of his family seemed to be—something which had perplexed Lucy.

Mr Parnassus approached them now, distracting her from her thoughts. He and Aristotle had already gone to his study for a private meeting as soon as they'd arrived. Now this old and stooped man, who walked with a cane, looked Lucy up and down with a wink. They'd been introduced earlier.

He said to Aristotle, 'Well, Ari, do you think we can trust her?'

Aristotle's voice was deep and authoritative. 'Absolutely. She's been with my firm for over two years now.'

As they continued to converse, Lucy decided that she liked Parnassus. He had a friendly twinkle in his eye. Suddenly he declared that Aristotle should go and mingle so that he could 'take this beautiful young woman outside for a turn around the patio'.

At a pointed look from her boss that Lucy couldn't really fathom, she gave her arm to Parnassus and led the way outside. It was night and the sky was clear, stars twinkling over a commanding view down into Athens. Momentarily relieved to be out of Aristotle's disturbing orbit, Lucy breathed in. 'It's so beautiful here. You have a lovely home, Mr Parnassus.'

'Please, call me Georgios.'

Lucy smiled. 'Very well. Georgios.'

He looked at her with shrewd eyes. 'He must trust you very much. This merger is very important. Not even his own family know about it.'

Lucy's belly clenched painfully. It wasn't so much about trust as necessity and desire, but of course she couldn't explain that. She frowned slightly. 'I'm aware of that.' She didn't want to say more. She didn't know Aristotle's reasons for not divulging this to his family, and she knew the only reason they were here in Athens was because Parnassus had requested it.

'He's driven.'

Lucy was lost in her thoughts for a moment. She almost didn't hear what the man said. But he was continuing, looking down at the view laid out before them.

'He reminds me of myself when I was his age.' Parnassus smiled, but it seemed sad. 'He reminds me of my own son. In exile. Driven to succeed at all costs. And for what?'

Lucy was nonplussed. Parnassus caught her look and chuckled. 'I'm sorry—you don't want to hear an old man's ramblings. We should go back inside.'

She put out a hand. 'Oh, not at all… I just… I don't know Ar—' She blushed. 'That is, I don't know Mr Levakis all that well.'

Parnassus stalled and looked at her closely. He gestured with an arm to encompass the view and the villa. 'See all this?'

Lucy nodded and sat back against the balustrade, captivated by this wizened man, by his deeply ingrained accent which he obviously hadn't lost despite living in the US for decades.

'It's taken me years to build it up. My family left this country in shame, and all I've ever wanted was to come back in a blaze of glory.'

Lucy frowned. 'But…that's what you're doing with this merger, isn't it?'

He shrugged one bony shoulder. '*Ack*. In some ways. It's not how I imagined it, even though I'll get what *I* want for my children, whether they want it or not: re-introduction and acceptance into Athens society. But the ultimate glory will belong to that man in there, and he's welcome to it.'

They both looked to where Aristotle stood, surrounded by a fawning crowd. Lucy shivered slightly despite the treacherous heat curling down low in her abdomen. He reminded her of a lone wolf. Head and shoulders above everyone else, supremely confident, supremely sexy and yet…*alone*. She hadn't really thought of him like that before, and didn't like the tender feelings it aroused.

At that moment a very glamorous-looking middle-aged woman came out to the terrace. Parnassus introduced her as his wife, bade Lucy goodnight and went back inside. Lucy turned to face the view again, her mind full of questions. She wrapped her arms around herself, feeling a sudden cool breeze. What did Parnassus mean about Aristotle? Did he somehow see him heading for an empty life, driven by a need to succeed? Clearly he wasn't far wrong. Aristotle had said himself that this merger was the most important thing, and yet—

She jumped when she felt a warm blanket of heat settle around her shoulders and heard a deep, 'We should get going. We've got a busy day tomorrow.'

His jacket was warm with his body heat and scent. It enveloped Lucy, making her sway a little as they went back in. She didn't say a word. Every nerve was twanging at the thought of sharing a car with him again, and her head was bursting with all the enigmatic questions Parnassus had posed.

But she needn't have worried. Aristotle couldn't have made it clearer he had no intention of touching her. Lucy sat in her corner and watched as they were driven down the hill towards the city centre. Feeling somehow compelled, she turned to face Aristotle and asked, 'Don't you have a family home here?'

She sensed him tensing, but he just said, without looking at her, 'Yes, it was my father's home, but I prefer to stay in a hotel.'

And then, before Lucy could halt her runaway mouth, she heard herself asking, 'Why don't your family know about the merger?'

His head whipped around so fast that she nearly flinched back. The lines in his face were stark. 'What makes you ask that?' The thread of warning was explicit.

Lucy shrugged. 'I just…wondered.'

'None of them are aware,' he said curtly. 'And I've already told you they must not know. As far as they're concerned I'm here for three weeks to check up on the Athens side of the business.'

Lucy's jaw clenched. 'I know all that, and of course I won't be telling them anything. I'm well aware of the terms of my *contract*.'

She turned her head away, stunned to feel a welling of emotion and discover that she had sudden tears stinging the backs of her eyes. What on earth was *that* about?

When she felt her hand being taken by a much larger, warmer one, her heart tripped. She looked around warily. She couldn't really see Aristotle's face in the dark gloom.

He sounded weary all of a sudden. 'Look, it's complicated, OK? It's family stuff between them and me and they just don't need to know. It's for security reasons…'

'That's all you had to say.' Lucy took her hand from his and took off his jacket, handing it back to him. 'I'm warm enough now, thanks.'

Boss/assistant. The lines of demarcation were unmistakable. Aristotle cursed himself again for having lost control earlier. In all honesty the depth of that desire still shook him up. He took the jacket and watched as she turned her head to look out of the window again. The curve of her cheekbone, the fall of her hair was an enticing temptation to turn her face back, seek out those warm lips, sink into her yielding soft body again.

He swore under his breath. He'd vowed he wouldn't take her like some randy over-sexed teenager, but here he was mentally stripping her, moments away from trying to seduce her all over again. He sat rigid in his seat the whole way back to the hotel. *Never* had a woman caused him this much frustration.

When they got back to the hotel Lucy skittered away from him like a scared foal. He let her go, bidding her goodnight, then went into the bar and ordered himself a shot of whisky. It was going to be a long three weeks.

Towards the end of that first week, Lucy half heard a question from Aristotle as they sat in his office in the centre of Athens. In essence they were conducting separate lives: presenting a benign face to his Athens-based company, and conducting top secret meetings with Parnassus at the same time. The meetings with Parnassus' side were complicated and technical, calling on all of Lucy's skills and much of the small amount of legal training she'd done.

She'd met his stepmother Helen and half-brother Anatolios, at a general board meeting that morning. The stepmother was tall and thin and cold, effortlessly supercilious. His half-brother was nothing like Aristotle. He was blond, shorter and had a spoilt, weak-looking face. It hadn't taken Lucy much to deduce that his brother had a serious jealousy complex as he'd frowned sulkily throughout the meeting, clearly hating having Aristotle back to remind everyone who the *real* boss was. After meeting them, she didn't entirely blame Aristotle for wanting to keep his distance.

'…to put in an appearance at the charity ball tonight.'

Lucy realised she was being spoken to and looked up. 'I'm sorry…?'

Her voice drifted away as she was caught by the gleam in Aristotle's eyes. They were sitting close together, side by side at a table, with papers strewn everywhere. For the whole week, ever since the night they'd arrived and that earth-shattering moment in the car, she'd been rigid with tension, happily throwing herself into work to try and escape from dealing with…*this.*

But it hummed around them now, this awareness. She'd been so careful not to let it catch her unawares, but she had failed in this instance. And in all honesty she knew that it was largely to do with Aristotle's own restraint. He'd been cool and solicitous all week. Not a hint of what had happened in his behaviour. At first it had thrown her, she'd been absurdly suspicious, but now… She realised it had been there all along. She knew it and he knew it, and much to her utter shame a flutter of dark excitement erupted deep in her belly.

She tried to ignore it. 'I'm sorry—what did you say?'

Aristotle looked at her and stifled a groan. Her eyes were huge pools of swirling grey, like a stormy ocean, with lashes so long and dark he could already imagine them fluttering against his cheek. *How* he'd managed not to touch her all week he couldn't really fathom. It had taken super-human restraint, but he'd been determined to prove to himself that she didn't exert that much control over him. Except it had been an exercise in failure, because she did. His mind had constantly been taken from business.

It didn't help that because of the wardrobe he'd provided, which was perfectly respectable, she was unwittingly displaying more of her luscious body. He knew she was deliberately choosing the most *un*revealing clothes, but conversely they were making him want to unwrap her like a delicious parcel.

At the board meeting earlier, when he'd seen his own half-brother's eyes riveted to Lucy's cleavage, he'd wanted to reach across the table and punch him in the face. Being driven to violence by a woman was a very novel experience, and he had to put it down to sexual frustration.

He cleared his throat and dragged his eyes back up, vowing silently to himself that he'd have her in his bed within twenty-four hours. He couldn't take much more of this.

'The charity ball tonight. Everyone will be there—including Parnassus. Needless to say it'll be seen entirely as a coincidence that we're there too. When we meet any of his people we'll affect no knowledge of having met before.'

Lucy had seen the extent of the security detail that both Aristotle and Parnassus commanded, so there had been no chance of a leak. Again the size and importance of what they were working on stunned her.

She asked abruptly, '*Why* is it so important that nobody knows of this, exactly?'

Aristotle's mouth thinned. 'Because our two companies merging will put a lot of noses out of joint. We'll effectively be blowing any competition out of the water; the only companies who will remain safe are the ones who are huge enough to withstand the pressure—people like Kouros Shipping, for instance.'

Lucy nodded, she'd heard of Alexandros Kouros. 'But…your family?'

His eyes flashed at her persistence, but he answered tightly, 'My stepmother and brother would oppose this absolutely. Helen would see it as a dilution of my father's name and a threat to her security. If my brother had even an inkling of this happening he'd do his best to derail it just to get at me. That's why we have to be vigilant. And they'll be at the ball tonight too.' His mouth twisted. 'Although I wouldn't worry about *him* too much—no doubt he'll be more concerned about scoring the best drugs and the best women.'

Lucy hid her shock at this evidence of little love lost. She quashed her immediate questions. She had no desire to know about Aristotle's family history. None at all.

CHAPTER SIX

THAT EVENING, after they'd eaten a sumptuous dinner, Lucy found herself separated from Aristotle. She was feeling almost relaxed, which she knew had something to do with the fact that she'd been seated apart from him, even though she'd felt the weight of his gaze from across the table, periodically.

She'd been seated next to Kallie Kouros, the wife of Alexandros Kouros, who'd proved to be down to earth and utterly charming, giving Lucy hilarious tidbits of information about Athenian society. When her gorgeous husband had come to whisk her away they'd looked so in love, and he'd been so innately protective, it had made a very secret part of Lucy ache... It surprised her, as she'd never found herself envious of happy couples before.

Lucy craned her neck to try and find Aristotle, not even sure why she felt compelled to do so when he was clearly only too happy to leave her to her own devices. Finally she saw him across the room, with his head bent towards a very blonde and very beautiful woman. She saw him smile and it impacted her deeply. He'd never smiled at *her* like that. *Yes, he did*, reminded a little voice. *That night outside your apartment.*

Immediately she could feel her blood cooling, the colour draining from her face. A strange falling feeling made her feel shaky all of a sudden. On a complete reflex, to deny her reaction and the fact that it might possibly be stemming from feeling *jealous*, she whirled around and made blindly for the ladies room.

After collecting herself she went to the sink and splashed some cold water on her face. When she stood up again she nearly jumped out of her skin to see Helen Levakis, Aristotle's stepmother standing beside her, reapplying her blood-red lipstick.

She looked at Lucy and said, 'Lizzie, wasn't it?'

Lucy shook her head, fascinated by this woman's brittle shell. 'Lucy.'

The woman smiled insincerely. 'My apologies. Ari seems to have a new assistant every time he comes home.'

Lucy washed her hands briskly. 'It's no problem.'

Helen Levakis turned and rested back against the ledge. 'You're sleeping with him, aren't you? I saw that little look outside, when you saw him with another woman.'

Lucy tried and knew she was probably failing to keep the shock from her face. This woman had stuck a knife right into the tender heart of her, and to realise that was huge.

She found her voice. 'Excuse me, but I really don't think it's any of your—'

'You're right,' the woman dismissed cuttingly. 'However, I thought I'd do you a favour. Ari may *sleep* with a woman like you, but he'll never marry a woman like you. That's more than likely why he's home. He'll be looking for a suitable bride soon. A man like him? He'll want to have an heir to secure his inheritance. He'll do anything to stop his brother getting what's rightfully his.'

Lucy watched the tall thin woman disappear back out into the bustling throng with a last glacial glance. She turned to face the mirror, realised that she was holding her breath and let it out in a big whoosh. What on earth had precipitated that? And what did she mean about his brother? And was Ari really looking for a suitable bride as well as the merger? And was she really that transparent?

Lucy forced herself to stand tall and looked at herself critically. She'd chosen one of the less revealing dresses, but still she wanted to yank it up and pull it down. One-shouldered, silk, it cut across her bosom far too low for her liking, and showed a veritable acreage of pale skin, which she was very conscious of in this milieu of much skinnier, more sun-kissed people.

The dark grey seemed to make her eyes stand out too large in her face, and her hectic flush had nothing to do with make-up and everything to do with embarrassment that everyone in the room must have seen her mooning after her boss. Well, it ended here. For the next two weeks it was work only. She'd keep Aristotle at arm's length however she could. A dart of doubt struck her. How did she know he hadn't already transferred his affections to that blonde? Perhaps he'd finally grown weary of chasing his too tall and too buxom secretary?

Choking back a frustrated cry at her own awful weakness and feeling so vulnerable, she left the bathroom—every intention of going back to the hotel. She got out to the lobby and retrieved her coat. She'd just leave a note for—

'Where have you been?'

A hard hand whirled her around so fast she lost her balance and ended up plastered against Aristotle's chest, looking up, slightly winded. When she realised what she was doing she scrambled back, inarticulate anger rushing through her. 'I'm going back to the hotel. I'm tired.'

'Well, I'm not—and we're not finished here.'

'It's a social event. Surely you don't need me to work.'

'I…' Ari faltered. He'd been about to say, *I do need you.* But she was right. It wasn't for work, and if it wasn't for work then what was it? Had he got so used to her calm, insightful presence? Had he really missed her throughout dinner?

He made the only decision he could. 'Fine, then I'll escort you back.'

A huge neon danger sign flashed over Lucy's head. 'No!' She tempered her response. 'I mean—you stay. I don't want to drag you away…' *From that blonde you were obviously enjoying so much.*

But in his usual arrogant way he'd already taken her arm and was leading her outside, where as if by magic his car drew up in front of them.

She tried again in the car. 'Really, you should stay.'

He quirked a small hard smile, leaning back easily, studying her. 'Oh, really? Should I?'

Lucy's hands twisted in her lap. She felt something intangible shift between them. The energy was palpable. 'Yes…' Why did her voice sound breathy all of a sudden? 'Yes,' she said again, stronger. 'You should. You obviously have…people to talk to.'

Aristotle grimaced when he recalled trying to evade the clutches of Pia Kyriapoulos just now. A very beautiful and very wealthy divorcee, she'd made it quite clear what he could expect if he wanted to indulge in an affair while in Athens. Before, he might have been tempted—she was offering just what he liked, no-strings sex—but now…the only woman he wanted was sitting just a few inches away from him, and he couldn't contemplate sex with anyone else.

'You're wrong, Lucy,' he drawled in deep honeyed tones. 'There's no one I want to talk to, and I am only too happy to escort you back.'

Lucy stifled a retort and looked out of the window, a mixture of dread and excitement licking through her when she remembered the last time he'd insisted on taking her home.

Far too soon they were pulling up outside their hotel. Lucy scrambled inelegantly from the car before her door could be opened. But of course her attempts were futile. Aristotle caught up with her easily and took her arm again, leading them over to the gleaming lifts.

Once inside, standing apart from him, Lucy looked up resolutely. She nearly collapsed when she heard Aristotle say innocuously, 'Do you remember the first time we met in a lift?'

Shocked and aghast, she looked at him—and realised too late that it was a mistake. 'The first time we…?'

'Met in a lift,' he said easily, turning to look up at the display. 'Funnily enough, the day you walked into my office to interview for the job I remembered it.' He looked back down at her. 'In vivid detail.'

Lucy was barely aware that she was still standing. She wanted to put out a hand to hold onto something, but the only solid thing was *him*. She prayed she wouldn't collapse.

She shook her head. 'No,' she croaked…and then knew she couldn't lie. 'That is…yes. I remember you using the staff lift, but I don't remember much else.'

Her heart was thumping as all she could remember right then was how hard his body had felt underneath hers. A lot like it had felt *over* hers the other day in the car.

The lift doors opened and Lucy almost fell out. Aristotle walked alongside her easily. Her legs were trembling. As she tried and failed to stick her keycard in her door she felt it taken out of her hand imperiously, and watched helplessly when he effortlessly opened the door.

When she stepped in he said quietly, 'Who knew you were such a consummate liar, Lucy Proctor?'

She turned around, affronted. 'What's that supposed to mean?' She saw that he'd neatly stepped into the room too, and when the door closed behind him her heart seemed to spasm in her chest. 'And what do you think you're doing in here?'

'Proving what a liar you are, Lucy Proctor.'

And then he reached out, two big hands encompassing her waist, and pulled her inexorably towards him, towards that searing heat. Lucy, gripped by an awful feeling of inevitability, stumbled right into his chest.

'This is much better,' Aristotle growled as she fell against him, and he lifted his hands to cup her face and thread fingers through her hair. 'Now I have you exactly where I want you.'

Lucy couldn't help a groan of reluctant supplication when he bent his head and took her mouth. It felt as if he'd injected some kind of life force into her body. Every nerve came tinglingly alive, her heart-rate sped up, her skin seemed to glow… and down below, between her legs, she could already feel her traitorous body responding hotly, wetly.

His tongue swirled, sought hers, sucked it deep into his mouth. She felt fireworks explode in her head. Then he was nipping gently at her lower lip and sucking it, exploring the gap in her teeth and saying throatily, 'Bite me…'

A feeling of exultation took her over. She felt him push her coat off her shoulders to the floor and hardly noticed. Experimentally, shyly, she bit down on his sensual lower lip, feeling its cushiony springiness, soothing with her tongue where she'd bitten.

He growled something indecipherable, and then she felt him searching for and undoing the zip at the side of her dress, pulling it aside so that one lace covered breast was bared. He lifted a hand and cupped its weight. Lucy bit her lip. She felt heavy, aching with a pooling of desire, and it was such an alien feeling it held her in its grip.

One of his big hands reached down and cupped her round buttocks, drawing her up and into him, where she could feel his arousal digging into soft flesh. She felt more liquid heat and instinctively closed her legs against it.

He was palming her breast, a thumb hovering teasingly over the puckered tip, Tension mounted until Lucy wanted to scream, and finally he lowered his head. Her own fell back when she felt that tight, aching lace-covered tip being drawn into the hot, sucking spiral of intense desire that was his mouth.

His hand gripped her buttock and she strained upwards, urging him to suck harder, her hips moving sinuously against his.

She was seeking for a pinnacle that she'd never experienced before, but she knew it was there somewhere.

Something made Lucy open her eyes, and she drew in a shocked breath when she saw their reflections in the mirror across the room, highlighted by the one dim lamp in the corner. They must have moved from the door somehow, although Lucy knew that an earthquake might have happened and she wouldn't have noticed. The image shocked her to the core. It was so explicit…and so like something she'd witnessed as a child, when she'd walked in on her mother unannounced one day.

Sanity and reality didn't trickle back—they exploded in her face. In a second she'd pushed Aristotle away and was pulling up her dress to cover her heaving breasts. She shook violently.

'Get out of here—*now*.'

She spied something from the corner of her eye and moved, grabbing the hotel robe from the end of her bed and pulling it on, wrapping it tightly around her, belting it firmly. She went and stood near the window, her brain hurting and her body throbbing with unfulfilled desire.

'*Please* just get out.'

'No, Lucy, I won't.' Aristotle's voice was unbearably harsh.

She could only imagine how angry he must be with her. She knew what men called women who—

'Look, I'm sorry. I should never have let that happen—it's entirely my fault.'

'You didn't *let* it happen, Lucy. You weren't helpless. You wanted it as much as I did.'

She shook her head dumbly and felt tears threaten.

Aristotle stepped forward then, and stopped a few feet away. His face looked as if it was carved from stone and Lucy quaked inwardly. She wanted to say sorry again, but didn't. His bow-tie was askew, his hair ruffled. Had she done that?

He frowned, as if trying to understand. 'Lucy, did someone do something to you? Did someone hurt you?'

She shook her head quickly. 'No…nothing like that.'

He shook his head. 'Well, if it's not that…what is it?'

She felt like crying in earnest now. How could she get into her tangled emotional history? Into how threatened she felt by the way he made her feel?

'I just… I don't want this. I don't want to *feel* this way.' It was the closest she could come to an admission.

Aristotle was unsympathetic. 'Well, tough—because you do and I do. It's called chemistry and it's unavoidable.'

'What if I leave?' Lucy asked hopefully.

He shook his head. 'We've been through this. You're not going anywhere.'

Her shoulders slumped, and she missed the flash of something that crossed Aristotle's face.

'Look,' Lucy began awkwardly, 'I'm not experienced—I'm not like the women you go for. I won't know how to…'

'You already do, sweetheart, without even trying.'

She looked up. It seemed important to say it. 'I'm not a virgin… I've had sex before.' *Once.* 'But I didn't feel anything. So I know that…it won't do anything for me.'

He came close and tipped her chin up. Lucy tried to avoid his eye but it was impossible.

'Are you seriously trying to tell me that you think you won't enjoy having sex?'

She shrugged, feeling very silly.

'Lucy, in case you haven't noticed, you're a sensualist. That's the only word I can find to describe you. Even though you seem determined to deny it, and I've no idea why that is. Don't you know why you have a taste for exotic underwear?'

'It's because…' Lucy stopped, remembering all those shopping trips with her mother—how she'd had it drummed into her how important it was to buy decent underclothes. But of course other teenage girls hadn't had the privilege of shopping with the scandalous Maxine Malbec.

'It's because I developed too early. I'm too…' her face burnt and she was glad of the dim light '…big. To get the right sizes you have to pay more…'

His hand still gripped her chin. 'Lucy, there's a whole nation of women out there bigger than you who wear woefully fitting underwear. Can't you just admit that you're drawn to it? To the feel of it against your skin? How it fits and makes you look—'

She tore his hand away and stepped back further. 'No.' But she knew his words had made an impact. *Did* she instinctively like it? *Was* she a sensualist, despite everything—just like her mother? Well, she'd proven spectacularly that in all other respects their shared genes certainly seemed to be showing themselves.

'No. Look… I have my reasons for not wanting this. I just… want you to respect that.'

Ari fought the most intense battle of his life as he looked at her downbent head and the tightly drawn belt on the robe. His body burned and ached. He felt hard from tip to toe and couldn't believe she was denying them this.

But he found some strength from somewhere. He stepped close again and saw the way Lucy's body tensed even more. In that instant something inside him melted. He wanted this woman with a passion he'd never known before, but he didn't want to force her. He felt an uncomfortable level of concern grip him as he tipped her chin up to see her face. She avoided his eyes. He felt her grit her jaw against his hand and his stomach clenched. He rubbed his thumb back and forth over silky smooth skin. The bones felt unbelievably delicate. Her jaw finally relaxed, and something akin to triumph moved through him.

Suddenly the urge to take Lucy to bed was superseded by his wanting to reassure her. He had the insane impulse to pull her close and tell her everything was going to be OK. Something deeply ingrained within him kept him from making the move, but it made his voice husky.

'I'm going to leave, but I want you to think about this, Lucy. What's between us is more than a banal attraction that happens every day of the week. This is…' His own words surprised him, and so did the emotion he could feel behind them, but he told himself it was just because he wanted her so badly. ' This is something much stronger. I don't know what demons you're fighting, and I can't fight them for you. Only you can do that. I'm going to leave the interconnecting door to my room open. I'd like you to use it, Lucy… I want to explore what this is with you…'

His mouth twisted. 'I've no doubt it'll burn itself out, but it's not going to go away until we do explore it. It's just going to get stronger. It's up to you. If you're strong enough to resist this then by God I hope you have enough strength for the both of us.'

Lucy's breath had stalled, and because it was hard not to she found herself staring directly into his eyes. What she saw there made her heart twist. It wasn't the heated intensity she'd expected—well, *it was*—but it didn't make her feel threatened. It made her feel quivery and achy, as if she wanted to throw caution to the wind and say *yes*.

For a long moment they stood like that, his words hanging heavy in the air, and all Lucy's nerves seemed to centre on the hand which felt so warm and oddly reassuring on her jaw. But then Aristotle was taking that hand away and stepping back. He turned and walked to the door. In a second he was gone, and the room felt huge and cavernously empty. Bereft. In mere seconds she heard him opening the interconnecting door on his side and flinched slightly at the sound.

She went and sat heavily on the bed, feeling sick in her belly, his words swirling in her head. Was he right? Would this only get stronger? The ripples of sensation still pouring through her body mocked her. Who was she kidding? She'd fooled herself that it had receded this week, but he was right—especially if her reaction just now was anything to go by.

She'd also, she had to acknowledge, fooled herself into thinking she was frigid. Right now she felt like the least frigid person on the planet. She had to recognise that in losing her virginity she'd subconsciously gone out and deliberately chosen someone she didn't feel attracted to—as if to try and convince herself that she wasn't like her mother, that she wouldn't spend her life craving sex.

She frowned at that. It sounded wrong as she thought it now. She'd always believed her mother to have craved sex…but in actual fact it had been the men, their power and attention. She'd sought validation from *that*. When Lucy really thought about it, her mother had always been quite cool and clinical about sex. She'd never become so passionate about a man that she'd lost sight of practicalities.

The way Lucy felt about Aristotle right now had nothing to do with being cool and clinical. He could be the hotel doorman and he'd still have this effect on her. While Lucy knew for a fact that her mother would never in a million years have spared a mere doorman a second glance.

Seeing herself and Ari reflected in the mirror, the look on her face—it *hadn't* been the same as her mother's that day. She'd never seen her mother look like that. So…desirous, so caught up in the moment.

The revelation stunned her now. Because of her mother's profession, and how overtly sexual it had been, she'd always assumed that Maxine's myriad liaisons had been all about sex. But they hadn't. They'd been about money and power and her mother's self-esteem. Not sex. That had merely been a tool she'd used. Lucy had *known* this, but it had taken the awakening of her own desire to really *see* it for the first time.

One of Lucy's biggest fears had to do with losing her independence by depending on men as her mother had done. But wasn't this a totally different situation? She was working; she already had a job. She wasn't hoping to get anything out of Aristotle—certainly not money or gifts. And he seemed to be as surprised by this flaring of attraction as she was. She had no doubt that if he had a choice he'd prefer this to be happening with someone in his own social group.

So didn't it stand to reason that once this thing had *burnt out*, as he'd said, things would get back to normal? Although Lucy had to concede she didn't know what it would mean to get back to *normal* in the office after something like this…her mind skittered weakly away from that.

She was pacing now, the thought of sleep impossible to consider. She bit at her nail, a tight feeling growing in her belly. For the first time in her life the fears she'd carried for so long about turning into her mother and all that meant seemed flimsy—they didn't hold water any more. *She was different.* The warm feeling of reassurance she'd imagined she'd felt just now surged back even stronger. And it scared her slightly, as she'd never in a million years have said that Ari was a *reassuring* type of man.

She stopped pacing. What if she could do this? Instead of running away, why not face this and vanquish the demons that had been plaguing her? Already she felt different; she had to admit she'd enjoyed the less restrictive wardrobe, and even though her reflex was still to cover up it was diminishing. She'd caught some of the men looking at her earlier in the ballroom, and instead of wanting to hide away she'd found herself straightening up, feeling a very fledgling sense of confidence trickling through her.

Had Aristotle helped her come to this? It didn't feel like the diminishing needy power that she'd seen her mother crave. It felt like an innately feminine power, pure and strong.

She thought about it again, tested the words: what if she did this? Just went over there to that door, opened it and walked through.

Before she knew her legs had even carried her Lucy stood at the door, breathing short shallow breaths, her heart thumping. She'd once read a book: *Feel the Fear and Do it Anyway.* Was she brave enough? To step across the line?

As if in answer to her own question, an intense yearning spread through her. She wanted this—wanted this man and what he promised more than she wanted to look at all the reasons for not doing it. He was right. The thought of repressing this desire was…inconceivable.

With a shaking hand she touched the doorknob, took a breath and turned it. She shut her eyes as the door opened silently. A lurid mental image of Aristotle lounging back against black silk sheets, hands behind his head with a mocking smile, nearly made her slam it shut. But she resisted the impulse and opened her eyes.

It took a second for Lucy's eyes to adjust, and the scene greeting her was as erotically charged as she could have imagined and yet surprisingly benign. Through the open bedroom door, across the wide expanse of opulent sitting room, Lucy could see the reflected figure of a sleeping Aristotle in his bed in a slightly open mirrored wardrobe door.

Far from black silk, the sheets he lay on were white, like hers. He'd thrown off the main covers and lay now, half propped up, with just a sheet hitched up to his waist. She'd seen his naked torso the other day, but now she looked her fill. It was long and lean and bronzed and hard, and exquisitely muscled. More superlatives filled her head but she couldn't articulate them. He was simply the most devastating specimen of a man she'd ever seen—not that she'd seen many, she had to acknowledge wryly, but she felt fairly sure that Aristotle could take his place among some of the most beautiful men on the planet.

Unruly inky black hair flopped with incongruous youthfulness onto his forehead, making him look much less like the feared CEO of Levakis Enterprises and instead like someone altogether more vulnerable and human.

Lucy's breath snagged when her eyes rested on those lean hips and then moved down lower, to where the strategically placed sheet was tented slightly over his lap. Hot colour poured into her cheeks at the intense and immediate reaction to even such subtle provocation.

A sound made her eyes dart up, and suddenly the sleeping god of perfection was no more—he was awake, light green eyes darkening even as she looked at him. Lucy belatedly realised that, as if in a dream, she'd walked right into his room and was now standing at the foot of his bed, the dim light of one lamp imbuing everything with innate intimacy.

Her hands gripped the sides of her robes together, knuckles showing white. Reality slammed into her, and she suddenly wondered if she'd suffered some kind of paralysis as she couldn't seem to move.

'I…'

Aristotle was completely still, awake and watchful now.

'You…?'

The sound of his voice resonated deep within her.

'I… I don't think… That is…perhaps I should—'

'Come here.'

The words were uttered with deep implacability, and Lucy's legs felt shaky. She'd come too far to go back now, so she moved forward jerkily, around the bed, until she was standing just a few feet away, eyes glued to his, mesmerised.

He lifted a hand and gestured. 'Come closer.'

Lucy looked desperately for any sign that he mightn't be as *über*-cool as he looked. And at the last second, just when she was contemplating running while she still could, she saw it: the light sheen of sweat beading his brow and the pulse beating fast at the base of his neck.

But, even so, it was as if the old, safe Lucy was calling her back through the doors, willing her to slam them shut between her and this man and this craving, aching need within her. She even turned and looked, as if to judge the distance.

Immediately her hand was taken in a ring of heat. Lucy looked down to see her wrist dwarfed by his bronzed hand. She looked at him, and gulped.

'Lucy, are you sure you want this? Because if you stay there's no going back.'

And in that instant Lucy mentally shut the doors behind her.

She didn't want to go back. She wanted to go forward and free herself of this unwanted baggage she'd been carrying.

She shook her head and felt her hair slip around her shoulders. 'I'm not going.'

He pulled her irrevocably towards him, and then she was there, legs leaning weakly against his bed, His eyes never left hers as he brought her wrist to his mouth and pressed a kiss against the pulse, his tongue flicking out. She gasped and felt as if he'd branded her, even with that small move.

And then he let her hand go and leant on one elbow. 'Take off your clothes.'

When he said the words, Lucy felt only an intense explosion of heat in her pelvis. She was far beyond disgust or shock. Without breaking eye contact she undid her thick robe and let it drop to the floor. She still wore the dress, which gaped open, and her shoes. She stepped out of the shoes and bent to put them neatly under the chair. Then she stood and looked at Aristotle again.

He had made no move, but his eyes had turned so dark with lust that the green looked almost black. His gaze burnt into her.

With a tremor in her hands she pulled the zip down all the way, and then slowly peeled the dress off her shoulder and down, baring breasts only just confined by a strapless lace bra. Her awful self-consciousness seemed to have faded away to another place. Another person.

Hands on her hips, Lucy wriggled slightly to ease the dress down and over her womanly shape. The veritable waves of heat coming from Aristotle as his eyes followed the path of her dress nearly had Lucy melting on the spot. The heavy silk pooled at her feet, and she stepped out with an innate grace she was entirely unaware of.

Seeing a heavily brocaded chair beside the bed, Lucy lifted one leg to rest her foot there and started to peel one stocking down, only belatedly becoming aware of the eroticism of her pose. She sensed it in the way Ari had stilled even more, felt it in the intensity of his gaze on her, and for the first time in her life, found herself glorying in her innate femininity.

Aristotle knew that the only thing keeping him from jumping out of the bed and burying his aching hardness into her as she bent like that over the chair was the knowledge that, given one touch of her skin, he'd lose all control. When he'd seen her standing at the foot of the bed like a vision, his feeling of pure desire twinned with what had felt suspiciously like joy had made him act gruffer than he would have liked. He gripped the sheets tight in both hands now. It felt hard to breathe. The fact that he also felt more out of control than he'd ever felt with another woman was uncomfortable. Finesse in this kind of situation was a distant memory.

A curtain of dark hair swung forward, restricting his view of the bountiful breasts threatening to spill from that completely inadequate bra, and instinctively he leant forward and brushed it back over one pale shoulder. She turned her head and looked at him, her lower lip caught by her teeth, sending a shudder of pure arousal through his body, tightening the erotic notch on his flimsy control.

She put down that leg and lifted the other, repeated the exercise. By the time she was done Ari could feel sweat rolling down his back from the effort it took to stay still.

Lucy registered the almost indecent bulge in the sheet covering his lap and her throat went dry.

'Your bra,' he said hoarsely. 'Take it off too.'

Lucy reached around behind her and felt for the clasp. She had to pull the bra tighter in the motion it took to undo it, and she saw Aristotle's Adam's apple move convulsively as he registered the movement. The clasp was undone, and Lucy held it for a long moment…*this was it.* And then, with an almost defiant movement, she pulled it away and threw it down, releasing her heavy breasts. She stood before him in nothing but her silk and lace pants. In some dim and distant part of her still-functioning brain Lucy had *no idea* how she was doing this—the enormity of the moment was too huge to contemplate—but the beat of her blood was drowning out everything but the need to be here right now, *with him.*

His eyes seemed to glaze over as he looked at her, making her skin tighten and tingle all over, especially her breasts. She could feel the tips puckering and growing unbearably tight. She didn't have time to feel self-conscious. Aristotle reached out with two hands and grabbed hers in both of his, pulling her close to the bed. The sheet moved down. Lucy had a stomach clenching view of narrow hips and dark hair just above—

With a smooth move she never saw coming he tumbled her down, so that she lay flat on her back. He loomed, huge and dark over her, his hands still capturing hers, held against her belly, his knuckles brushing the sensitive undersides of her breasts. Her heart was beating so fast she felt dizzy, but then his head was lowering to hers, his mouth slanting over hers, and within seconds dizziness had been replaced with heat and sensation. His naked torso crushed her chest. He released her hands and she instinctively wound them around his neck as she arched voluptuously towards him.

Never had she imagined feeling like this. This rightness. She fitted him; he fitted her. The moment she ached for him to touch her somewhere he touched her; the moment she wanted him to deepen the kiss he deepened it—sucking her tongue deep, biting her lip, pressing fiery kisses down over her jaw and further, until he hovered teasingly over her breasts.

He cupped one and then the other, caressing their firm smoothness. Lucy's breathing was fractured, jerky. She looked down but couldn't bear the eroticism of seeing her breasts in his hands like that. So she closed her eyes and cried out when he took one burning nipple into his mouth and sucked hard, rolling the tip, flicking it with his tongue, grazing it with his teeth before suckling hard again.

Lucy was burning up, her hands in his hair as he cupped both the voluptuous mounds together, his mouth tasting and testing each peak until they were throbbing with arousal.

'Please…' she begged brokenly.

Her hips moved in a silent and primeval rhythm, her lower body on fire. She looked down to see Aristotle looking up at her, eyes dark green, cheeks flushed. His huge broad shoulders blocked out the light as he finally released her breasts and came over her on strong arms, lean and awe-inspiring.

'Are you ready?'

She nodded jerkily. She wanted to say yes to anything this man said, not even caring what he meant.

'Are you sure? I think we should check, just in case…don't you?'

'Yes,' Lucy gasped. 'Whatever—just do it…'

He smiled down at her even as she registered that the sheet had fallen away and his powerful erection nudged her belly. On pure instinct she reached down and covered him with her hand, heat suffusing her face and neck as she registered the size of him—fully aroused.

He grimaced as her hand tightened on him and he took it gently away. 'That's why we have to see if you're ready Lucy, *mou*…patience.'

She didn't know what *mou* meant, but then he disappeared, and Lucy gave a yelp when she felt him drawing her pants down, over her hips and down her legs, before he spread her legs apart with big hands. Lucy tried to resist the movement, which felt far too intimate, but he was ruthless, eyes on hers, holding her, *telling her to trust him* as his head lowered. She closed her eyes and put a fist to her mouth to hold back the groan when she felt his breath feather in the intimate space between her legs, and then the sensation of his mouth and tongue on her nearly sent her shooting into the stars.

He licked her, exploring her secret folds, thrusting deep into her, circling and sucking on her clitoris until her hips were lifting off the bed, wantonly jerking towards him, her teeth biting down on her fist.

When she felt two fingers slide deep into her slick heat everything in her body teetered on an edge that she'd never known before; every nerve pulled tight. But then he was withdrawing for a moment. She heard a drawer slam shut, a foil wrapper, and then he was back over her, strong, hair-roughened thighs parting her own smoother ones even more.

She could feel his erection nudging her down there, where she burned. He moved back and forth, drawing his penis along the moistened and plump folds of her sex, eliciting a deep groan from somewhere deep within her. She was almost mindless for the need for *something*…she wasn't sure what it was…it hovered just out of reach.

Lucy put her hands on his shoulders. They glistened with sweat, and the feeling of something so earthy made her rejoice.

'Ari…' she breathed. 'Please—I'm ready.'

And that was when Ari's control broke. He heard her husky words, felt her tip her hips up towards him, reach down to take hold of him, forcing him to impale her slightly. And then he drove in deep and hard, knowing instinctively that this woman was made for him alone and they would fit like a glove.

Ari stilled his movements—both of them did. Lucy's eyes were wide with shock at the sensation of him filling her, but it wasn't painful…it was delicious.

She moved again, experimentally, and Aristotle sank into her even more, pushing her down into the bed. Lucy wrapped one leg around his waist and threw her head back, hands still clinging onto his shoulders as he slowly withdrew and then impaled her again. He continued with his slow, voluptuous rhythm, the pleasure building and building. Lucy could feel her body starting to shake as he took her other leg and bent it back, opening her up to him even more, changing the angle slightly, going even deeper, and as his movements started to get faster and more urgent Lucy could feel the onset of something so huge, so terrifying as it came hurtling towards her, that she tensed—even though everything in her was urging her to meet it head-on.

Aristotle bent his head, his body holding her suspended with his movements, and kissed her deeply. Her breasts were crushed against his chest, her arms clasping his neck. 'Let go, Lucy… It's OK…let go.'

Holding on tight, she took the final, terrifying leap and let go…and was thrown so high and so far on the wave of her orgasm that she was hardly even aware of Aristotle's own explosive loss of control as his big powerful body jerked and still rhythmically thrust into hers as the never-ending ripples of her orgasm held him suspended in a halfway world he'd never known before.

CHAPTER SEVEN

ARISTOTLE WAS RUNNING AWAY. And the fact that he was aware of what he was doing made him nearly incandescent with rage. He didn't *run away*. And yet after last night, with Lucy, all he'd known was that he needed space—and fast. His brain was still too hot and far too tangled to even pretend he could deal with a banal morning-after scenario. He'd received a call from his New York PA while Lucy lay sleeping, and on the flimsiest of pretexts had declared he'd fly over for the weekend to take care of something that ordinarily he wouldn't have touched with a bargepole.

Lucy had woken to find him dressing that morning. He'd seen her wake through the reflection of the mirror as he'd knotted his tie with unsteady hands. Unsteady because he'd wanted to strip off all his confining garments and go over to where she lay in such gloriously voluptuous naked abandon and take her all over again. But the truth was he wasn't sure if he could take that intensity of experience again.

Wasn't sure if he could take that intensity of experience again? Ari's hand clenched around the crystal glass, the design digging into his palm as he looked unseeingly out of the plane window. Since when had sleeping with a woman been too intense for him? *They* were the ones left weak and dizzy and sated. Not him.

He closed his eyes and threw his head back. And then opened them again abruptly when all he could see was Lucy's passion-glazed eyes as she'd looked up at him the moment he'd filled her, the moment he'd been completely sheathed in her hot moist warmth… It had felt…it had felt like nothing he could have imagined. He could remember the feel of her breasts pushing against him, their peaks as hard as bullets against his chest, could hear their heartbeats even now, thudding slow and unsteady, and then, as he'd started to thrust deeper and deeper, the beats had got faster…until—

Aristotle swore softly. He needed to numb that *intensity.*

His mouth twisted and he called himself all sorts of a fool for running away. So it was the best sex he'd ever had? That was it. It didn't mean anything. It hadn't touched any part of him that hadn't been touched before. *So why did it feel as if it had*?

Ari blocked out that assertion. He was immune to feeling, immune to emotions. He'd started to shut them away when his mother had died, and then when Helen Savakis had come into his life, and then finally on that first night in a cold boarding school in England at the age of five. It was the last time he'd cried and now… His gut clenched. *Now he only cried in his sleep.* He reiterated it to himself: he didn't *do* emotions.

Perhaps he'd sensed that Lucy did, and that was why he'd run. A sense of calm stole over him. That was it. She wasn't like the women he went for…she was bound to be less versed in how this would work. He'd seen the look on her face that morning, slightly nervous, biting her lip… And suddenly he was right back to square one—a raging erection pushing against his trousers, thirty thousand feet in the air, and the only chance of alleviating it far behind him on Greek soil.

He just had to lay it on the line with her, that was all. Make sure she knew what not to expect. And then…then he would take her again, and these demons would not be hovering over his shoulders. Ari smiled cynically. Who would have thought he'd be growing a conscience now, after all these years?

Lucy had got over Aristotle's abrupt and cold departure yesterday morning. She told herself stoutly that she was back on an even keel. But if she allowed images to surface for a second—She stumbled slightly in the street and a kindly old woman caught her arm and smiled up at her, saying something in Greek. Lucy smiled weakly and mumbled something back. So much for an even keel. If she even *thought* about the other night for a second she lost her balance… Self-disgust ran through her.

She spied a taverna on the other side of the street and made her way there, sitting gratefully in an empty chair. She ordered sparkling water and fanned herself with a menu, thinking that perhaps it was the heat getting to her. Who was she kidding? The heat was getting to her all right, but it had nothing to do with the sun.

And along with the heat was a lingering hurt—Lucy brutally cut off her thoughts there. She wasn't hurt. *She wasn't.*

She tried to focus on her surroundings, the pretty and quaint area of Anafiotika, a hidden gem of old Athens within touristy Plaka, just beneath the Acropolis. She'd climbed up there earlier, the exertion doing little to clear her head of the tangled knots. She took a sip of water, but with annoying precision her mind slipped back again to that excruciating moment when she'd woken the day before.

She'd felt so heavy, so lethargic, so replete. She'd lazily stretched and opened one eye before realising that she was naked, and that muscles ached where no muscle had been before. In an instant she'd been alert, and staring into the cool, wide-awake green eyes of Aristotle as he'd knotted his tie in the mirror.

She needn't have worried about the embarrassment of the morning after as he'd coolly informed her he had to go to New York urgently on business, that he didn't need her, and that he'd be back late on Sunday. It was almost as if nothing had happened. Lucy had even wondered for a paralysing moment if she'd sleep-walked into her boss's bed and he was merely being diplomatic and ignoring the *faux pas*.

And then he'd gone, leaving her there, shell-shocked, the only evidence that anything had happened in the tremors that had started through her body along with the ache when she moved.

After he'd left her mind had gone to some numb place where she wouldn't have to process what had happened, answer the questions that were piling up. Was that it? Had he just been scratching an itch? Would things revert to normal now? Was he that cold with everyone? Lucy had remembered the way he'd treated Augustine Archer and she'd doubled over in her steaming shower, feeling sick. *How could she have let this happen with a man like that*?

Because, she realised now, as the everyday hustle and bustle went on around her, she simply had not had a choice. He'd overwhelmed her—her response had overwhelmed her. And she was grateful for the space and time to process what had happened.

At that moment a group of handsome young Greek men passed her table, and they all turned to look Lucy over appreciatively as they backed down the street. One of them cheekily wolf-whistled. The shock of the attention when she wasn't used to it made her freeze. She felt acutely self-conscious in her khaki shorts and V-necked black T-shirt. The waiter in the restaurant bustled over and shouted something at the boys. They ran, laughing, and he started apologising to Lucy, but she assured him smilingly that it was fine and put some money on the table, getting up to go.

She had to acknowledge as she walked away that it wasn't an entirely unpleasant experience to be noticed like that. She'd hidden away for so long that she'd never had a chance to just play with situations like this.

The sun beat down and she tipped her head up to it for a moment. She felt an alien sensation of lightness, as if she were finally letting go of a weight. It was also a sense of freedom, and she desperately wanted to cling onto it. One thing she knew: *if* Aristotle thought they could take up where they'd left off when he returned, that sense of freedom might disappear. She'd indulged in the experience once; it would have to be enough. She knew too much about him, about his cold methods, and she knew that she didn't have the hide of someone like Augustine Archer to be able to take it.

But she had a mortifying, sickening feeling that he'd had enough already, and it killed her to admit to feeling other than overjoyed at the prospect.

She set off back in the direction of the hotel. Just before she rounded the corner a flash of movement caught her eye, and she looked over to see Aristotle lounging against an ancient wall, hands thrust deep into jeans pockets, a faded white T-shirt making him look indecently handsome. Dark glasses hid those amazing eyes, but added to the overall devastating package.

It was so like something she might have conjured up out of a fantasy that she blinked and blinked again. *Was* it a mirage? He was dressed more casually than she'd ever seen him. He moved, strolled towards her. Stopped in front of her. Her heart stopped and kick-started again with heavy thuds.

This was no mirage.

'You're…back.' Despite the drink of water, Lucy's mouth felt like a desert.

Ari smiled a hard smile and in that second Lucy knew it was him. Despite his hardness something melted inside her, all her good intentions of moments ago disappearing like pathetic wisps of cloud.

He lifted his glasses onto his head. 'I left New York in the middle of the night.'

The shock of seeing him like this and the force of those eyes on hers made her brain feel fuzzy. 'But you…you had to work.'

'I sorted it out. I needed to get back here.' *I shouldn't have left,* he surprised himself thinking, as lust slammed into his gut.

'You did?' Lucy was mesmerised by his mouth, remembering what it had felt like on her skin. Heat bloomed between her legs. People jostled past them and Aristotle took her arm and led her to the side, to the wall. He pushed her back against it and stood close—far too close. She could feel him, smell him… God, she wanted to taste him.

'Ari…'

He bent his head, feathering a kiss to her neck. 'Yes, say that again. That's why I came back.'

'Ari.'

His hands rested on either side of her head, his pelvis was tight against hers, and she could feel how aroused he was—right here in the middle of the street, with people passing by.

'I'm going insane for you, Lucy.'

Lucy opened her mouth, but her words were stolen by his lips coming down hard and swift, demanding and eliciting a flash-fire of response. After a long drugging moment Ari lifted his head, his eyes glittering down into hers. Amazingly, she could see herself reflected in his eyes, looking up, dazed, and that sent sanity rushing back. Somehow, with superhuman strength, Lucy found the will to put her hands against his broad chest and push.

He budged only minutely, a frown drawing those black brows together.

'No.' Lucy was starting to panic. The speed with which he'd appeared and made her conveniently forget all logic was making her burn inside.

He quirked a devilish smile. 'You're right. Here isn't the place.'

He took her hand and started to pull her away, clearly misinterpreting her reasons for wanting to stop. Lucy dug her heels in and pulled her hand back. He didn't let go, just looked back impatiently when she wasn't moving.

'What—?'

He took one look at Lucy's mutinous face and it sent something cold through him. 'I'm sorry—did I misunderstand?

Maybe you *want* to be made love to in front of Athens strollers and their families?'

'I don't want to be made love to, full-stop,' Lucy hissed, very conscious of the stares they were getting—primarily from admiring women.

Ari gripped her hand tight and Lucy, very reluctantly, let herself be pulled towards him.

Ari was frowning again slightly, something like ennui trickling through him, making him feel absurdly disappointed. 'If this is about the way I left…'

Lucy emitted a sharp laugh that disguised the dart of pain and the surge of anger at how easily she'd given in to his charm and fallen into his bed the other night. Faced with him now, the fact that she desired him even more acutely was making her regret it all the more fiercely. 'Of course it's not. I'm well aware of how you conduct yourself… I guess—oh, I don't know—I expected at least a bunch of flowers. After all, isn't that what you give all your one-night stands?'

He stood stock still, staring down at her, the lines in his face tightening and growing harsher by the minute.

'Well, let's make this more than a one-night stand, and then you'll get a priceless piece of jewellery. Is that what it'll take, Lucy?'

He looked around for a moment and spotted something Lucy didn't see. With that tight grip on her hand, he began hauling her away again. Trepidation slithered down her spine. He'd looked ready to throttle her.

He growled back, 'Tell you what—why don't we cover all bases now? That way we're clear, left in no doubt as to where we stand, because to be perfectly honest I don't think I'm going to be satisfied with just two nights.'

'What—?'

Ari stopped abruptly at a flower stall and picked out the biggest bunch of flowers the man had. Then, to Lucy's horror and the flower stall man's delight, Ari presented it to her with a mocking flourish.

Lucy took them purely because she couldn't *not.* She pasted a smile on her face for the benefit of the flower seller, and after paying Ari was leading her away again. The flowers were huge and cumbersome. Lucy tried to get his attention, pulling on his hand, but it would have been easier talking to a block of wood. He led her relentlessly through a veritable maze of streets until they emerged into a charming square and Lucy spotted shops with designer names.

Again without pausing for a moment, Ari tugged Lucy along until she found him leading her into an exclusive jewellery store, the iconic name of which made horror slam into her. As the door hissed quietly closed behind them, and the security guard clearly recognised Aristotle Levakis, Lucy tugged fiercely on Ari's hand—but to no avail. He led her over to where an eager assistant, already smelling a large sale, stood.

He drew Lucy in close to his side with an arm of steel and sent her a devotedly loving look. Only Lucy was aware of the hard glitter behind it. Hardly breaking that eye contact, he said, 'I'd like to buy something for this beautiful woman.' He flicked a glance at the sales assistant and smiled urbanely. 'Although I'm sure you'll agree that there couldn't possibly be anything in this shop to rival her beauty.'

The sales assistant cleared her throat obsequiously and looked Lucy up and down, taking in the T-shirt and shorts, the flat gladiator sandals and dusty feet. Lucy cringed from head to toe under the snooty woman's scrutiny, and right then she hated Ari more than she'd ever hated anyone in her life, hearing his well-practised patter.

Hellbent on proving *something,* Ari was still so incensed that he dragged Lucy from display to display, forcing her to look at priceless bracelets, necklaces, earrings and brooches. Every now and then she tried to entreat him, to tug on his hand, but he ignored her. A heavy mass of dark, twisted emotion was weighing him down inside.

Why hadn't her eyes lit up when they'd got in here? And *why* had he felt that punch to his solar plexus in the street when he'd believed her to be exactly the same as every other woman? And *why* was she contradicting that now, insisting on leaving? Making him feel confused and out of his depth. He heard her speak again.

'Ari. *Please.* Let's just go. I don't want anything here.'

He turned to look down, and the stunning natural beauty of her face and those stormy grey eyes nearly floored him. He could feel the thrust of her soft breasts against his chest. She looked pale. But he did not know how to get himself out of this situation except by saying, his voice harder than he'd ever heard it, 'We're not leaving until you choose something, Lucy. There's not a woman in the world who would say no to that, so please don't play the wide-eyed innocent with me. It won't work.'

Lucy's belly clenched at the look of pure cynicism that crossed Ari's features, twisting them. Suddenly her anger dissolved, and all she felt was sad. She tore her eyes away and looked around futilely, hating every single item of jewellery on display. This whole scenario was making her skin crawl. But she knew he meant it. They would not leave until she'd chosen something.

She tugged her hand, and for the first time Ari let go. Moving away, feeling tears film her eyes, Lucy searched and searched, barely even seeing the glittering gems arrayed in glorious profusion.

But then something did catch her eye, hidden away at the back of one of the cabinets. It was a necklace of such stunning simplicity that it took her breath away. It was a butterfly design; she'd always had a sentimental thing about butterflies, and her mother had used to buy her presents with butterfly motifs. Seeing this now was like some kind of sign, and Lucy had to fight back the tears.

The wings of the design glistened with what she could only assume were tiny diamonds, and three delicate silver strands linked it on each side to the catch.

She pointed with a trembling finger. 'I like that one.'

A startled gasp of disbelief came from the sales assistant, clearly seeing her month's worth of commission disappearing down the drain.

'*That* one?'

Ari had heard the exchange and was behind Lucy, looking over her shoulder. She tensed as the fine hairs stood up on the back of her neck.

The sales assistant couldn't keep the pain out of her voice. 'Well, yes, it is a nice piece…' She laughed nervously, 'If you like something more…subtle…and the designer is local. But *really…*'

Lucy heard a scathing, 'Less than one thousand euros? I don't think so…' come from behind her, and then she felt his mouth close to her ear, so only she could hear which he said. 'I think I want a lot more than a two-night stand Lucy, *mou*, so I think you're worth a lot more than that…'

Before she knew it Ari had arrogantly picked out a completely different necklace, with a huge sapphire stone surrounded by diamonds, and the ecstatic sales assistant was wrapping it up efficiently before they changed their minds.

Outside the shop, Lucy broke desperately from Ari's grasp, but he caught her again effortlessly and swung her round. She closed her eyes and to her utter horror could feel tears welling. She couldn't stop one from slipping out. She felt a tense stillness come into his body.

'Lucy…' He sounded exasperated now. Lucy didn't doubt that he'd moved women to tears after buying them jewellery before, but for entirely different reasons.

Ari took hold of Lucy's arms. They felt slender and fragile under his hands. He saw the tear slip down the pale softness of her cheek and cursed himself silently, feeling like an absolute heel when he didn't even know why. He'd just spent a fortune on her! And in his experience money equalled a satisfied woman. He was floundering badly, had never been in this place before, and had certainly never expected a reaction like *this*. She looked almost green.

Seeing her still holding onto that crazy bunch of flowers, Ari grabbed them out of her hand and passed them to a woman strolling past. He was unaware of her gasp of delighted surprise as she took them, entirely focused on Lucy again. More tears were slipping down her cheeks. He was used to women's histrionics, but this was different. She was doing it so silently. And he could tell that she hated that she was crying.

'Lucy…look—'

She seemed to come to life and lifted a hand, knocking aside one of his as she wiped her cheek. Finally she opened her eyes, and their swirling depths made him want to pull her close. But everything about her screamed *stay back*.

Her voice was heart-achingly husky. 'I've never been so hu… humiliated in all my life.'

Ari raked a hand through his hair. He wanted to go back to when he'd seen Lucy in the street, taken her in his arms and kissed her, and start all over again. But when she'd pushed him away and then said those things about the flowers he'd lost all perspective. Without wanting to look too closely at why, he just knew it had something to do with her reference to those other women. That this was exactly the same… A small voice crowed, *Wasn't it?*

Lucy couldn't look up at Ari any more. She broke free and started to walk back towards the hotel. She could see it in the distance; they were closer than she'd thought. She felt numb.

When she felt Ari take her hand again she stopped dead and took a deep breath before turning around. 'Look—'

'No, *you* look.'

She did—right up at him, emotion still swirling dangerously in her breast. She'd never felt so vulnerable, like every one of her childhood fears was being taken out and exposed to the harsh sunlight.

Ari felt tight. 'Those women in London—the flowers… They weren't one-night stands. They were pathetic attempts to negate your effect on me and to keep up appearances.' His mouth twisted. 'I'd agreed with Parnassus that it might help distract people from investigating the merger if I was seen to be out and about as usual.'

Lucy's head went into mind-melt.

'I'm sorry for leaving you so abruptly the other morning. I'm sorry for the flowers, and I'm sorry for dragging you into that shop and forcing you to choose something you didn't want.' *Even now he couldn't understand her reaction, or why he was explaining himself when he never had before.* And he couldn't really believe he'd felt compelled to defend his actions in London. But he wanted Lucy more than he wanted to understand right then…

Fresh tears threatened and Lucy wailed inwardly, *Don't be nice!* I can't handle nice.

She pursed her lips even as her anger drained away spectacularly. *He hadn't slept with those women?* She felt very wobbly and vulnerable, and knew her words lacked impact. 'Your behaviour was unforgivable. Spending that kind of money just to make a point is disgusting.'

His face tightened. He held up the bag. 'What do you want me to do with it?'

Lucy felt wrong-footed by his immediate response. The Ari she'd thought she knew was morphing out of all recognition. She thought for a second. 'I don't think that lady in the shop deserves commission when she couldn't be bothered to promote local talent. I don't know…it'd be nice to give it to someone who'd really appreciate…'

She looked around. In the thronged square, back at the jeweller's shop, she could see a young couple clearly in love, looking wistfully through the window at the engagement rings. Lucy could see the pain on the young man's face at his girlfriend's quickly disguised yet crestfallen expression as they walked away. She glanced up at Ari and could see that he had followed her gaze and witnessed the little exchange.

She saw his jaw clench. He let her hand go and strode through the crowd to the young couple. Lucy saw the conversation, saw Ari gesture back to her with a rueful smile and hand the young man the elaborately wrapped box. The young couple's faces were shocked as Ari walked back to Lucy and took her hand again.

He led her away, but looked back for a moment and said, 'Satisfied now?'

Lucy nodded jerkily. She couldn't quite believe he'd done that, and asked a little shakily, 'How…how much was it worth?'

He tossed back a figure and she felt the colour drain from her face. She bit her lip and said quietly, 'Oh, well, it'll buy them a nice engagement ring…or three.'

She felt the earth shift as she realised she was seeing a completely different side to Ari. She was very much afraid that she'd stuck her head into the lion's mouth and he was about to bite down—hard.

By the middle of the following week Lucy was as drunk as she'd ever felt, and all without touching a drop of alcohol. She couldn't stop her mind drifting back to last Sunday afternoon, now as she sat waiting for Ari to come out of a private meeting with Parnassus being held in his villa in the hills above Athens.

When they'd got back to the hotel an unspoken inevitability had vibrated between them, intensifying the closer they'd got to her room. Once inside, as if to stave it off, as if she could save herself from the burning flames, Lucy had said breathlessly, 'Wait…what is this now? What are we?'

Ari had rested back against the door, hands behind him, those lean hips in the low-slung jeans making Lucy's mouth dry and her head ache with the effort it took not to look down.

'We are two consenting adults, exploring a strong mutual attraction, and this is…the second time we make love.'

Heat had exploded all around her. He'd pushed off the door and come towards her. Lucy had put out a hand, as if that could stop him, and had watched as he'd nonchalantly stripped off his T-shirt.

She'd swallowed. 'But…what about us…working together? How can we do this…?'

He'd caught up with her effortlessly and pulled her into him, tight. She had felt the bulge of his arousal pressing against his jeans, pressing just above the apex of her thighs, and her legs had nearly buckled.

He'd bent his head and whispered at the corner of her mouth, '*This is* how we do this…'

Things had escalated swiftly. Clothes pulled and yanked, they'd stumbled and staggered towards the bed, Lucy falling back into the softness, somehow naked except for her underwear.

She'd watched as Ari yanked down his jeans and briefs in one go. She'd gazed at him in all his bronzed, aroused glory, she'd realised in that moment that ever since that day she'd bumped into him in the lift *this* image had been hidden deep in the recesses of her darkest fantasies. A fantasy she never might have acknowledged if this man hadn't wanted her too.

Was that why he'd got under her skin so thoroughly from the start? The revelation sent her pulse soaring, pounding through her veins and under her skin, even now, as she sat on the chair with her legs tight together and Parnassus' own assistant sitting just feet away.

Even that couldn't halt the images, though. Ari had come towards her like an avenging god and pushed her legs apart, where they dangled over the bed. On two hands he'd rested over her. After looking down at her for an intensely long moment, he'd pushed down one bra strap and then the other, and then pulled down the cups of her black bra so that her breasts were exposed, upthrust by the confining underwire.

When he'd bent his head to blow softly Lucy had groaned deep in her throat, in between her legs a deep, endless ache. When his tongue had flicked out and teasingly licked around the rapidly hardening peak of one breast she'd arched her back, willing him to suck it deep, like he had before.

When he hadn't, she'd looked at him, felt sweat breaking out on her brow. He'd smiled devilishly, and she'd cursed him silently, her eyes flashing in a mute appeal.

He'd shifted her back onto the bed and with far too practised ease managed to dispense with her bra. His big hands on her thighs had held her apart. He'd looked at her with such desirous intensity she'd felt trepidation lick through her, feeling that she *had* to be imagining this.

She'd spoken huskily, and winced now at the memory. 'How can you…how can you find me attractive? I'm not like… I'm too big… I'm *plump…*'

He'd merely hooked fingers into the side of her pants, said throatily, 'You're perfect…' and started to pull them down, dropping them summarily on the floor. He'd stood again, blatantly aroused, making a mockery of her words. Making her feel as if she was all woman and the only woman for him.

He'd bent over her and she'd felt his erection teasing her, hot and hard against her desire-drenched sex. She'd felt so *wanton*, but had bitten her lip and forced herself not to move her hips towards him as she'd wanted to do so very badly.

Lying right over her, so she could feel his chest against her, he'd stretched her arms above her head, the movement causing her breasts to rise as if offered to him like succulent desserts.

Holding her hands captive with one of his much larger ones, he'd trailed his other hand down the side of her body, teasing the side of one breast, and whispered in her ear, 'You are quite simply the pure embodiment of my every fantasy of what the perfect feminine form is… I didn't know it till I saw you, and now I can see nothing else…'

Lucy's heart had stopped altogether. She'd searched his eyes as he'd lifted back and looked down, so dark and hot they'd scorched her alive.

'You…really mean that?'

Lucy hoped desperately now that she hadn't sounded as vulnerable as she'd felt in that moment.

In answer Ari had bent his head and laved one of her nipples with his mouth and tongue, before sucking it deep, causing her back to arch again helplessly.

Releasing her hands for only a second while he'd put on protection, he'd come back and captured them high again. Lucy's hips had bucked of their own volition.

He'd then slid into her, inch by torturous inch, and when he was in as far as he could go, when she didn't know where she started or he ended, he'd leant close to her mouth and kissed her deeply, before saying, so quietly that she almost didn't hear, 'Yes… I really mean it.'

And then, with slow, deep thrusts which built and built to a stunning crescendo—

The door in front of Lucy opened suddenly, and she jumped up at the same time as Parnsassus' assistant, a guilty flush staining her cheeks, breathing as if she'd just been running. A pulse throbbed between her legs and she was caught by a pair of glittering green eyes.

She saw Ari smile sardonically, as if he knew *exactly* what she'd just been thinking about, and Lucy flushed even redder. He strolled over and took the file she was holding out of her hands, his fingers caressing hers underneath for a lingering moment, making her pulse beat even faster.

Lucy nearly groaned out loud, and then he said *sotto voce*, 'Have Helios bring the car round. We'll be out of here in less than ten minutes… I'll tell Parnassus we can work from my office for the rest of the afternoon.'

Lucy just nodded, not capable of much else, and certainly not capable of anything like *work*. She felt feverish, distracted, more elated than she'd ever felt, and knew that right now she had neither the strength of will *nor the inclination* to resist this man.

'We've been invited to my father's house for dinner on Friday night.'

'You mean *you've* been invited for dinner.' Lucy shuddered inwardly, she didn't fool herself for a second in thinking that Helen Levakis had included her in that cosy little invitation.

Ari shook his head and marvelled at this woman in front of him. They were having a private dinner in her bedroom at the hotel, late in the evening. She looked so beautiful in just a bathrobe, with her dark hair spread around her shoulders, not a scrap of make-up, that delicious cleavage just visible in the gap of her robe. When he thought of how they'd barely made it back to the office the afternoon before— He stopped his rampant mind. He was far too susceptible to this woman. And, worryingly, he didn't feel at all complacent or triumphant about the fact that he'd got her into bed. If anything he just felt a growing sense of hunger. The fact that that was not the usual way for him and women was conveniently pushed aside. He reminded himself that Lucy was different, from a different class—world. It was the novelty of that, *that* was all. And for now he was loving the novelty.

Reaching for her hand, he tugged her up and over until she fell into his lap, making a spasm of lust arrow straight to his groin.

He shook his head, and before he bent to kiss her said, 'Where I go, you go.'

Lucy accepted the kiss, drowned in the kiss, but a sense of guilty anticipation made her shiver slightly. No matter that they were spending time together like this. Ari was still as open as a closed book when it came to anything but the most general conversation. And now the thought of getting a chance to learn more about this man, who was fast tangling her head into one big knot of confusion and reducing her body to little more than a slave to his, was proving to be far headier than was healthy for her heart.

When the kiss deepened, and as Ari carried Lucy over to the bed and came down on top of her with his delicious weight and told her how beautiful she was, how desirable, she conveniently blocked out the clamour of voices in her head telling her to be careful, not to be weak, and not to be so easily seduced—and above all *not to fall in love.*

On Friday evening Lucy was sitting ramrod-straight on a rigid divan in the main drawing room of the grossly opulent Levakis house. Tonight had to be one of the most excruciatingly uncomfortable evenings of her life. From the moment she'd arrived, with Ari's hand on her arm, it had been clear she wasn't welcome.

Lucy had held her head high and thanked her lucky stars for her chaotic but expensive education; every time Helen had directed some snide comment her way, or had tried to undermine her, Lucy had answered with the utmost dignity. Helen had even been so rude as to conduct some of the conversation between the few guests in French, but her eyes had almost popped out of her head when Lucy had replied fluently.

Lucy felt inordinately proud of her mother's legacy.

Ari was now on the other side of the room, talking to the same beautiful blonde who'd captured his attention at that function the first week. Lucy tried to ignore the poisoned darts that seemed to be arrowing into her heart, and tensed even more when she saw Anatolios, Ari's half-brother, head her way.

He sat down, far too close for comfort, obviously drunk, and Lucy tried to edge away, smiling weakly. He merely moved with her, crowding her. She felt intensely vulnerable.

Anatolios's blue eyes followed where her gaze had just been and he said, 'Beautiful, isn't she?'

Lucy flushed. 'I'm not sure I know what you mean.'

She looked at Anatolios reluctantly. She guessed she couldn't be much older than her own twenty-three years, and hoped the revulsion she felt didn't show on her face.

He smiled sleazily, and then, shockingly, ran a fleshy finger up and down Lucy's bare arm. She flinched, but couldn't move, hemmed in as she was.

He gestured with his head. 'That's Pia Kyriapoulos. She used to be a famous model, and now she's famous for being wealthy and divorced and looking for a new husband.'

Lucy swallowed painfully and looked across the room. They did look amazing together—blonde contrasting with dark. Pia had her hand resting on Ari's arm, and he certainly didn't look in a hurry to move it. At that moment he looked up and straight at Lucy. Feeling inordinately exposed, Lucy smiled brilliantly and looked back at Anatolios as if he'd said something funny. Not as if he'd said something to make her heart feel as if it was being ripped, still beating, out of her chest.

When she felt Ari's gaze move again Lucy ripped her arm away from Anatolios, who glowered sulkily at her. His eyes dropped to her cleavage and Lucy screamed inwardly. The guy was a total creep.

Just then Helen swept into the room and said something to Ari who, after a moment's hesitation, followed her from the room, his face hard. Sensing a chance to escape, Lucy mumbled something about needing the bathroom and fled, vowing to get out of there even if she had to leave on her own.

Wherever I go, you go. Ari's words resounded mockingly in her head. At least until the next available, infinitely more beautiful woman came along, she surmised grimly.

She was coming back from the bathroom and passing a partially opened door when she heard raised voices. *Ari and Helen.*

Without being conscious of what she was doing, she slowed down and heard Ari say, a low and blistering voice, 'I'll never marry someone like her; she's completely inappropriate. And anyway, don't you think it's a little late to be doing the concerned mother act?'

CHAPTER EIGHT

LUCY'S HEART FROZE like ice in her chest as the words registered. Was Helen afraid that their affair was more than just a fling? She had to swallow back a semi-hysterical cry, putting a hand to her mouth. Well, Ari had certainly reassured her of that.

The next words from Helen were indistinctly shrill, and then Ari's voice came again. Lucy stood rooted to the spot in some kind of sick, paralysed fascination, and heard him say something along the lines of, '…useless waste of space of a brother…'

There was an awful silence, and then the sharp crack of what could only be a hand across a cheek.

Knowing that it wouldn't have been Ari, and acting on a surge of adrenalin that was pure primal instinct, Lucy pushed open the door and flew into the room, aiming herself straight at Helen, who still had her hand raised, her eyes glittering almost feverishly.

Lucy was unaware of their shocked looks. She saw only Ari's proud stance, the livid handprint and the trickle of blood from the corner of his mouth. She saw red, and for the first and only time in her life considered striking another person. It was only Ari's quick reflex action, pulling her back behind him, that stopped her.

Helen lowered her hand and her eyes took on a malevolent

glow. She smiled cruelly. 'Well, well—if it isn't the quiet little secretary, come to save her lover.' The woman's obsidian eyes flicked up and down and she added cuttingly, 'Or perhaps I shouldn't say *little*.'

Lucy made to move again and Ari held her firm, glancing back with a hard expression, 'Leave it, Lucy.'

He turned back, and Lucy could feel the ice in his gaze even though he wasn't looking at her.

'She wouldn't balk at striking you too. After all, you never had any qualms about striking a five-year-old—did you, Helen?'

Helen's focus moved back to Ari, and Lucy could see the older woman's face grow mottled with anger. Abruptly Ari turned and pulled Lucy with him, and within a blur of minutes they were sitting in the back of his car, leaving the house behind.

Lucy was still shaking, a mixture of powerful anger and shock coursing through her. She glanced at Ari. He was looking resolutely out of the window. When she saw his mouth her heart lurched painfully.

'You…you're bleeding.'

He turned abruptly, and the dead look in his eyes scared her. He smiled harshly. 'Want to kiss it better for me, Lucy?'

He flicked out a handkerchief nevertheless, and dabbed at the blood. Overcome with an emotion she couldn't name, Lucy reached out and put her hand to his cheek, where it still felt warm.

'How could she have hit you when you were so small?'

A surge of emotion so powerful that it made him tremble caused black spots to dance before Ari's eyes. His breathing grew shallow. The feel of Lucy's hand like a cooling balm on his hot cheek, the look on her face… He'd never, *ever* had someone rush to his defence so unreservedly. He'd felt the fine vibrating tremors of her anger as he'd held her back, and he didn't doubt that if he hadn't stopped her she might very well have struck Helen. The realisation was cataclysmic, earth-shattering.

A hardness entered him. He certainly wasn't going to shatter along with it. Everyone wanted something out of him—especially women. Lucy was just taking advantage of a vulnerable moment.

Lucy's wrist was gripped and pulled down. Ari's eyes glittered at her, but at least some life had come back into them. 'Quite easily,' he bit out. 'I was an easier target then.'

He kept hold of her wrist, almost painfully, but Lucy didn't say anything.

'Don't pity me, Lucy Proctor. I don't need anyone's pity.'

The fierce pride on his face nearly made Lucy weep. She shook her head and managed to pull her hand back, cradling it with her other one. He saw the movement and sighed deeply, raking his hair with barely concealed anger.

Lucy looked away for a long moment. The rest of the evening was coming back—what had happened just before she'd gone to the bathroom, and then the words she'd heard. *What was wrong with her?* Sitting here mooning over a man who quite patently needed no one and was biding his time with her until he flitted to the next woman.

She started hesitantly, 'I didn't mean to… I was just passing and heard her…'

'How did you know it wasn't me hitting *her*?' came the sardonically amused question.

Lucy turned around, a fierce expression on her face. 'Because I know you would never do anything like that.'

His belly clenched. It was harder not to touch her than to touch her and risk that emotion rising again, so Ari reached out and tugged a resisting Lucy onto his lap. He felt an unusual peace steal over him. He buried his head in her neck and after a moment felt her relax, her curves softening into him with delicious inevitability.

But then he felt her tense again, and he looked up and said with a growl, 'Stop it. Relax, Lucy, *mou*.'

She was biting her lip and avoiding his eye. He turned her jaw so that she had to face him, and she said, almost defiantly,

'I saw you with that woman. I won't…won't be some substitute. If you'd prefer to be with her, then please…just go back.'

The thought of going back to that house made Ari shudder. He'd known it would be a mistake to go at all, and hated the fact that he had done so. Hated the fact that after all these years there was still a tiny sliver of yearning left for something he'd never experienced. Harmony. Even as that thought materialised in his head he blocked it ruthlessly, focused on the woman on his lap, reducing his world to the here and now.

He shook his head, amazed that Lucy could have seen him and Pia together and not have known that he'd all but itched to go back across the room to *her*. Then he remembered the moment before Helen had come into the room and asked to speak to him. Lucy had been with Anatolios, looking at him and laughing gaily. Anatolios had been practically sitting in her lap.

Dark anger surged. 'From what I saw of you and my brother, you looked very cosy also… Are you sure it's not you who wants to go back to him?'

Lucy couldn't help the shudder of disgust run through her as she said quickly, '*No.* I was just—we were just…talking.'

The relief that surged through Ari made him feel weak. He pressed a kiss to Lucy's bare shoulder and she shivered again, but this time he recognised desire and it was heady.

'Then, please believe me, I too have no desire to go back to that house. Pia Kyriapoulos is a woman who is looking for her next wealthy protector. She thinks I could be it, but this evening I told her in no uncertain terms that I have no interest in signing up for the job. And anyway…' Ari brought Lucy's hand between them to his lap, where she could feel the stirrings of his growing arousal. 'She doesn't have this effect on me.'

Ari felt Lucy's fingers flutter over him and held back a low groan as his arousal soared. In that second he had a flash of an idea. Without stopping to consider what he was doing, he said, 'When we get back to the hotel, pack some things for the weekend. We're getting out of Athens…'

* * *

When Lucy woke the next morning she knew immediately that she was alone in the strange bed, but she was too deliciously lethargic and sated to worry about it. She heard nothing except beautiful stillness and the gentle lapping of water nearby.

They had travelled here, to this island, which Ari had told her was called Paros, by helicopter last night. It had all been a little overwhelming to Lucy. When they'd arrived Ari had driven them in a Jeep to this place, which Lucy hadn't been able to make out in the dark.

Now, without opening her eyes yet, as if superstitious for a moment that it might disappear, Lucy knew that there were doors open nearby. She could feel the warm breeze, could smell the tang of the sea and feel the bright sunlight.

Finally she opened her eyes. They took a second to adjust, and then as if in a dream she got up, blindly threw on a T-shirt and walked to the open French doors and the tiny balcony. She simply could not take in the beauty of her surroundings for a moment. The balcony seemed to be perched right over the Aegean Sea, which stretched out in glittering blue before her, other islands visible as shapes in the hazy distance under a clear cerulean sky.

The modest house was whitewashed and all but clinging onto the rocky coast, nestling alongside equally bright houses either side. Lucy frowned slightly. She'd seen Ari's portfolio of extensive properties around the world, and knew he had a luxurious villa on Santorini, but she'd never seen pictures of this house. She looked around. Admittedly, it was more humble than anything she might have expected of him. And all the more intriguing.

She heard a sound behind her and turned to see Ari, shouldering his way in through the door with arms full of supplies. Her breath snagged at remembering how he'd stripped her bare last night and taken her to heaven and back on the modest double bed. He was wearing long shorts and a faded T-shirt, and looked impossibly young and handsome at that moment—a million miles from the proud, successful, arrogant billionaire.

He pressed a lingering kiss to her mouth and proceeded to spread out a veritable feast of a breakfast on an ancient wrought-iron table. Bread, jams, fruit… Then he disappeared, presumably to the tiny kitchen downstairs, and came back with steaming fragrant coffee in two cups.

'Cat got your tongue?' he asked lightly as they sat down and Lucy still hadn't said a word.

She shook her head and tried to communicate with him what she was thinking, feeling. She made a half-gesture around them, encompassing the view. 'It's so beautiful… I can't even begin to describe…' She looked at him then. His face was shuttered, dark glasses shielding his eyes. 'This property isn't listed with your other ones…'

Ari's jaw clenched. He looked out towards the glittering Aegean. When he'd made the decision to come here he hadn't stopped to consider Lucy's reaction to the basic nature of the house. He knew very few women who wouldn't have turned up their noses and shuddered disdainfully. A ridiculous feeling of disappointment ran through him and he drawled, 'You'd prefer to be on Santorini? The villa there certainly is…larger.'

Shock coursed through Lucy. 'No! That's not what I meant at all. I'd much prefer to be here…' She hated that he'd jumped to that conclusion. 'I just mentioned it because I hadn't seen it. That's all.'

Ari flicked her a glance. 'It's not listed because I've deliberately kept it private. It was my mother's house—where she grew up.'

'Oh.' There didn't seem to be anything more to say, and Lucy could feel a wall spring up between them. Clearly he wasn't going to elaborate. It seemed important to make him believe so she leaned across and took his hand. 'Ari, I'm glad you brought me here. Really.'

* * *

After a long day in the sun, exploring the island's beaches and eating a basic picnic, drinking sparkling wine in the shade on an empty beach, making love until their bodies seemed boneless and sated, Ari couldn't stop thinking about Lucy's words and expression from that morning. She'd seemed sincere. He'd believed her to be sincere when she'd professed to liking the place.

He held her hand in his now, as they wandered through the ancient winding streets of his mother's birthplace. He repressed the urge to ask her if she'd really meant what she'd said—if she really loved this humble little place as much as she seemed to—because he hated how important it felt to him that she did.

A little later Ari sat back in his chair in the small taverna he'd brought her to, and Lucy's belly flipped over at his expression. He was looking at her so intensely she had to ask, 'What…? Have I got something on my face?'

He shook his head and smiled, and her heart turned over. She had once thought he was incapable of smiling, but the younger-seeming, softer side of this man was altogether far too enticing.

'Just a lot of freckles. Who would have known you'd freckle so easily?'

Lucy grimaced. 'I have celtic ancestry.'

He smiled wider, lounging back, cradling a half-empty wine glass. 'They're cute.'

Lucy scowled at the word. 'Unfortunately we can't all go a deeper shade of bronze in the sun.'

She tried to stop her eyes roving over his powerful form but couldn't resist. His T-shirt strained over broad shoulders and clung to that lean torso; low-slung jeans were so low slung that she could see a sliver of taut dark flesh just above the button, the dark shading of hair making her heart trip.

'Stop devouring me with your eyes, or I'll carry you back to bed over my shoulder, Lucy Proctor.'

She looked up again and blushed. He leant forward and captured her hand.

'It's amazing that you can blush when you're so incredibly sensual…when you wear such decadent underwear…'

Lucy groaned.

'…and have a body to put the Venus de Milo to shame…'

'I don't… *Stop.*' Lucy glanced around, mortified, in case someone had heard him. He laughed out loud.

'Yes, you do—and it's entirely appropriate that we're here, because this is the island that supplied the Parian marble for the sculpture.' He kept her hand and asked then, 'Tell me, Lucy, why is it that you have these two different sides? And why did you fight not to fall into my bed? Was it all a game?'

His voice had hardened, his hand had tightened, and Lucy looked at him and felt nervous. It suddenly seemed very important to be honest with him.

Even more so when he added, 'And how is it that you speak at least two other languages fluently and can hold your own in the snobby dining rooms of Athens?'

Lucy was silent for a long time. She looked out of the window that they were seated beside and saw the dark ocean, and fishing boats twinkling under a moonlit sky. And then she said haltingly, 'My mother was one of the most celebrated burlesque performers in the world…'

And before she knew it she was telling him everything, and he was listening, as rapt as she'd ever seen him. She told him about living in Paris, and before that Rio de Janeiro, New York… London. The ever-changing schools, the nomadic nature of their lives.

Lucy wrinkled her nose. 'Her real name was Mabel Proctor, but she changed it to Maxine Malbec.'

Ari frowned. His thumb stopped making little circles of sensation in her palm.

'*The* Maxine Malbec?'

Lucy nodded, feeling slightly sick. Was he going to judge her now or, worse, judge her mother? She started to pull her hand back, but he gripped it again.

He was shaking his head. 'Lucy, that's an amazing story… The picture I saw in your flat—I thought there was something familiar about her.'

She smiled wryly. 'That's what I was afraid of. And it's not a story—it was my life.' She shrugged, feeling self-conscious. 'Having a mother who was so overtly…sexual made me wary, I think, of that side of me.' Her mouth tightened. 'It's also why I have an aversion to expensive jewellery…trinkets… Seeing my mother fobbed off by so many rich men over the years… My father was one of those men, married with his own family. He had no desire for a love-child.' Lucy's voice trailed away. She was shocked she'd revealed so much so quickly.

She didn't elaborate on how precarious her life had been until she'd grown older and taken control of herself and her mother. She also didn't elaborate on the fear she still had of becoming dependent on a man, on how her father's rejection had fostered a deep feeling of insecurity she was only just beginning to let go of.

Ari winced inwardly when he recalled her reaction to his asking her to buy something for Augustine Archer, and then dragging her around that jewellery shop. He remembered the innately sexy way Lucy had stripped for him that first night. 'You've obviously inherited her natural sensuality—*that's all.* She sounds like she was an amazing woman, and it must have been hard, raising a daughter on her own.'

Lucy was struck somewhere very vulnerable by his easy understanding. She nodded and smiled weakly, feeling emotion rise. 'She was…*is* an amazing woman.'

Ari frowned. 'She's still alive?'

Lucy nodded. 'Yes, but…' She told him about her mother's illness and the home that she was now in.

He said quietly, 'It must be hard to see her like that… diminished.'

Lucy just nodded, terrified she might start crying. 'It is.'

To her relief he seemed happy to let it drop there, and discreetly paid the bill before tugging her up and leading her back down the quiet winding streets to the humble little house.

A few hours later Ari lay on his back, his arms around Lucy's sleeping form, her breasts rising and falling gently against his bare chest. Even though he was recently sated, that subtle movement made him hard again. He shifted minutely and bit back a groan when Lucy moved too, and he felt her nipples against his side like two hard berries.

For the first time in his life he'd put himself in a situation where he couldn't just get up and leave a woman behind—after all, where could he go? And for the first time it wasn't sending that usual feeling of suffocating claustrophobia into his belly.

The following evening Lucy was changing while Ari had a shower in the small bathroom downstairs. The house *was* tiny, and rustic and beyond basic, but she loved it. Ari had told her earlier of how his mother had grown up there with her sister and her mother, his grandfather having died when they were small.

She went to the balcony and smoothed the plain dark red sundress over her hips. Her skin tingled from being in the sun, and she felt freer than she'd felt in a long time. She'd called her mother's home earlier, and she was obviously having a good day—although Lucy had had to explain again why she wasn't able to visit for another week. It seemed as if her mother was making friends with some of the other residents, and the matron had assured her again that she was being well cared for. The relief was enormous.

A sound made her whirl around from where she was leaning against the balcony rail, watching the sun go down over the sea. Ari stood in the doorway with just a towel around his lean hips.

She looked up, throat dry, and met his eyes. They glowed with dark, decadent promise. He put his hand to the towel and with a flick of his wrist it was gone. Lucy's body flamed.

'Come here…' he said softly.

Lucy tried to resist the feeling of hot insanity. 'Ari, I've just changed…'

'Come *here*.'

On shaky legs and bare feet Lucy walked over and said, 'Has anyone ever told you that you're extremely bossy and arrogant?'

He shook his head and pulled her right into him, reaching for her dress and pulling it up, at the same time pulling her pants down. Excitement made Lucy shiver uncontrollably.

'Only you seem to have the nerve to say these things…' he growled, mock angrily.

And then talking stopped for a long, languorous moment.

Much later, when the moon had risen and the stars were out, they headed out for dinner. Lucy had put on a light cardigan as the late spring evening had a slightly cool edge. Her eyes drank Ari in as she trailed him, her hand firmly clasped in his. She never would have imagined him to be so tactile, but he was always reaching out to touch her, to take her hand, rub the back of his hand down a cheek… She sighed inwardly. He was wearing black trousers and a snowy white shirt, and he was more gorgeous than any one man had a right to be.

This part of northern Paros was a sleepy fishing village. The summer hordes hadn't descended yet, but in the distance Lucy heard music and recognised a traditional Greek tune as they rounded the corner into an idyllic little square where a taverna was all lit up. A mad profusion of flowers erupted from every windowsill and around the door.

Lucy heard shouts and laughter, and as they went in Ari ducked his head to avoid hitting the doorframe. An even bigger shout went up, and suddenly a crowd was thronging around them and a huge man was dragging Ari's face down and kissing him soundly.

When he could, Ari pulled Lucy forward, feeling an incredible lightness in his chest. He'd missed coming here. A gut-wrenching sense of homecoming nearly floored him with its intensity. London and the merger and Athens and Helen all seemed to be light years away from this moment.

But as if he couldn't hold it down the thought rose up like a spectre: *the emotion...* The threat of it was rising up to swallow him whole. That was why he hadn't been back.

He felt for Lucy's luscious curves and let her distract him from those dark thoughts, introducing her to his mother's old friends and even to some distant cousins. He could see a few of the young bucks eyeing her up, but with one warning look from him they retreated, shamefaced. Ari kept her close when they were seated in the corner with Costas, the owner, who pulled up a chair and ordered a veritable feast on their behalf.

Lucy sat back a while later and groaned, wiping her mouth with a napkin, 'I've never eaten as much as I have these last two days. And I do *not* need any extra padding.'

Ari looked at Lucy from under hooded lids, his eyes drifting down to that delectable cleavage in her red dress. It made him remember taking that dress off her only hours before, unhooking her bra and letting those voluptuous mounds spill into his hands. His body tightened and grew hot with annoying predictability. She turned him on with such ease…

She caught his eye and smiled and leant forward, crossing her arms so that her breasts were pushed together and forward. 'See something you like?'

Ari's green gaze glittered and darkened. He leant forward too and said softly, 'Witch. I'll punish you for that.'

They looked at each other, everything fading into the background for a long intense moment, until Costas came over and pulled Ari up, breaking the spell. It was only then that Lucy saw the tables and chairs had been pushed back, the volume of music had been raised and Ari stood now with Costas, arms high, as they started to do a mesmeric Greek dance.

Lucy's breath caught in her throat. It was so beautiful. It should have made Ari look effeminate, but it did the opposite. A couple of the older ladies dressed in black got up and danced with the men, their steps in sync as the music started to increase in tempo. As more people, young and old, joined in and linked arms, the music got faster and faster. The next thing Lucy knew she was being hauled up to join in.

She hissed at Ari. 'Don't you *dare*.'

But he didn't listen, just drew her into the melee, and Lucy found herself laughingly trying to keep up with everyone else. The women were showing her the complex steps, it was frantic and captivating, and as the last evocative chords died away she stumbled right into Ari's arms.

Something potent and silent was vibrating between them, and without further ado Ari grabbed Lucy's cardigan and they left, a silent intensity surrounding them all the way until they returned to the small house. Barely had the door closed before their mouths were fused, hands seeking desperately to touch bare flesh. They didn't even make it up the stairs. Ari took her there and then, fast and furiously.

It was only later, after they'd made it to the bed and made love again, that Lucy woke from a tangled dream to a strange sound. She was curled close to Ari's big body and she looked up to see that he had an arm flung over his face. His breathing was fast and shallow and he was speaking in Greek.

Lucy put her hand on his arm, tried to draw it down, and it was only when she did that she saw the tracks of tears on his face. Her heart turned over.

At her light touch, he was awake in an instant, eyes alert, straight on hers. Lucy's voice was incredibly husky. 'You were…' She faltered, nearly saying *crying* but instinctively stopping herself. 'You were having a dream…you sounded upset.'

He did nothing for a moment, and then his face closed over and became so cold she nearly shivered. His expression was quite clear in the bright moonlight streaming in through the open doors.

In an instant he'd jackknifed off the bed to go and stand with his back to her at the balcony railing, looking out to the dark expanse of the sea. He was naked, and his physique was so gloriously powerful that it took Lucy's breath away for a moment. He was also extremely tense.

She got up and pulled on a T-shirt, went over silently to stand next to him. She noticed that his hands were wrapped so tight around the railing that his knuckles shone white. Instinctively she put her hand over his nearest one, and he flinched minutely as if he'd been unaware of her presence. When Lucy looked up at his face it was unbearably harsh, and she knew instantly that this man was worlds apart from the one-dimensional playboy tycoon she'd first believed him to be.

She didn't say anything, just kept her hand on his, and after a long moment he said, so quietly that she had to strain to hear, 'I remember being here…in this house…with my mother and father on holiday, just before she died. Ya-ya was still alive too, and my aunt…and we were happy. Really happy.'

Lucy didn't interrupt.

'My father had met my mother when he'd come here on a day-trip with some friends. They were typical Athenians—cocky, arrogant, rich… But he saw her, and within a month he'd taken her back to Athens to be his wife.'

'He must have loved her a great deal.'

Ari jerked his head to look down at Lucy. She felt tension spike in his form as if he'd just realised that he'd spoken out loud and had a witness.

'Loved her so much that after she died he married again within the year? *Please.* My father left me here with my grandmother, and the next time I remember seeing him he had Helen Savakis with him. His new wife.' His lip curled. 'She convinced him to send me to boarding school, where I was conveniently out of the way, so that she could have her own son and raise him to be my father's golden child.'

Lucy's shock at Helen's cold-hearted ruthlessness was palpable. 'But your father left everything to you…?'

Ari nodded, looking back out to sea. 'Which is why Anatolios hates me and Helen despises me even more now than she did when I was a child. She hates the fact that she needs me for her security. She hates the fact that I'm not in Athens, where she can try to make me marry a woman of her choosing to control me even more…'

Lucy winced reflexively at his mention of marriage and remembered his caustic response to Helen's obvious fear that what was between *them* might be serious. She guessed in that moment that Ari's memory of this place and that time when his parents were together ran deep for a reason. If they'd had a halcyon time here, only for his mother to die so suddenly and his father disappear, it must have been heartbreakingly confusing for a small child. How would someone so tiny make any sense of loving a place when it was also the scene of such sorrow?

But from the sounds of it, if his father had been a successful young man, with the world at his feet, it must have been love for him to marry Ari's mother, who would have been very poor.

'I can only imagine how hard it must have been for your father to leave you behind…perhaps that's why he married again so soon…'

Ari turned then, and looked down at Lucy properly. She felt very exposed in the face of his deep hurt and unmistakable cynicism.

'Yes—and why he found it no chore to send me away to school on his new wife's recommendation.'

'Ari, I've seen the way a woman can enchant a man. Maybe he was just—'

Just enchanted the way you're being enchanted right now? The revelation made Ari's voice harsh. 'What, Lucy? Please don't try and feed me some psychobabble nonsense. This subject is closed for discussion.' His eyes flashed a warning in the silvery light. 'And you're far too overdressed.'

Ari picked Lucy up with an intensity that sent a flutter of fear through her. Instinctively her hands tightened on his shoulders. And then something happened. Almost instantaneously she sensed a different intensity run through him. The mood altered. He looked down at her and she could see feral desire mixed with something almost like confusion in those dark green depths, and her heart ached with a mirror emotion.

The fact that she could sense his need to dilute the emotion he'd just revealed with physicality made her reach up and touch her mouth to his. She felt him tremble slightly, and as she wrapped her arms around his neck and deepened the kiss he responded.

He took her over to the bed and laid her down with a gentleness Lucy would have bet he hadn't been feeling just moments ago. The fact that she was so aware of him, aware of what was going on inside his head, made her reel anew. His body covered hers with a delicious weight and Lucy brought a shaky hand to his face. When he turned to press a kiss to her inner palm she felt another flutter of fear—but this time it was because she knew for certain that she'd fallen in love with this complex, proud man who presented one face to the world and another here with her.

When Lucy woke the next morning she wasn't surprised to see Ari up and dressed and sitting on the balcony. Dark glasses shielded those amazing eyes. There was a stillness to his body and a sternness to his features that told her the sensual cocoon they'd inhabited last night was gone. The revelation of admitting she'd fallen for him made her feel intensely vulnerable in the harsh light of day. She pulled the sheet up over her body and Ari's head turned. Her skin prickled when she imagined the slow appraisal he was giving her from behind those shades.

She came up on one arm and pushed her heavy mass of hair back, feeling very rumpled and lethargic. Ari had been ruthless in his pursuit of pleasure last night, *hers and his,* surprising her with the depth of passion he'd incited within her. It had seemed as if their lovemaking had gone to another place, and Lucy cringed inwardly now to remember that she'd been moved to tears after one shattering climax after another.

Now Ari just uncoiled that long lean body from the chair and said coolly, 'We need to get back to Athens. We've got work to do and a heavy week coming up.'

Lucy felt as if he'd slapped her. Her body went cold. Boss/assistant. Back to work. Back in her place. The intense vulnerability made her feel slightly sick.

'Of course,' she said through numb lips, when she felt like saying something like, *I never asked for this, you know, and I certainly never expected to be brought here to this idyllic little hideaway where you couldn't contain your emotions.*

When Lucy stood under the shower a short time later her belly clenched painfully. She could see exactly why he'd brought her here now: no possibility of paparazzi catching them out, no one who knew him apart from the locals he'd known as a child…*no chance for her to be getting any ideas.*

There was a knock on the door that made her jump, and Lucy heard a curt, 'The helicopter is on stand-by. As soon as you're ready we're leaving.'

'Fine,' Lucy called casually, belying the unsteady beating of her heart and the sick feeling gripping her gut. His words and cool manner were an all too mocking confirmation of her fears and her own stupidity. He was hustling them out of here as if there had just been some kind of dire weather warning, making it patently obvious how much he regretted bringing her there in the first place.

As she switched off the shower and stepped out, she knew that she would have to start distancing herself. She couldn't go on like this. She was being served a timely reminder of what she could expect out of this relationship—which was nothing but a very bruised heart.

That evening, when they returned to the hotel from Ari's Athens office and Lucy felt Ari take her arm as they stepped out of the lift, she drew on all her strength to pull away from his touch.

They approached her hotel room door and she prayed silently that he wouldn't try to come in. She sent him a quick glance, while swiping her door open at the same time, thanking God that her hands were steady.

'I'm tired. I'm going to go to bed…'

Her door opened and she heard a drawling, 'Not a bad idea.'

Lucy turned in the door and looked up. '*Alone*. As you said yourself earlier, we have a heavy week. And I—I am tired.'

Ari looked down at Lucy and felt the knot of frustration which had started the minute he'd left their bed earlier this morning intensify. Every moment he spent not touching this woman meant dealing with a level of frustration he hadn't experienced before. He looked at her properly for the first time. He'd tried to avoid looking directly at her all day—if he was honest since last night, when she'd— His belly flipped over and he ruthlessly quashed the memory of such weakness. He still couldn't believe it had happened…

But now she did look tired, with faint circles of violet under her eyes. She also looked a little strained, and a dart of guilt struck him when he remembered the urgency he'd felt to get off Paros and back here, bringing them straight to the office and working them both like dogs.

Lust was a force within him, crying out for satisfaction… but he would not admit to that. She wanted to go to bed alone? Well, he was damned if he was going to let her see that the notion of that went against every clamouring instinct to throw her over his shoulder and carry her to his own bed.

So he backed away, and did not like the visible look of relief that crossed her face. He almost stopped and gave in to his primal urges—had to clench his fists not to.

'We leave for Parnassus' villa at nine a.m. I'll see you in the lobby.'

She nodded and then disappeared into her room, shutting the door between them with a firm click that seemed to resonate all the way through Ari's body right to his feet.

* * *

On Thursday evening Lucy thought back to the gentle exhaustion she'd felt the previous Sunday and could have laughed. Since then it had been like the first week—a frenetic blur of work, whizzing from Parnassus' villa, back to Ari's office, and back to the hotel. Ari had been out late nearly every evening, having private meetings with Parnassus and their legal teams, and much to Lucy's relief hadn't thought it necessary for her to be there too.

She'd carefully locked the interconnecting door on her side each night, even though all she'd fantasised about was slipping naked between Ari's sheets and awaiting his return.

Instead, as she'd thumped her pillow, she'd told herself that this was the best way. Nip it in the bud now, and when they got back to the UK she'd calmly inform him that this brief moment of madness was over. Her mind froze at the thought of calling women for him, arranging dates, seeing him come in in the morning with that satisfied look on his face, slight shadows under those amazing eyes from not sleeping—

'Lucy, what are you doing hiding over here? Has Ari told you to stay out of sight in case people realise he's sleeping with his PA?'

It took a moment for Lucy's focus to return to the room and realise that Anatolios was standing in front of her, with a smarmy look on his face. She could almost feel sorry for him now that she knew he'd been rejected in the end, despite his mother's vast efforts to secure him number one place in his father's affections.

'I'm not hiding.' She felt defensive. She *had* been guilty of hiding, hoping to get a glimpse of Ari and compose herself before going over to him. 'I've just arrived and I was looking for Ari.'

They'd come separately to this, another charity ball which was being held in their hotel in honour of Parnassus' contribution to helping the homeless in Athens. It was going to be the precursor of the announcement of the merger, which would be made the following morning, with the papers being signed at a press conference.

Lucy felt a prickle of unease skate up her spine when she saw how Anatolios's eyes were all but devouring her breasts, and she realised she was hemmed in between him and a wall. She moved to try and edge past him, but he moved too, surprising her with his agility.

He came and stood close, effectively blocking her from the room, and Lucy was very aware of how intimate it might look. She was plastered against the wall behind her now, could feel Anatolios's breath, smell the alcohol. Her belly spasmed.

'Anatolios, I have to go and find Ari. Would you excuse me, please?'

He laughed, and it was nasty. He didn't move. 'You English, you're always so polite—please and thank you. You're not going anywhere until you tell me what Ari is cooking up with Parnassus.'

Lucy flushed, and her eyes were immediately caught by Anatolios's. He couldn't hide his look of triumph.

'I *knew* it. I knew there was something big going on.' He grabbed Lucy's arm then, making her wince.

'Tell me what it is *right now,* I have a right to know what my brother is—'

Abruptly Anatolios was moved out of the way bodily, and then Ari was standing there. Lucy felt weak with relief.

He gestured with a hand for her to come with him, and she went gratefully, her legs feeling like jelly. She didn't look back, and when Ari said to her, 'What was going on there?' she avoided his eye and shook her head, saying, 'Nothing. He just…we were just chatting, that's all.'

The whole scene, with its air of menace, was making her feel sick, but she didn't see the point in rising Ari's ire now, when the deal was all but done.

Lucy made sure to stick close to him after that, figuring the devil she knew was better than dealing with Anatolios or Helen, who she'd also seen in the distance.

Just before everyone started to disperse Ari pulled her aside and took a sheaf of folded documents out of his inside jacket pocket. He handed them to her and they were still warm from his body heat. Even that made her tremble.

'Put these up in the safe in my room, would you, please? They're the official merger documents for tomorrow.'

She just nodded, avoiding his eye, and hurried out of the ballroom, glad of the respite and a chance to get herself back under control.

Ari watched Lucy leave the room, his eyes drawn helplessly to her glorious body in the figure-hugging strapless dress. His hunger for her was like a wild thing within him—a beast clawing to get out.

He rationalised it: it had to be because she'd been holding him at arm's length all week, her door firmly closed by the time he'd come back each evening. His mind had been helplessly distracted, despite the fact that he'd told her *not* to come to those late-night meetings, but now— His body tightened unbearably. The thought of her right now, in his room… He glanced around and knew he wouldn't be missed for a few moments. His blood surged at the thought of tumbling her onto his bed and sating this demon desire inside him.

Lucy was walking over to where the safe was hidden in the wardrobe of Ari's bedroom when she heard something at the door. She turned and went back, thinking it might be the turn down staff. When she saw Anatolios slipping into the room she froze.

'What are you doing here? How did you get in?'

He smiled nastily, and she saw his eyes take in the documents in her hand. She hurriedly put them behind her back.

He kept coming towards her, and she started to back away into the bedroom.

'Oh, let's just say I'm in Athens a lot more than Ari these days, so I have my contacts. Now, why don't you show me what you have hidden behind your pretty back?'

He was coming straight at her and Lucy froze for a second, fear gripping her like a cold, clammy hand. He was almost on her before she turned and stumbled, making for the safe before he could get the documents from her.

She felt her arm grabbed in a merciless grip and cried out, tipping off balance. Anatolios jerked her back painfully.

'Let me *go*.'

He was reaching around her, trying to get the papers, his face red and flushed. In a bid to get away, though his arms were wrapped tight around her now, Lucy dropped the papers behind her and used her hands to try and push him off. He saw the papers and lunged, knocking them both to the ground. He fell as a heavy weight on top of her, reaching underneath her for the papers.

Lucy was struggling in earnest now. She could feel her dress riding up her leg, her chest being squashed by his heavy weight. 'You… Get off me. I can't…*breathe…*'

'What the hell is going on here?'

CHAPTER NINE

BEFORE LUCY KNEW which way was up, the heavy weight of Anatolios was being plucked off her by Ari, as if he weighed no more than a bag of sugar. He literally held Anatolios by the scruff of his neck. The man was spluttering now, clearly terrified of his much stronger older brother.

'She told me to come up here. She told me she had something for me. *There!*'

He pointed to the papers, now strewn on the ground.

'Is this true?' Icy green eyes and an even icier voice were directed down at Lucy, who realised that she was still on the floor, dress hitched up, breasts heaving with her breath. She scrambled up, but then had to subside onto the side of the bed when her legs wouldn't hold her. Reaction was starting to set in.

She shook her head. She couldn't look at Ari—or *him*. 'No, of course it's not true. He followed me up here. He must have seen you give me the papers.'

Anatolios spluttered even more. 'Come *on*. Why on earth would I want to see some stupid papers? It's not as if there's anything going on—is there?'

Ari stilled. Right until that moment his vision had been blurred because he was so angry. When he'd seen Anatolios on top of Lucy he'd felt an awful weakness pervade his limbs before he'd kicked into action. And then, when he'd seen the papers… His heart was telling him one thing, but his brain was refusing to listen.

He dragged Anatolios to the door of the suite and said blisteringly, 'If I find out that you were the instigator of this incident you can kiss goodbye to working for Levakis Enterprises once and for all.'

And with that he threw his brother out of the suite and faced back to the bedroom, thinking to himself, *If, on the other hand, I find out it was Lucy...* His brain seized.

She appeared at the bedroom door. She looked unsteady on her feet, one shoe on, one shoe off. Her dark hair was tumbled in glorious profusion around her milky pale bare shoulders, the curve of her breasts outlined by the top of her strapless dress. As if seeing the direction of his gaze, she put her hands there and hitched the dress up. He noticed they were shaking, and yet he couldn't give in to his overwhelming instinct which was to go to her, to take her into his arms. He *couldn't*—because she might very well have just tried to betray him in the most heinous way.

He suddenly thought of the way he'd seen her earlier, backed into a corner talking to Anatolios as intimately as if they'd been lovers. And thought too of all the distant warning bells he'd ignored in his pursuit of her. The fact that work had taken second place, especially at such an important time, was starkly clear now.

Lucy sucked in a sharp breath. Ari clearly wasn't leaping to see if she was all right as he stood there, all but glowering at her. The fact that he believed she *might* have led Anatolios up here with a view to giving him or showing him the documents was screamingly obvious. Her hand gripped onto the doorframe as sheer hurt at his fundamental lack of trust nearly floored her.

He moved suddenly, and she flinched, but he just went over to the drinks board and poured a measure of what looked like whisky into a shot glass and brought it over to her.

'Here—drink this.'

She looked up as she took the glass. 'Ari, please let me—'

'I don't want to hear it. Not right now anyway.'

And he stepped past her and into the room, where she looked back to see him pick up the papers and put them in the safe.

Feeling numb, Lucy bent to take off her one shoe and went into the sitting room to sit down. She took a sip of the liquid, wincing as it burnt its way down her throat.

Ari came back out and stood with arms folded, all but towering over her. She refused to cower back into the chair, and put the glass down jerkily on the table beside her.

'Ari—'

'Did he see the papers? Does he know about Parnassus?'

'Of course not. How can you think that?'

'Because tonight is the second time I've seen you deep in conversation with my brother, and now, the night before the biggest merger in Greek history is announced, he happens to be conveniently in the same room as you when you're putting the papers in the safe.' His mouth thinned. 'Although obviously you both got distracted—'

Lucy stood, quivering from head to toe. 'Stop that right now. That's not how it happened. He followed me up here and got in somehow. He must have got a key from someone on the staff. Before I knew it he was…' She shuddered convulsively as she remembered the instant panic at feeling him crowding her, all over her.

Lucy stopped talking and looked into those devastating and yet icy green eyes, that harsh face. Her words might as well have been addressed to a marble statue. He was so remote, so *untouchable*. And something slammed into her consciousness. It was cold and stark reality. Despite his cool behaviour that last morning on Paros, had she really fooled herself for a second into believing that something amazing had happened between them? That against all the odds they'd gained some sort of mutual trust and respect? She was just the secretary and he was her boss… She gasped audibly as it became even more clear, her hand going to her chest as if to stop the lancing pain. But it didn't.

Even Ari frowned. 'What is it?'

Lucy figured dimly that all the colour must have drained from her face. She felt icy cold all of a sudden, and tried to formulate words through numb lips. 'That's why you appeared—you didn't even trust me to come up here and do this. You suspected something all along.'

She watched as his face flushed a dark red, and found herself sinking back down onto the chair.

'All this time you've thought that I might do something like this.' She shook her head and looked up, pain shattering her insides as she had to ask, 'Is that why you slept with me? Because you thought it might be easier to control me?'

His lack of response and that stony visage was confirmation enough. As if watching a movie in slow motion, Lucy went all the way back to when she'd tried to resign and Ari had told her she couldn't. It must have been then. He must have decided at that point that she might be a liability and planning some kind of revenge.

She somehow found the strength to stand again. She felt even clammier now. She'd always known what Ari was, the kind of man he was, but somehow in the past few weeks she'd let herself forget it.

He put out a hand towards her but Lucy flinched back, moving behind the chair,

'Lucy—'

'*No.* I don't want to hear it. I know it's over. It's all over. That's the only reason you slept with me. I've been really—' She stopped and bit her lip before she could say *stupid.* She lifted dead eyes to his. 'Blood really is thicker than water, isn't it?' She smiled a small harsh smile. 'Perhaps this is a step forward in fostering a new regard for your half-brother?'

Her smile faded. 'Anatolios doesn't know about the merger.

It happened exactly the way I said it did. The reason I passed off the conversation earlier as nothing was because he was beginning to suspect something and asked me about it. I didn't tell you because I figured he'd never find out before the morning and you didn't need the hassle.'

She hitched up her chin. 'I intend to resign once the press conference is over, I can't see why you wouldn't agree to that now.' She smiled with brittle brightness. 'After all, I can't imagine you want to be faced with an assistant you had to sleep with for business every day.'

Lucy turned and walked stiffly to the door, then looked back, somewhere in his general direction. 'I can organise my own flight home tomorrow after the press conference. I'd prefer that, and I'm sure you would too. I'll work out my notice if you insist, but I'm happy to collect my things from the office on Monday too.'

And, opening the door, she slipped out.

Ari watched the door for a long moment. The earth was shifting underneath him. He *had* been about to refute her reasoning behind why he'd slept with her, but then, when she'd interrupted him and obviously decided that that had to be the case, he hadn't spoken up.

He could have stopped her from leaving. He could have told her. *Why* hadn't he?

Ari sat down heavily onto the ornately brocaded sofa behind him. Without the awful stomach-churning red mist of anger that had gripped him, he had to concede that of course he trusted Lucy over his opportunistic brother any day of the week. This whole scene had all the clumsy and unoriginal hallmarks of Anatolios. But he'd just seen them together and…his mind had imploded.

His fists clenched when he saw how easily he'd misinterpreted the situation. She was wrong in this case. Blood was most certainly not thicker than water. If Lucy had been guilty she'd never have jumped to the conclusion she had. She'd have defended herself vociferously, she'd have cajoled and enticed, perhaps even tried to seduce him into bed to distract him. But he didn't need reminding that she hadn't come near him since Paros. His mouth twisted. And could he blame her? When he'd all but hustled her off the island like a fugitive. But he had just been so…so overwhelmed that she'd witnessed his excruciating weakness. *She'd seen him cry.* And she hadn't turned away in horror, she'd been gorgeous, sympathetic, understanding… It had been too much.

He couldn't deal with that. No one had seen that side of him. It had been locked away for so long—he'd been alone against the world for so long…

And that was why he'd let her stand there and believe he'd seduced her deliberately. His life hadn't been on an even keel since he'd started noticing her, desiring her. That had been part of his knee-jerk response tonight—the knowledge that he'd been so hungry for her that he'd followed her to the room for *that* and not because he might have suspected her of espionage. He'd felt intensely vulnerable for the brief moment when he had contemplated that that could have been the reality.

He stood abruptly and made for the door. He had to go back downstairs, had to smile and pretend everything was OK, when he felt as if his insides were twisting tight in his gut. Lucy was right. It was over. Where could it go from here anyway? He would not let her see him be weak one more time. No woman was worth that.

The next morning, when the press conference was over, Lucy avoided the scrum of shocked and chattering press and went up to her room. She picked up her one small bag, she was leaving all the bought clothes behind, and went down to the lobby to check out.

She was just arranging for a taxi to take her to the airport when she felt her arm taken in a spine-tinglingly familiar grip and a smooth voice spoke over her to the concierge. 'My driver will look after her, thank you.'

She stiffened under his touch, her whole body crying out shamefully for more.

'That's really not necessary.'

He smoothly moved them away, his hand still on her arm. Lucy fought not to pull it free, afraid he might guess how badly he was affecting her.

'Lucy—' he sighed heavily '—about last night—'

'Please. You don't have to say anything.'

'I do.' His hand tightened, and she looked up against her better judgement. His eyes were so green that she felt pole-axed.

'You were wrong, I never slept with you because I thought you were capable of espionage. I read the situation entirely wrong and I'm sorry. But you're right…it's…this—*us*—is over.'

Lucy tried to school her features, even though she felt as if someone had just stabbed her in the belly. Relief that he *had* trusted her was eclipsed by sheer pain that she shouldn't even be feeling. 'What about…your brother?'

Ari grimaced. 'I'll deal with him. It's not for you to worry about.'

No, thought Lucy faintly, still reeling and hating herself for it. Because she wouldn't be working for Levakis Enterprises any more.

'Look, I'm leaving for New York from here for about ten days, to make sure the merger goes smoothly over there. If you still intend to resign—'

For a second Lucy heard nothing but a roaring in her ears—*what other option did she possibly have?* It cleared just in time for her to hear him say, 'That should give you time to sort yourself out.'

Lucy nodded dumbly. Even though she *wanted* this, had asked for this, to be faced with it now was like no other devastation she'd ever felt. But how on earth had she thought it might play out? she admonished herself. Aristotle Levakis would never keep a discarded lover hanging around like a bad smell. And of course they couldn't go back to a benign working relationship, no matter how she'd thought it might happen.

Ari walked her out to the entrance, where his car was waiting. He handed her in and said, 'I want to thank you for all your work. This merger wouldn't have happened nearly as smoothly without you.'

Oh, please just don't, she almost said. Their affair was reduced to this—trite thanks for her work on the project and for pleasuring her boss in bed in between meetings. The glaring cliché of it all nearly made her want to be ill. Before she could lose control, Lucy grabbed the door handle and pulled it closed firmly, shutting Ari out, but not unfortunately, the pain.

She didn't look back as the car pulled away, so she didn't see Ari standing there, his features drawn and almost grey in the glorious Athenian sun. And anyway, even if she had she wouldn't have believed it.

It was Friday evening, a week later, and Lucy was packing her final bits and pieces into a box, looking around the now empty office. It had been infinitely easier to do this without Ari here, though it had been heart-wrenchingly painful to talk to him on the phone every day, when he'd called to check in or give instructions and hear how interviews were going for a new assistant.

'I trust you. After all, you've been the best assistant I've had,' he'd said when she'd protested that she couldn't be responsible for hiring someone new.

He'd made no effort to ask her to stay, and even though Lucy didn't even want that, couldn't contemplate that, she'd found it nauseating to shake the hand of the best candidate just the other day and had forced a brittle smile when the girl had said, 'Is it true what they say? Is he really that astoundingly gorgeous?'

Lucy shook her head now, to try and clear it, and pulled on her beige trenchcoat. She'd dressed down today, not having seen the point in making an effort, and was wearing jeans, an oversized black jumper and battered sneakers. Her thoughts in that moment went guiltily to her mum, and she bit her lip as she hefted up the box. She had to find another job, and soon. She'd be OK for the next few months or so, but after that—

'Lucy.'

Lucy whirled around at the familiar deep voice. It tugged on her insides and made a fire of sensation race across her skin. Her movement had been so sudden that the full box wobbled precariously out of her arms and fell to the floor, upending everything in a big mess.

She barely registered Ari standing at the door like a huge, dark and threatening presence, and bent down to start picking the things up, her hands shaking. He moved fast and crouched down. Lucy put out a hand. 'Please—don't. I can do it.'

But he ignored her, picking up books and stationery, putting things back in the box. Lucy had to break the taut silence. 'I thought you weren't coming back till the weekend.'

Had he been wining and dining some new woman already in New York? She slammed a book more furiously than she'd intended into the box, in reaction to her wayward thoughts and the jealousy that spiked through her gut.

Ari didn't seem to notice, calmly packing the box. His scent reached out and wrapped her in a heat haze of lust.

'I wrapped things up early. I wanted to get back here.'

His voice was cool, devoid of emotion.

Lucy's movements became brisker. She just wanted to get out of here—right now. 'I think you'll like Gemma, your new assistant. She was far and away the most qualified person.'

Everything was back in the box, and there was an awkward moment when Lucy and Ari went to pick it up at the same time. Lucy had to let him take it, or it would have fallen again.

'I thought I told you I don't like your hair tied back.'

Lucy's eyes flew to his in shock. He sounded almost *flirty.* And his eyes were dark, glittering in a way she hadn't seen since— Once again she cursed her fevered brain. 'That's hardly relevant any more.' She took the box firmly out of his hands and held it to her like a shield. She stepped neatly around him, her breathing feeling short and jerky. 'Well, I'd better—'

'You haven't found a new job yet, have you?'

Lucy turned around. When would this torture end? She longed to be able to say yes, feeling inherently ashamed that she hadn't found a job, as if it made her look unemployable. But every single company she'd approached had stonewalled her—hadn't even allowed her an interview. She couldn't understand it. With a glowing reference from Ari himself, she'd have thought it would be at least easier than it had.

She shook her head and could feel her low ponytail move as she did so. 'Not yet.' She lifted her chin. 'But I'm sure I will, sooner or later.'

Ari sat back on the edge of her desk and fire raced into Lucy's cheeks as she remembered one day in his office in Athens, when he'd perched her on the edge of his desk, spread her legs and— She nearly dropped the box again.

'Look, I have to get going. I have to visit my mother.'

'How is she?'

Lucy wanted to scream. What was this? Twenty questions?

Her throat felt constricted. 'She's fine…well, as fine as she can be. She's comfortable—that's the main thing.'

Ari stood up then, hands in pockets. 'Lucy, I want to offer you another job here in the company. You don't have to work for me, you can work for the legal team again. A position has become vacant.'

She shook her head immediately, panic gripping her at the thought of not being able to escape from this man's devastating orbit. 'No, I don't want— That is, I'd prefer to seek employment elsewhere.'

He said nothing for a long, ominous moment, and then said quietly, 'You might find that more difficult than you think.'

Sick realisation sank in. The box slipped precariously in Lucy's arms but she gripped it tight. She thought of all the jobs she'd gone for in the past few days. The dead ends when she'd known that they were seeking people yet had turned her away.

'Did you—have you stopped me from getting jobs?'

Ari's jaw clenched. He didn't have to answer—he saw the dawning realisation on Lucy's face. 'I've changed my mind. I want you to stay here with Levakis Enterprises.'

His jaw clenched even harder. He'd changed his mind as soon as he'd seen his car pull away with her in it that day in Athens. 'I want to see you again, but I know it can't happen if you're my assistant. It wouldn't be fair on you. But this way it'll be much more acceptable.'

Shock, horror, *heat*—a complete mix of emotions rushed through Lucy with such force that she nearly fainted. She saw black spots before her eyes, but through them she saw Ari—tall and proud and hard and implacable. And as ruthless as ever. Because he hadn't finished with her. *Yet.*

'You've changed your mind, you say? Well, I'm sorry,' she bit out, 'but I'm not available for the position of convenient mistress.'

He stood straighter, his face flushing. 'It doesn't have to be like that, Lucy. I'm asking you to be my lover. We were good together. I can't get you out of my mind…'

She shifted the box. Her arms were starting to ache. But when Ari saw the movement and made as if to take it out of her arms she jerked away. *'No.'*

This moment was so important to her—how she acted right now. Because if she followed the craving call of her body to give in she would be going the way of the doomed, of her mother. She would have learnt nothing. Her heart was bound up inextricably with this man, and he would crush it completely.

She felt a deep sadness well within her that she'd fallen for someone who could never love her as she now knew she ached to be loved. She ached to find the fulfilment she'd never seen as a child. To have the security that came from being in a committed, equal and loving relationship. The kind of thing she'd seen in Kallie and Alexandros Kouros.

'I don't want that, Ari. I don't want you…not like that. I'm worth more than a sleazy work affair, and, no matter how you try and pretty it up, that's all it would be.'

'There is another option. You don't have to work here. It could be much easier than that. I could show you the best that this world has to offer, take care of you and your mother—'

Lucy felt bile rise. She shook her head vehemently, her ponytail slipping over one shoulder. 'I won't be set up like that. I grew up with that, and it's something I just won't settle for. I can look after myself and my mother just fine. We don't need you or any other man.'

Lucy saw Ari's fists clench at his sides at her rejection of his offer. His voice had a rough quality that somehow jarred with his autocratic behaviour, but Lucy didn't have time to dwell on the meaning of that. 'Well, good luck finding a job, Lucy… I'll be waiting for your call when you realise you won't get one. I've marked you as exclusive to this company—no one will touch you with a bargepole.'

Lucy felt tears prick the backs of her eyes when she thought of what a precarious position that would put her mother in. '*Why* are you insisting on doing this?'

He said something guttural in Greek, his face unbearably harsh. 'I told you. I want you. This isn't over between us. I'll expect you to be in Theo's office on Monday morning. I know you can't move from London without jeopardising your mother's treatment.'

Right then Lucy hated Ari, and yet even as she thought that her heart clenched—because she knew she didn't. She couldn't. She tried to make her voice sound as cool and calm as possible, and prayed that for once her every emotion wasn't showing on her too-expressive face.

'I will not be manipulated like this, and I *won't* be falling back into your bed. You'd have to knock me out and drag me there like the neanderthal you're behaving like now.'

His face flushed again, but she didn't mistake the glint of triumph, despite her petty barb. He thought he had her right where he wanted her, but Lucy vowed not to succumb—no matter what he might try or what he was threatening. She turned and stalked from the room, realising that she'd never see him again, at least not in person, and the pain that ripped through her nearly made her stumble and fall.

It was only his softly spoken mocking words that came from behind her that helped her to keep going.

'See you on Monday morning, Lucy.'

CHAPTER TEN

ON MONDAY MORNING Ari strode authoritatively through his own building. The gasps and shocked murmurs as he passed people by merely bounced off him. Aristotle Levakis never frequented any office or floor of the building but his own. His blood was humming, anticipation a taut wire of need, and all because he was going to see Lucy any second now—and because seeing her the other day after a week's absence had shown him that even one day was too long. He vowed there and then to make sure it didn't happen again.

He was too far gone to try and deny the fact that she had him wound so tight around her little finger that he couldn't think straight. For the entire weekend his conscience had been pricking him but he'd quashed it down with a strength of will that was matched only by the strength of his desire for this woman. As he walked towards her office he finally had to acknowledge that he felt out of control for the first time in his life. One thought and one thought only had dominated since he'd seen her last: he wanted her, he needed her, and anything was better than her leaving—

He stopped in his tracks when he pushed open the outer door to his legal team's offices only to see an empty chair where Lucy should have been sitting—*where the hell was she?*

The immediate hollow ache in his solar plexus stunned him with its force. Just then Theo strolled out of his office, a frown on his face.

'Ari? What's up?'

What's up? Ari felt dizzy for a second. He bit out, 'Lucy Proctor—where is she?'

He was hardly aware of Theo's frown and obvious confusion. 'I thought you knew…? She rang this morning and said she wouldn't be taking the position—said something about wanting some time off. I won't lie, I was delighted when you said she was going to be back working for us, but now…'

Ari didn't hear the rest of whatever Theo said. He left. When he got back up to his office he shut the door on his new PA's concerned face and found that he was shaking. Actually shaking. Aristotle Levakis—shaking like a leaf.

With a roaring in his ears he went over to his drinks cabinet and poured himself a drink. He downed it in one. For the first time in his life he did not know what to do. He sat down heavily in his chair and stared vacantly into the distance.

She'd gone. She'd not been playing coy. He'd not backed her into a corner with his threats to derail her chances of getting work. And, if anything, to remember what he'd done and said, the lengths he'd gone to to keep her near, made him feel ill. Especially when he thought of her mother and how much it meant to Lucy to have her taken care of. Immediately he went to reach for the phone, to call her and tell her that everything would be fine, that he'd look after her mother. He stopped.

He'd already done that. He'd already offered her his protection, the exalted position of his mistress, and she'd turned him down. Again bile rose as he realised he'd offered her the one thing she'd refuse even if her life depended on it. Ari sat back and closed his eyes, something awful like dread trickling through him, gathering force as it did so.

Lucy felt as brittle as a Chinese Ming vase teetering on the edge of a table. It had been two weeks since she'd *not* walked back into Levakis Enterprises to take the job that had been so ungraciously offered to her. She still felt sick to her belly to know that despite everything, despite all she'd shared with Ari of her life, he'd turned around and offered to *take care of her.*

And yet as she sat here now in her mother's bedroom, holding the book she'd been reading from aloud, she missed him with an ache that seemed to be growing more acute and stronger by the minute. She was constantly bombarded with images of their time together, and, worse, she'd even caught herself in a daydream of them together, *with a family*, before she could stop herself. Having never believed she was the slightest bit maternal, it was as if she'd suddenly tapped into some universal compulsion to have a baby. With him.

Her mother shifted restlessly and Lucy looked at her, smoothing some hair off her brow. She'd fallen asleep as Lucy had read to her.

Lucy hadn't had the heart to fight the uphill battle to look for a new job yet, so she'd spent the last two weeks coming to see her mum every day, but time was running out. She needed to get work fast. Her mouth firmed as the familiar pain rose. More than that, she needed to forget about—

'Lucy, love, someone here to see you.'

Lucy looked up and blushed. She'd been so caught up in her thoughts she hadn't heard the woman come in. She stood up, and as she followed the nurse out she wondered who on earth it could be…here of all places.

When she came out into the corridor the world swirled crazily. So crazily that she must have swayed, because before she knew it Ari was in front of her and holding onto her, looking down into her eyes.

With a deep inner cry of dismay Lucy wondered if she was conjuring him up, and if it was in fact just her mother's consultant. She blinked. Ari. She blinked again. *Ari.*

From somewhere deeply welcome she came back to earth and pulled herself free of his touch. She stalked to a small empty waiting area nearby. She crossed her arms and turned around, feeling her cheeks grow hot as she took in the reality of facing him again. Those recent images of small dark-haired babies mocked her.

'What are you doing here?' She injected all the frost she could muster into her voice, but when Ari winced imperceptibly she treacherously felt nothing but remorse.

He looked awful. As if he hadn't slept in a week or shaved in days. He was wearing jeans and a sweater, nothing like the cool urbane businessman she'd first seen at a distance two years ago. He was more like the man she'd seen on Paros. Her heart clenched painfully.

He looked at her, and she quailed inwardly but tipped up her chin. When he spoke she had to strain to listen.

'I thought that here might be the only place you'd speak to me. Please forgive me for intruding on your personal space with your mother.'

One fire died in Lucy's belly and another started. Her arms relaxed fractionally. How was it that he still had the power to surprise her, damn him?

'Lucy, I want you to come back to Greece with me. Right now. I want to show you something. I need to talk to you but I can't…' He looked around for a moment. 'Not here…'

Lucy's arms tightened again. She shook her head fiercely. *Go back to Greece?* He had to be kidding. The thought of being in close proximity to this man was about as dangerous as skydiving without a parachute.

He registered her reaction and Lucy saw something flicker in his eyes.

'Lucy, *please*.'

Something in the quality of his voice made her stop, but still she shook her head. Nothing on this earth would persuade her to set herself up to be hurt again. She crushed the treacherous need to know answers: why did he want her to go to Greece? Why wasn't he sweeping in here and demanding to know why she hadn't taken the job? It was what she might have expected. Why wasn't he acting like the proud, arrogant man she knew? And—the worst question of all—why had it taken him two weeks to come after her?

Ari's jaw clenched and something trickled down Lucy's spine. She saw a glimpse of the man she knew. Hard and implacable.

'Very well, if the only way I can persuade you to come is by threatening to reveal to the press that your mother is here, then so be it.'

Lucy gasped and went icy cold. On some level she was certain that Ari would never do such a thing, but on another level she wasn't absolutely sure, and the fact that he was even threatening such a thing made her feel acutely disappointed, and if she was disappointed what did that say about her own pathetically skewed judgment?

'You absolute *bastard*.'

He stepped forward and she stepped back, seeing colour flash through his cheeks. He held out a hand imperiously, and when she didn't move he just dropped it and said, sounding utterly defeated, 'I don't know where that came from. I'm sorry. Of course I wouldn't do that to you or your mother. I just want you to come with me so that I can show you something and talk to you… I promise that if you want to return after you've seen it and we've talked, I'll bring you straight back here.'

Lucy looked at him for a long moment. She was already starting to drown in those green depths. The real and awful truth was that she'd go to the ends of the earth if this man asked her. A very weak part of her was saying, *Go, go, go,* and she could already feel resistance washing away. He was confusing her with his behaviour, with the vulnerability she'd glimpsed but couldn't quite believe. Even so, she had every intention of keeping him to his word.

She said tightly, 'You promise? Then you'll leave me alone and let me find another job?'

He nodded. 'I'll make sure nothing stands in your way.'

Lucy waited for what seemed like an interminable moment, and then finally said, 'I'll get my jacket and bag.'

A scant few hours later they were landing at Athens airport, and Lucy still felt slightly winded at knowing that she'd been sitting at her mother's bedside just hours before. The steward opened the plane door and Ari stood and held out a hand. Lucy looked at it. They hadn't spoken a word on the flight. Ari had been sternly cold.

Feeling intense trepidation, she put her hand in his and let him pull her up. He led her out, and then they were climbing into a nearby helicopter, which was lifting into the clear blue sky within minutes.

Lucy's hands were tightly clasped in her lap, and she avoided looking at Ari as much as possible. After a while Lucy could see that they were circling an island, and she recognised Paros. A mixture of sheer pleasure and intense pain gripped her. If he'd brought her here just to—

But the helicopter was landing, and then they were out, and it was just Lucy and Ari, standing by the same Jeep they'd used the last time. Memories were too intense.

Lucy backed away and mocked herself inwardly for having such a weak and delayed reaction. He'd got her here by barely saying please. She was pathetic.

'Ari, if we're just here so that you can—'

He came and stood close—too close. 'Lucy, please, just trust me. A little further, that's all.'

Where could she go anyway? Lucy looked around. They were miles from anything. Silently she got into the Jeep. Ari got in too, and then they were driving. When she recognised the signs for his mother's tiny village Ari turned and went eastwards. After another ten minutes he took a sharp left turn down towards the coast, and they stopped at a set of ancient wrought-iron gates, nearly overgrown with vegetation.

Ari came round to meet Lucy. He helped her out but when he saw her open her mouth as if to speak he put a finger to her lips. He'd never been so terrified in his entire life; his heart was hammering painfully.

'This is what I wanted to show you.'

The feel of her soft lips against his finger nearly undid him, but he controlled himself.

He led her in through the gate, which was hanging off its hinges, then down an overgrown path and out into a huge clearing where an old and rambling villa, clearly dilapidated, stood on a bluff overlooking the sea.

Lucy's hand tightened reflexively in Ari's. It must have been stunning in its heyday, and the view was priceless. Already she could imagine what it might be like if it was done up, restored to its former glory.

'What is this place?'

Ari brought her over to the other side of the house and an unimpeded view of the sea to where a trail led down to a private beach.

'I bought it…signed the papers just yesterday.'

Lucy felt a little bewildered. He'd brought her here to show her his latest acquisition? 'Oh…well, congratulations.'

He turned and looked at her intently. 'You like it, don't you?'

Lucy frowned, feeling very vulnerable. 'Well, of course I like it. It's beautiful, idyllic, but what does it matter what I think about it?'

He didn't say anything for a long moment, and then he said, 'Because I bought it for you…for us.'

Lucy tried to make sense of his words, feeling a little spaced-out. 'You mean…?' Something struck her then, and anger flowered deep down. She took her hand from his. 'Ari, if you've bought this as some kind of…of love-nest, just so that I can be your mistress—'

He was shaking his head, a curious light in his eyes. 'No. I want it to be a home—a place where we can come…perhaps even with a family…'

Lucy was starting to flounder badly. His words were making all sorts of things bloom in her heart, making it beat faster. How could he know of her deeply secret daydreams? It felt as if he was looking straight into her head. 'Ari—I don't… What are you talking about…?'

He brought a shaking hand to her face, his eyes so intense it nearly hurt to look at them. 'Lucy, I brought you here because *here* is the only place I know how to be me, where I can say what I need to say. I've been going crazy these past two weeks. At first I told myself I didn't need you, that I wasn't devastated beyond belief when I found out you hadn't taken the job with Theo. And then one night, at three o'clock in the morning, when I found myself driving to your flat and sitting outside like a stalker, I had to face up to myself.'

He took a deep breath. 'I think I fell in love with you when you appeared like a whirling dervish to defend me against Helen. I've never had anyone stand up for me before—*care about me before*. I've never *needed* it. But you made me realise how lonely I've been all my life.'

His mouth twisted. 'I thought I had it all figured out. I'd keep you on in the company if you insisted on working, but essentially I wanted you as my mistress. It was only when I said the words out loud I realised what an insult it was—especially to you, after all you've been through. And it was then that I knew I wanted much, much more than that. I wanted everything. A life together. *A marriage.*'

He laughed harshly. 'Of course I denied it to myself. *Love?* I'd cut myself off from anything like that when I was sent away to England and it became my home. Helen effectively cut me off from my father, wouldn't even allow a normal relationship to develop between me and my brother. That's why I'd locked away my memories of here and my mother… I couldn't believe it had existed. But meeting you, falling in love with you, made me believe in them again. It made me remember the love I felt.'

Lucy was more than shocked. She was in danger of floating away from her body. But at the same time she felt welded to the ground, incapable of processing his words, because she realised just how badly she wanted this. And yet…

'But I heard what you said to Helen just before she hit you… about never marrying someone like me…'

Ari looked confused for a moment, and then his face cleared. '*Thee mou*, that wasn't about *you*. Helen was suggesting I marry Pia Kyriapoulos, which would have suited her ends perfectly and kept me marginalized. Pia is not exactly the epitome of the blushing Greek bride.'

'Oh.' Lucy tried to look down, away from his intensity, but Ari wouldn't let her budge.

He took something out of his back pocket and held it out to Lucy. It was a small velvet bag. She looked at him and he just said, 'Open it—please…'

She was all fingers and thumbs, so Ari helped her, and then it was open and something fell into her hand. It was the stunning butterfly necklace she'd seen all those weeks ago and it glinted up at her now. She felt her eyes film over with tears. Ari took it and placed it tenderly around her neck, making tingles run up and down her spine. He tipped her chin up again, forcing her gaze to meet his. His eyes blazed into hers.

'So will you, Lucy Proctor—marry me? Please? Because I cannot imagine going forward from this day or this place without you by my side.'

Emotion was cracking open inside Lucy, and it was the most gloriously painful thing she'd ever felt in her life.

'I never wanted to feel this much.'

Ari's mouth quirked. 'It's painful, isn't it?'

It was the sudden complicit feeling of mutual emotion and how similar they really were in their hearts that made Lucy's eyes water in earnest. Her mouth wobbled precariously. 'I thought I'd settle for someone boring—someone who wouldn't make me face up to myself, to the desires I kept hidden. But you made me believe I had nothing to be scared of… I love you, Ari. I fell for you the day you gave that stupidly expensive necklace to two strangers in the street. And it was when you brought me here that I knew I'd fallen in love with you. And, yes, I'll marry you.'

Lucy could feel the tremor in his hands as they framed her face.

'Thank God,' he said huskily, and bent his head to seal their vow with barely restrained passion.

When they broke apart she could still feel his hands trembling, and his face had such an endearing mix of expressions—pure Ari arrogance and then something she'd never seen before, sheer childlike *joy*—that she couldn't help smiling at him.

He returned her gaze, and for just a moment Lucy caught a glimpse of something achingly vulnerable cross his face before he said haltingly, 'That night I was sitting outside your flat, apart from lurid fantasies featuring a certain tight skirt, I found myself imagining you pregnant…having a baby…*our* baby. I suddenly wanted a family. And not just for an heir… but to create something—a secure foundation. It scared me to death, and it's the only thing that's held me back from coming for you sooner.' He quirked an unsteady smile. 'That and the fact that you might reject me. But the thing is… I've no idea how you feel about kids…'

Lucy looked up at him and wondered how her heart hadn't exploded into tiny pieces. 'Funny you should mention that…'

In more or less exactly the same spot where Ari had proposed to her three years before, Lucy shaded her eyes and looked down to the private beach, where her husband was holding their son high in the air before dunking him back in the glittering sea. The childish shrieks of delight made her smile and she sat down, rearranging the tiny baby in her arms so that she could feed her from the other breast.

'You're very happy, darling, aren't you?'

Lucy looked over to her mother, who was sitting in a wheelchair in the shade on the other side of the table, and smiled. 'Yes, Mum… I am.' Her mother looked away again, out to sea, with an enigmatic smile of her own.

Maxine had these moments of lucidity every now and then, ever since Lucy and Ari had moved her here to the refurbished villa on Paros permanently, with a full-time nursing staff to take care of her every need. Her Alzheimer's hadn't improved, but it seemed to have slowed its development, and sometimes when Lucy looked at her she knew her mother was imagining herself to be in this beautiful place being cared for by one of her besotted suitors.

Lucy had insisted on Ari keeping his mother's house nearby exactly as it was, and sometimes they went back for a night on their own, and revelled in their private space that no one knew about.

Just then a dripping wet Ari appeared, holding an exuberant Cosmo steadily on his shoulders. He smiled widely, his eyes flashing with secret promise and something much deeper and more enduring—*love*. Lucy couldn't remember when she'd once wondered what he'd look like if he smiled. She smiled back, for life was good.

* * * * *

A Merger By Marriage

Cat Schield

Books by Cat Schield

Harlequin Desire

Meddling with a Millionaire #2094
A Win-Win Proposition #2116
Unfinished Business #2153
The Rogue's Fortune #2192
A Tricky Proposition #2214
The Nanny Trap #2253
**At Odds with the Heiress* #2279
**A Merger by Marriage* #2304

*Las Vegas Nights

Other titles by this author available in ebook format.

CAT SCHIELD

has been reading and writing romance since high school. Although she graduated from college with a B.A. in business, her idea of a perfect career was writing books for Harlequin. And now, after winning the Romance Writers of America 2010 Golden Heart Award for series contemporary romance, that dream has come true. Cat lives in Minnesota with her daughter, Emily, and their Burmese cat. When she's not writing sexy, romantic stories for Harlequin Desire, she can be found sailing with friends on the St. Croix River, or in more exotic locales like the Caribbean and Europe. She loves to hear from readers. Find her at www.catschield.com. Follow her on Twitter, @catschield.

Dear Reader,

I know when most people think of Las Vegas, they picture high-energy casinos and spectacular shows that once featured showgirls and now costumed acrobats. For me, it's the history of the town and the people who lived—and died—to make it what it is today.

The idea for my second Las Vegas Nights book came to me after reading several books on Las Vegas history. Back when the mob ran the town, lots of people disappeared. It led me to consider how many people travel to Vegas and how dangerous the issue of identity theft can be.

So I wondered what if my hero's father wasn't who he claimed to be? What if there was no definitive proof that he'd stolen someone's identity?

Trusting those closest to him wasn't something JT Stone developed growing up. Violet Fontaine knows this and is working hard to convince her new husband she only wants what's best for him. But she knows a secret that, if it comes out, may cost her the man she loves.

I hope you enjoy this second installment of Las Vegas Nights. Find more information about my books at my website, www.catschield.net.

All the best!

Cat Schield

For Kevan Lyon, my fabulous agent.

CHAPTER ONE

WITH HIS ARM stretched across the back of the black leather couch, JT Stone sipped one of Rick's signature cocktails and brooded over a woman.

Tonight Violet Fontaine wore a black, skin-tight mini with long sleeves and a neckline that concealed her delicate collarbones. Despite the snug fit, the dress looked modest when viewed from the front. But the back of the dress. Oh, the back. A wide V bared an expanse of golden skin, crisscrossed by spaghetti thin straps from her nape to the indent of her waist. As he suspected the design intended, his gaze was drawn to the curve of her tight, round backside.

His fingers twitched as he imagined holding those luscious curves in his hands. Before he'd met Violet six years ago he'd been a diehard breast and thigh man. These days he was on a mission to find a butt better than hers. To date he hadn't found one. Good thing she had no idea what she did to him or he might lose something more irreplaceable than his favorite bartender.

The resident mixologist of Fontaine Chic's lobby bar Baccarat, Rick was a genius when it came to creating unique cocktails. Tonight JT was having Rick's version of a dirty martini in the lounge. His excuse for showing up six nights a week was that he was wooing Rick back to Titanium where he belonged.

JT finished the last of his drink. Who was he kidding? In the year since Rick had switched employers, JT was here most nights because Violet swung through on her rounds at exactly eleven-fifteen and lingered to chat with the clientele. As the proprietor of the Fontaine Chic, she was very hands-on.

"Another drink, JT?" The waitress cocked her head and smiled warmly at him.

"Sure." Why not? He nodded toward Violet. "And whatever she's drinking."

Charlene followed his gaze. "You know she doesn't drink when she's working."

"Maybe tonight she'll make an exception for me."

"Maybe." But Charlene's tone said something completely different.

"Would you send her over?"

The nightly ritual made the waitress's lips curve in wry humor. "Sure."

Violet herself brought his drink over, setting it before him with practiced ease. "Rick said this is what you're drinking tonight."

"Will you join me?"

When she shook her head, the diamond drops dangling from her earlobes swayed seductively. "I'm working."

"And I'm your best customer."

"You're a fan of Rick's, not Fontaine Chic."

"I'm a fan of you," he murmured and her eyes widened briefly as if startled by his admission. Was it possible she was oblivious to his interest? Not one of the waitresses thought he came here every night just to drink.

It did no good to remind himself that he liked his women curvy, blonde and agreeable. That with her long lean frame inherited from her showgirl mother and her father's wavy brown hair, she was not his type. Or that her strong-willed personality had been cultivated by his estranged uncle, Tiberius Stone, her surrogate father. A man who blamed JT's father for orchestrating his disinheritance.

"You can take a couple minutes," he said, gesturing to the empty space beside him.

Her eyebrow arched at his implied command, but she settled sideways on the couch and crossed her long legs. She'd fastened her waist-length hair into a high, sleek ponytail. The look was both modern and retro and showed off her large brown eyes and bold cheekbones to great advantage.

With the toe of her black stiletto a mere inch from his pant leg, she propped her elbow on the back of the couch, rested her cheek on her palm and waited for him to speak. Quick to smile, she was the most upbeat, optimistic person he'd ever met. She was sunlight to his shadow. Forever close, always untouchable.

He sipped his drink and surveyed her over the rim. The dark circles beneath her eyes told him she was working harder than ever since Tiberius had been murdered several weeks ago.

"You should take some time off," he said, aware that what she did was none of his business.

"And do what? Sit around and grieve?" She must have heard the edge in her tone because after a long sigh, she continued on a milder note. "I know it's what most people do when they lose a parent, but I can't think of a better way to honor Tiberius's memory than to work."

JT nodded in understanding. "I'm sure he'd approve."

Although he'd been given the middle name, Tiberius, after his mother's younger brother, until the last few months JT had never had the chance to know his uncle by anything other than reputation. JT had been raised in Miami where Stone Properties had their headquarters. Tiberius rarely left Vegas. And the bad blood between Tiberius and his brother-in-law and JT's father, Preston Rhodes, made any chance of a relationship between JT and his uncle impossible.

The hard feelings between Tiberius and Preston went back twenty-five years. According to what JT had gleaned from family friends, Preston had accused Tiberius of embezzling from Stone Properties and had convinced James Stone to fire his son. Then, five years later, James had died and JT's father had used his influence over his wife, Fiona Stone—bowing to pressure from her father, she'd never taken her husband's last name—to get the board of directors to vote in favor of making him chairman and CEO.

"Thanks for coming to the memorial service this morning," Violet said. "I know you and Tiberius weren't close, but lately he'd talked a lot about how he regretted all the years he kept you out of his life and how he wished he'd gotten to know you."

Regret tightened in his chest. "I had no idea Tiberius felt that way." JT sucked in a deep breath and let it out slowly.

When he'd arrived in Las Vegas to run the local family operations, his opinion of his uncle had been formed by what he knew about Tiberius from his father and grandfather. Although relations between him and his uncle stayed tense for many years, after seeing how much Violet admired Tiberius, plus all the positive things said about his uncle by other Las Vegas businessmen, JT had begun to suspect that if Tiberius had done what his father had accused him of, there'd been a good reason.

"When it came to your family, he could be hard-headed," Violet said with a faint smile. "And he really hated your dad."

"The feeling was definitely mutual."

Violet remained lost in thought for a moment. "Lately he'd mentioned quite a few times that he thought you'd do a terrific job running Stone Properties."

The compliment landed a direct hit in his gut. He wished he'd had a chance to get to know his uncle the way Violet did. Now it was too late. "I'm leaving the company."

JT heard himself say the words and wondered at his impromptu disclosure. He hadn't divulged his inner thoughts to anyone. Not even his cousin, Brent, and they were as close as brothers. JT peered into his drink. Had Rick infused some sort of truth serum into the cocktail? JT set the glass down. When he looked up, he caught Violet staring at him in surprise.

"Why would you do that?"

"When I turned thirty two months ago, I gained control of my trust fund and the thirty percent of Stone Properties shares my mother left to me when she died. This enabled me to dig into the finances and see what my father has been doing lately."

"And?"

"The properties are overleveraged. My father's been borrowing too much trying to expand and with each property that gets built, our resources are stretched closer to their breaking point." In his gut was a ball of frustration that had been growing steadily these last sixty days.

"I had no idea." Sympathy made her voice soft. She felt sorry for him and he hated it. "Have you shared your concerns with your father?"

It wasn't like him to disclose his difficulties to anyone, least of all someone as tightly connected to the competition as Violet. But then, she wasn't just anyone. She was special. Through her he was linked to a part of his family he'd never known and just being around her made him feel less alone.

JT picked up his drink once more. "He won't listen and since he controls the majority of the shares, I don't have leverage to affect current policy."

"If you leave Stone Properties, what are you planning to do?"

He'd never been one to show his cards, but Violet's attentiveness made her easy to confide in. She acted as if she had all the time in the world to listen to what ailed him and offer sensible feedback. He'd be a fool not to listen to her opinion as a businesswoman. But it was her friendship he craved. And if he was honest with himself, her body he longed to devour.

"I've been cultivating some investors," he said. "I'm going out on my own. My uncle didn't need the family business to be successful and neither do I."

"Are you sure that's the best idea? Tiberius let your father drive him out of the business and never stopped regretting it."

"No one drove him out," JT corrected her. "Tiberius was caught stealing from the company and was fired."

Her disappointment in him was like clouds passing in front of the sun. "He was framed." She truly believed that. "By your father."

JT sat perfectly still beneath the weight of her accusation while his thought raced. A normal person would rush to defend their father against such slander, but JT had seen the company's financials for himself and knew his father was not telling the stockholders everything. That made him a liar in JT's books. Nor would he ever champion his father after the way Preston had treated JT's mother.

But he wasn't ready to jump on the bash-Preston bandwagon either. As conflicted as JT was about his father, he put a high value on loyalty.

"If that's true," he said, his tone neutral, "all the more reason to break with the company and my father."

Determination flared in her eyes. "Or you could stay and fight for what's yours."

While JT appreciated her spirited defense of his inheritance, he'd been contemplating the wisdom of staying with Stone Properties for a couple years. It was worse now that he had seen the company's financials.

"I hate being powerless to stop him from taking apart all that my grandfather built."

"I can understand that." Without warning her gaze sharpened. "These plans of yours, do they mean you're leaving Las Vegas?"

Was she hoping he wouldn't? The thought of not seeing her every day made him grim. Did it bother her as well?

JT searched her eyes for answers, but saw only curiosity. With Violet, what you saw was what you got. Her openness fascinated him. She never seemed to worry about guarding herself against hurt or disappointment.

It was a major factor in why he'd never pursued her.

Not long after he'd arrived in Las Vegas, he'd run into his uncle and Violet at a charity event. Despite his instant attraction to the twenty-three-year-old, he knew better than to act on his interest. The bad blood between her adopted father and his biological one was a significant barrier. So was JT's playboy lifestyle.

Before he'd moved to Las Vegas, JT had made quite a name for himself in Miami's social scene. Going at life at a reckless pace whether it was fast boats, expensive cars or unavailable women, he hadn't cared whom he hurt as long as he displeased his father.

He liked Violet too much to subject her to his unhealthy family dynamic. Besides, she wasn't a good choice for him. Unlike the women he usually pursued, she would expect things from him. Things he couldn't give her. Openness. Joy. Trust. In order to be with her he'd have to surrender the defenses that muffled his emotions and protected him from pain and disillusionment. She'd lure him out of his comfortable dark cave and require him to find happiness. How was he supposed to do that when his childhood hadn't given him the tools?

His father believed anything that got in the way of business was bad. As a kid, JT had had that philosophy hammered into his head. His mother had been weakened by her hunger for love. Being ignored by the domineering husband she adored had made her life hell, and she'd started retreating into drugs and alcohol around the time that Tiberius left town. By the time he turned twelve, JT was used to being ignored by his parents, forgotten by his grandfather and alienated from his uncle. Nor was there any family on his father's side. The only person who'd showed any interest in him was his grandmother and she split her time between Miami, Virginia and Kentucky.

Traditional family. Love. JT had never grown up with these things.

Being around Violet gave him a glimpse of what a normal

personal life could be. The love she had for her sisters, her mother and Tiberius made him long to be included in her circle. But he couldn't take the steps needed to put himself there. Nor could he leave well enough alone either. The need to connect remained. A tantalizing temptation. One of his deep, dark secrets.

So he visited Fontaine Chic night after night and sat in the bar. He craved a relationship with Violet, but had no idea how to go about having one. In casino terms, he was betting the minimum. He'd never win big, but he wasn't going to lose everything either. Playing without risk was not how he lived. He got a rush from flinging his body into danger, but gambling with his heart was something else entirely.

"I don't know what the future holds," he responded at last. "Will you miss me if I go?"

The question caught her off guard. Her eyes widened and her lips parted, but no words came out. Usually their exchanges hovered on the verge of personal without either of them crossing that line. Tonight, he'd changed the game by giving her a glimpse into what was bothering him, by trusting her with his plans for the future.

"I'll miss your business," she retorted with a wry smile that didn't quite reach her eyes. She uncrossed her legs, signaling their conversation was at an end.

"Violet." He caught her hand before she could rise. The casual contact created a complex chain reaction in JT's gut. He wanted her. That had never been in doubt. But what lay below the lust was dangerous beyond belief. "I'm really sorry about Tiberius."

He gave her hand a gentle squeeze and released her. It rattled him how hard it was to relax his fingers and set her free. What he wanted to do was draw her into his arms and let her soak the shoulder of his suit coat with her tears. He knew it was impossible. They didn't share that level of intimacy. The fact both relieved and frustrated him.

"Thank you." Two polite words, but her tone carried a wealth of emotion. She dabbed at the corner of her eye, catching teardrops on her knuckles. “I’m such a mess.”

“I think you’re beautiful.”

Such a simple statement from such a complicated man. Unvarnished and without subtext, the words shook her. Needing a second to compose herself, Violet made quick apologies and headed for the bar to snag a couple of drink napkins to soak up her tears. Feeling steady once more, she returned to where JT now stood.

“Are you okay?”

The hard, unyielding businessman was back. As Violet nodded in response to his question, she breathed a sigh of relief. Whatever glimpse she’d had behind the curtain, however brief, made JT that much more interesting. And that was problematic.

Long ago she’d accepted that one look from him set her hormones off like Roman candles. Lust she could handle. She was a modern girl with a healthy appetite for sex. Maybe she didn’t indulge often, but that didn’t mean she wasn’t interested. Just cautious.

It was the way her heart sped up whenever she spotted JT that concerned her. Getting romantic notions about a man as emotionally unavailable as JT would only lead to heartbreak. And she’d seen the effects of that sort of misery up close. Violet’s mother had been abandoned by her married lover and left with a baby to support. Ross Fontaine had taken everything Lucille Allen had to give and moved on without a backward glance. Yet despite her heart being a shattered mess, Violet’s mother still loved Ross and would to her dying day.

No. Violet was way too smart to end up like her mother. The instant the uncharitable thought surfaced, Violet regretted it. She loved her mom like crazy. It was just that being Lucille’s daughter had forced Violet to grow up too fast. If not for Tiberius, she’d have had no childhood at all.

He’d adored Lucille. Taken on the responsibility for her and her daughter. They'd been his family. Not legally, of course, because even though he loved Lucille and wanted to marry her, she refused to give up on the hope that one day Ross Fontaine would return to her.

When Violet gave her heart, it would be to someone available, emotionally as well as legally. His reputation as a smart, fair businessman impressed the hell out of her, but when it came to personal relationships, he never went all in.

Not that he'd given her any reason to believe he thought of her as anything other than a competitor who'd stolen his favorite bartender. Tonight that had changed. Tonight he'd asked if she'd miss him if he left Las Vegas and made her believe his next heartbeat hinged on her saying that she would.

Violet brushed away her fanciful thoughts, but she couldn't ignore how her pulse had hitched at the gentle strength of his hand on hers. This was just simple desire. Nothing more. The man was six-feet, one-inch of rock solid male. Handsome with his black hair and bold eyebrows. The slight downturn of his chiseled lips. The fathomless ocean blue of his eyes.

Her instincts said he was a man who could use some help and she was a girl who loved cheering on her teammates. Only he wasn't on her team or even part of her circle. She would be wise to mind her own business where he was concerned. If she became too invested in offering him help that he did not want, she'd end up getting burned.

"I'd better get going or I'll be completely off schedule," she said, but couldn't bring her feet to move. Something had changed between them tonight and walking away from JT was proving difficult.

"I'd better get going as well," he told her, glancing at his watch. "If you need anything I hope you'll call."

More surprises. "Sure." She couldn't imagine what sort of help she'd turn to him for. Most of the time she was pretty self-sufficient. She'd had to be. Her mother was too easily overwhelmed by the least difficulty. Violet had learned to take care of herself from an early age, even when life had grown less challenging after they'd moved in with Tiberius when Violet was six. "That's nice of you."

For a brief moment his eyes softened. Before she could draw an unsteady breath he'd retreated behind his reserve once more.

"It's not being nice," he said, neutral and polite. "We're family."

His declaration was the cherry on top of a triple scoop sundae of surprises. "How do you figure?"

"It might not be the most traditional connection, but you were my uncle's daughter."

"Not legally." Violet wasn't sure how to cope with a connection of this sort with JT. If things became affectionate between them she might just step out of the neutral zone and into treacherous territory.

"Do you really think that mattered to Tiberius?"

"No." Violet cocked her head and regarded him. "But I would have thought it mattered to you."

"Why?"

Violet floundered. Confronting people didn't come naturally to her. It was a skill she'd worked hard to develop during her years in management positions and when she did speak her mind, it was after careful preparation.

But JT had flustered her tonight and she'd spoken without thought.

"The truth is I really don't know."

"But you had a reason to say it," he persisted, his interest laser-sharp.

Admitting her flaws wasn't something she did often, but Violet felt she owed JT an explanation after he'd been so kind to her tonight. "I didn't like growing up the bastard daughter of Ross Fontaine," she explained. "Being treated as if I didn't exist by the entire Fontaine family gave me a huge chip on my shoulder."

"That's changed now. Henry Fontaine not only welcomed

you as his granddaughter, he gave you a hotel to run and a shot at becoming CEO of the family business."

Violet nodded. "And most days that amazes me. But sometimes I regress to that eleven-year-old girl who was ridiculed by her classmates for bragging that I was Ross Fontaine's daughter when everyone could tell he wanted nothing to do with me."

"I can see where that would be hard."

She had a difficult time believing JT could sympathize with her situation. The sole heir to Stone Properties, he'd grown up knowing who he was and where he belonged. Maybe things hadn't been perfect with his parents and maybe the company was struggling with his father at the helm, but that could be turned around with the right moves.

"So, you think we're family," she said, aiming for a warm smile. She could tell by JT's expression that she missed the mark.

"I didn't have a chance to know my uncle," he explained. "I think I missed a lot. You knew him better than anyone. I feel connected to him through you."

It took a second for Violet to register that JT was reaching out to her. All of a sudden she felt a little giddy. "Your uncle was my father in all ways but legally." She sounded a tad breathless as she finished, "I suppose that makes us cousins."

JT cocked his head and regarded her. "I suppose it does. Good night, Violet."

He departed Baccarat without touching her again and Violet was dismayed by her disappointment. She could get used to having his hands on her. Was that creepy now that they'd agreed to consider each other cousins?

Violet continued on her rounds, and contemplated what her sisters would make of her conversation with JT. With her traditional upbringing and ambitious professional goals, Harper would give her sensible and conservative advice. Younger than Violet by a few months, Harper was nonetheless the voice of pragmatism. She would encourage Violet to keep her distance from a complicated man in a tricky family situation. Violet's relationship with Tiberius had made her by extension an enemy of Preston Rhodes, JT's father. If she and JT became friendly, it would only complicate what she sensed was a strained relationship with his father.

While Harper's rational arguments would appeal to Violet's head, Scarlett's opinion would go to work on her heart. A few weeks ago Scarlet had pointed out that there was more to JT's nightly appearance at Baccarat than simply that he missed Rick's mixology expertise. Scarlett would encourage Violet to get to know JT better; she was convinced that something would ignite between them. Shock waves pummeled Violet's midsection as her thoughts ventured down that path.

Sex with JT would be explosive. Tonight when he'd squeezed her hand, she'd been hard-pressed not to lean over and plant a very uncousinly kiss on his well-shaped lips. Her skin tingled at the thought and she gave her head a vigorous shake. She couldn't go there. Shouldn't even think about going there. Trouble was when she was around JT, she had a hard time thinking clearly.

Angst and passion simmered beneath his expensive suits and professional demeanor. During the six years she'd known him she'd occasionally caught glimpses of deep pain, and her instinct had been to offer comfort or help. But JT was a man who stubbornly resisted admitting to any vulnerability or weakness. From Tiberius, Violet knew JT's childhood hadn't been ideal. His father was a ruthless businessman who'd manipulated his father-in-law into disowning his only son. His drive for power had caused him to neglect his wife.

JT's mother had not taken the banishment of her brother well. She'd retreated into alcohol and pills. Tiberius had kept tabs on her through friends, but he'd been unable to do more than stand by and watch her fade away. What Violet had never understood is why she'd never divorced Preston. She might have had a chance at happiness if she had.

Violet finished her rounds and returned to her large executive office. Even though it was three in the morning, she didn't expect to sleep. Reports awaited her attention.

The hotel's management offices occupied a small chunk of the third floor. She spent little time here, preferring to be on the floor, eyes on the action taking place in her hotel.

It's what she'd learned from shadowing Tiberius around the Lucky Heart. Her throat closed as she stared down the Las Vegas strip to where the small hotel and casino sat. Built in the sixties, it lacked the amenities of the modern hotels and casinos: five-star restaurants, extravagant décor and luxury suites. The ceilings were low. The carpet needed replacing. And the clientele came in for the cheap bar drinks and stayed for the loose slots. But for Violet it would always be home.

Which is why she'd been surprised how Tiberius had reacted when Henry Fontaine approached her about coming to work for him. She'd expected Tiberius to discourage her from joining the family business. Quite the opposite. Tiberius knew how hard it had been for her to be Ross Fontaine's bastard daughter. Unlike Scarlett, Ross's other illegitimate daughter, Violet had grown up in Las Vegas within the long shadow of the gorgeous hotels and casinos that were owned by the Fontaine dynasty.

The older she got, the more being an outsider frustrated her. Without Tiberius as her champion, constantly making as if she was the smartest, most capable person he'd ever known, she might never have accepted that she didn't need approval from the Fontaines to make her happy.

Maybe that's why she sympathized with JT. If his grandfather hadn't died when JT was ten, Preston would never have taken over Stone Properties and ousted his brother-in-law. The company would have stayed in Stone hands. First Tiberius's, then JT's.

Attending his uncle's memorial service today must have really upset him. She had no other explanation for why he'd shared with her his concerns regarding Stone Properties. They'd known each other for six years and as much as he made her pulse dance, he'd always just treated her like a business acquaintance. Was it any wonder his behavior tonight had thrown her off balance? Did he regret telling her about his worries for his family's company? It just wasn't like him to be so…forthcoming.

She smirked as she imagined him kicking himself the entire way back to Titanium.

It was a spectacular property. He'd spent his first two years in Vegas rebuilding the hotel and casino. It was larger than both Fontaine Chic and Richesse combined, with a huge convention facility and an eighteen-hole golf course in the back. Admiring the hotel's style, she'd used the same design company to bring to life her vision for Fontaine Chic.

What would happen to Stone Properties if JT left? As hurt as Tiberius had been that his father believed Preston's lies and disinherited him, Tiberius's biggest concern had always been for the company beneath Preston's stewardship. He would be worried that JT was quitting.

"Not my problem," she muttered, but already the wheels were turning in her mind.

Tiberius would have wanted her to help JT. Despite all the years they'd been estranged, right before his death, Tiberius had started reaching out to his nephew.

And Violet was confident she could keep her head screwed on straight and her hormones in check long enough to figure out a way to help JT save Stone Properties. With the decision made, Violet headed to her suite for a hot shower and a good night's sleep.

CHAPTER TWO

VIOLET STARED AT the shelves of law books that covered the walls of the lawyer's office, her eyes gritty and dry. In contrast, her mother sat beside her, weeping softly. In the weeks since Tiberius's death, Lucille had gone through a dozen boxes of tissues.

A part of Violet was ashamed that she'd moved swiftly through the five stages of grief while her mother had gone straight to stage four—depression—and stayed there.

"That takes us to the Lucky Heart," John Malcolm, Tiberius's lawyer continued. "As you probably know, the casino is deep in debt."

Violet nodded, absently squeezing her mother's hand in comfort, relieved that Tiberius had invested his personal fortune wisely and set aside enough for Lucille to never have to worry about money. "I don't understand why. The entire time I worked there, it always operated in the black. Nor has business fallen off in the last five years. Tiberius was too savvy to let that happen. So where did the debt come from?"

"He was mortgaging the Lucky Heart in order to buy stock."

"Stock?" That didn't sound like Tiberius at all. "Why would he do that? He didn't trust Wall Street. Said it was a sucker's bet."

"He was buying private stock."

Even more curious. A rhythmic ache had manifested in Violet's temples. She rubbed to ease the pain. "So can we sell the stock and get the Lucky Heart out of debt?"

"Unfortunately, you're not going to be able to do that."

"Why not?" Making bad business decisions was something Tiberius had never done. "What sort of stock was he buying?"

"Stone Properties stock."

Violet leaned forward. Had she heard the gray-haired lawyer correctly? "Why would he do that?"

John's solemn blue eyes were the gatekeepers of a thousand clients' secrets. "He had his reasons."

Her thoughts rushed through a dozen scenarios as to why Tiberius had kept something this huge from her. Then she contemplated her conversation with JT a few days earlier. "How much stock did he have?"

"In the three months before his death he'd managed to get eighteen percent."

Violet's curiosity spiked. Did his purchase of Stone Properties stock have anything to do with why he'd been reestablishing his relationship with JT? Together they would've controlled forty-eight percent of Stone Properties, not enough to take over and force Preston out, but if they could secure another three percent…

Is that what Tiberius had been up to?

"Did he leave the stock to JT?"

John Malcolm looked surprised. "No. He left it to you."

Any normal person who'd just inherited eighteen percent of a multi-billion dollar company might be dancing around the lawyer's office or at the very least grinning. Violet had no desire to celebrate. The price tag for her windfall was too high. She'd lost the man who'd been her father in heart and soul if not by blood or marriage.

"Why me and not my mom?"

"Because he trusted you'd know what to do with it."

"First Scarlett inherits a warehouse full of secret files and now this," she muttered, thinking about all the private information Tiberius had gathered over the years on acquaintances and family. "What other surprises does Tiberius plan to unleash on the Fontaine sisters?"

"Now, as to the conditions of the inheritance."

"And there it is," Violet grumbled. She loved Tiberius, but he was a cagey bastard.

John Malcolm ignored her outburst. "You can't sell the stock, donate it or give it away." The lawyer smiled ironically as he said this last bit, if he couldn't understand why anyone could part with that much money and expect nothing in return. "Until the death of Preston Rhodes."

Obviously Tiberius wanted to make sure his brother-in-law never got his hands on the stock.

"Chances are it won't be worth anything by the time that happens," she murmured.

"And there's one other issue," John Malcolm continued as if she hadn't spoken. "You can't vote the shares because you're not family."

Violet sat back in her chair and regarded the lawyer in utter bafflement. Why hadn't Tiberius just left the shares to JT? The answer occurred to her an instant after the question had formed. Because his relationship with JT hadn't reached that level of trust yet. Tiberius probably thought he had months to get to know his nephew. It wasn't like he was planning on getting murdered.

"Thank you for all your help," Violet said, standing to shake hands with the lawyer.

"Yes," Lucille echoed. "Thank you. I know you were a good friend to Tiberius all these years."

"Sometimes I felt more like a co-conspirator," John Malcolm with a wry smile. "But it was my pleasure to call him both friend and client."

Violet and her mother left the lawyer's office and headed to the parking lot.

"I can't believe Tiberius left you all that stock," Lucille said, "without there being anything you can do with it."

"Did he talk to you about what he was up to?"

Lucille's beautiful smile was always a little bit sad, but since Tiberius's death it had become downright melancholy. "You know he didn't talk business with me."

No. Tiberius had always made it his mission to bring all things joyful and fun to his conversations with Lucille. He'd loved when her eyes sparkled. Discussing something as upsetting as staging a coup against Preston Rhodes would never have happened.

"Maybe I'll check his office when I drop you off," Violet said. "There might be something in his files."

When they arrived at the house Lucille had shared with Tiberius for years, Violet discovered that her mother was right. There were ten files pertaining to the stock acquisition. Two contained the paperwork for the stock Tiberius had purchased. The other eight contained information on family members he hadn't yet contacted. Her interest rose as she read through Tiberius's notes. Gaining another three percent wouldn't be easy, but she had a notion of how it could be done. Not that it did her any good. She owned eighteen percent of a stock she could neither get rid of nor vote.

So, what the hell was she supposed to do with it? Better to ask, what would Tiberius want her to do with it?

The thought of becoming embroiled in the intrigue surrounding Stone Properties gave Violet a bad taste in her mouth. She was quite content with her own piece of the Las Vegas strip. From the second she'd been put in charge of Fontaine Chic, she'd known complete happiness. It was all she needed. She didn't care if she won the contest their grandfather had created to decide which of the three Fontaine sisters would succeed him as CEO. Violet was realistic about her chances. With Harper's education and hotel training, it was her contest hands down. Besides, it was her birthright. Just like Stone Properties was JT's.

If only there was something Violet could do to make it so he could claim his rightful place. Not that he wanted her help. She dismissed that as insignificant. She needed to focus on keeping alive Tiberius's plan to reclaim his family's company. But how?

When the answer came, she was stunned by its simplicity and foolhardiness. She couldn't. The idea was crazy. On the other hand, maybe crazy was what the situation called for.

And there was only one way she was going to know for sure.

JT was about to leave his usual spot in Baccarat and head back to his hotel when he spotted Violet approaching the bar. Tension he'd not been aware of released its grip on his muscles. He relaxed his clenched teeth and felt a scowl melt from his forehead.

Since finding out what his father had been up to with Stone Properties, he'd been frustrated and in great need of a confidante he could trust. He trusted Violet. Sharing his problems with her had eased his mind.

For the last five days she'd been absent from the lounge. Either she'd been detained by hotel business or she'd been avoiding him. Thinking she might be avoiding him had been a bitter pill to swallow.

He'd stepped across the line at their last meeting. Claiming her as family had pushed their association past the boundaries of casual acquaintances. But no matter how much it worried him that he might become dependent on her, he couldn't stop craving her support.

To his unreasonable delight, the instant she entered the bar, her gaze sought his and she immediately headed his way. As she drew near, the spicy scent of her perfume preceded her and he had just enough time to draw a heady lungful before she sat beside him. Tonight's black dress was a knee-length sheath with a deep scoop neckline that showed off the upper curves of her breasts. Keeping his attention on her face proved challenging as she gathered a deep breath before speaking.

"I'm glad you're here tonight," she said, her voice brisk, expression resolute.

He resisted the urge to remind her that he was here every night. She already had him eating out of the palm of her hand. Why give her more power?

"You look beautiful," he told her, letting his gaze drift over her.

His compliment caused her to blink. "Thank you." For a moment she looked as if she'd lost her train of thought.

Despite the bar's low light, he spied a rush of color in her cheeks and noticed an uneven hitch to her breath. In that instant he realized she'd felt the impact of his attraction for her, even if she wasn't ready to admit it.

The revelation inspired a rush of longing to touch her smooth skin, to pull her body tight to his and hear her sigh beneath his lips. He imagined sweeping his tongue across her breasts and hearing her cry out. Not seeing her these last few days had fueled his hunger for her. He'd spent far too much time pondering exactly how he would make love to her.

"JT, are you listening to me?"

He shook his head and dispelled the evocative images lingering there. "Sorry. I was distracted. Is that a new perfume you're wearing?"

"It's something Tiberius gave to my mother last Christmas. Since his death she can't bear to wear it, but I love the scent so she gave me the bottle."

"It's nice," he murmured.

"Thank you." She paused and regarded him through narrowed eyes. "We went to Tiberius's lawyer for the reading of his will a couple days ago."

JT wrestled his libido back under control as her words registered. "And he left everything to you and your mother."

"Yes." She scowled at him as if he was supposed to comprehend a deeper meaning to what she'd said. "But it's *what* he left that caught me by surprise."

"His house, bank accounts, the hotel." JT ticked the items off on his fingers. "What else?"

A smug grin bloomed on her full lips. "How about eighteen percent of Stone Properties stock."

The news dealt him a sturdy blow. "How did he get it?"

"He mortgaged the Lucky Heart and bought every share he could."

"But why?"

"To take on your father?"

"Eighteen percent wouldn't do him any good. When my mother died she left my father thirty percent of the company. Combined with the rest of what my family owns, he has enough votes to control the company."

"Until two months ago when you turned thirty. Your father controlled your trust fund until then, didn't he?"

"Yes." JT didn't know what to make of what he was hearing. "You think my uncle wanted us to join forces?" He recalled the dinners Tiberius had invited him to. "He never said anything of the sort."

"I think he wanted to get to know you before he committed to anything."

For the first time in years JT felt a flutter of excitement. Combining what he'd inherited with Violet's shares left him three percent away from taking the company back from his father and repairing all the damage that had been done.

"How much do you want for your stock?"

Violet had been watching him closely, grinning at his reaction to her news, but now delight drained from her expression. "That's where things get a little tricky."

Suspicion flared before JT remembered that this was Violet he was dealing with. She was loyal and a team player. She wasn't here to get something from him. She honestly wanted to help. But none of his trust reflected in his tone as he asked, "Tricky how?"

"The terms of Tiberius's will don't allow me to sell, trade or donate the shares in any way." She looked as if she expected him to explode in frustration. "Otherwise you have to know, I'd let you have them."

Although disappointed by his uncle's unorthodox terms, JT knew there was a way he could work this to his advantage. "But you can give me your proxy vote." Of course, he only had eighteen percent, but if Tiberius had convinced several of their family members to part with the stock, surely that meant JT could do the same. He only needed three percent more.

"That's the other problem," she said, apology in her tone. "The way your grandfather set up the stock, only family members by blood or by marriage can vote. Since, I'm not family, my votes can't count."

JT exhaled in exasperation. "So we're back to square one. With your votes voided, my father remains in control of the majority of the stock."

But Tiberius's plan was still a viable option. JT and his father each had thirty percent of the shares. With Violet's eighteen percent excluded, that left twenty-two percent up for grabs. If he could buy twelve percent of the shares belonging to the rest of the family or failing that, convince them to swing their votes his way, he could take the company back.

"Not back to square one," Violet said, interrupting his train of thought. "If I was family, I could vote the shares."

"If you were family, yes," JT agreed, his gaze fixed on the lights racing around above the bar. "But you're not."

"I could be."

Something in her tone caught his attention. A tentative smile trembled at the corners of her lips. She was trying to tell him something, but his mind was darting in too many directions to grasp the nuances of her meaning.

"How?"

"We could get married."

If she'd nailed him with a cattle prod he couldn't have been more stunned. "Married?"

"In name only, of course." She offered him a cheeky grin that didn't reach her eyes. "There's nothing in my uncle's will that prevents me from marrying the shares away."

"Since he knew we'd never get married, it probably never crossed his mind."

She cocked her head and regarded him solemnly. "And how did he know something like that?"

"I told him I had no intention of starting anything up with you."

Violet sat up very straight. Her eyes narrowed. "You two talked about me?"

JT nodded. "When I first arrived in town. Tiberius had heard about my activities in Miami and was worried that if I pursued you, you might get hurt. I agreed to keep my distance."

"How noble." Her tone dripped with scorn.

"Not that noble," he retorted, deciding if they were going to consider her wild scheme, she might as well hear the whole truth. "It was an easy promise to make. You really aren't my type."

Mouth tight, she stared at him for several seconds. But then her hand stole across his leg, mid-thigh, and lingered.

"You aren't my type either." But her husky tone and the come-get-me-big-boy look in her eyes said the exact opposite. "So that should make a marriage in-name-only a snap."

JT kept his expression bland. No need for her to learn the truth. He'd promised himself that nothing would happen between them. He needed her in his corner far more than he needed her naked in his bed. He wasn't about to ruin their fledgling connection over something as fleeting as lust.

"It should." But he didn't feel as confident as he sounded. "And it isn't forever."

"Right. We only need to be married long enough for me to

vote my shares at the annual meeting. It's at the end of August, right?"

"August twenty-fifth."

"That's only six weeks away."

JT had another thought. "Your family isn't going to be happy if you marry me without some sort of a prenup."

"At the moment I'm not worth more than the stock I inherited from Tiberius and what I've saved towards retirement. We can sign a simple agreement that states we leave the marriage with what we arrived with."

She made everything sound so reasonable. So why was he resisting?

Sure, marriage wasn't on his to-do list. He enjoyed playing the part of confirmed bachelor. Las Vegas was the perfect place to find attractive, single women looking for a little fun. They came in for a weekend and he gave them the royal treatment. Then they were gone. No fuss. No muss.

Violet was a whole different package. She was in Vegas to stay. Getting involved with her would be complicated and undoubtedly end in heartbreak. His.

But it wasn't as if they were getting married for real. He just needed to remember that.

"So are we going to do this?" She'd plucked her palm from his thigh, leaving behind a distracting tingle.

"You're sure you want to marry me?" His heart thumped hard against his ribs as he reminded himself this was a business deal.

"Want to marry you? Absolutely not." Her lighthearted laugh had a slightly wicked edge. "But I feel like I owe it to Tiberius to finish what he started. And I'd like to see you take back your family's company."

He scrutinized her lovely features, finding only altruism in her expression. Her self-sacrifice made him uncomfortable.

"I get that you feel an obligation to Tiberius, but I'm not sure this is the best idea."

"I don't feel obligated."

From her earnest expression he could tell she didn't. And that's what worried JT the most.

"Okay, but you're also looking for a way to make your shares pay off too, right?"

She cocked her head and regarded him in silence for several seconds. "You yourself said the company isn't doing well with your father at the helm. If he continues, the shares will lose value. Maybe even become worthless. I know you'll make a much better CEO. I'm protecting myself the best way I can."

Her answer rang with conviction. JT's resistance eased minutely. Still, he should refuse. The only way this wasn't going to backfire on them both was if he turned down her help. But the idea of getting that much closer to Violet was a temptation of the hard-to-resist variety.

But marriage? Was the opportunity to rescue Stone Properties from his father's clutches worth the danger of getting too attached to Violet? He already liked her far too much for his own good. Watching her walk into the lounge was enough to make his day. What if he started to rely on spending lots of time with her? He knew himself well enough to know that just being friends wouldn't cut it. He wanted her. Badly. It was only a matter of time before he did something about it.

After a fast and furious debate, JT kicked self-preservation to the curb.

"Then I'm in." He was on the verge of getting on one knee and proposing to her properly when she spoke up.

"I think we should do this sooner rather than later. Before either one of us comes to our senses."

"How soon?" She'd saved him from going all romantic—even if it was just for show—and making an ass out of himself. "Like Saturday?"

"What about now?" Seeing his shock, she rushed on. "Too fast?"

"A little." But what the hell. If they waited, the anticipation might prompt him to do something stupid. Like let her see how badly he needed her. "But it's doable. Your chapel or mine?"

"How about someplace neutral. The Tunnel of Love Chapel?"

Some of JT's tension faded. She really was approaching this as a business arrangement and he needed to do so as well. But ignoring her effect on him was easier said than done.

"Positively romantic," he said, his tone dry.

"Good." She glanced at her phone. "I booked it for midnight."

"You were feeling pretty confident I'd say yes."

She shrugged. "It made perfect business sense that you would."

But business was the furthest thing from his thoughts at the moment. He was contemplating all the delightful things a husband did with his brand-new wife. "Are you going to leave the booking of the honeymoon suite to me?"

She looked positively horrified. "Perhaps I wasn't very clear. A marriage in name only means no sex."

"Not even on our wedding night?" he couldn't resist asking. She was so delightfully earnest. It made teasing her a pleasure.

"I thought I wasn't your type." Her voice lacked any trace of amusement.

"Since you're going to be my wife," he said, "I figured I should make an exception just this once."

"It's a lovely thought but we should really keep this all business between us."

"Whatever you say."

"It will make things easier."

She was oh so wrong about that. Nothing about being married to Violet was going to be easy. In fact, he'd better brace himself because things were about to get a whole lot harder.

CHAPTER THREE

On her way across Fontaine Chic's lobby, Violet decided it was okay if a bride felt excited and slightly terrified on her wedding day. Especially if the groom was sexy and enigmatic and the decision to marry was somewhere between logically conceived and wildly impulsive.

Wearing an off-white lace dress she'd bought on impulse that morning from one of the hotel's shops, Violet's heart double-timed to each click of her heels on the black marble floor. She clutched an overnight bag and a briefcase filled with Tiberius's files on the holders of Stone Properties stock. Against her better judgment, she'd let JT talk her into spending their wedding night together at his house. In separate bedrooms, of course.

She wasn't worried that he'd take advantage of her. He'd already pointed out that she wasn't his type. That declaration still stung. With his reputation as a player, she hadn't suspected he had a type beyond female, single and young. She was all those. So what about her didn't appeal to him?

Was she the wrong height? Too thin? Too fat? Not pretty enough? Not sexy?

Violet slammed the door on curiosity. It didn't matter if she was his type or not. Their marriage was a business arrangement. She needed to remember that. And to guard against demonstrating the way her body came alive whenever he drew near.

A bright blue BMW convertible stood at the ready in the hotel's circular driveway. JT leaned against the car's hood, wearing a dark gray, almost black suit and white shirt with a blush-colored tie that emphasized his potent charisma. He hadn't spotted her yet so she had a private moment to observe his relaxed posture and utter gorgeousness as he joked with one of her bellhops. Thanks to anxiety, her muscles hadn't been responding properly to the signals from her brain for the last hour; now they were positively spastic.

He was still laughing when their gazes met. The power of his smile knocked the breath from her lungs. Wanting his eyes to light up with pleasure at seeing her, she was crushed at how fast he sobered.

"Right on time, I see." He stepped forward to take her bags.

Was he used to waiting for the women he dated? They probably took longer to primp and fuss than she had. In truth, her nerves had prevented her from applying eyeliner with a steady hand so she'd just dusted her lids with neutral eye shadow, buffed her cheekbones with blush and used a little powder to keep down the shine. It didn't occur to her that she hadn't applied lipstick until his gaze locked on her mouth.

A bride shouldn't attend her wedding in such a state. She dug in her purse, but all she found was some lip balm. "Damn," she muttered. "I don't have any lipstick."

"You don't need any." He opened the passenger door for her and gave her plenty of room to get by him. It was almost as if he was avoiding her. But why would he need to do that?

"I'm not sure I feel completely dressed without it."

"I assure you, you're completely dressed."

Was that humor she saw in his expression? Oh how she wished she could read his mind. It would be nice to know how the man she was about to marry thought, but it wasn't likely to happen now, or ever. He would make certain of that.

"I wonder what else I forgot to pack," she mused, her brain on autopilot. "I had some last-minute things to take care of with my assistant. I was afraid I was going to be late."

"And that I might change my mind?"

"The thought occurred to me." She slid into her seat and watched him circle the car. "What about you? Did you think I might chicken out?"

"No. I think you are the most dependable person I know." His statement made it sound as if he knew more about her than their limited association had led her to believe. He slipped behind the wheel and started the engine.

Violet regarded his strong profile, admiring the precise cut of his jaw and his ridiculously long eyelashes. "What makes you say that?"

"From your reputation around town. Whenever you make a commitment to a cause or a promise to a friend you come through. No matter what."

As the car rolled toward South Las Vegas Boulevard, Violet put her hands to her cheeks and found them hot with embarrassment. "I don't do more than anyone else."

"And then you rarely take credit for all the good things you do." The light turned green as they approached it and JT was able to turn onto the strip without stopping. "It causes people to take advantage of your generosity."

Was he trying to warn her that this is what he was doing? If he was, it was too late. She was already committed to their goal.

"You make me sound like a sap."

"I was trying to pay you a compliment."

"A backhanded one, maybe. *You're a dependable doormat.*" She made a face. "That's a fine way to talk about your bride-to-be."

An impatient sound erupted from him. "In the future I'll remember that flattery makes you prickly."

"See that you do. I prefer honesty to sweet talk." She stared at him in silence until he'd stopped at a light and looked her way. "Are you going to have a problem with that?"

"Not at all."

"Good. Just think of me as a fellow businessperson and we'll get along just fine."

JT merely nodded his agreement.

Ten minutes later, they swung into the Tunnel of Love Chapel. It wasn't Violet's first trip through the tunnel. Her best friend from high school had tied the knot here the day after graduation and two short months before baby Cory was born. JT, however, looked like he'd never seen anything like the blue ceiling adorned with cupids and stars.

He stopped the car before a booth with a sign that read "The Little White Wedding Chapel Drive Thru Window," and they filled out the paperwork for the marriage license. Getting married in Las Vegas was a simple matter. Maybe too simple? Time for second thoughts came and went in the blink of an eye. As the opening words of the wedding ceremony began, a strange buzzing filled her ears.

Was she really marrying JT Stone? Violet glanced from the man framed by the booth window to JT. Her lips twitched uncontrollably. As first JT then she repeated the vows spoken by the minister, Violet was overwhelmed by the dreamlike aspect of her wedding. She didn't feel attached to the body sitting in the car beside JT. And she didn't recognize her voice promising to love and honor him. It wasn't until JT pulled out two platinum rings and she felt the cold metal slide onto her finger that she crashed back to earth.

She had only a second to scrutinize her ring's antique setting. The setting was square, the diamond round, the corners filled in with ornate filigree. Violet guessed the stone to be over two and a half carats. Smaller round diamonds flanked the center stone. He slipped the ring on her left hand. The instant she realized it fit, all her agitation disappeared and she was struck by the rightness of what she was doing.

The minister interrupted her thoughts. “Now the bride.”

JT handed her the other ring, this one embossed with waves and swirls. Repeating the vows that symbolized love and commitment, Violet slipped the ring onto JT’s finger. She couldn’t look him in the eye. Her wild idea to marry JT so she could use her stock to put him in charge of his family’s company was on the verge of becoming legally and morally binding.

“I now pronounce you man and wife,” the minister proclaimed.

Violet’s heart had been erratic since JT had agreed to marry her. Now it was positively aflutter. They’d done it. For good or for bad, there was no going back.

“You may kiss the bride.”

Mouth dry, Violet waited for her first kiss from JT. Her stomach had been in knots for the last several hours since they’d agreed to get married. How would he kiss her? Would it be passionate? Romantic? Would he sweep her into his arms and steal her breath or would he woo her with slow, sensual kisses? Either way, she knew it would be perfect.

She’d never dreamed he’d catch her chin in his fingers and plant a quick kiss at the corner of her lips. Lost in a fog of disappointment, she automatically went through the formalities that followed and accepted the congratulations of the witnesses with a heavy heart.

And then the car was rolling out of the Tunnel of Love Chapel and emerging into the noise and lights of Las Vegas once more. While JT negotiated the traffic on his way to the freeway, Violet stared at the ring on her hand. How had he gotten a set of wedding rings on such short notice? And such unique ones at that.

“It’s my grandmother’s,” JT said as if reading her mind. “And this is my grandfather’s.” He held up his left hand. “I drove to the ranch before picking you up.”

Rendered speechless at the significance of wearing a family heirloom, Violet gaped at him. Harper would laugh at her for believing that jewelry held the energy of the wearer, but what else could explain the tranquility that came over her the instant she'd put on his grandmother's ring? They'd married without love. She didn't deserve to be wearing something so dear.

"Is something wrong?" he prompted.

"We could have bought rings at the chapel."

"Why, when these were collecting dust in my safe?"

"But it's your grandmother's ring."

He eyed her. "And I trust that as soon as it's no longer necessary, you'll return it."

"Of course." It was beginning to annoy her that he wasn't getting the significance of the jewelry he'd just pledged his troth with. Heaving a sigh, Violet decided to let it drop. In a few months it would be back in his safe where it belonged.

As the car streaked through the Nevada night, the adrenaline rush she'd been riding for the last two days began to fade. Her confidence waned as well. She was now married to a man who was for all intents and purposes a virtual stranger. And with the strength of his deflector shields, he was likely to stay that way no matter how delicately she probed. Which she really shouldn't do.

What she had to remember was that despite the marriage vows they'd just exchanged, theirs was a union of expediency. Mutual benefit. JT got the chance to reclaim his family's business. She would finish what Tiberius had started and preserve the stock's value.

It was a business arrangement. He would resist her efforts to dig around in his private thoughts in an attempt to get to know him better.

"Now what's bothering you?" JT quizzed.

"Nothing, why?"

For the last half hour they'd been heading north out of town on I-25. His sixty-acre ranch sat just beyond the outskirts of the city. At first she'd resisted being away from the hotel on such short notice, but since Tiberius's death, she'd been working herself hard and could really use a night off.

"You haven't said a word in fifteen minutes," JT said. "It's not like you."

"Was it crazy, what we just did?"

"Completely." He exited the freeway and turned left onto a two-lane highway. "Have you changed your mind?"

"No." And she was surprised at how strongly she felt about staying the course. "It's all going to work out. We just need to get the last three percent Tiberius had been working on before the next stockholders' meeting."

JT nodded. "One way or another, we can be divorced before fall."

Her stomach fell at his eagerness to be rid of her and she chided herself for reacting so foolishly. That was the deal they'd made. She had no right to wish for something else.

"Then we'd better get to work immediately," she said. "I brought all the files from his desk at the house. He was about to approach eight more shareholders. Four of the leads look promising."

"I'll look at them first thing in the morning."

His use of first person singular wasn't lost on her. Before she returned to Fontaine Chic tomorrow, she was determined to make him understand that this undertaking was going to be a team effort. She'd married him and was determined he would not do battle with his father alone.

"This is going to work, you know."

He shot her a dour look. "Are you always this optimistic?"

"You make it sound like a bad thing."

"It's not bad, but I'm not sure it's realistic. Don't you ever worry?"

"Not about the future." She lifted her face to the wind streaming off the windshield. "Why bother? It's a blank slate, full of possibilities."

He didn't reply and she tried to be comfortable in the silence that filled the space between them once more. But the unfinished conversation itched like a case of hives.

"All the brooding you do in the bar every night. Tell me what good it does you to worry about things that haven't happened?"

"It's not the future that concerns me, but the past. Things I'd like to take back, do differently, but can't."

Delighted that JT was on the verge of a revelation, she prompted, "Such as?"

"Nothing I feel like talking about."

And just like that she was shut down. Violet heaved a sigh and lapsed into silence. What a puzzle he was. She knew his childhood hadn't been one to brag about. His father's ambition. His mother's retreat into alcohol and drugs. Emotional injuries he'd suffered at a fragile age had turned him into a wild teenager. When JT had first arrived in Las Vegas, Tiberius had warned her to stay away from him. He was not a bird with a broken wing or a kitten who'd been struck by a car. He was a grown man who only knew how to use people and cast them aside.

Tiberius's initial opinion of his nephew had been right on, but Violet suspected it wasn't the whole picture. Curious about the Stone family, she'd conducted an internet search and discovered what sorts of trouble a party boy from Miami could get into. Although her contact with him had been limited these last six years, she didn't think he was the type to act out without cause. But whatever motivated him was locked deep inside and given the firm set of his jaw, likely to remain so.

"So you have a hard time letting go," she said. "How can you think that's good for you?"

"Reliving past events helps me avoid similar situations in my future."

When Violet considered her life, she decided she could probably spend a little time learning from her experiences. How many men had she dated who'd needed her to be their cheerleader or their psychologist or their financial advisor or their life coach? Too many. And here she was doing it again. Only this time she'd gone too far and had actually married someone.

JT turned down a long driveway bordered by landscape lighting and stopped the car in front of a massive stucco-and-stone prairie-style house. Curved planting beds held desert plants and tropical flowers. Their round lines softened the home's square architecture.

"This is definitely worth the commute," Violet said as she exited the car. The covered walkway to the front door was flanked by pillars covered in square stone and lighted by sconces. The effect was elegant and welcoming. "I can't get over how quiet it is." For a girl who'd practically grown up on the strip, the silence was a bit unnerving.

"Wait until morning. The view from the living room is what sold me on the property." He collected her bag from the trunk and gestured for her to precede him toward the front door.

The house continued to impress Violet as JT gave her a quick tour. From the expansive two-story foyer he led her into the combination living room-dining room. Such large spaces could seem cold and uninviting, but the coved ceilings, inset lighting and desert tones made it very homey. In the living room, sliding glass walls opened out onto a wide patio. The gourmet kitchen was almost as large as her suite at the hotel and contained all restaurant-quality appliances as well as a large wine chiller.

"I wish I knew how to cook," Violet said, gliding her palm along the center island's cool granite.

"You don't?" JT had fetched a bottle of champagne and a couple of glasses. He popped the cork and filled both flutes.

Violet accepted the champagne he handed her. "Just the basics. Not well enough to do justice to all this." She was proud of herself for standing her ground as JT stepped into her space and held up his glass.

Finding out that Tiberius had left her the stock. Her wild proposition to JT. The quick drive-through wedding that followed. And now, being alone with JT in his house. So much had happened. She was feeling a little exposed and emotional. Primed to do something stupid like demand a far better kiss than the one he'd deposited on her in the Tunnel of Love.

"To our successful merger," JT declared, touching his flute to hers. Crystal chimed in the large room.

"To getting Stone Properties away from your father." Violet drank sparingly. The man before her was a heady concoction. She didn't need to add alcohol to the mix.

"It's after one. Do you want me to show you to your room?"

"So I can do what?" Violet quizzed, walking toward the breakfast nook's bay windows. "Pace for hours? I don't know about you, but I rarely get to bed before three." She spied a turquoise pool behind the house. "Can I use that?"

"As of twelve-fifteen the house became half yours. You don't need to ask."

Violet gasped, all thoughts of a moonlit swim forgotten. "Oh, no. That's not what we agreed to. And when we get divorced, we'll just go our separate ways—I don't want half of your house."

"Maybe we should renegotiate our deal. I might need to demand alimony in the divorce settlement."

"Why would you need alimony?"

"Because if our plan fails my father will surely kick me out of the family business and the way he's running things, the stock won't be worth much." He leaned back against the counter and crossed his arms over his chest. "While you will be worth millions as Fontaine's CEO."

Because she couldn't tell if he was poking fun at her or not, Violet refrained from commenting on her chances of winning her grandfather's contest. "I never imagined that I would end up supporting you," she replied. "Perhaps we should get an annulment—"

"While we still can?" JT interrupted, his silky voice spreading shivers along her skin.

"Stop kidding around." She tried for lightness, but a hint of anxiety crept into her tone. "Just because we're married and alone in this house on our wedding night…" Violet trailed off. What point was she trying to make?

"Doesn't mean that we'll fall prey to our basic urges," JT finished.

"Exactly."

"Even if those urges are fueled by champagne and curiosity?"

Violet set her glass down and dismay sparked when she realized it was empty. "I think it's time you show me the bedroom. My bedroom," she corrected, feeling her cheeks heat. "Where I'm going to sleep. Alone."

JT picked up her bag and gestured back the way they'd come. "It's upstairs."

Violet attributed her lightheadedness to the champagne, refusing to believe that she was overwhelmed by the thought of spending the night alone with JT in his house. Was his room way down the hall from hers or a convenient few steps away?

Get a grip. You're not a virgin at your first frat party. You're a successful businesswoman and this man is a colleague. Keep your head and everything will be fine.

"Here you are." JT opened a door and gestured her inside. The large room contained a queen-size bed with matching cherry nightstands, a triple dresser, and a small seating area in front of a gas fireplace. He set her overnight bag on the bed and returned to where she stood just inside the bedroom door.

"This is nice. Thank you."

"I'm the one who should be thanking you. If this wild idea of yours works, I'll be able to save my family's company. And that's a debt I can't repay." JT leaned down and kissed her gently on the cheek. "Good night, Violet. I'll make sure I have green tea ready for you in the morning."

He knew that she didn't drink coffee? She vaguely recalled having a tea versus coffee discussion with him long ago. And he'd remembered.

"That's nice of you. And one more thing." Before she considered the wisdom of her actions, Violet lifted on tiptoe and coasted her palms along JT's massive shoulders. Shoving aside rational thought, she tunneled her fingers into his hair and murmured, "You didn't give me a proper kiss at our wedding."

"Then let me rectify that right now." He lowered his lips to hers.

Her breath stopped. Every nerve in her body screamed to life. Newly sensitized, her skin prickled at the slide of his cotton shirt against her bare arm as he cupped the side of her head to hold her in place. His lips were firm, but softer than she'd expected. The friction of his mouth on hers dragged a moan from her chest.

The sound spurred him to intensify the pressure of his kiss, but he retreated before she could act on her rising passion. His teeth caught at her tender flesh and gently tugged. She arched her back, seeking closer contact. This was so much better than she'd ever imagined.

He flattened his palm against her back, locking her in place before treating her to the first delicious lick of his tongue. A slow thrust followed. Warm. Wet. Skilled. He claimed her mouth as if he'd done it a thousand times. Taking his time, he explored every corner of her mouth, tantalizing her with his leashed passion. What happened if his control snapped? Violet was fast losing her wits. Much longer and her stance on a sexless marriage would topple.

Anticipation built as his hands coasted over her ribs, thumbs whisking provocatively over the outside curves of her breasts. She pulsed with need, craving his possession, and shifted restlessly against him to ease the ache.

JT tore his lips from hers and gulped air into his lungs. "Better?"

Better? Glorious was more like it.

Chest heaving, knees like pudding, she blinked to clear her vision and was startled to see they hadn't moved from the doorway. How was that possible when he'd turned her entire world upside down?

"Now I feel married," she said.

"You'd feel even more so after a proper wedding night," he murmured, letting his lips graze temptingly close to hers once more.

Unsure whether he was serious or merely taunting her, Violet clutched at his strong shoulders and leaned back in order to survey his expression. With eyes that glittered, JT probed her gaze. His compelling curiosity alarmed her. What was he looking for? Proof that his kisses rendered her insensible?

He swept his hands down her spine, fanned his fingers against the small of her back. Ever so slowly he pressed her hips forward, easing her against the hard length of him. Violet's legs trembled. She wanted nothing more than to be filled by him. To lose herself in his evocative touch.

Damn. She never should have asked for that kiss. If she'd just ignored the tension building between them, her body wouldn't be throbbing with unfulfilled longing nor would she be fighting temptation at the idea of one night with him. One incredible, mind-blowing night.

"JT, I..."

Before she figured out what she intended to say, shutters dropped over his gaze and she was left staring at an insurmountable wall. The speed with which he'd shut her out acted like a bucket of ice water on her overheated hormones.

"You don't need to explain." He relaxed his hold on her and stepped away. A sardonic smile tugged at his lips. "I know our marriage is only for show."

And she'd been seconds away from forgetting that fact. Humiliation chased away any lingering traces of desire. No question, she'd just dodged a bullet. So why was she so miserable about it?

"It's not that," she began and then frowned. "Well, it's mostly that, but the truth is, I don't know you very well and I'm not in the habit of falling into bed with a man this quickly."

"You know more about me than most of the women I date."

Really? Did that somehow elevate her above the numerous women that passed through his life? She bit her lip, disturbed by the yearning to be more than just another of his conquests. That was a dangerous road to travel. Better that they keep things all business between them.

"It'll just be easier if we keep everything strictly hands off." Who was she trying to convince, herself or him?

"Then I suggest you refrain from asking me to kiss you in the future." His icy tone was meant as a reproach, but Violet had tasted more than passion in his kiss. Or was she merely hoping that was the case?

"It was one kiss." She heard the defensive ring of her voice and dug her nails into her palms. "What's the big deal?"

"The big deal—" a muscle jumped in his jaw "—is that when I start something like what just happened between us, I like to finish it."

Why was he so exasperated? Not because she'd turned him down. Surely women had said no before. Hadn't they? "Haven't you ever kissed a woman without expecting to sleep with her?"

"Not since high school."

If he was trying to annoy her with his self-satisfied smirk, he was doing a fine job. "So, are you saying you don't bother to kiss a woman unless you're going to have sex with her?"

"I'm saying after I kiss a woman, she rarely says no to having sex with me."

This was so obviously a declaration of JT's reality that Violet crossed her arms over her chest and scowled. "Then I'm thrilled to be included in that minority of your female acquaintances."

"You forget that you are not one of my acquaintances. You are my wife."

JT took possession of her left hand and lifted it to eye level. His grandmother's ring caught the overhead light and sparkled. He couldn't explain why he was so angry with her at this moment. Could it be the unrelenting desire rumbling through him? Going to bed alone and horny was not how he'd expected to spend his wedding night—or it wouldn't have been if he'd ever considered getting married before now.

But the odd hollowness in his gut had begun the instant she'd dismissed the earth-moving kiss as *no big deal.* When he'd pulled her into his arms, he'd expected the urgent need to get her clothes off and have his way with her. It was the other sensation he'd experienced, the one not tied to anything corporeal, that would require privacy and time to sort out.

"I'm your business partner," she retorted, snatching her hand back.

Damn. She was beautiful with her brown eyes shooting sparks and outrage painting her high cheekbones with rosy patches. As quickly as it had flared, his temper dissipated. She wasn't someone he could afford to alienate even if it would make keeping his distance that much easier.

"And you're doing me a huge favor." He inclined his head. "I'm starting to understand why you took sex off the table. Things between us are a little too volatile, aren't they?'

Violet nodded in obvious relief. "I think we will be fine as long as we stick to the plan."

"A plan we can start to flesh out after a good night's sleep."

"I'll see you in the morning."

JT walked out the door and heard the click of the latch behind him. He strode down the hall to the master bedroom and without turning on a light, crossed the room to the double French doors that led out onto the terrace. Throwing them open, he stepped into the night. His nerves were a tangle, too raw to allow him to enjoy the desert air or the crescent moon that hung low in the clear sky.

Did Violet have any idea how close she'd come to being ravished tonight? First she'd shown up for their wedding in that romantic lace dress. Then she'd flirted with him over a glass of champagne. The final straw was complaining that he hadn't given her a proper kiss at their wedding. Was she trying to drive him mad or did she honestly not have a clue what she did to him?

It was the latter, JT suspected, gripping the terrace railing hard. And where she was concerned, he was his own worst enemy. When she'd stared at him with her big soulful eyes all soft and earnest, the consequent firing of all his nerve endings had short-circuited his self-preservation.

So now what was he supposed to do with all this pent-up hunger for her?

It had been one thing when he sat in her bar night after night, driving himself crazy with lurid fantasies he'd never act on. He could enjoy tangling with her verbally, knowing that her open, sunny nature would eventually grow tired of his talent for closing himself off. She'd said it herself. She knew nothing about him. He hadn't let her in. He never let anyone in.

And yet, she knew things about his past few others did. His uncle had told her about his mother's addiction so Violet had some idea how miserable his childhood had been. She would want to talk about all the things that had happened when he was young. He would resent her questions. Withdraw even further. When it came to intimacy and love, he lacked the skills to find happiness.

She wouldn't want to be with him until she'd solved all his problems. Made him see the silver lining in everything that had happened in his past. She'd expect him to come around to her positive way of thinking and would grow frustrated when he didn't.

A splash from the pool below drew his attention. Violet swam through the turquoise water, her stroke powerful and elegant. JT watched her as she came up for air at the far end of the pool. Once again she dove under. She used her feet and legs to push away from the wall with great power. When she surfaced, she headed for the opposite wall in a strong freestyle.

He watched her lap the pool for fifteen minutes. Her focus

and determination amazed him. It was how she approached everything, he decided. Once she set her mind to something, she wasn't going to be deterred.

At long last her energy seemed to burn itself out. She lazed in the middle of the pool and her stillness roused JT to the uncomfortable realization that she was naked. Cursing, he pushed away from the railing and headed for the stairs that led down from his terrace to the pool house and lounge area.

He enjoyed throwing parties and often his guests forgot to bring a suit along so he kept a stock of bathing suits in the pool house for their use. By the time he found a bikini he thought might fit Violet, she had gotten out of the pool and had wrapped herself in a towel. She looked up in surprise as he approached.

"Next time you decide to go swimming," he began, holding up the bikini he'd selected, "I'd appreciate it if you didn't skinny-dip."

"I'm sorry," she murmured, taking the bathing suit from him. Water streamed from her long dark hair, dampening the towel. "I didn't realize you'd still be up."

It eased his irritation a little that she looked so utterly mortified to have been caught. "Like you, I'm often still working at this hour."

"Thanks for the suit. I won't bother you any further tonight."

Was she kidding? He'd never get to sleep with the tantalizing glimpses he'd had of her naked body parading through his thoughts. JT ground his teeth as she retreated toward the house. Only when her towel-clad form had disappeared from view did he return to the master suite.

At least one positive thing about this marriage in name only was that they didn't have to live under the same roof. After less than an hour alone in his house with her, he was a finger snap away from tossing her over his shoulder and spiriting her off to his bed.

Thank goodness he wasn't going to share his living space with her day and night. His control would snap like a dry twig if he had to put up with her sassy humor and artless sensuality. Before she could remind him of their agreement, he'd have her in his bed, her beautiful body writhing in pleasure.

Making love to her would only be the beginning. Soon she'd be ferreting out all his ugly childhood secrets and he'd be living in fear that something she discovered would be so awful she'd cut him out of her life.

And then he'd be alone again, turned inside out, his raw emotions exposed for all the world to see. No. That was something that could never happen. And if he kept her at arms' length, it wouldn't.

CHAPTER FOUR

AT EIGHT THE next morning, Violet found JT in the room he'd dubbed his playroom. She paused just outside the door, needing a second to collect her wits before approaching him.

Clad in worn jeans and a black cotton button-down shirt, he was bent over what looked to be an antique pool table. With his left hand, he rolled the eight ball toward the far bumper and caught it as it returned, all the while studying the papers scattered over the table's beige felt. The briefcase she'd filled with Tiberius's files sat empty on the floor beside his bare feet.

Being confronted by so much casual masculinity first thing in the morning wasn't fair. Especially not after she'd lain awake staring at the ceiling until the sun starting lightening the horizon, regretting that she'd kissed him, wishing she'd dropped her towel when he confronted her on the pool deck. Her conflicting desires were tearing her apart. She'd have to choose one path and commit to it.

"Did you get some tea?" he asked without glancing her way.

His question made her realize she'd been silently staring at him for far too long. "Your housekeeper made me a cup. It's delicious." She didn't need to ask why his kitchen was stocked with four different blends of green tea. She already suspected the house saw a lot of guests. While in Miami, JT had been known for his parties. She doubted much had changed in the last six years. "Find anything that might help us?"

"My uncle accumulated copious amounts of information and enjoyed making detailed notes on all his business dealings. Every share he bought is documented. What I'm missing is the information on the family members who turned him down."

She drew close enough to the table to see that he'd created two lists of names. From past experience she knew how much Tiberius loved to collect information. The files from his home office overflowed with details—some of them helpful, most of them too trivial to waste time on.

"Let me help. Maybe I can speed things up."

She waited for him to acknowledge her offer, but he remained lost in thought. Had he not heard her, or did he want to handle everything himself? If it was the latter, too bad. She'd come up with this plan and intended to be involved at every stage. Running her gaze down JT's list of relatives who still owned their stock, she saw he'd notated which ones were definitely in Preston's pocket.

"You should know Paul and Tiberius had a huge argument three years ago," she said, indicating his mother's cousin. "Something about a rare comic book that Tiberius and Paul supposedly bought together using Tiberius's money when they were eight. Paul kept the comic book, but never paid Tiberius for his half and now it's worth like ten grand."

She shook her head. No matter what the comic's worth, it was silly to still be feuding about it all these years later, but Tiberius wasn't one to forgive a slight. She glanced at JT's strong profile. It was a characteristic Tiberius shared with his nephew.

"Thanks." JT made a note next to Paul's name and returned to the file he'd been reading.

"You've gotten a lot done." She assessed how he'd organized the files, and then pulled five out to make a third pile. As she finished, she noticed JT's glare. "What?"

"I had a system."

"And now it's better." She flipped open the top file and pointed to a gossip article about his third cousin. "Casey is in the middle of a nasty divorce. He has a mistress with very expensive taste tucked away and I believe she sees herself as the next Mrs. Casey Stone. Then there's the problems he's been having with his investment firm. He'd probably be receptive to an influx of cash."

JT looked no less displeased. "My father has done several favors for Casey. He has no interest in selling his stock to me, nor would he throw his votes in my direction."

Violet opened her mouth to argue, but decided from JT's set expression that she'd be wasting her breath. Instead, she set Casey's folder aside and opened the next one. She sifted through several documents before arriving at the one she wanted. "Your great aunt Harriet has recently come under the influence of a rather clever con man who has convinced her to fund his charity in New Orleans." Seeing the flicker of interest in JT's gaze, she sidled closer. "I can be a big help. No one knew the way Tiberius's mind worked better than me. Did you know that over the past thirty years Tiberius had collected a storage unit full of Las Vegas history? Some of it was significant. Most of it was trivial nonsense. He left the entire collection to Scarlett for her *Mob Experience* exhibit."

"I'm sure that's fascinating, but you've done enough." He pushed away from the pool table and nodded toward the open door. "Have Pauline fix you some breakfast. I'll take you back to Fontaine Chic when you're finished."

She repressed a protest. Assuming he'd accept her as his business partner just because she'd come up with the idea of getting married was shortsighted. A man as closed off as JT wasn't going to jump at the chance to work with her. If she didn't accept that, frustration was going to make her crazy.

"Before we head back to town, there are a few things we should talk about."

"Such as?" He crossed his arms over his chest.

"How would you like me to explain this?" She held up her left hand and indicated the ring with her right pointer finger.

For a moment he didn't speak, just stared at the ring. "However you'd like."

Violet gnashed her teeth and tried a different approach. "What are you planning to say about our impulsive wedding last night?"

"If it comes up, I will say we've been involved for almost a year, but we've been keeping it quiet."

"And that's it?"

"I do not expect anyone will press me for details."

"Truly?" How could he not comprehend people's curiosity? "You don't think someone will ask where we met? How long we've been seeing each other?"

"They won't."

"Isn't there anyone in your life you share things with?"

His isolation continued to baffle her. Did he choose to keep everyone out of his life or was he such a pain in the ass that no one was interested?

"My staff knows better than to show an interest in my personal life and those I see socially aren't interested in my business dealings. Since our arrangement falls in neither of those categories, I won't have to explain our marriage to anyone."

"That's great for you," she retorted sarcastically. "But I have two sisters and a mother, who when they hear I got married, are going to expect me to share every juicy detail of what we're doing and why."

At last he gave her his full attention. "There are no juicy details."

She shoved her hands into the back pocket of her jeans to keep from acting on the desire to jolt him out of his stoic calm. "Can I tell them what we're really doing?"

"Do you trust them to keep the truth to themselves?"

Given his tendency to play his cards close to the vest, the

question shouldn't have shocked her as much as it did. "I trust them completely."

She bared her teeth in a spiteful grin. "But if you don't think I should, I could tell them that you've pined over me for years, but were too afraid that Tiberius would ruin you if you made your feelings known."

Irritation tightened his mouth into a thin line. "They won't believe something so ridiculous."

"Scarlett will." Violet gave free rein to the demon riding her shoulder. Being reasonable hadn't worked, and she badly wanted a peek at the hand he held. Time to play dirty. Maybe if she antagonized him, he'd let something slip. "She already has it in her head that you show up in Baccarat every night because you want me."

If he denied it, she wouldn't be surprised.

"And she bases that on what exactly?" His even tone gave nothing away.

Violet found herself in deeper water than she expected. Nothing for her to do but swim hard for shore and hope she wasn't eaten by sharks. "The way you look at me."

"And how exactly do I look at you?"

Violet frowned, trying to remember exactly how her sister had phrased it. "She said you look hungry."

JT might be a master at hiding his thoughts, but Violet swore she saw a slight widening of his eyes. To her delight, she'd scored if not a direct hit, then one fairly close to the mark. Fascinating. She was pondering the possibility that he wasn't as disinterested in her as he'd claimed when he spoke up.

"Your sister has a flare for the drama," he said. "She's fallen in love and sees nothing but potential love matches all around her."

"You're probably right."

But he hadn't actually come out and denied it. Violet decided she'd pushed enough for one day. Much more and she'd run the risk that he'd become even more enigmatic. By allowing herself this tiny win, she now had something she could build on. It was like gaining the trust of a wild creature. Better to use short positive sessions to get them to drop their guard than to try and rush things and make it more skittish.

"Have you eaten?" she asked.

"An hour ago."

She masked her disappointment. "I'll eat something quick and be ready to go back to town in half an hour if that works for you."

"I think I'm in a place where I can take a break and I could use another cup of coffee." He scooped an empty mug off the edge of the pool table and followed her out of his playroom.

Violet's pulse kicked into high gear. Maybe she'd learned the secret to dealing with JT: she'd pretend she didn't care if he spent time with her or included her in his plans to take over his family business and wait for him to come to her. It wasn't the way she was accustomed to dealing with the men she got involved with. Most of the time they liked her to take the lead.

That would never be the case with JT.

"You were right about the view," she remarked a half hour later. She and JT were sitting in the breakfast nook just off the kitchen. The wall-to-wall windows offered a panoramic view of the desert and the mountains to the north that speared an impossibly blue sky. "Do you miss the ocean? Growing up in Miami, I would think the desert would be hard to get used to."

"At first I was worried that I'd hate the dust and the heat, but the mountains make it all worthwhile. And if I need to get on the water, I have a boat on Lake Mead."

Something about the view or sharing a meal—he'd sampled her eggs and stolen half the fruit off her plate—had worked some sort of magic on him. For the last half hour he'd been almost…charming. And Violet was loath to break the spell. So she sipped tea and nibbled on toast, delaying the end of the meal so she could prolong her time with this more accessible version of her new husband.

"Sounds like the best of both worlds." She popped a grape into her mouth. "I am curious though, why are you living on a horse ranch out here instead of closer to Titanium?"

"My grandmother grew up on a horse farm in Kentucky." He took Violet's left hand and regarded the ring he'd put on her hand to seal his wedding vows. "Even after she married my grandfather and moved to Miami, she kept several show jumpers. Starting when I was five, my mother used to take me to watch her. I'd sit in the stands and marvel at how she and her horse flew over six-foot-high jumps."

As he spoke, his gaze grew less focused. He'd stopped seeing his grandmother's ring and was revisiting a happy moment from his past. The muscles of his face relaxed into a fond half smile. Violet watched him with dawning wonder. This wasn't the first time he'd opened up to her—after all, he'd shared his decision to quit his family's company. But it was the first time he'd shared a happy memory from his childhood.

Based on their interaction to this point, she'd labeled him as guarded and brooding. She'd assumed his unhappy childhood had left him emotionally shut down and incapable of letting joy in. But maybe it wasn't that he didn't feel but that he felt too much? If he was a powder keg ready to explode, what happened when someone lit a match?

"She insisted I learn to ride," JT continued, oblivious to the thoughts churning inside Violet's head. "During the summer, she would take me to her family's horse farm in Kentucky and we would spend hours riding. When I was good enough to compete, she took me to horse shows. It all stopped when she died."

JT had lost his grandmother when he was ten. Hearing him speak so warmly of her, Violet suspected he'd been devastated to lose the one person who'd showered him with love and attention. She remembered what a tough time Tiberius had gone through when his mother had died. He'd taken Lucille and Violet to the funeral and she remembered how unwelcome they'd been.

"I never had any grandparents around when I was a kid," she

told him. "My mom left Cincinnati when she was seventeen and never looked back." She smiled wryly. "And you know the situation on my father's side."

"I've never met any of my father's relatives. His parents died when he was very young."

"I remember Tiberius saying something about that. I guess I didn't realize Preston didn't keep in touch with his family. Wasn't he from California? Have you ever thought about looking some of them up?"

The shutters were back over JT's eyes. As soon as he'd mentioned his father, his expression became as remote as the mountaintops that made his view so extraordinary.

"No."

His abrupt answer discouraged further conversation on that topic. Violet sighed as she realized JT was done sharing.

"If you don't mind," she began, setting her napkin on the table beside her plate. "I think it's time I headed back to Fontaine Chic."

"I'll get my keys."

While JT waited in the foyer for Violet to collect her overnight bag, he replayed their conversation in his mind and revisited every expression on her lovely face. He'd enjoyed sharing breakfast with her. So much so that instead of giving her a brief, dry explanation of why he'd chosen ranch life over a house in the city, he'd gone all sentimental on her and let her see how his grandmother had influenced him.

Nor did it surprise him how tempted he was to trust her. Her earnest curiosity and upbeat outlook weren't a clever cover for ulterior motives. She honestly wanted to help. Her impulsive suggestion that they get married so he could get control of Tiberius's Stone Properties stock had demonstrated she was far too quick to believe in people.

Take him for example. She expected him to stick to their understanding that this wasn't a real marriage. Which meant hands off. And the best—no, only—way he could think of to honor their agreement was to stay as far away from her as possible.

"Ready when you are," she said, as descended the stairs. She was a feminine marvel in a pastel floral dress with thin straps that bared her delicate shoulders and a full skirt that flirted with her knees. Pink sandals with three-inch heels drew attention to her spectacular calves and her hair was swept up into a loose top-knot. She made his mouth water.

With a slight bounce, she stepped from the stairs onto the foyer's marble floor and crossed to where he stood by the front door, tongue-tied, his hormones in an uproar. As she neared, he snagged her luggage and opened the door.

"I don't think we should live together," he stated, his voice short and clipped.

"How are people going to believe we are married if we don't?"

"We both work a lot. No one will notice."

Her lips thinned. "That's not going to work."

"We'll talk about it when I return to town."

She eyed the second overnight bag he held. "Where are you going?"

"As soon as I drop you off, I'm heading to North Carolina." The sooner he secured the necessary shares of Stone Properties, the sooner he could replace his father as CEO. And the sooner he could be free of this marriage-in-name-only before he did something to change their relationship forever.

"Who's there?"

"My cousin Brent. His dad's Alzheimer's has made it necessary for him to take charge of the finances in the last few months. He has several thousand shares. It's not all that I need, but every bit helps."

"I don't recall seeing him in Tiberius's files."

JT held the passenger door open and gritted his teeth against the sweet seduction of her perfume as she brushed past him and slid into the car. Damn, but she was a tempting armful. Resisting the impulse to reprise last night's kiss actually caused a dull ache in his gut. When he'd agreed to marry her, he'd underestimated just how challenging it would be to keep his hands to himself.

"He's not." After depositing their bags in the trunk, JT got behind the wheel and started the BMW. "I don't know why Tiberius didn't include him."

The car picked up speed as he drove down his long driveway toward the highway and JT noticed that the airflow in the open convertible whipped Violet's skirt into a frenzy of dancing flowers and bared a whole lot of lean, toned thigh. He daydreamed about sliding his hands along the soft, smooth length of her leg and finding her hot and wet and eager for him. It wasn't until a truck flashed past on a perpendicular course that he realized they'd reached the end of his driveway. JT slammed on his brakes and the BMW skidded to a halt.

"Are you okay?" he asked, glancing her way.

She regarded him curiously. "I'm fine. Are you?"

Not even close. "I think we'll be more comfortable with the top up." He hit the button that raised the convertible top and while it was closing, stared at his grandfather's ring on his left hand.

Yeah, staying as far from her as possible for the next couple months was the only way he was going to survive this marriage with his heart intact.

On the thirty-minute ride to Las Vegas, he kept his eyes to himself and his thoughts on the trip ahead. Violet seemed to understand his need to plan because she kept her gaze on the passing landscape, only occasionally glancing down at her ever-vibrating smartphone.

Finally, JT had to ask, "Is it always this way for you?"

"I'm sorry?" She blinked as if she had a hard time refocusing her attention on him.

"Your phone. It's been going off non-stop since we got in the car."

A wry smile curved her lips. “It’s my sisters. I’m not usually off the grid for twelve hours.”

Envy stabbed at JT. What would it be like to have someone fret about your wellbeing? Nice? Smothering? “They must be worried about you. Why don’t you answer them?”

“I sent them a text last night. They know I’m safe.” Her smile developed sharp edges. “I told them I was with you.”

JT ignored the way his pulse leapt at the challenge in her manner. She would take any opening he gave her to provoke him; what she didn’t realize was that once unleashed, his emotions would overwhelm them both.

“Did you explain that we got married?”

“I didn’t want to do that in a text.”

“Then what do they think you are doing with me?” His body tensed, but the sensation was pleasurable rather than distressing.

“Probably what most of the women do when they spend the night at your house.”

Damn her sass. “Why would you want your sisters to think we slept together?”

She didn’t answer him immediately, and when she did speak, all amusement had fled her voice. “I suppose that’s something else we should discuss.”

“Aren’t we already discussing it?” Her change of topic made him feel as if he was spinning in place.

“Do you intend to bring women home while we’re married?”

Her question sparked a ridiculous urge to snatch her into his arms and kiss her silly. He wasn’t allowed to make love to her, but she didn’t want him having sex with anyone else? “I hadn’t really thought about it.”

“I know our marriage isn’t real, but I’d appreciate it if you could refrain from dating other women until we can get divorced.”

“I think I can last a couple months.”

“What if you can’t get the shares or the votes you need in time for the annual stockholders’ meeting?”

"What are you asking?"

"Our goal was to make you CEO," she said, her manner matter-of-fact. "If that doesn't happen in the next few months it's because we didn't have enough time. You aren't horrible to be married to. I could see sticking it out for another year."

A year of being married to Violet with the temptation of making love to her eating him alive? JT recoiled from the thought. "We'll get divorced in the fall regardless."

Her expression was inscrutable as she nodded. "Then we'll get divorced."

Conversation dried up after their exchange. Fortunately they'd reached the city limits and traffic wasn't as backed up as usual, so their journey to her hotel was accomplished quickly. He swung the BMW into Fontaine Chic's circular driveway and stopped the car by the lobby doors. Before he could shut off the car, Violet put a hand on his arm.

"If you just open the trunk, I'll grab my bag."

In that instant, JT realized the last thing he wanted to do was fly off and leave his brand-new wife to her own devices. What an idiotic notion. They weren't really married. It wasn't as if they'd shared a grand night of passion he couldn't wait to duplicate. But she was already far more important to him than a casual acquaintance, which—their connection to Tiberius aside—was all they were.

"I'll call you and let you know how things went in North Carolina." He slipped the garage remote off the visor and extended it to her. "Here."

Her brows came together briefly. "Why would you give me that?"

Because he liked the idea of her sleeping—and skinny-dipping—in his home.

"Our house," he corrected her. "I might need some information from Tiberius's files. It would be useful if you could get to them."

"Let me get this straight." A playful light glinted in her eyes.

"You're going to let me help and you're going to trust me alone in *our* house?"

"Are you planning on digging through my underwear drawer?"

She leaned close and whispered, "Is that where you keep your secrets?"

No, those were all locked up in his head. "Please feel free to investigate and see."

"It doesn't bother you to have me snooping?"

To his surprise, it didn't. "What do you think you'll find?"

"I don't know." She plucked the opener from his grasp. "But everything about you is such a closed book I'm sure I'll find the most mundane of things utterly fascinating."

With a sassy wink she slipped from the car and collected her bag. JT watched until she'd sashayed through the lobby door before shifting into drive. He'd been married to her for less than twenty-four hours and already he was noticing cracks in his defenses. Sunshine was seeping in, illuminating emotions that hadn't seen the light of day in over eighteen years. He felt lighter, more optimistic as if her positive outlook was contagious.

It took all his determination to put aside thoughts of his new wife and her unsettling effect on him, but by the time JT reached long-term parking, he'd managed to focus his attention on the trip ahead. Earlier that morning he'd had his assistant book a flight from Vegas to Charlotte. He'd decided to fly commercial instead of borrowing the company jet. He didn't want his father to start questioning why he was traveling all over the East Coast.

After parking his car, he headed to the terminal. An email message arrived on his phone as he exited security. His secretary had forwarded his itinerary for the coming week. He was booked from Charlotte to Atlanta to Louisville and finally up to New York City. Four cities in six days. He hoped like hell it would be a profitable trip.

CHAPTER FIVE

AS SOON AS Violet entered Fontaine Chic, she headed straight for her office. Since no one had called her in a panic, she assumed nothing earthshaking had happened in the last twelve hours, but she wanted to touch base with her assistant. Patty brought Violet a cup of tea and the previous day's report. Violet crossed to the seating area near the window and sat down on the couch. A quick scan assured Violet that her hotel continued to run smoothly in her absence. Now to address the problem of convincing her sisters that marrying JT didn't mean she'd lost her marbles.

I'm back.

She sent the text to both Scarlett and Harper and wasn't surprised how fast the responses came.

I'm on my way. From Scarlett.

Give me twenty minutes and don't tell Scarlett a thing until I get there. From Harper.

With a fatalistic sigh, Violet set the phone down on the coffee table. Exhaustion washed over her as her night of little sleep caught up to her. She let her muscles relax. Her head fell back against the comfortable leather couch. Almost immediately she was besieged by hysterical amusement. Had she seriously just married JT? Demanded that he give her a proper kiss? Not that there was anything proper in the way his tongue had coasted against hers. She shivered as the memory swept over her.

"I demand to hear every last detail immediately," Scarlett proclaimed from the doorway.

Violet's eyes flew open. She hadn't even realized she'd closed them. "Harper said to wait."

"You don't seriously think I'm going to sit here in suspense for twenty minutes, do you?" Scarlett flopped onto the couch beside Violet and pinned her with a steely glare. "Spill."

Now that the moment had arrived, Violet decided it was harder to justify her actions than she'd imagined. "I really think we should wait. I don't want to explain myself twice."

She wasn't sure she wanted to explain herself *once*.

Scarlett waved Violet's objection away. "What's there to explain? You finally gave in to the chemistry between you and JT. Was it fabulous? Is he an intense lover? He has such great hands and those lips..."

Violet choked back a laugh. "Scarlett!"

"What? Harper will want to lecture you on moving too fast. I won't get to hear any of the hot stuff once she shows up."

"There is no hot stuff."

"Really?" Scarlett's face reflected disappointment. "I would have thought there'd be major fireworks between you."

"It wasn't like that."

"Then why are you blushing?"

Violet put her hands to her cheeks and found them on fire. "He caught me skinny-dipping in his pool."

"And...?" Scarlett leaned forward, her eyes wide and encouraging.

"He handed me a bikini and told me to wear it next time I wanted to take a swim."

Scarlett sat back and regarded her sister in absolute confusion. Violet had never seen her so utterly baffled.

"I thought your text said you spent the night with JT."

"I did. Only not the way your naughty mind thinks. I slept at his house."

Before Scarlett could reply, Harper breezed into the room. She was slightly out of breath as she demanded, "What did I miss?"

"Not a darned thing," Scarlett muttered in disgust. "Apparently there's nothing for her to tell."

"What about that?" Harper settled next to Scarlett and reached across her to point at Violet's left hand.

Scarlett snatched up the hand and stared at the ring. "You're engaged?"

"Not exactly," Violet murmured.

"That looks like an engagement ring."

"Actually it's a wedding ring. JT and I got married last night at the Tunnel of Love Chapel."

"Married?" Scarlett gaped at her sister.

"JT Stone?" Harper shook her head. "Have you told Grandfather? Are you at all worried how he'll react when he finds out you're married to the competition?"

"I'm going to call him in a little while." Violet was all prepared with a rational explanation for her actions. "He'll understand when I explain what happened."

"What did happen?" Scarlett asked. "The last time I mentioned him being interested in you, I got the distinct impression you had no intention of letting anything develop."

"It hasn't exactly developed the way you think," Violet said.

"You're married," Harper pointed out. "Something had to happen between you."

"It's all a little complicated."

"Did Rick slip something special into one of his signature cocktails?" Scarlett narrowed her eyes. "By that I mean, were you drunk?"

"I was perfectly sober." Violet rushed to answer the question in Harper's eyes. "So was he."

"So, you didn't just spend the night at JT's house," Harper clarified. "You spent the night with JT?"

"No. It's not that kind of marriage."

Harper regarded her gravely. "What sort of marriage is it?"

"It's strictly a business arrangement."

"But not funny business obviously," Scarlett groused.

Violet ignored her. "Mom and I went to the lawyer a few days ago and it turns out Tiberius had been purchasing Stone Properties stock from other family members."

"I thought he didn't want anything to do with the company after what Preston did to him," Scarlett said.

"I think it was more a matter of not being able to do anything to get his brother-in-law removed as CEO. Preston controlled the shares he inherited on his wife's death as well as the ones that were in JT's trust. Shares that JT took control of on his thirtieth birthday two months ago."

"How much stock had Tiberius managed to buy?" Harper asked, her keen business mind catching on quickly.

"Eighteen percent."

"And how much was in JT's trust?"

"Thirty percent. Preston owns thirty and the other twenty-two percent is split up among the family."

"So what does this have to do with why you and JT got married?" Scarlett asked, returning the conversation to what she was interested in.

"Obviously Tiberius left her his shares," Harper said.

Scarlett shot her sister a pained look. "I get that, but why marry JT when she could sell him the shares?"

"Because according to Tiberius's will, I have to keep the stock until Preston dies."

"You know you didn't have to marry JT," Harper pointed out. "You could have just thrown your support behind him."

Violet felt her features take on the same injured expression Scarlett had just worn. Once in a while she wished Harper would acknowledge that she wasn't always the smartest one in the room.

"Only family can vote the shares," she explained.

Scarlett clapped her hands in delight. "So, now you're family. That's brilliant."

"Thank you." Violet appreciated having Scarlett's support because she could see that Harper wasn't done with her objections.

"But with your eighteen percent and JT's thirty—"

Violet interrupted. "We still need three percent to control the vote." She glanced at the clock on her phone and realized JT was probably boarding his flight to Charlotte. "He's heading out to talk to some of his relatives, hoping he can persuade enough of them to either sell or throw their vote his way so he can take control of Stone Properties and get his father out."

"And you found out about this a few days ago?" Harper frowned. "Aren't you moving a little quick? I would think you'd both want to protect yourselves before getting married."

"You haven't seen the way JT looks at her," Scarlett interjected. "I don't think that man has the patience to last any longer."

To Violet's intense dismay, she felt her cheeks heating again. "It's not like that between us," she protested. "And we signed an agreement that we'd walk away with what we came into the marriage with. Really, it's just a business deal. A marriage in name only."

"How long do think that's going to last?" Scarlett's lips wore a lusty smile. "The two of you share the same house night after night. Him just down the hall? I give you a week tops before you crack. JT…" She cocked her head and considered. "Maybe three days."

"We're not going to live together," Violet explained, growing lightheaded as she remembered how hard it had been to fall asleep the previous night after kissing JT. But in the future there would be no more such kisses, passion-drenched or otherwise. They'd both agreed on that.

"You're not?" Scarlett looked scandalized at the thought.

"Lots of married couple don't," Harper said. "My parents being one of them."

And their marital separation was what had led to Ross's numerous affairs and the two daughters he'd never acknowledged. Or maybe his affairs had led to his estrangement from his wife. Violet had never asked Harper what she thought. As close as the three girls had become in the last five years, some topics remained uncomfortable.

"Are you sure you know what you're doing?" Harper continued. "I mean, how well do you know JT?"

"Not as well as she's going to get to know him," Scarlett put in slyly.

Violet shot her a repressive look. "I don't know how to explain it, but he feels like family. I know until recently that Tiberius refused to have anything to do with him, but he talked so much about his sister and what life was like for JT as a kid, I feel as if I know him." She regarded each of her sisters, trying to gauge if she was making sense.

"I get how sometimes you can feel as if you know a person even though you've never met," Harper said, a note of tension in her voice. "But often the reality is very different and you have to be careful."

Was Harper referring to JT or her own problems with celebrity chef Ashton Croft, whose latest restaurant was supposed to have opened in Harper's Fontaine Ciel hotel two weeks earlier? The charismatic executive chef-turned-television sensation was unconventional and passionate about food and adventure. Since starting negotiations with Harper for the restaurant, he'd been a thorn in her side with one outrageous demand after another.

Violet suspected her sister had been a Chef Ashton fan long before the restaurant deal. Harper's DVR was filled with Croft's television series, *The Culinary Wanderer*, in which he traveled around the world in search of the perfect meal. Why such an adventurous wanderer appealed to someone as methodical and strategic as Harper, Violet would never understand.

"I'll admit that what I know of JT is already proving incomplete." Violet considered what she'd learned over breakfast. He'd opened up to give her a glimpse into his past. A happy moment in what she suspected was a turbulent childhood. "But I don't think he has any intention of cheating me." And any heartbreak that happened would be because she'd let it.

Harper shook her head. "I just hope you know what you're doing."

"So do I," Violet muttered. "So do I."

JT should have known that letting Violet's optimism rub off on him was reckless, but he'd been seduced by her earnest smiles and luminous brown eyes. Now, with a tumbler of excellent scotch on his knee, he allowed his gaze to drift around his cousin's mahogany-paneled study and tried not to let his disappointment show.

"Sorry, JT." Brent looked as if the weight of the world rested on his shoulders. "My dad sold the shares to Preston five months ago. You're welcome to the hundred I received on my eighteenth birthday."

"Thanks for the offer, but I'd rather you remain a stockholder and help me convince the rest of the family that my dad's management isn't doing the company any favors." No wonder Tiberius hadn't created a file on Brent's father. What was the point when the shares were already lost? "Any idea why your father sold the shares to my dad? It's not as if the two of them got along."

Brent snorted. "That's an understatement. My dad hated yours. He blamed Preston for your mom's death."

Brent's father Ted was Tiberius and Fiona's first cousin. He'd been as close to them as a sibling, but Ted and Fiona's relationship had grown a bit strained over what had happened to Tiberius When Brent's dad had told Fiona her husband was out of control, she'd resolutely defended her husband. Preston became a sore spot between them, but their love remained as strong as ever.

"Then why did he sell him the shares?"

"After it happened, he felt horrible. Preston convinced him that your mom wanted more shares for you."

"Your father didn't remember that my mom's been dead for eighteen years?"

Brent grimaced. "I knew then I had to get power of attorney and take over his finances."

"He's getting worse faster than you expected, isn't he?"

"His lucid moments are fewer and fewer." Father and son had enjoyed a close connection that JT had long envied.

"Sorry," JT said. "I can't imagine how hard this is for you."

"Most people can't." Ted had been an intelligent, intuitive businessman. It had to be tearing Brent apart to lose his father this way. To watch him slip away a little more each day, knowing there was no way to ever get him back. "It's tough watching a clever, bold businessman like my father forget the dog's name or where the kitchen is in the house."

The deep throb in Brent's voice made JT's chest hurt. "Is there anything you need? Anything I can help with?" He regretted that in his preoccupation with his own troubles, he'd not kept up with his cousin the way a friend should.

Brent cleared his throat. "That's the worst of it. There's nothing anyone can do." He swallowed the last of his scotch. "But I appreciate the offer. You're not just family, you're a good friend."

A year apart in age, they'd spent time together as kids, forming bonds that made them close as adults. Fiona Stone had often traveled to Charlotte to visit her favorite cousin. JT remembered how, in this Neoclassical-style house, built more than a hundred years ago, his mother hadn't needed drugs or alcohol to cope with her life. She'd smiled all the time and given him big hugs and spoiled him with ice cream sundaes and trips to the zoo and museums. Getting his mother back had been like a miracle. But neither the trip nor his mother's happiness could last forever.

"So, why don't you tell me what's going on. Why you're suddenly buying up stock."

"I want to get control of Stone Properties."

"Seriously?" Curiosity flared in Brent's gray eyes. "And how are you planning to do that?"

"For the last six months, Tiberius had been quietly buying shares."

"That clever son of a bitch," Brent exclaimed in admiration. "So, you two were going to team up?"

JT shook his head. "I had no idea what he was planning. You know Tiberius."

"Kept his cards close to his chest. And who could blame him after what your dad did to him. How much of the company had he managed to get?"

"Eighteen percent."

"And with the thirty you came into on your last birthday, you are three percent short of control."

"It's a little more complicated than that," JT explained, thinking of Violet and her damned skinny-dipping. "Turns out, Tiberius didn't leave me the shares."

"Really?" Brent got up to refresh their drink.

"Thanks to my dad, my uncle and I weren't on the best of terms, but in the last month or so we'd started to reconnect." JT considered all the tales his father had told him about Tiberius and wished he'd been smarter about where he'd put his loyalty.

Brent frowned. "So who owns his shares?"

"Tiberius's unofficially adopted daughter." JT held up his left hand and showed off his grandfather's ring. "Last night we got married."

The number of times JT had successfully surprised his quick-witted cousin could be counted on one hand. Today marked the fifth one.

"You're married to…oh, what's her name?" Brent snapped his fingers as he searched his memory.

"Violet Fontaine."

"Tiberius took in her and her mother, didn't he?" Uncertainty fogged Brent's gaze. "But I thought her last name was Allen?"

"Turns out she's Ross Fontaine's illegitimate daughter. After he died, Violet's grandfather—Henry Fontaine, head of Fontaine Resorts and Hotels—came to Vegas to find her and make amends for his son's neglect. She's in line to succeed the old man as head of the company."

"And you married her instead of buying the stock?" Brent asked, sounding very much as if he thought JT wasn't thinking clearly. "If you're short on cash, you could have come to me."

A year ago Brent had sold the company he'd started and had not yet found a place to invest the four billion he'd made.

"The terms of Tiberius's will don't allow her to part with the stock in any way until my dad dies."

"Good old Tiberius." Brent grinned in admiration. "And until you married her, she couldn't vote because she's not family."

JT knew he could count on his cousin to grasp the entire problem. "That sums it up."

Brent blew out a worried breath. "When your dad finds out about this, things are going to get nasty."

"That's why I need to meet with as much family as I can before he finds out."

With regret tugging his dark eyebrows together, Brent said, "I wish I could help you out."

"Me, too."

His cousin was one hell of a businessman. His father had taught him well. Again JT felt the twinge of envy. Why did bad things happen to good people while manipulative bastards like JT's father sailed through life unscathed?

"Where are you off to next?" Brent asked.

"Atlanta."

"Cousin Skip." JT's cousin rolled his eyes. "I don't envy you."

CHAPTER SIX

AT MIDNIGHT, Baccarat's couches and barstools were occupied by a twenty-something clientele with palates sophisticated enough for Rick's special blends. As Violet crossed the threshold into the lounge, her pulse escalated but she immediately told herself to calm down. Even if JT was in town, it was too late for him to be at the bar. She usually swung through here at eleven-fifteen, but tonight she'd been held up by the manager of the sports book.

The only contact she'd had with JT in the last several days was a series of terse text messages, each less hopeful than the last. He was having no luck finding more shares to buy. His father had either bought up what he could or had convinced his family to vote with him.

Her phone vibrated, indicating a text message had come in. Someone at the front desk was looking for her. Violet left Baccarat without catching Rick's attention and headed for the lobby.

As she approached, she saw a tall man standing with the night manager. The stranger had his back to her, but when Violet was five feet away, he turned his head and she glimpsed his profile.

She almost stopped dead in her tracks. Preston Rhodes? What the hell was he doing here?

JT's father hadn't spotted her yet, but she was too exposed

to make a run for it without drawing unwanted attention. Gathering a deep breath, Violet stiffened her spine and marched forward.

"Good evening," she said, doubting her ability to pretend she had no idea who Preston was. Although the man had never appeared in Vegas before, she recognized him from articles she'd read about him. And then there was the resemblance to JT around the man's eyes and chin. "Preston Rhodes, isn't it?"

While the night manager returned to his post, Violet held out her hand and wasn't surprised when Preston clasped it in a punishing handshake. Of course the man would choose to demonstrate his power with brute force. That he wouldn't pull any punches just because she was a woman wasn't as flattering as it might have been if he were someone else.

"Ms. Fontaine." His smooth tone did little to hide the poisonous nature of the man's character. "Or should I call you Violet since we're now family?"

She tried to keep her surprise from showing. His thin laugh let her know that she hadn't been successful. JT hadn't mentioned that he'd told his father. Irritation flared. She wished he'd warned her. Facing someone like Preston without preparation was better suited to Harper, who had a knack for staying calm no matter what the catastrophe.

"Mr. Rhodes—"

"Preston," he corrected, a viper's smile twisting his lips. "Unless you'd prefer Dad. I know you never had anyone you could call by that name."

It wasn't in her nature to call him what he deserved. "Preston," she acceded. With that one word, she was out of polite things to say to the man who'd ruined the most important man in her life and who cared little that his son distrusted him.

"Why don't we go have a drink and get to know each other a little better."

Preston caught her by the arm and turned in the direction of Lalique, a stylish two-story bar inside a spectacular three-story crystal chandelier that was Fontaine Chic's centerpiece. Her grandfather hadn't said a word about the three million dollars she'd spent on this single item. Crystal was Violet's signature décor. Throughout the hotel and casino, multifaceted crystals sparkled above the gaming tables and from the fixtures that lined the walkways. Pillars sparkled with embedded lights made to resemble crystals and all the waitresses and dealers wore rhinestone-accented black uniforms.

Preston's firm grip left her feeling very much like a disobedient child being led to her punishment. Annoyed at being manhandled in her own hotel, Violet nonetheless went with JT's father. A scene would harm her more than him and she was certain he knew that. Preston was a master manipulator. It was how he'd gotten the best of his wife's younger brother.

Once they were seated in a quiet table near the railing on the bar's second floor, Preston signaled the waitress. "A bottle of Cristal. We must toast to becoming family."

Violet's skin itched where he'd touched her. The thought of being legally connected to this man, no matter how briefly, made her physically ill.

"I don't drink when I'm working," Violet protested.

"Nonsense. This is a special occasion."

"Then shouldn't we wait to celebrate with JT?"

"My son is running around the country visiting family." Preston's smile didn't reach his hard eyes. "Telling them his good news, I'm assuming." JT's father pinned her with merciless scrutiny. "And yet he left you—his brand-new bride—here. Why is that?"

Again Violet feared her face would betray too much. Tiberius had told her over and over that she made a lousy poker player. She couldn't bluff to save her soul.

"It wasn't a good time for me to be away from the hotel."

"No honeymoon for you then? Stone Properties has a wonderful five-star resort in the Cayman Islands. I could call and have a suite made available for you two."

"Please don't bother."

"It's no bother at all."

The waitress arrived with their champagne and a pair of flutes. Violet appreciated the momentary distraction. She needed to stop reacting and get ahead of Preston. Why had he come? Nothing he did lacked motivation. If he knew JT was traveling, he'd shown up in Vegas to catch Violet alone. Anxiety flared, but she pushed it down. No matter how vile the man, he was powerless to do more than intimidate her.

Once the champagne was poured, Preston handed her a flute. "To wedded bliss. May your life with my son be as happy as mine was with his mother."

More a curse than a blessing, Violet thought as she put the flute to her lips and wet them with the champagne. "Thank you." She set the glass down. "Now, if you'll excuse me, I really have some pressing matters to attend to." But before she could rise, Preston covered her hand with his.

"How long have you and my son been together?"

"A while."

"You must be good at keeping secrets because your wedding caught everyone by surprise."

"JT's very private." And for once she was glad. "We run rival hotels. He wanted to maintain a low profile until we were sure of our relationship."

"You certainly managed that. No one had a clue that you and he were dating, much less falling in love." Preston leaned forward, his eyes intense. "You are in love with my son, aren't you?"

Violet hesitated before answering. Preston knew something was not on the up and up between her and JT. She saw the challenge in his gaze as if daring her to lie.

"JT is the most amazing man I know. How could I not be?"

That she didn't answer the question directly wasn't lost on Preston. His calculated smile was back.

"And I'm sure he feels the same way about you. I'm glad. I would hate for you to have married him for the wrong reasons."

"Such as?" The instant she spoke, Violet knew she should have insisted she loved JT.

"For his money."

Violet raised her eyebrow and glanced around her. "Do I look like I need money?"

"From what I understand, all this belongs to Fontaine Resorts and Hotels, not to you."

"Regardless, I don't need JT's money."

"That's good." Preston finished his glass of champagne and stood. "I'm very protective of my son. If I thought someone intended to hurt him, I would take steps to see that didn't happen."

She couldn't believe what Preston was saying. He'd done more to hurt his son than the entire rest of the world combined. "I have no plans to hurt JT. Quite the opposite."

"Good. So are you planning on giving up your suite here and moving to my son's ranch?"

Again he'd caught her unprepared. "We haven't decided yet."

"Because two people living apart isn't much of a marriage."

"We'll figure it out."

"And soon, I hope. Because if you're not living together, someone might assume that your marriage is a fake and that would lead to questions."

The entire conversation had been charged with subtext and Violet grew more concerned with each exchange. She suspected Preston had figured out she and JT weren't a love match. Not that there was anything he could do about it.

"Why would anyone care?"

"I care." Preston at last dropped all pretense of being civil. "I know why he married you. To get at the stock Tiberius bought. Well, that only gives him forty-eight percent. Not enough to challenge me."

The speed at which JT's father had figured out what they were up to startled Violet. And yet, should it? The man was devious. He would see a game being played from a mile away. How were they going to get ahead of him if he anticipated all their moves?

"You look worried, Violet."

Preston obviously enjoyed having the upper hand and rubbing his opponent's nose in the fact.

Composing her expression, Violet replied, "I have nothing to be worried about."

"Because you and JT didn't get married so he could use the stock Tiberius left you to stage a coup against me?"

Goose bumps broke out on Violet's arms, but she kept her gaze locked on Preston's cold, flat eyes. "I have no idea what you're talking about."

"Of course you do and when I prove that you two aren't married in good faith, I'm going to sue you for fraud and take back the stock in your possession."

"You can't do that."

"Maybe. Maybe not. But I can tie up the stock in a lawsuit long enough to get rid of my son the same way I got rid of my brother-in-law."

While Violet sat in stunned silence, unsure if she'd ever experienced this level of malice, Preston topped off the champagne in her glass and stood.

"Drink up, Violet. You and my son have embarked on a grand adventure. I only hope you know what you've gotten yourself into."

Preston strolled away before Violet could wrap her thoughts around his threat. Her phone buzzed and she checked the message. JT's plane had just landed at the airport. He had news.

Well…she texted back, agreeing to meet at his house in an hour…so did she.

The drive from Las Vegas to his desert ranch had never bothered JT before. But then again, he'd never had a woman like Violet to come home to either. He banished the thought the instant it entered his head. This was a business meeting. Simple as that.

Violet had used the garage door remote he'd given her and let herself in. He found her curled up on the couch in the living room, staring at the cold fireplace. He had to say her name twice before she realized she was no longer alone. There was a split second of utter delight in her eyes before she frowned.

"You look exhausted. Sit down and let me get you some tea."

"I'd rather have a beer."

"The tea will relax you and soothe your nerves."

"The beer will have the same effect, plus I prefer the way it tastes."

"Fine." When she returned, she held two bottles. He raised his eyebrow as she handed him one, and she shrugged. "You really shouldn't drink alone."

It was on the tip of his tongue to remind her that he drank alone all the time, but decided not to push her away. Instead, he held out his free hand and pulled her down onto the couch beside him. She landed close and he slung his arm over the back of the couch above her shoulder. Her body fit nicely against his side. He sipped his beer and sighed.

"How's your week going?" he asked, resisting the urge to nuzzle his nose into her silky hair. She'd taken it down and it cascaded around her shoulders in soft waves.

"Until an hour ago, better than yours. You had no luck at all with your family?"

Her first comment snagged his attention. "What happened an hour ago?"

She tensed, and didn't immediately answer. Perplexed, JT glanced down at her. She was staring hard at the beer bottle.

"Violet?" he prompted, growing uneasy.

"We have a problem."

Keeping a sudden flare of concern from his voice, he asked, "What sort of problem?"

"Your father knows what we're doing."

JT cursed silently. "How do you know that?"

"Because he came to see me at Fontaine Chic. He basically told me if he finds out that our marriage isn't real that he'll sue us for fraud."

Fury held him immobile. How dare his father threaten Violet. This was a battle between businessmen. But JT should have been prepared for this. It wasn't the first time Preston Rhodes had intimidated someone who tried to take him on.

"I'll deal with him." JT took a healthy swallow of his beer and swallowed his irritation. No need to get Violet any more worked up than she already was. This wasn't her fight. It was his. That his father chose to confront Violet instead of him let JT know that he was feeling threatened. "It's just a threat to distract us while he shores up support amongst the other shareholders."

"But he said that it would tie up the stock until after the August stockholders' meeting. And that if he keeps control of the company he's going to do to you what he did to Tiberius."

As threats went, it lacked teeth. "There's no immediate family to turn against me," JT reminded her. "As for ejecting me from the company, I was ready to go out on my own before we found out about Tiberius buying stock." JT liked her fierce defense of him. It gave him an urgent need to pull her into his arms and offer her his ardent thanks. "Besides, if he wanted me gone, he could make that happen at any time. He hasn't. He doesn't want to risk losing the support of what shareholders he has at the moment."

"I suppose." She didn't look convinced. "But why should we risk the lawsuit and your reputation when there's a simple solution."

JT grew apprehensive when he realized she'd concocted a plan in that nimble brain of hers. "And that is?"

"We appear as if we're truly married. I'll move in here. We'll let ourselves be seen around town looking like lovebirds. Meanwhile you keep talking to your family."

A simple solution? Maybe on the surface. Definitely for her.

But with Violet living here, JT knew it was only a matter of time before he trampled their bargain and made her his wife for real. And then what? He just let her go in a month? Impossible. Once he made her his, there was no going back.

"Sounds perfect," he heard himself say and wondered just how long it would remain so.

Beneath Scarlett's watchful eye, Violet packed a suitcase full of essentials and ignored most of her sister's questions.

"At least tell me this," Scarlett said. "Are you going to give the man a chance to rock your world?"

Violet sat down on the bed beside her sister. "I'm afraid that if I do that by the time we get divorced I'll be madly in love with him."

"But wouldn't it be worth discovering he's madly in love with you, too?"

"JT's right. Your happiness with Logan makes you want everyone else to find love." Violet shook her head. "It's not where JT and I are heading."

"You're just afraid. Before Logan, I was afraid, too. But trusting him—trusting myself—let me see with my heart as well as my head. All I'm suggesting is that you do the same thing."

"JT doesn't want to let me in. Trying to get to know him is like slogging through mud. Forward progress is slow and exhausting."

"But it's still progress."

"And what if I do get to know him only to discover that he's been damaged so badly he won't be able to accept love much less return it."

"If anyone can fix him, that person is you."

Scarlett's faith strengthened Violet. Was it possible that what had started out as an inspired business strategy could become a viable, satisfying and permanent merger?

"We're having a party at JT's ranch on Tuesday. I need you, Logan and Harper to come for moral support."

"Of course we'll come, but you don't really need us. You and JT will do great together. I think you make a wonderful team. I'll bet Tiberius did too. It's probably why he left the stock to you instead of to JT with the caveat that you couldn't dispose of it until far in the future."

Ever since the reading of his will, Violet had wondered about Tiberius's motivation for doing so as well. Why had he given her the stock and forced her to hold on to it knowing that she wouldn't be able to vote?

Plagued by questions she'd never know the answer to, Violet drove to JT's ranch and arrived at three in the afternoon. JT's housekeeper took charge of Violet's luggage and informed her that JT was in the barn. Curious, Violet went in search of him.

To describe JT's property as a ranch was a little misleading. What he had was a first-class training facility for show horses. The barn was a state-of-the-art structure with an impressive lobby whose walls were lined with large photos of expensive-looking horses doing dressage or jumping fences. The centerpiece of the room was a large bronze horse and female rider. Violet wondered if it had been modeled after JT's grandmother.

Off the lobby were several offices, currently empty. A door toward the back had a sign on it that indicated it led to the barn. Violet pushed her way through. She expected to be hit with heat, noise and stench, but it was a comfortable eighty degrees, and the few sounds that reached her ear were muted crunching and an occasional nose clearing. As for the smell, whatever air conditioning JT had incorporated into his design also pulled the dust from the air as well as the strongest of the horsey odors of hay, sweat and manure.

The concrete floor between the stalls was newly swept and free of dust. Violet wandered along, peering into stalls as she went. With each step she took, she found herself growing more and more calm. By the time she rounded a corner and spotted JT, down on one knee, wrapping some sort of poultice around a horse's knee, she was humming.

"Hi," she said, stopping ten feet from the large horse.

JT glanced up at her greeting and offered her a lopsided grin that made her heart jerk almost painfully. He wore camel-colored jodhpurs and knee-high boots. A navy polo shirt showed off the strong column of his throat and his powerful biceps.

"I'll be just a couple minutes more, then I can give you a tour of the place."

"Take your time."

She was enjoying the view. After not seeing JT for five days, she'd almost been able to convince herself that the way she'd melted beneath his kisses had been a symptom of her shock at learning what Tiberius had left her and reaction to her impulsive and speedy wedding. Then he'd returned and she'd proposed that they move in together. She could deny her feelings to Harper and Scarlett, but it was a lot harder to lie to herself.

She was hoping the chemistry between her and JT would combust and land them in bed together. Admitting it made her giddy. She'd disavowed the truth long enough. She wanted JT Stone in a big way and her subconscious had positioned her perfectly to act on those feelings.

"You ready?"

While she'd been coming to grips with her desires, JT had finished with the horse and a groom was leading it away.

"Sure."

JT guided her down the row of stalls, telling her a little bit about all the different horses.

"Until I stepped into the barn, I didn't realize this was a training facility," she exclaimed as he opened one of the stall doors and stepped inside. "How many horses do you have here?"

"We have fifty in training. They're all housed on this side. Across the arena is a whole other line of stalls where we keep horses for sale and the mares who are either in foal or who have babies. There's another forty over there."

"So, this is much more than a hobby for you."

"Not really. Vic manages the facility and deals with all the clients. Ralph is in charge of the training. Sid handles the sales. Bonnie keeps everyone healthy and watches over the mares. The place doesn't need me to run."

But from the way everyone they met asked his opinion or updated him on the barn's occupants, she gathered he was the heart and soul of the operation.

"This is Milo." JT laughed as they approached a stall and he had to push the horse's nose away from his pocket. "You get treats after you work, not before."

"Is he yours?"

"No. He belongs to a very talented ten-year-old girl. I've been his trainer for two years."

Keeping her gaze off her husband's handsome face—relaxed and unguarded for the first time she'd noticed—was necessary to avoid embarrassing herself with renewed pleas for his kisses. Instead, Violet stared at the horse. His back was well over five and a half feet off the ground. "A little girl rides this horse? That's a long way to fall."

"She's been riding since she was three. She has an amazing seat. The sort my grandmother had. And a real feel for the horse. She and Milo are quite a team. She'll be by for a lesson tomorrow. You can see for yourself."

"I'd like that."

JT slipped a halter over the horse's head and led him out of the stall. He held the lead rope out to her. "Can you hold him for me while I get my saddle and bridle?"

"Me?" She squeaked out the word after sizing up the enormous animal. "I've never handled a horse before."

"He's a big pussycat." JT put the rope in her hands. The horse took a step toward her, his ears forward. "Blow lightly into his nostril. He likes it and it will help you two get acquainted."

If it had been anyone but JT she might have assumed she was being pranked. Still, she felt silly following his instructions until the big horse pricked his ears and breathed back at her. On some sort of horse level they were communicating. By the time JT returned with a saddle and bridle, she had grown brave enough to pet the horse's soft nose and scratch his cheek.

"Looks like you two have hit it off," JT observed, setting the saddle carefully on the floor. He held out a brush. "Feel like giving me a hand?"

"Sure." She sounded more confident than she felt, but as she applied the brush to the animal's rich brown coat, she was overcome by a sense of peace. No wonder JT enjoyed his horses. Being with them grounded him firmly in the moment. Nothing mattered but the stroke of a brush against Milo's warm flank. It was the perfect counterpoint to the Las Vegas strip. "It's very Zen," she remarked.

"This is where I spend my days. I can handle just about any crisis after a few hours with the horses."

JT tossed the saddle onto Milo's back and fastened the cinch. While he worked, he spoke softly to the horse. Mostly nonsense, but it was his melodious tone that the horse listened and responded to. And he wasn't the only one. Violet found herself lulled as well.

"Can you hand me his bridle?"

His question snapped her out of her trance. Spending time with him like this meant she risked falling beneath JT's spell. Eventually, reality would intrude and she'd be in too deep. She just had to decide if getting hurt was worth the ride.

"Here you go."

The horse stood patiently while JT slipped off the halter and replaced it with the bridle. His actions were smooth and efficient. Remembering Scarlett's opinion about JT's hands, Violet watched as he fastened buckles, double-checked the fit of the cinch and soothed the horse with a stroke along his shoulder. By the time JT turned the horse toward the door that led into the arena, Violet was experiencing waves of heat that had nothing to do with the air temperature.

"You can watch me work Milo from there." JT pointed to the far corner where several chairs sat on a raised platform. He handed her a small towel. "We use crumb rubber as a footing to keep down the dust, but you'll probably want to wipe off the chair."

She glanced down at her flat sandals and pale blue skirt. "I guess I'm not really dressed for the barn, am I? If I'm going to visit in the future, I'd better wear jeans."

"And boots as well. Not everyone is as careful where they put their feet as Milo. I wouldn't want your pretty toes crushed."

"You think I have pretty toes?" His offhanded compliment made her grin.

His eyes glowed as he gave her a quick once-over. "I think you have pretty everything."

It was on the tip of her tongue to shoot back that he hadn't seen her everything, but then she recalled how he'd caught her skinny-dipping. At the time, he'd been so annoyed, it hadn't occurred to her to wonder how much he'd seen. Now, she suspected he'd glimpsed more than he let on.

"JT…" She had no idea how to convey what she wanted without giving away too much.

"Don't read too much into that," he told her. "You're beautiful. I find you attractive. It doesn't mean I can't control myself around you."

His words acted like an ice bath. "I'm not sure whether to be insulted or relieved."

Teeth flashing in a wry grin, JT led Milo to the center of the arena, leaving her standing in an emotional stew of her own making. When she'd set out to discover JT's true identity, the one a painful childhood had forced into hiding, she'd done so thinking that it would do him good to connect with people.

But after seeing the way he related to his barn staff and the joy he received from working with the horses, she realized he wasn't the damaged train wreck she'd assumed. He had a healthy outlet for his passion. A place of peace that benefited others. He wasn't exactly the loner she perceived him as—and felt sorry for. What else had she gotten wrong?

As Violet watched JT swing his long lean form into the saddle, she felt her perceptions shift. Her ego had fooled her into believing JT needed her when it was so obvious that he had things all figured out. He didn't need her to run to his rescue with a marriage of convenience or to draw him out of his shell for his own good. He'd been doing just fine on his own. Yet he'd accepted her help. It wasn't as if anyone could force JT to do something he didn't want to do.

Milo moved through a series of maneuvers that looked complex, but which the horse executed with ease. JT sat quietly in the saddle, appearing on first glance to be more passenger than active participant. But his concentration told a different story. Violet paid closer attention to his hands and legs. Still she couldn't discern what JT was doing to make the horse sidepass one direction for a few steps and then abruptly switch and go the other way.

JT was asking the horse to dance for him. His control over the animal was amazing. And sexy as hell.

After fifteen minutes he dropped the reins onto Milo's neck and patted the horse on both shoulders. His broad grin made Violet catch her breath. So this was what it felt like to swoon over a guy. She'd never experienced anything like it and wasn't sure how to behave now that her body had a mind of its own.

"That was amazing," Violet called, stepping off the platform.

JT dismounted and led Milo toward her. He stroked the horse's neck. "He did all the work." A slight sheen had developed on JT's forehead, contradicting his assertion.

"I don't believe that."

Their eyes connected and locked. JT's smile faded. What had been warm flesh a moment earlier became solid granite, and Violet's heart sank as she watched the doors slam shut over his thoughts. After several heartbeats, JT sucked in a deep lungful of air.

"I lied to you earlier," he said, his gaze probing hers, searching for answers, but giving nothing away.

The disappointment she'd felt seconds earlier faded slightly as her heartbeat accelerated beneath his intent expression. "About what?"

"About—"

"If you're all done with Milo, Boss, I can take him." A groom stepped into the arena. "Bonnie is in with Bullet and wonders if you can come look at the foal. She's wondering if we should call the vet."

"You're busy," Violet said, taking a half step back. "And I promised Harper I'd come in early today so we could discuss a joint promotion." As excuses went, it wasn't the best, but she needed time to regroup and figure out what she really wanted from JT before things started to happen. "We can talk after work tonight."

He caught her arm and kept her from moving away. The groom was fast approaching. Violet's heart thumped hard against her ribs as JT lowered his lips toward her ear.

"Your sister was right," he murmured, his warm breath sliding seductively over her skin. "I am hungry for you."

And then he was handing Milo off to the groom and striding away from her. Violet stared after him, her knees pressed together for stability because the strength had gone out of her muscles.

He was hungry for her?

He was hungry for her.

Well, that was good because she was hungry for him as well.

CHAPTER SEVEN

THE RANCH HOUSE was quiet and dark when JT let himself in at two in the morning. He'd cut his night short, unable to concentrate on business with thoughts of Violet bombarding him. He liked that she'd shown up at the barn today. Watching her overcome her anxiety about Milo had demonstrated that her interest had been genuine. Having her gaze follow his every move in the arena had been a pleasant distraction. He'd stepped up his game and showed off for her like a smitten teenage boy.

What he'd seen in her eyes made him want to throw her over his shoulder and carry her straight to his bedroom. Was she reconsidering the arrangement? He hoped so. But if she needed more convincing, he was ready for that as well.

Taking the stairs two at a time, JT headed down the hall to her bedroom. The door stood ajar, the room beyond dark. He let his eyes adjust and saw that the room was unoccupied. Reaching in, he flipped on the light. The room wasn't just empty. It showed no sign that anyone was staying there.

If JT hadn't seen Violet's car in the garage, he would've assumed that she'd changed her mind and returned to Fontaine Chic. Perhaps she'd chosen a different room. There were four others she might prefer. But none showed signs of life. So where was she?

JT headed for the terrace outside the master suite. As soon as he stepped outside he heard the sound of splashing. She'd gone for a swim. He grabbed a set of swim trunks from a drawer and changed. It wasn't until he entered the closet to hang up his suit that he realized which bedroom she'd decided to sleep in.

His.

What had once been the empty half of the enormous his-and-hers closet was now filled with black dresses, casual daytime wear and several pairs of jeans. The shoe racks overflowed with pumps and sandals. He returned to the bedroom and discovered half his drawers filled with lacy lingerie, knit tops and scarves. The countertop in his bathroom bore perfume bottles and creams.

Holy hell.

He marched down the stairs at a deliberate pace, formulating how to approach Violet about this new development. It was one thing to perpetuate the myth of their happy marriage by living together. But sharing his room—his bed—with her was taking the playacting way too far.

JT stalked through the living room and stepped onto the pool deck. Violet stroked through the water, naked limbs breaking the surface and plunging back in again. Damn, but she was beautiful. Her movements were lazy, content. The exact opposite of the riotous emotions surging through JT.

He was standing at the edge of the pool before he even realized he'd moved. "I found all your things in my room. What's going on?"

"I got to thinking your dad might have spies in your employ. I don't want to give him any ammunition against you." She didn't meet his gaze, which made him wonder what she had to hide.

"I think you're giving him too much credit."

"Come for a swim. We can talk about it later."

He wanted to get it resolved right now. JT dove in and swam underwater toward her. With just the pool lights to see by, he didn't realize that she was naked until he was close enough to touch her.

He came up coughing.

"Are you all right?" She set her hands on his shoulders and peered at him.

"I thought we had an understanding about your skinny-dipping."

To his immense shock, she hooked her fingertips into the elastic waistband of his swim trunks and pulled it a couple inches away from his stomach. Her touch against his bare skin brought him to a swift and fierce arousal. He clenched his teeth to contain a groan.

"You should try it," she murmured, her smile come-hither. A second later he felt the snap against his belly as she let go. In a flash she was gone. Water splashed against his cheeks and blinded him as she dove sideways, swimming beyond his grasp in seconds.

Sputtering, he shook his head to clear his eyes and took off after her with a growl. It wasn't until he caught her at the edge of the pool and pinned her against the wall that he remembered she was naked. Her thighs tangled with his and she hooked one foot around his calf to anchor herself to him.

"Kiss me," she demanded, sliding her palms up the side of his neck and latching onto his hair. "Soft, slow, hard, deep. I don't care. Just make me lose myself."

His lips captured hers in a relentless assault that definitively declared that this time there would be no backpedaling, no stopping, no mercy. She accepted every stroke of his tongue, every nip of his teeth and gave him back frenzied desire and impatience. Her nails bit into his skin, her moans heightened his already explosive hunger. She writhed against him, her hips moving rhythmically against his erection, driving him wild.

He sucked the water from her neck, tasting chlorine and below that the sweetness of her skin. His breath caught as she threw her head back and offered him even more access. He wrapped his fingers around her delicate ribcage and lifted her until her perfect breasts bobbed above the water's surface. She wrapped her thighs around his waist as he locked his mouth over one hard nipple. With her wet heat pressed tight to his abdomen, he sucked and nibbled first one breast, then the other until her breath came in short, tight pants.

Her lithe body trembled in his arms as he grazed his fingertips down her spine and splayed his hands over the firm planes of her butt. She'd been working her hips in an ever-increasing rhythm. What she wanted, she wasn't getting and she unhooked her ankles from around his waist and let her feet drift to the pool bottom.

Once again he felt her tug on his trunks. This time she forced the fabric downward, freeing his erection. He hissed through his teeth as the pool water hit the sensitive head. The sound was followed a second later by his strangled moan as she closed her fingers around his hard length.

He slammed his mouth down over hers, plunging his tongue inward, all technique lost in the savage need to claim her. She matched his kiss with sweet ferocity, using her tongue and teeth to drive him wild.

"Give it all to me," she murmured, stroking him in ever more tantalizing sweeps as he sucked on her neck.

She parted her thighs and placed the tip of him at her entrance. He nudged firmly against her hot wet core, and almost cried out at the agony of holding back, but remained perfectly still.

"Protection," he garbled out the word, unsure how he was going let her go, walk all the way upstairs and fetch a condom from his nightstand.

"I'm on the pill." She arched her back and rocked her hips forward, embedding him inside her before her words fully registered.

The tightness of her encased him and nothing JT had ever dreamed of matched the reality of Violet naked and in his arms.

He put his hands on her hips and settled himself deeper still, hanging onto his control for dear life so he could make the moment into something they would both find satisfying.

"You are amazing," he murmured as they rocked together in the pool, stirring the water as they kissed and caressed.

Time slowed. JT's world narrowed to the rush of air through his lungs, the surge of heat in his groin and the warm silk of Violet's skin caressing his.

"This is so much better than I imagined it would be," she whispered, her breath tickling his ear.

"You thought about it?"

He wandered his hands over her back and down her thighs as his lips drifted along her shoulder. She'd locked the soles of her feet against his calves to anchor herself in the weightlessness of the water. It gave her the leverage to add a little twisting motion to the rhythmic movements of her hips. The power of that move was close to blowing a hole in his willpower. He ground his teeth against a groan.

"Night and day since you first started showing up at Baccarat."

Her confession prompted him to offer one of his own. "Losing Rick to you was the best thing that ever happened to me."

"You don't say." Her chest vibrated with a sexy laugh, making her breasts shift tantalizingly against him. Her tight nipples were searing points of heat that quickened his breath.

"Or it was," he amended, unable to stave off the quickening of sensations any longer. "Until now."

He moved more strongly into her and felt her close tightly around him, forming a tight sheath. The friction was almost too intense to handle. But if her body brought him acute pleasure, her dreamy smile was a balm for his spirit.

And then he felt her body tighten and her focus sharpen. Using all his willpower to hold off his own release, he watched her climb higher and higher. Her eyes flew open. Her sharp gasp was followed by a shudder. Only then did JT let himself go.

His orgasm came with such speed and intensity he wondered how he'd held it off as long as he had. The pool, Violet's face, all vanished behind a wave of black. He was cast into the heavens. A thousand pinpoints of lights guided his flight. They rushed at him, through him. Each one left a mark, a permanent reminder of this perfect moment.

He came back to earth and realized that his chest hurt. The pain was caused by either his tortured lungs or the impossibly swift beat of his heart.

"Best sex ever," Violet murmured, framing his face with her hands and smiling at him. Equally winded, she seemed less shaken by their turbulent lovemaking. "I knew it would be great with you, but wow."

He couldn't match her openness. What he felt for her was too immense, too raw.

"Yes." It wasn't eloquent, but it was heartfelt. "Wow."

The corners of her eyes crinkled as her grin grew. "Am I still banned from skinny-dipping?"

Captivated by her happiness, he shook his head. "In fact, I plan to burn every bathing suit in the place."

"You're smiling a lot this morning," Harper commented, eyeing Violet over a glass of orange juice.

It was Tuesday morning and the Fontaine sisters were meeting for their weekly breakfast, this morning in Scarlett's office at Fontaine Richesse. Usually they met on Wednesdays, but Violet and JT were having their belated wedding reception at the ranch that evening and they all figured it would be a late night.

"Am I?" Violet sipped her green tea and tried to look nonchalant.

"Of course she's smiling," Scarlett put in. "She and JT have been shacked up for three days of postnuptial bliss."

"I don't think it can be called 'shacked up' if we're married," Violet corrected her.

Harper frowned in confusion. "You're living together now?"

"If you'd pay attention to something other than your hotel once in a while," Scarlett began, "you'd know that Preston showed up here and threatened to sue JT and Violet for fraud if their marriage wasn't real."

"He can't possibly have a case," Harper said.

Scarlett smirked. "Not anymore."

"What I mean," Harper continued, shooting Scarlett a look, "is there's nothing in the corporate bylaws insisting the marriage must be real, just legal."

"We were concerned that by taking us to court, he could prevent me from voting my shares at the upcoming shareholder meeting and remain CEO."

A line formed between Harper's brows. "I guess that's possible. I just don't know how likely."

"We didn't want to take the chance."

"And because of that your relationship has become physical?"

Violet resisted looking Scarlett's way for fear that her sister's expression would make her laugh. Harper was a little too literal and that often kept her from finding the humor in a situation.

"Not exactly…"

"He's crazy about her and vice versa," Scarlett explained. "Unlike you and Ashton where you make each other crazy."

"I have every right to be crazy," Harper insisted. "The restaurant is behind schedule because he hasn't been here to make decisions. And when he does make decisions, it puts us even more behind schedule because he wants to change things."

Scarlett gave her sister a doubting look. "To say nothing of the fact that he's gorgeous and sexy and your DVR is full of his television series."

Harper's scowl would have been more intimidating if she'd been able to meet Scarlett's gaze. "It seems to me that you and Logan were in that drive-each-other-crazy place less than a month ago."

Scarlett and her security-expert fiancé were so madly in love these days it was hard to remember just how much they used to antagonize each other

"That was then. Now we just drive each other crazy with passion."

Harper's response was a rude noise. Violet chuckled. She loved her sisters. To outsiders, it sometimes appeared as if the three of them didn't get along, but in fact for three women who'd not known each other until their grandfather introduced them five years ago, they were as tight as siblings who'd grown up together. Maybe even tighter because there were no childhood battle scars.

"Putting aside all the *crazy* talk for a second," Violet said, turning to Scarlett, "you said you had something important you wanted to discuss with me."

After some meaningful eye contact with Harper, Scarlett went to her desk and brought back two files. She held one suspended in Violet's direction and said, "I know I've told you a little about the files I inherited from Tiberius. This one is about Preston Rhodes."

Curious, Violet accepted the file and quickly scanned it. The contents included old newspaper clippings about a flash flood drowning in the desert near Las Vegas as well as a grainy group photo of seven rough-looking young men. Below that was a piece of paper with a woman's name and contact information on it. Charity Rimes.

"What am I looking at?" Violet asked.

"Grady and I think the man we know as Preston Rhodes is actually a local Las Vegas kid who was supposed to have drowned during a flash flood back in 1970."

Violet glanced at Harper and saw in her sister's expression the same skepticism she was feeling. "So, the newspaper report got it wrong? It wasn't this George Barnes guy, but Preston Rhodes. How is that possible?"

"I think JT's father—whose real name I think is George

Barnes—switched identities with Preston Rhodes after Preston was killed in the flash flood."

"That's a pretty wild theory," Harper interjected.

"Why would he do that?" Violet wanted to know.

"From what information Tiberius had gathered about George Barnes, he'd been a juvenile delinquent on his way to a bad end. Preston Rhodes had a bright future ahead of him. A rich kid with no family. He'd left California, where he'd grown up, to take a road trip to the East Coast where he would be attending college. Think of how easy it would have been for George to simply step into Preston's shoes."

Violet skimmed the clippings, and realized that Scarlett's explanation was sounding more reasonable by the second. And after meeting JT's father, she had no trouble believing the man was ruthless and unscrupulous enough to steal another man's identity and fortune. But what would this mean for JT? She imagined how devastating this revelation would be to him. Finding out your father had stolen someone's identity was a far cry from merely worrying that he was making poor business decisions.

With her stomach in knots, Violet set aside the file. "I don't know what you want me to do with this."

"You should talk to Charity Rimes. Tiberius tracked her down for a reason."

"Who is she?" Harper asked.

"She's the writer doing a story on a series of killings in Los Angeles back in the sixties. I don't know much about the story other than they never caught the guy. I let the whole matter drop when I realized it wasn't any of my business. But things have changed. JT married you. That makes him family." Scarlett extended a second file. "Which brings me to this. I don't know if you want to read it or not, but since you're now involved with JT, I thought I should at least give you the choice."

"Tiberius had a file on JT." Violet wondered why he hadn't kept it in his home office. "Have you read it?"

"I was tempted to when I first suspected his dad of stealing Preston Rhodes's identity, but then I decided it wasn't my place to know his secrets." She extended the file to Violet.

The amount of paper contained in the manila folder took Violet by surprise. This wasn't a simple summary of his unhappy childhood and adolescent acting out. Tiberius had spent time and energy researching his nephew. Probably in preparation for renewing their relationship.

Reading the file would be a shortcut to learning most everything that had gone into developing JT's character. No doubt she'd learn things about him he wouldn't appreciate her knowing. But maybe talking about the most painful events would help him to heal. And if he healed, perhaps he could then open himself up to love.

As soon as the thought occurred, Violet reined it in. Was she hoping that if she fixed him he'd be so grateful he'd never want their marriage to end? They'd been married less than two weeks and she was already figuring out ways to manipulate him. Better to let JT tell her what he wished her to know when he wanted her to know it.

"I shouldn't." Violet tried to hand the folder back to Scarlett, but she put up her hands.

"Keep it. Burn it. Give it to JT. I don't care, but I don't want it back in my possession." Scarlett glanced at Harper who was glaring at her smartphone. "I'm already the keeper of more secrets than I'm comfortable knowing."

Violet knew Scarlett was referring to the file she'd found on Harper's mother. The one with the potential to turn Harper's life upside down. From her calm demeanor, Violet suspected that Scarlett hadn't yet decided to share with her half sister what was in the file.

"I have to go," Harper said, getting to her feet. "I emailed Ashton another round of head chef candidates and he has fifteen minutes of free time to talk about them."

As soon as Harper left the room, Scarlett fetched another file from her desk. "I wasn't kidding when I said I'm uncomfortable with the secrets I'm keeping."

"Are you planning to tell her what you discovered about her mother?"

"I'm going to tell you what's going on and I want you to help me decide."

"Very well." When Violet had first found out about the file on Harper's mother, she'd sympathized with Scarlett's dilemma. Now she had a similar problem—what to do with the files on JT and his father. "What did Harper's mother do?"

"She had a brief affair during an extended period of time where her husband was away on business."

"Penelope?" Violet couldn't believe Harper's uptight mother could have done anything that rash. "It's so unlike her."

Scarlett opened the file and displayed the black-and-white photos of a young Penelope Fontaine and a handsome man in a hot embrace.

"Apparently being married to our father could push even the most conservative person into reckless behavior," Scarlett remarked, sounding more tired than wry.

"I'm sure Harper will be shocked and embarrassed by her mother's actions, but it was a long time ago." Violet wanted to reject what her eyes were seeing. "But I don't understand why you think it will devastate her."

"Because she was born nine months later."

It took several seconds for Scarlett's meaning to penetrate. "You mean…?"

"Harper isn't a Fontaine."

"Are you sure?"

"Unfortunately, yes." Scarlett closed her eyes. Pain raced across her features. "How can I tell her that?"

When Harper found out the truth about her parentage, she'd be destroyed.

"I don't think you should," Violet said at last.

Harper had the education and the business savvy to run Fontaine Resorts and Hotels, not to mention the ambition and a seemingly inexhaustible store of energy, and she'd spent her whole life preparing to run the family business. In the last five years Violet had learned enough about Harper's character to guess she'd bow out of the contest to determine the next CEO.

A year ago Violet would have been excited at the prospect of moving into the lead. She had Harper's ambition and drive, but of late she'd been thinking less about her career and more about her personal life. The transition had been subtle, but she suspected it had begun around the time JT started showing up at Baccarat.

As for Scarlett, the former child star had recently decided to return part-time to acting. Splitting her time and attention between L.A. and Las Vegas meant she'd already decided not to actively compete for the CEO position. Nor was Violet convinced Scarlett had ever truly given herself props for the work she'd done to make Fontaine Richesse the standout hotel it was.

Scarlett nodded somberly and returned the photos to the file. "It's what I think, too. No good will come of telling her."

With too many secrets weighing her down, Violet left Scarlett's office and headed to her suite to find a dress to wear to her belated wedding reception. She'd been so preoccupied with the details for the party that she'd forgotten all about herself.

In the back of her closet was a pale pink chiffon dress embellished with blush and silver sequins on the bodice. Three years ago, she'd bought it to wear to a charity event that at the last minute she'd been unable to attend. Despite having spent a fortune on the dress and the matching pink slingbacks, Violet couldn't bring herself to return the ensemble. She knew eventually she'd be attending a party where she could wear it. Her wedding reception fit the bill.

As she was exiting her suite, her gaze fell on the files Scarlett had given her. She hadn't decided what to tell JT yet. He'd been through so much already. But she didn't want to go behind his back on something as serious as his father stealing another man's identity. Leaving JT's file on her home office desk, she slipped Preston's and the one containing information on Charity Rimes into her briefcase and exited the suite.

CHAPTER EIGHT

"YOU LOOK GORGEOUS." Impatient for a last minute alone with her, JT linked his fingers with Violet's and tugged her toward the stairs. They had fifteen minutes until their guests were due to arrive.

"Is it silly that I'm nervous?" With her free hand, she smoothed her skirt and tugged at her neckline.

"Yes." He lifted her hand to his lips and kissed her knuckles. "Everyone here tonight will be a friend. And I'll be at your side the entire evening."

To his gratification, she looked reassured. "And you're sure I look okay?"

"You're perfect." He wasn't accustomed to her lack of confidence and wondered how someone as beautiful and charming as Violet could doubt herself.

"Because the dress is three years old."

"It looks brand-new."

"That's because it is. I've never worn it."

The subtleties of a woman's mind when it came to fashion were lost on JT. "Let's go have a glass of champagne. I want to make a toast."

He led her outside to the pool deck. Because of the number of guests who would be coming, they'd opted to open the living room's glass walls so people could enjoy the night air. Tiny white lights decorated the palm trees and shrubs, adding a festive air. A bottle of champagne and two flutes awaited them in the outdoor seating area.

JT popped the cork and poured the sparkling liquid. He handed one to Violet and cleared his throat.

"To you. Thank you for marrying me. It's been a long time since anyone has acted in my best interests instead of their own. Your optimism and knack for thinking outside the box have enabled me to shake loose the cobwebs and let in the sunlight. No matter what happens a month from now, I am ready for whatever the future brings."

The toast was awkward and sappy, but Violet didn't seem to notice. Her eyes remained riveted on him as he spoke. Her faith had given him wings. His father could throw every vile trick in the book his way and JT would let it all roll off him. It was impossible to convey the depth of his appreciation for all Violet had given him.

"I'm glad to hear you say that," Violet told him, clinking her glass to his. "And I hope I can continue to make good things happen for you."

"All I need is for you—"

"There's the couple of the hour," a man announced from the living room. It was Brent. He'd flown in from Charlotte earlier that day and was staying at Titanium.

Fighting back a sigh at the interruption, JT towed his wife to greet his cousin. After introductions were made, JT caught a subtle nod of approval from Brent and relaxed. His cousin's opinion mattered. Everyone else could go to hell.

Shortly after Brent's arrival, the floodgates opened and guests began to pour in. In addition to family and friends, they'd invited many business associates from Las Vegas.

Waitstaff circled with glasses of champagne and fancy hors d'oeuvres. With the help of her catering manager, Violet had organized the party within a week and the entire evening flowed without a hitch. And with each hour that passed, JT found himself a little more enthralled with his wife.

She charmed everyone with her quick laugh and positive outlook. He was glad the evening called for them to navigate the room as a couple, because he couldn't bring himself to move more than an arm's length away.

The floral scent she wore made his head spin with shameless thoughts of what he intended to do with her later. He had a hard time keeping his hands off her bare arms.

"You've been monopolizing your wife the whole evening," Scarlett complained, tugging Violet away. "Harper and I need a couple minutes with her."

JT continued to move about the room, but what little enjoyment he'd had in the evening had been leached away the second Violet had gone. More than anything he wished everyone would just go home.

After what seemed like hours, but had been no more than fifteen minutes, Violet returned to him.

"I missed you," he murmured, after welcoming her with a quick kiss.

By the end of the night, he accepted that he was the luckiest man in the world. As they stood in the doorway and bid the last of their guests goodbye, JT became aware of a raging need to have her all to himself. The instant she closed the front door and let out an enormous sigh of relief, he lifted her onto his shoulder and headed upstairs.

At first she was too startled to protest, but she'd rediscovered her voice by the time he reached the second floor.

"Have you lost your mind? There are still things to clean up and I need to thank the caterer. Put me down."

"She left twenty minutes ago. You and I are all alone." He deposited her on the king-size bed in the master suite. "Finally."

"We've been alone these last four days," she reminded him, sliding his shirt buttons free.

He tugged the thin strap off her shoulder and buried his face in her neck. Her scent had been driving him crazy all night. It reminded him of two days ago when he'd…

JT's brain short-circuited. Her busy hands had unfastened his zipper and slipped inside his pants to cup him. He groaned, his erection growing impossibly hard beneath her clever touch.

"Slow down," he commanded, snagging her wrists and pinning them onto the pillows above her head. "We have all night."

"But I need you now." She slowly gyrated her hips in the way she knew made him crazy. "And we're both ready. Why can't you just go with it?"

Because he'd been *going with it* for four days and had yet to learn all he wanted to about pleasing her. Their chemistry was so explosive. He'd never been with anyone like her. Eager, passionate, sexy as hell. She could look at him from across the room and he'd want her. His obsession grew worse every day. It interfered with his ability to focus at work and distracted him from the purpose of their marriage in the first place: gaining the stock he needed to oust his father.

"You want me to go with it?" he asked, rolling off the bed so he could strip off his shirt, pants and underwear.

"Very much." She watched him with greedy eyes as she got to her knees and stripped off her fancy cocktail dress. Clad in a strapless bra and silk bikini underwear, she waited for him in the middle of the bed, her hands on her hips in brazen challenge.

"Very well." His smile acknowledged that if she wanted to play, he could too. "Turn and face the headboard."

Surprise and uncertainty flickered in her eyes for a moment, but after a short hesitation she did as he asked. Peering at him over her shoulder, she asked, "Like this?"

"Just like that."

He moved onto the bed and came up behind her. Her beautiful back was a feature he'd not had much opportunity to explore these past few days and it was worth his attention. The first thing he did was pop the catch on her bra so he could appreciate her delicate spine without hindrance.

The elastic that held the bra in place had created indentations on her skin. He bent his head and kissed the marks while drawing his fingertips along her narrow shoulders. She quivered beneath his light touch and her breath hissed out in a long sigh.

Little by little she relaxed as his fingers explored the contours of her shoulder blades, lightly massaged her nape and drifted down her arms. As he sucked on the place where her neck and shoulder came together, she leaned back against him and savored the prod of his erection against her butt.

"That's nice," she murmured, arms straight at her sides, palms resting on his thighs. "But what can I do for you?"

"Enjoy this. That's all I ask."

Violet didn't ask what *this* was. She was feeling lazy and aroused. Her skin was delighted to receive all the consideration JT was lavishing on it. Despite the insistent throbbing between her thighs, she hoped he'd treat her entire body to the same attention to detail.

"You have a beautiful back. I love the dimples right here." He pointed out the particular spot with a soft caress.

"You know there's a whole 'nother side of me that would love some attention."

He kissed her neck. "Such as?"

"My breasts."

Following her command, he grazed his palms up her sides. She caught her breath as his long fingers stroked across her sensitive nipples, and exhaled as he swallowed her fullness in his hands.

"Better?"

"Much."

"Where else would you like me to touch you?"

She sucked her lower lip between her teeth and bit down as his hands moved over her abdomen and caressed the tops of her thighs. She rotated her hips as the ache built deep in her loins. Undulating waves of longing pulsed through her.

"Here."

Shaking with need, she snagged his strong hands and urged them toward her mound. He'd knelt with his knees on either side of hers. Now, he nudged her thighs apart, spreading her legs wide, opening her. She gulped at the brush of cool air against her tender flesh. Anticipation of his possession aroused her still more until she thought she'd go mad with longing.

"JT, this is not fair."

"What's not fair?"

He turned her face toward him and rubbed his lips over hers, mingling their breath, but not giving her the satisfaction of his tongue. She wanted a deep, penetrating kiss. Something to momentarily take her mind off the painful throbbing at her core.

"You aren't taking advantage of having me in this position."

"No?" He nipped at her neck. "What should I be doing?"

She wagged her hips, rubbing herself against his erection. He groaned. At last his fingers slid into the cleft between her thighs. She almost cried out at the pleasure.

"You're so hot," he muttered, his tone guttural and low. "It makes me crazy how wet you get."

"Show me." She bent forward at the waist and let her hands fall to the mattress.

From between his teeth came a savage curse. JT seized her hips and in one swift move plunged into her. The position offered Violet a whole new range of sensation and she released a soft "oh" of surprise.

JT kissed her back. "Are you okay?"

"Wonderful. Perfect." She sucked in a breath and laughed. "In fact, it's fabulous. Keep going."

Snorting his amusement, JT began rocking against her. Faster than Violet would have imagined, she felt an orgasm rising to meet her. And when JT reached between her thighs and plucked at the knot of nerves, she went off like a rocket.

"Yes!"

JT picked up his pace and continued to fondle her. To Violet's intense shock, she didn't settle to earth on a golden cloud like normal, but felt another pulse of pleasure stab her. She quaked as her second climax roared through her.

Before she had a chance to marvel at the wonder of it all, JT dove into her hard two more times and was claimed by his own release. He collapsed onto her back, his chest vibrating with laughter.

Catching her around the waist, he shifted his weight and rolled them onto the mattress. They landed in a tangle of limbs. JT pushed himself up so he could peer into her face. He had to brush her hair away from her eyes before he could meet her gaze.

"Did you just come twice?" he demanded in amazement.

She grinned. "I believe I did."

"You are the most incredible woman I've ever been with."

His words were sweet music to her ears. She'd never had a man appreciate her lovemaking the way JT did. And the feeling was mutual. He made her feel like a goddess. It was heady stuff for a girl who'd too often been self-conscious in bed.

"It's only because you're such a wonderful lover."

He sobered. "Don't do that."

"Do what?" She couldn't imagine what she'd said to make him look so unhappy.

"Downplay how terrific you are."

She squirmed a little beneath his intense regard. "I get uncomfortable when anyone says nice things about me."

"Why is that?"

"I guess I don't always believe that I deserve it."

"That's ridiculous."

She lifted one shoulder and let it fall. "Ever since I was three, I knew my father didn't want to have anything to do with me. I thought that was my fault."

"But you know it wasn't."

It was easier to talk about her insecurities when she was staring at his chin. His outraged expression made her feel even worse. “These days, sure. But it hurt for a long time and I forged some armor that I wear when I’m feeling vulnerable.”

“You don’t need to wear it around me.”

He kissed her with reverent gentleness, endeavoring to heal her hurts with tenderness. Violet’s chest ached. Falling deep in love with him was so easy when he offered her his support like this. But she couldn’t help but be saddened by the fact that he wouldn’t let her help him in kind.

In the calm after their earlier passion, JT and Violet snuggled in his big bed, their hands offering comfort and connection, their lips meeting in affection. They exchanged no words. The union of their bodies was an effortless way to communicate.

Violet didn’t return to the problem of how to broach the subject of his father’s possible identity theft until almost five in the morning. JT lay on his stomach beside her, hands buried under the pillow, his features softened by sleep. She reclined on her side, head propped in her hand and watched him. Memories of their lovemaking moved through her nerves like a breeze through a weeping willow. Her hormones stirred lazily in response.

Too wide awake to sleep and knowing she’d be tempted to rouse JT if she kept staring at all his naked glory, Violet slipped from the bed and put on a robe. The moratorium regarding her skinny-dipping had been lifted and she padded downstairs. Earlier, their hasty retreat to the bedroom meant that the living room’s glass walls had not been closed. Nor had the lights been turned off anywhere. Violet moved through the various rooms and left a trail of darkness in her wake.

The warm night air pressed against her skin as she stripped off the robe and used the stairs to enter the pool. Despite the water’s comfortable temperature, she shivered. Swimming had always been both a way to exercise and a method for sorting through whatever problems she was having.

She’d been on both her high school and college swim teams. Maybe she hadn’t been the fastest competitor, but driven by a fierce desire to catch her father's attention, she'd worked harder than most. All in vain, of course, because it wasn't as if he'd ever attended a meet. Eventually she'd accepted that their lack of a relationship was her father's loss not hers, and she'd learned a valuable lesson in loyalty. Never would she let anyone down. If she gave her word, she would move heaven and earth to keep it.

Which brought her to the file on Preston Rhodes. Tomorrow she would show JT what it contained. With the stockholder meeting approaching and his father still holding all the cards, if they had the chance to discredit him, they needed to take it. But was JT ready to destroy the last member of his immediate family?

Violet left the pool and grabbed a quick shower in the pool house before returning to the master suite. Dropping the damp towel on the floor, she climbed naked between the sheets. Convinced she'd left and returned without waking JT, she was surprised when his arms snaked around her waist, drawing her firmly against his side.

With his face buried in the crook of her neck, he murmured, "You smell like chlorine."

"Impossible. I showered before coming back here."

"It's barely detectible, but there." He pressed his lips against the pulse in her throat. "I wouldn't have thought you'd have enough energy for a swim. I guess I'll have to do better at wearing you out."

She laughed at the sting of his nip. "I didn't swim. I waded. It isn't always about burning off excess energy. Sometimes it just feels good to hang out and enjoy the scenery."

"Is that what you were doing tonight? Enjoying the scenery?"

"And thinking."

"About what?"

She hesitated, unsure she wanted to disrupt JT's good mood. "About the upcoming stockholders' meeting and the shares we still need."

JT stopped kissing her neck and lay very still. "I don't want you worrying about that. This is my battle to fight, you've done enough."

"This is my fight, too." Although she was certain he was merely trying to protect her, Violet bristled. "Don't shut me out. I can help."

"My father. My problem."

"We're married. Our problem."

"It's a paper marriage."

"Don't do that," she told him, an ache building in her throat. "Don't shut me out."

He heaved a sigh and rolled away from her, coming to rest on his back. She pursued him across the mattress, sitting up so she could peer down at his face. His eyes remained hard, but his hand scooped her hip, thumb moving rhythmically against her waist.

"You never stop pushing, do you?"

She set her left hand on his chest. His grandmother's ring snared the dawning light drifting in through the open window. They both stared at it.

At long last she asked, her voice scarcely rising about a whisper, "Do you want me to?"

They both knew what she wanted to know. Did she take off the ring and walk away from the marriage? Or did she stay and did they both commit to making their relationship grow and strengthen?

"What you're asking from me isn't easy."

"I know." Relief made her dizzy. He hadn't immediately challenged her bluff. "But we're a good team and we need each other."

"You need me?"

"Don't sound so surprised." Being with him she felt a part of something bigger than either of them could ever be alone. "I'm not as unselfish as you believe." She laid her cheek on his chest and snuggled against his side. "You make me feel safe and secure. I know I can count on you."

"You never seem as if you need anyone's help."

"I may be everyone's cheerleader, but once in a while, I appreciate it when someone has my back." She lifted her head and met his gaze. "I like it when you're that someone."

"You know you will always be able to call on me for anything."

She gave him a wistful smile. It wasn't a passionate declaration of love, but it was a heartfelt promise he would never betray. And she accepted at this moment it was everything he was capable of giving.

In close proximity to the kitchen, an extensive covered patio contained a barbeque pit, a seating area with fireplace and flat screen television and a table that seated eight. Unless he was entertaining, JT rarely used the space. Most often he ate a quick meal in the kitchen before heading out to the hotel or the barn. But since Violet had moved in, he'd spent a fair amount of time enjoying all the amenities.

This morning, the table was strewn with bowls of fruit, plates of bacon, eggs and waffles. More food than either of them could eat. But as soon as Violet had handed him the file on his father, he'd lost all appetite.

"This can't be real." He set the file aside and rubbed the bridge of his nose where a headache was starting.

"Maybe," Violet replied, her tone neutral. "Maybe not."

"Have you read the whole thing?"

"Twice."

"It's ridiculous. My father grew up in California. I've heard him speak about his parents and his childhood in Los Angeles. He's not some wannabe thug from Las Vegas."

"That was my exact attitude when Scarlett brought it to my attention. I thought the whole thing was crazy and told her so."

A chill formed in JT's chest. "Who else knows about this?"

Her gaze sharpened as she caught onto his irritation. "Just

Harper. She was there when Scarlett gave me the file. You don't need to worry about her. She won't say anything."

"Do you have to share everything about me with your sisters?" His aggrieved tone made her flinch, but his resentment bit too deep for him to apologize. He'd barely gotten comfortable sharing bits of himself with Violet and it made him surly to think that her sisters knew a devastating secret about his father.

"They won't say anything," she said, using her fork to shred the uneaten waffle on her plate.

"I don't know that."

His logical side reminded him that behaving as if he didn't trust her would create problems between them. But he couldn't ignore his emotions as they sliced him with a double-edged sword of alarm and resentment.

"Well, I do."

Hearing the conviction in Violet's tone, JT let the matter drop, recognizing the true source of his disquiet was not Violet or her sisters. He didn't want to believe his father had stolen someone's identity.

Because if his father wasn't just greedy or ambitious, but despicable beyond belief, couldn't that badness have been passed down to his son?

Wasn't JT the reason his mother had died? He'd been acting out, defying her, and she'd died of an overdose. His adult brain could reason that she'd chosen to take the pills, but he was haunted by the question of whether she'd been so upset with him that she'd taken too many. And there was no denying if he'd come home straight after school that day, she might still be alive.

He stared at the information contained in the file about George Barnes and Preston Rhodes and wondered what the reporter from L.A. knew. "When were you planning to call this Charity Rimes person?"

"I thought it was something we should do together. Perhaps even go to Los Angeles and meet with her in person." She shrugged. "Or we could drop it entirely. Like you said, it's ridiculous that your father stole someone's identity in 1970."

Violet was too forthright to be able to hide her confusion or disappointment at his rejection of the information she'd brought him. Nor could JT point to where this surge of loyalty was coming from. What did he think he owed his father? Preston had never done anything with JT's best interests in mind.

"Let me think about it," JT muttered and Violet nodded, the gesture stiff and jerky.

Because if they discovered his father actually was George Barnes, JT would then have to decide if he should send his father to prison or simply use the information to blackmail Preston into stepping down? Neither appealed to JT. He'd much rather defeat his father the old-fashioned way: by being a better businessman.

Violet finished applying her makeup and checked her appearance in the bathroom mirror. She'd done an acceptable job of hiding the dark circles under her eyes caused by her sleepless night, but nothing could be done about the churning in her stomach.

Right after breakfast, JT had headed to the barn where he'd remained for the rest of the day. As difficult as it had been to give him space when her instincts demanded she make him feel better, she'd stayed in the house and hoped he would forgive her for delivering such a difficult message.

Her wait had been in vain. At three she'd discovered that JT had already left for Titanium. He'd gone to work without letting her know he was leaving. That meant she'd have to be patient for a little while longer and hope uncertainty wouldn't eat her alive.

Instead of heading to Fontaine Chic where she knew a hundred decisions awaited her, Violet detoured to Scarlett's hotel and tracked her sister down in the casino. Scarlett would be eager to learn how Violet's conversation with JT had gone and Violet needed a sympathetic ear.

"I was right to fear that JT wouldn't react well to Tiberius's suspicions about Preston," Violet said, as they wound their way past a hundred slot machines to a dessert bar on the second floor. "And I couldn't blame him for being upset with me."

"You did nothing wrong," Scarlett reminded her.

"I feel as if I did. He was upset because you and Harper knew what was in the file and was worried you'd tell someone. He didn't believe me when I told him you wouldn't. I wish he trusted me."

"I'm sure he does. Remember you'd just brought him shocking information about his father. No matter how strained their relationship or how badly he wants his dad to step down as CEO, Preston is still JT's father."

"Is it crazy that I'm afraid the progress we've made in our relationship has been dealt a deadly blow today?"

"Not crazy at all. But I do think you're worrying for nothing." Scarlett looped her arm through Violet's and pulled her before a glass display case loaded with absolutely scrumptious-looking treats. "We'll take one of those chocolate shells filled with white chocolate mousse and a hazelnut gelato-filled cream puff with Kahlua chocolate sauce," Scarlett said to the counter person. Catching Violet staring at her in astonishment, Scarlett grinned. "What? Heartache calls for fancy desserts."

Violet carried the tray of desserts to a table by the window that overlooked the extensive, beautifully landscaped grounds at the back of the hotel. Scarlett arrived seconds later with cups of espresso.

"I don't know why I was so caught off guard by JT's reaction." Violet dug into the white chocolate mousse. "Barely two weeks ago we were little more than casual acquaintances and today I told him his father might be a criminal."

"Do you really think you two have ever been casual?" Scarlett asked. "You may not have been friends, but there was a strong pull between you. I saw it that night in Baccarat."

"I've been attracted to him since the first time I saw him."

"I'll bet he felt the same way. Wouldn't surprise me if Tiberius warned him off."

"I'm sure the issue never came up."

"So how did you two leave things?"

"JT is deciding if we should contact Charity Rimes."

"What do you think he'll do?"

Violet shook her head. "I think he'll want to do the right thing, but loyalty is really important to him and no matter how complicated their relationship is, JT will feel as if he's betraying his father." She finished the mousse-filled chocolate cup and began on the half of the cream puff Scarlett pushed onto her plate. "You know, I think he was almost as upset that I'm the one delivering this news about his father as he was by the thought that his dad might be a criminal."

"It makes sense," Scarlett said. "He's not a man who wears his heart on his sleeve. Watching you two last night, it was obvious you have pried the oyster out of his shell. He trusts you, but behaviors rooted in childhood trauma are difficult to overcome and the more vulnerable he feels, the more he will overreact if he something scares him." Scarlett's lips curved. "And baby, the way you make him feel terrifies him."

"I don't want him to be afraid." Doing the right thing shouldn't cause this much anxiety and hurt. "I want him to be happy."

"I know, and he'll get there."

But what if he never did? JT hadn't yet learned to make lemonade out of lemons and wasn't ready to rely on her for his well-being. The stockholders' meeting was less than a month away. If he refused to let her in, she was convinced he would demand the divorce they'd agreed to in the beginning. And that would be bad. He needed her. She reminded him to laugh and appreciated his romantic soul. And she needed him. He made love to her with a ferocity she'd never known before. In JT's arms, she wasn't a team player. She was a star.

Buoyed by Scarlett's assurances and a great deal of sugar,

Violet went about her day with a lighter heart. It wasn't like her to worry about what hadn't happened yet. Obviously JT was rubbing off on her. If only she were having the same effect on him.

At five her cell phone rang. To her delight, JT was calling. She answered, hoping to keep her emotional state from showing up in her voice. "Hello, husband."

"Hello, wife. I'm calling to apologize."

Lightheaded, Violet leaned against a nearby pillar and squeezed her eyes shut. "No need."

"As always, you are patient and understanding, but I simply must insist on making up to you for my bad behavior this morning."

"What did you have in mind?"

"Room service. Your suite. Fifteen minutes?"

"Sounds perfect." After hanging up with him, she called her assistant and rescheduled the next three hours of meetings. Then she raced toward the elevators and jabbed impatiently at the Up button.

Ten minutes later she'd ordered a steak dinner to be served in an hour, dabbed perfume in all the places JT enjoyed exploring and was waiting for him wearing a smile and a nightie that left just enough to the imagination.

Her approach had been perfect because two seconds after he shut her door, he whisked her into his arms and made straight for the bedroom. A half an hour later she sat astride his narrow hips, breathing heavily in the aftermath of a powerful orgasm, feeling him pulse inside her.

"I could get used to this," he said, cupping her face and pulling her down for a long, slow kiss.

"Me on top?" She gave him a cheeky smile.

"You period."

Her heart lurched. It was the closest he'd come to mentioning the future. She drew his lower lip between her teeth and sucked gently. Beneath her, his chest rose and fell unsteadily.

"No reason you can't," she murmured, showing him how much she had to offer.

"I guess it's something we should talk about."

In her head she was screaming, *Please, can we discuss it now?* What came out of her mouth was a restrained, "I'd like that."

When the door chimed announcing their dinner, JT slipped on his pants and went to let in the waiter. Violet took a second to throw on a robe and run a comb through her disheveled hair. By the time she entered the living room, her small table had been set for an intimate dinner for two, complete with candles, crystal and china.

"It smells wonderful," JT commented as he held her chair while she sat down.

Violet lifted the silver dish covers and set them aside. By now she knew JT liked his meat rare and his vegetables steamed seconds beyond crisp. "Sixty-day dry-aged steak straight from Fontaine Chic's award-winning steakhouse," she said. "With sides of potatoes rosti and asparagus with aged Parmesan and browned butter."

"What are these?" JT pointed to three small bowls.

"Red wine sauce, Béarnaise and a truffle sauce that I haven't yet tried."

"Sounds wonderful."

"Only the best for you." And she meant it. "And for dessert—"

"You're all the sweet I need."

With her insides turned to mush, Violet finished, "Berries with cream."

She watched JT put a piece of steak in his mouth and chew reverently. "This is amazing. There's nothing to compare at Titanium."

He was in such a good mood she hated to spoil it with the question that had plagued her all day: what was he going to do about the information Tiberius had dug up on George Barnes?

"I was lucky Chef Baron agreed to open his third restaurant with us," Violet said, squashing her curiosity.

"I'm sure luck had nothing to do with it," JT said. "You can be quite persuasive."

The compliment warmed her faster than a July day on the strip. "When I know what I want, I go after it."

"I'm very aware of that." A lopsided grin tugged at his lips. "In fact, I'm amazed that you haven't asked if I've decided to call Charity Rimes. I imagine you're dying to know."

"I'd be lying if I said it's the furthest thing from my thoughts." She carefully phrased her next words. "But I can't imagine what a difficult choice you have to make."

"If you'd found out Tiberius had done something terrible, what would you do?"

The question was fair, but it left Violet with a terrible conundrum. She'd always had faith in Tiberius. He'd taken her in and loved her like his daughter. Her faith in his honesty had never been shaken.

"I'd like to say that I'd turn him in and never doubt myself for doing so." Violet gave JT's hand a sympathetic squeeze. "But I don't think I'd ever forgive myself for being disloyal."

JT carried her hand to his lips and kissed her palm. "After dinner, let's call Charity Rimes."

"Okay." Delighted that JT trusted her to help, Violet tucked into the meal with gusto. "I'm glad I didn't order a heavy dessert," she said as they dueled over the last berry. "I don't remember the last time I ate so much."

"Everything tasted so good, it was hard to stop."

Leaving the dishes for later, JT tugged Violet toward the couch. Together they sank into its softness. With JT's left arm around her shoulder and his right hand playing absently with the tie of her robe, Violet waited for some sign from JT that he was ready to hear what Charity Rimes had to say.

"Do you think my father belongs in jail?"

"If he stole someone's identity, yes."

JT closed his eyes and for a brief moment sadness blanketed his expression. Violet's chest tightened sympathetically at his pain. She wished she could take it away. She wanted nothing but happiness for him. But she could only offer comfort and support. JT would have to resolve his ambivalence on his own.

"Make the call," he said, his voice hard and determined.

Reluctant to budge from the circle of JT's arm, but knowing she had to act while he was still in a mood to find out what the writer knew, Violet snagged her cell off the coffee table and found Charity's number. She dialed and then held the phone so JT could listen.

"Yes?" A male voice answered.

Violet and JT exchanged a puzzled look. "Hello. I'm looking for Charity Rimes."

"Are you a friend?"

The man's question awakened Violet's anxiety. "Not exactly. My name is Violet Fontaine. She spoke with my father several months ago about a book she was writing. I was hoping to find out what she told him."

"Can't you just ask him?"

She wanted to demand he let her speak to Charity, but some instinct stopped her. "He died." She left out the part where Tiberius had been murdered.

A long silence followed. At last the man spoke. "I'm sorry about your father, but Charity won't be able to help you right now. She was in an accident. Her car was T-boned by an SUV."

"Is she okay?"

"She has some broken ribs and a head injury that the doctors want to monitor."

JT frowned and stood. Violet's gaze followed his tense form as he paced across the room. She could only imagine his disappointment. Since this morning he'd had to assimilate potentially damning news about his father and decide whether or not to pursue the truth. No matter how damaged their relationship, inside JT was a little boy who'd once looked up to his father.

"Please tell her I hope she'll be okay. Perhaps I can call again at a later date."

"Do you want to leave your number? I can have her call you."

"That would be nice." Violet gave him the numbers for her cell and the direct line to her office phone. When she hung up a gust of air poured from her lungs. "How crazy was that?"

"It appears as if fate has once again beaten me to the punch," JT replied, his voice wearing a frustrated edge.

"We still have over three weeks until the stockholders' meeting and your cousin Phil has promised to throw his vote your way."

"That means we have forty-nine and a half percent. My father wins." He headed to the bedroom and retrieved the rest of his clothes. "I'd better get back to Titanium. There's one last relative I can call. I didn't want to reach out to her, but maybe the favor she will demand in return won't be as bad as I think."

Violet could tell this wasn't the right time to reassure JT that everything would be okay. He was obviously too disappointed in the phone call to Charity Rimes to believe that the future would work itself out for the best.

"I'll see you at home," she called before he shut the door behind him.

After a quick shower, Violet dressed and returned to her office just in time to make the first of her rescheduled meetings. Even though it was hard to concentrate, she gave it her all. JT's problems would work themselves out one way or another. All he needed to do was trust that when the time came, he'd choose the right path.

And what about her? Would he want her beside him? Violet knew she'd better brace herself in case he didn't.

CHAPTER NINE

"HE'S LEANING. You want to lift his inside shoulder," JT called. "Trot him in a tight circle." The young rider did as asked, and JT nodded. "Do you feel him balance himself?"

Her bright smile was answer enough.

JT followed her progress around the area, but his attention wasn't complete. Part of him was thinking about the stockholders' meeting a week away while another portion gnawed on his relationship with Violet and what he wanted for the future.

It was relatively easy to drop his guard with her. Her lack of an agenda, coupled with her unflagging positivity, and ability to distract him from his problems made her company a balm to his troubled soul.

She seemed to understand, though not appreciate, that he possessed secrets he didn't want to share. JT knew it was unfair. She'd given him so much of herself. That he continued to hold back made their relationship uneven. He didn't know how to fix it without risking losing her. But would she eventually get frustrated with him and leave?

In the beginning, they'd agreed to divorce after the shareholders' meeting. He hadn't yet decided how to ask her to give their marriage a little more time. He'd grown accustomed to having her around.

She'd coaxed him out of his shell. He was happy. But was she? And was it fair of him to take advantage of her generosity and give her little in return?

The question plagued him through the rest of the afternoon. He listed the pros and cons of being married to Violet, pitting logic against emotion and measuring the ratio of risk to reward. In the end, after he'd applied all his business decision-making skills, it all came down to what he needed to be truly happy.

That evening, as he waited for her to show up at Baccarat, he faced the troubling reality of his situation. No matter how many objections he'd unearthed for staying married, the biggest factor in his decision was that he was falling in love with his wife. "Good evening, husband," Violet said, sitting down beside him on the couch. "What has Rick concocted for you tonight?"

JT glanced at the drink in his hand and realized he'd consumed half of it without tasting a drop. "I have no idea."

"Let me." She plucked the glass from his grasp and sipped. "Blissful Ignorance. Plum gin, red wine syrup, egg white, lemon juice, rose water and balsamic. One of my favorites."

He blinked, a little surprised by her memory and vastly turned on by the way she licked her lips and smiled. Everything about her unleashed his desire. No sooner had he figured out one habit that aroused him than she exhibited another. To say she fascinated him would be an understatement.

"A client wants my opinion on a horse that's for sale in Kentucky," he blurt without preliminaries. "And I thought I'd take a side trip to my family's farm outside Louisville."

"I'm sure your family will be happy to see you."

"Come with me."

They could both use a change of scenery and he very much wanted to show her where he'd spent the happiest moments of his childhood.

"I'd like that. When?"

"Tomorrow."

"I'll clear my schedule." Her willingness to drop everything and run off to Kentucky said that she too felt the need to clear her head. "How long has it been since you've visited?"

"About six months. I try to get there a couple times a year." The farm was the only place he'd ever felt completely at home.

"It must be wonderful," Violet said. "I've never seen you look so happy."

"Never?" He lifted her palm to his cheek and gave her a wolfish smile. "Then you'll just have to pay close attention later tonight."

Her eyebrows rose. "I'll make sure I do."

After a night filled with lots of blissful smiles and very little sleep, they boarded the private jet JT's client had sent to take him to Kentucky.

"Nice," Violet murmured, accepting a mimosa from the flight attendant and relaxing into a butter-soft leather chair. "Fontaine owns several corporate jets, but none as nice as this one. Who's your client?"

"She's a member of the royal family of Dubai." JT smiled at Violet's wide-eyed reaction. "A princess who has a passion for horses and show jumping."

"I had no idea you were so well connected."

"We met in Miami many years ago and struck up a friendship. She knew my grandmother's reputation and likes to get my opinion when she's planning on spending six figures on a horse."

"I am impressed." Violet eyed him over the rim of her glass. "And more than a little turned on."

JT chuckled. "Then my work here is done."

The farm where JT was to evaluate the jumper was about an hour away from his family's farm, Briton Green. The plane touched down at the regional airport less than fifteen minutes away and JT's cousin Samantha was waiting to greet them. He dropped the suitcases an instant before she threw her arms around him and hugged him hard. Tall and slender, with long, dark blond hair and an infectious grin, she had always been a whirling dervish of energy.

"It's great to see you." As soon as she stopped choking JT, she turned her attention to Violet. "I'm Samantha."

"Violet. JT talked non-stop about you the whole way here. It's nice to meet you."

"Likewise." Samantha looped her arm through Violet's and drew her toward the waiting SUV.

JT followed the two women at a slower pace. Already he felt as if the weight of the world had fallen from his shoulders and they hadn't even arrived at the farm.

"How are things?" he quizzed as Samantha sped down the highway.

"Wonderful. Dancing Diva had a gorgeous colt. Mom's convinced he's the best foal we've produced in ten years."

"That's saying something." In the last decade, three national champions had been foaled at Briton Green. "I can't wait to see him. What can you tell me about the six-year-old I'm looking at over at Cal Rutledge's place?"

Samantha nodded. "Nice mover. Good legs. Athletic. I think they've had a few issues with his work ethic."

"Meaning?"

"He's lazy."

"Worth what they're asking?"

"I'd offer them thirty-five and see what happens." Samantha had always been a tough bargainer. "Is the princess open to looking at any other horses?"

"Who'd you have in mind?"

"A client of Roger Simmons has a really nice eight-year-old mare. She's done really well in the show ring, but she needs a smart rider. Roger's had trouble finding someone good enough for her."

"Never hurts to look. Any others you can suggest?"

Samantha laughed. "JT, I could keep you busy for a month looking at all the talent we have in the area."

"Unfortunately I don't have a month."

When they arrived at the farm, they were met by his mother's cousin, Phyllis, Samantha's mother. His grandmother and Phyllis's mother, Adele, had been sisters. When JT's grandmother had married and moved to Miami, Adele had stayed and taken over the running of the farm. They'd owned stock in Stone Properties, given to them by JT's grandfather in exchange for startup capital. Tiberius had bought their shares of Stone Properties stock from them months earlier.

JT hugged his aunt and introduced her to Violet. "The farm looks great," he remarked as they entered the large Greek revival house. "Samantha tells me you had a bumper crop of foals this year."

"She's dying to show them off to you." Phyllis led them into the large living room where a maid had just finished setting a pitcher of sweet tea on the sideboard. "Lunch will be served in half an hour. Would you like something to drink?"

Violet accepted a glass of tea and perched on a damask chair. The house had been built in the late 1850s and had all its original furniture. It was a vastly different from Violet's two-year-old, ultramodern hotel and she looked overwhelmed by the history embedded in every inch of the home.

"I see you're wearing my aunt's wedding ring," Phyllis remarked, her expression friendly, but slightly curious. "When JT called to tell us he was coming and bringing his new bride, we were very excited to meet you." She was too well-bred to admit her curiosity, but JT could see her eyes were bright with it.

"I was excited to meet you as well," Violet said. "I know JT spent a lot of time here as a kid."

"Where did you grow up?" Phyllis asked.

"In Las Vegas."

"What do you do there?"

"I manage a hotel and casino on the strip. Fontaine Chic. My grandfather is CEO of Fontaine Resorts and Hotels."

JT could tell Phyllis was surprised at his choice in wife. Before Violet, he'd gone for style over substance. It made it easier to remain unattached. With Violet, he had the best of both worlds. And he was in way over his head.

"That must keep you very busy," Phyllis remarked, glancing in JT's direction. "This one here has a very difficult time tearing himself away for a visit."

"Between Titanium and the ranch, he has way more on his plate than I do." Violet covered his hand with hers. "Most days I'm lucky if see him at all."

"I'm sure he understands that a wife should never be neglected," Phyllis remarked dryly.

No one in the room could have missed what Phyllis referred to. For several seconds there was complete silence. At last Violet spoke.

"It's fortunate that our work schedules are similar," she murmured.

"I'm sure." Phyllis then took pity on her and changed the subject to what was happening with JT's cousins since they'd last spoken.

After lunch, Samantha took them on a tour of the barns. There were three altogether, housing horses owned by JT's family as well as their clients. They began in the mare's barn. Violet lost track of how many horses she'd petted and how many foals she'd seen either peering out from behind their mother or boldly stepping forward to greet the newcomers. She was completely charmed by the time they headed to the training barn.

"Do you ride?" Samantha asked.

In addition to being a breeding farm, Briton Green had an outstanding reputation as a training facility.

"I'm learning." Violet glanced at JT. "He's given me a few lessons."

"She has a good seat for a beginner."

"We should all take a ride later."

JT glanced at his watch. "I don't think we'll have time. I

have a four o'clock appointment with Cal to see what he's offering to Husna."

Samantha looked disappointed. "How about you, Violet?"

"I don't mind going alone to my appointment," JT said.

As much as she'd love to see more of the farm by horseback, she'd come on this trip to spend time with JT. "Maybe tomorrow before we leave?"

With that settled, they quickly toured the training barn and then JT and Violet headed out.

"It's easy to see why horses got into your blood," she remarked as they raced along the country highway in the SUV they'd borrowed from Samantha. "There's something so grounding about them."

"They keep you in the moment. A smart rider is one who anticipates that even the most well-mannered horse might react badly to something in his environment."

"I guess focusing on the present is a good thing for all of us to do from time to time." She'd been spending too much time speculating about what would happen in the aftermath of the stockholders' meeting.

"Is that comment meant for me?" he quizzed, without a trace of acidity in his tone.

"Actually, I meant it as a reminder to myself. I've been doing a lot of thinking about the future. Our future," she clarified, searching his expression for some sign that he had picked up on what was troubling her.

"I've given it some thought as well." He stopped speaking, but didn't appear as if he'd said all he intended to so Violet waited him out in silence "The shareholders' meeting is a week away. We agreed to part ways after that."

Violet held her breath, hoping he felt the same way she did. This time JT's pause was longer. She couldn't keep quiet another second.

"I don't want to divorce you."

JT took his gaze off the road and let her see the yearning that filled his eyes. "I feel the same way." He captured her hand and lifted her fingers to his lips. "Having you in my life is the best thing that has happened to me in a long time."

"Me, too." And it made her realize that if she hadn't already been falling in love with JT she never would have suggested they marry in the first place.

"Are you sure you understand what you're getting with me?" JT asked, holding their clasped hands against his chest. "I'm not the easiest man to live with."

"I know." He still had secrets locked up inside him that caused pain and made him retreat from her. She might never know everything about him, but she'd come to terms with that before she'd decided to fight for their marriage. "I also know you don't fully trust me with everything that happened in your past."

"Are you sure you can live with that?"

How could she answer him when she didn't know herself? "I'm going to try."

As if admitting their heart's desire had drained the energy available for conversation, they both lapsed into silence. Violet stared at the green landscape around the car and waited for her rapid heartbeat to return to normal.

JT wanted to stay married. She made him happy. The thought thrilled her. But Violet wasn't a hopeless romantic.

What lay between them still required work and trust in order to grow, but the fact that neither of them appeared ready to throw in the towel gave them a fighting chance.

The conversation in the SUV had cleared the subtle tension between them. To Violet's delight, JT smiled more readily than she'd ever seen and his kisses grew abundantly more plentiful and passionate.

Snuggling with JT beneath the handmade quilt in the guest room, Violet sighed in utter contentment.

"I'd love it if we could come back here and stay longer," she told him. "I've really enjoyed meeting your family and want to get to know them better."

"I think they feel the same way."

"You're lucky to have them." She pondered her own lack of extended family and sighed. "Until Scarlett and Harper came along I didn't have any family but my mom and Tiberius."

"I get why you weren't in contact with the Fontaine family, but what about your mom's relatives?"

"She lost contact with them after coming to Las Vegas. I asked about them a couple times, but it really upset her so I stopped mentioning them." Violet had gotten the feeling that her mother had been running from an unhappy place when she left home.

"I'm sorry you grew up like that."

"It was okay. At the time I didn't know any different. The lack of family didn't really bother me until after college when I was in a friend's wedding." It had been a huge affair with six bridesmaids and groomsmen. The bride had looked radiant walking down the aisle on her father's arm. "I was the only one of the wedding party that wasn't a family member."

"Does it bother you that we got married without your family there?"

Violet didn't have to think about her answer. "A little. Mostly it bothered me that Tiberius wasn't there to give me away."

"When the shareholder meeting is over we should get married again. Properly this time. With friends and family around us."

"You don't have to do this for me." But she was thrilled that he'd suggested it.

"I'm doing it for us. We should make a fresh start." He kissed her on the forehead. "A real marriage deserves a real wedding. Don't you think?"

Violet tilted her head back so she could read JT's expression. His tender smile made her heart hiccup.

"It sounds like a perfect idea."

CHAPTER TEN

JT WAS IN his office reviewing a capital expenditure request for remodeling the exercise room and upgrading the machines when his assistant hailed him on his phone's intercom.

"Mr. Rhodes is on line one."

It was three days until the stockholder meeting and JT remained short of the votes he needed to oust his father as chairman of the board and strip him of his CEO position. Was Preston calling to gloat?

"Hello, Father."

"You didn't really expect to beat me, did you, son?" Preston gave the final word a disparaging twist. "I've taken on much more skilled players than you."

"I've no doubt you have."

"Then you won't be surprised when I tell you that I'm in negotiations to sell Titanium."

"Not surprised at all." JT had known that challenging his father would be a one-shot deal. He either secured the votes to get Preston voted out as chairman or went out on his own. JT wasn't afraid to do the latter. He'd been ready to abandon any hope of saving Stone Properties before Violet had inherited Tiberius's stock.

"I'm sure we can find you a hotel to manage somewhere,"

Preston said. “I think the general manager of Platinum Macao plans to retire later this year.”

JT saw no reason to react to his father’s taunt. “I’m certain you have a number of managers who would jump at the chance to take over that hotel. I have several opportunities I can explore.”

“Perhaps your wife can find you a job working for Fontaine Resorts and Hotels.”

“In fact we’ve already discussed that,” JT lied. Why was his father trying so hard to get him riled up? “Fontaine is negotiating to buy the Lucky Heart. They’re planning to demolish it and build a new hotel. They want someone who can oversee the entire process.”

More lies. JT had no idea what would become of the Lucky Heart now that Tiberius was dead, but investigating the fabrication would distract his father for a little while.

“You were lucky to marry your heiress when you did.”

“Is there anything else you’d like to discuss?” JT glanced at his watch and saw it was almost time to rendezvous with Violet. They’d taken to enjoying late dinners in her suite. “Otherwise I have a meeting I must get to.”

“Nothing else. I’ll see you in Miami in a few days.”

“Looking forward to it.” JT hung up without saying goodbye, unsure if it had been worth his effort to try and shake his father’s confidence.

Before leaving his office, JT signed off on the exercise room upgrade, then made his way to the first floor and strolled through the casino. As much as he loved the hotel and was proud of all he’d done to turn the property around in the last six years, JT had always known that his time here was limited. As CEO, his father called the shots. JT could stay working for Stone Properties and do what Preston wanted or abandon the company and strike out on his own. Leaving would have been better for him financially and professionally, but he knew his grandfather would want him to stay and loyalty was deeply imbedded in his psyche.

Even at nine o'clock at night the air on the strip hung hot and thick with exhaust and the sweat of many thousands of bodies. JT sucked in a lungful. Leaving Las Vegas had just become inevitable. The investment opportunities he'd been investigating had involved properties in California, Arizona and the Caribbean. He would be traveling a great deal and setting up his corporate office here didn't seem likely.

What did that mean for him and Violet? They had agreed to stay married. Maybe that had been shortsighted of him. Or she'd gotten him so accustomed to thinking positive that he hadn't truly believed he would lose. Tonight they would have to discuss what changes the future would bring.

Violet sent him a text as he entered the suite to say she was running fifteen minutes late and that the dinner she'd ordered would arrive before she did. JT saw her dining table was littered with copies of Tiberius's files on his family. They'd been going through them the night before, talking strategy. A waste of time. It would take a miracle to topple his father's solid base of supporters.

Was it idiotic of him to ignore the possibility that his father had committed a crime? Preston Rhodes, or George Barnes if he bought into Scarlett's theory, was a ruthless bastard to those who stood in his way. He'd schemed to turn JT's grandfather against his only son. He'd psychologically abused his wife until she'd turned to drugs and alcohol and overdosed. And he'd blackmailed a Stone Properties stockholder to manipulate the annual vote in his favor.

Maybe it was time someone pushed back. And who better than the son he was determined to hurt next.

Not wanting to start their evening by talking about his father, JT gathered the files and carried them into her home office. He set the pile on her desk and was turning to go when a lone file caught his eye.

JT looked closer and went cold as he spied his name in Tiberius's handwriting on the tab.

Violet had a file on him.

If Tiberius had investigated Preston's past, didn't it make sense that he'd have looked at JT as well? And when he'd left his files to Scarlett, of course she would share his file with her sister.

Dread collecting in the pit of his stomach, JT opened the file and stared at the top sheet. It was the police report on his mother's death. They'd ruled it an accidental overdose but right there in black and white was JT's darkest secret.

How long had Violet pretended not to know what he'd done? Had she played him for a fool from the start? Acted as if it was important that he confide in her when she'd already known every agonizing truth of his childhood. Bile rose in JT's throat at her betrayal.

Below the police report was a copy of the psychiatrist's initial assessment when JT had been hospitalized for a severe concussion and broken ribs after trying to jump his bicycle over his father's yellow Ferrari convertible. He'd attempted the risky stunt a month after his mother's death. Based on the timing, the doctor had determined he was depressed and put him on medication. But no pill had been capable of taking away JT's guilt.

A knock sounded on the suite's front door startling JT. For a long black moment he'd been twelve again, hearing the news that his mother was dead. Lightheaded, he backed away from Violet's desk and those horrible childhood memories.

His heart pounded madly as he shook his head to clear it. There was a second knock on the front door. Rousing himself, JT made his way through the living room and let in the waiter. The smell of the food turned his stomach as it passed and he stood in the doorway while the man unloaded the dishes onto the dining room table. Moving on autopilot, JT signed for their dinner and was about to close the door when Violet stepped off the elevator and headed down the hallway towards him.

"It smells wonderful," she said cheerfully, lifting on tiptoe to press her lips to his.

JT stood with his hands at his sides and didn't return her kiss. She pulled back with a frown and surveyed his expression.

"What's happened?" she asked, closing the door.

"You have a file on me."

Guilt flashed across her lovely features and drove a spear into his heart. "Tiberius had a file on all of us."

"All this time you've been lying to me." A heavy note of sadness weighed down his voice.

"That's not true."

"You've known everything all along and pretended you didn't."

"Scarlett gave me the file," Violet explained. "But I've never opened it. If I've done anything wrong it was in not handing over the file to you as soon as I got it."

"You really expect me to believe that you didn't satisfy your curiosity about me by reading what my uncle dug up about my life?"

"If I had, why would I bother to ask you to share your past with me?"

"To make me believe you were the perfect woman for me. It's all in there, you know. The psychologist's report explains that before my mother's death I badly wanted her love and when she chose my father over me I retreated into belligerence and bad behavior. The more I acted out, the less likely it was that anyonc would love me. And then you came along, and knowing what I most wanted was what I most feared, you did everything you could to make me trust you."

Violet looked stricken. "You don't know me at all if you believe I would ever manipulate you."

"No? You suggested we get married. You claimed my father threatened to sue us if we didn't act like a real married couple."

Now it was her turn to get angry. "I married you to help you."

"You married me to help yourself."

The part of him she'd touched with her compassion and optimism wanted very much to take her at her word, but he'd been protecting himself against being hurt for so long. It was a compulsion he couldn't resist.

"I spoke with my father tonight and he let me know he's selling Titanium. I'll be leaving Las Vegas to pursue some investment opportunities." He hadn't intended to present the situation so bluntly, but in lieu of what he'd discovered here tonight, he wasn't capable of being sensitive.

"How long will you be gone?"

"This is a permanent move. I'm going to sell the ranch and resettle elsewhere."

Violet recoiled as if he'd struck her. "Just like that without discussing it with me?"

"What would be the point? As per our original agreement as soon as the annual shareholder meeting is over, I'll be filing for divorce."

"Can't we talk about this?"

"There's really no point. Your life, your career is here. I have no reason to stay."

"You really don't get it, do you?" Violet's soft question resonated with compassion.

JT's chest ached to the point where he couldn't draw a full breath. "Get what?" he asked coldly.

"That I love you."

"I'm sorry you said that," JT told her, his voice low and flat.

Violet nodded. "I'm sure you are."

He'd torn out her heart and thrown it at her feet, but Violet wasn't about to let him think he'd won. His mask of indifference might have worked on her once upon a time, but she'd glimpsed his sensitivity. He'd rather be the most hated man on the planet than let people see his vulnerability.

Not that she was immune to what he'd told her. Stung by pain and disillusionment, he was going to isolate himself beyond anyone's ability to reach him. In her heart, she knew that was the last thing he wanted. If she'd shown him anything, it was that being alone only made him miserable.

"I don't think I'll stay for dinner." He stepped around her and put his hand on the doorknob.

"Before you go." Violet headed to her home office where she found the file that had destroyed any hope of happiness for her or JT. She straightened the pages he'd disrupted while reading and closed the cover. In less than a minute she'd returned with his file and the one on his father. "You should take these with you."

He looked ready to toss more angry words at her, but accepted the files in silence.

"If you need anything, just call," she added as he opened the door and stepped into the hallway.

His back stiffened as if she'd cursed at him. "Goodbye, Violet."

And then he was striding away, his long legs carrying him around the corner and out of sight. Only then did Violet turn into a puddle of shaking limbs and wracking sobs. She shut the door and slid onto the floor and wrapped her arms around her knees. Drawing a complete breath was impossible so she closed her eyes and let the storm roll over her. By the time she'd calmed enough to pick herself off the floor, half an hour had passed.

She stumbled into the living room and dropped onto the couch. Greeted by silence, she immediately grabbed her phone and texted her sisters.

I messed up. In my suite, could use some sympathetic company.

Harper was the first to respond. Bringing both red and white wine.

Scarlett texted a minute later. Got chocolate.

With a shaky smile Violet rubbed tears from her cheeks. How lucky she was to have two wonderful sisters who dropped everything in order to rush over to make her feel better. Fifteen minutes later, wearing sweats and feeling marginally calmer, Violet opened her door to admit Harper.

"Which one should we start with?" she quizzed holding both bottles out for inspection.

"Definitely the red," Violet replied, knowing Scarlett would vote for that as well. She led the way into the kitchen to find the bottle opener.

"What's with the uneaten dinner?" Harper quizzed.

"JT and I ended things before we had a chance to eat."

"What?" Scarlett demanded from the living room, having come through the door to the hallway Violet had left open. "How is that possible? You two were doing great." Scarlett came into the kitchen, and both her sisters stopped what they were doing.

Harper held up her hand as she took in Scarlett's outfit. "Before we get to that, can you please tell me what you're wearing?"

Scarlett looked surprised at the question. "It's Princess Leia's harem costume from *The Empire Strikes Back*."

"Were you wearing that in the casino?" Violet quizzed, imagining the ruckus her sister must have caused among the male customers.

"Don't be ridiculous. I wore it for Logan."

Harper looked sorry she'd asked.

"I didn't mean to interrupt your evening," Violet said.

"Don't worry about it. Logan understands that a call for help from one of my sisters will never be ignored."

Tears surged in Violet's eyes once more, causing Scarlett to curse and Harper to put her arms around Violet's shoulders.

"You guys are the best," she whispered past the lump in her throat.

Harper poured the wine and the three of them moved to the couch. Snuggled between her sisters, Violet sipped at the excellent red and told them about JT finding his file and accusing her of using its contents to trick him into marriage.

"How does he not realize that if anyone benefited from you two getting together it was him?" Harper demanded hotly.

"He's used to being manipulated," Violet said. "It's made him guarded and secretive."

Harper regarded her in dismay. “You’re still defending him?”

“She’s in love with him,” Scarlett said, patting Violet’s knee. “And if anyone is to blame in all this, it’s me. I never should have given you his file.”

“Not true. I could have given him the file immediately or shredded the thing. He never should have discovered it sitting on my desk.”

“But you aren’t to blame for the way he reacted,” Harper insisted.

“In a strange way, even though I never looked at what was in his file, I feel as if I betrayed him.”

Scarlett shook her head. “You’re acting far too reasonable. Rant. Cry. Call him terrible names. He deserves it.”

That wrung a weak smile from Violet. “You know I’ll never do that.”

“Any chance this will just blow over?” Harper asked.

Violet exhaled shakily. “Maybe if it had happened weeks ago, but we’ve grown really close recently. We’ve talked about the future and agreed to give our marriage a chance.”

“That could still happen.” Scarlett looked hopeful.

“Preston is selling Titanium. JT has no reason to stay in Las Vegas.”

“Bastard,” Scarlett muttered. “I think for JT’s sake we need to find out the truth about his father.”

Before tonight Violet might have protested that it was JT’s business not hers, but since he’d called it quits, she no longer had to consider his feelings in the matter. Still, guilt tweaked her. What if he didn’t want his father exposed?

“I spoke with Charity Rimes earlier today,” Violet admitted. “I was going to talk to JT about it tonight before…”

“What did she have to say?” Scarlett demanded, her expression alive with curiosity. “Why did Tiberius contact her?”

“Remember how she was doing research on a serial killer who was operating in Los Angeles in the sixties? He invaded homes and attacked families. The police never caught him.”

"How is that related to Preston?"

"Turns out one of the families killed was named Rhodes. They left behind a ten-year-old son, Preston, who'd been spending the night with a friend."

Harper had been leaning forward, fully engaged. Now she sank back against the couch cushions with a whoosh of exhaled air. "That's awful."

"Charity was blogging about the families who were killed and Tiberius had been running internet searching on Preston when he stumbled on her."

"So, how does this help us?" Harper persisted.

"After speaking with Tiberius, Charity got curious about Preston and tracked down his high school yearbook."

"And," Scarlet prompted.

"She promised to send me the photo."

Harper prodded. "Did she?"

"After what happened with JT I haven't thought to check."

"Where's your phone?" Harper was on her feet.

"I left it in my home office when I went to get the files for JT."

All three women raced to find Violet's phone. Sure enough, an email from Charity Rimes sat in Violet's inbox. She opened the message and held it so both her sisters could survey the image.

"That's not JT's father," Harper intoned.

Scarlett agreed. "No it's not."

Violet felt a peculiar lightness envelop her. In her hands was a way to save JT. But did he want to be saved? More importantly, would he want to be saved by her?

"We need to go to the police," Harper said.

"Which police?" Scarlett asked. "It won't do us any good to take it to the Las Vegas PD because Preston lives in Miami." She plucked the cell phone from Violet's grip and began typing. "I'm going to send this to Logan. He'll know the best way to handle it."

Twenty minutes later, Scarlett's fiancé sat on the coffee table and scowled at each of the three sisters in turn. When his gaze settled on Scarlett, he growled, "I thought I told you to drop it."

"I did." She gave him a winning smile. "Right after I gave Charity Rimes's phone number to Violet."

Logan sighed and shifted his hard gaze to Violet. "Have you spoken with JT about this?"

"We aren't on speaking terms at the moment."

That seemed to surprise Logan. "He should know what you've discovered."

She shook her head. "I doubt he'll take my call. Would you tell him?"

"You're his wife. It would be better coming from you."

"I'm the woman he married to get access to his family's stock," she corrected him. "And tonight he found out I had a file that Tiberius had put together on him. That I never looked at," she added when Logan's expression grew even grimmer.

"Every one of those files should have been burned," Logan growled, shooting his fiancée an unhappy look.

"What's done is done," Scarlett replied unapologetically. "We need to move forward. Preston Rhodes is an imposter and it's time that caught up with him."

Clad in a towel, JT stood in the enormous walk-in closet off his master suite and stared at the array of feminine fashions that occupied half the space. In addition to Violet's clothes, there were twenty pairs of shoes and assorted purses. Her jewelry was on his bureau, her lingerie in his dresser drawers. The scent of her clung to the sheets. Her cosmetics occupied the bathroom countertops. Traces of her lingered everywhere.

"Damn."

He'd been unable to sleep the night before so he'd sat in his living room, alternately staring out at his empty swimming pool and reading the file Tiberius had put together on Preston. He'd grown queasier with each page he'd turned. A dozen times he'd started to close the file, but then he'd hear Violet's voice and knew he could no long pretend that his father hadn't maliciously sabotaged his competition and blackmailed friends. He'd fled the truth for too long. His father was evil.

Sometime around dawn he'd drifted off. When he woke around six, he'd been having a dream where he chased Violet through a casino, calling her name, but she was always far out of reach. The memory of it left him with a cottony taste in his mouth and an ache in his temples. Interpreting the dream was easy. He'd lost the best woman he'd ever known because he was too closed down to give her the intimacy she deserved.

In the center of the large master suite, his empty king-size bed stood as a reminder of all the things he'd never enjoy again. Violet's body moving beneath him. Her soft moans. The bite of her nails as she climaxed. The brilliance of her smile in the aftermath of their lovemaking. The utter peace he felt with her nestled beside him.

He could burn the sheets, replace the mattress, hell, even toss out all the furniture, but he'd never be free of the mistakes that had led him to shove her away. Worse, he suspected she'd forgive him for being such an ungrateful jerk if he'd just share with her his feelings about what haunted him. But he'd clung to the secret for so long. It was impossible for him to set it free.

For a moment he was almost grateful to his father for selling Titanium. Staying in Las Vegas would have been impossible. Only with a change of scenery could he hope to adapt to life without her. Not that it was going to be easy. He'd given her access to places inside him that no one else had ever seen. Or was that true? Thanks to the file Tiberius had put together on him, didn't she already know all his secrets?

From the nightstand, his cell began to ring. Teeth locked together in irritation, JT left the closet and went to answer it.

"Yes?" he snapped.

There was a momentary pause before a man spoke. "JT? This is Logan Wolfe."

The security expert's connection to the Fontaine family immediately roused JT's suspicion. "What can I do for you, Logan?"

"I was wondering if we could meet. I have something to talk to you about and it shouldn't be done over the phone."

"If this is about Violet, you can forget it. We're done. End of story."

Another short but significant pause followed JT's declaration.

"Actually, this is about your father."

"I don't know what he's up to but he can go to hell. I'm done with him. I'm done with Stone Properties. I'm done with everything." Aware that he was working himself into a rant, JT sucked in a breath to steady his emotions. "Sorry," he muttered more calmly. "It's been a bad twenty-four hours."

"I get it," Logan said, sympathy in his voice. "I was there. And I have to tell you that the way you're feeling right now is not worth taking out on a terrific woman like Violet."

The unsolicited advice was a sucker punch to his gut. "You have no idea what I'm going through."

"Trust me, I do," Logan said, and the words were so heartfelt that JT believed him. "Scarlett and I almost didn't make it because I overreacted to something that happened. I would have been the sorriest son-of-a-bitch on the planet if she hadn't forgiven me for taking it out on her."

JT's anger faded, leaving a sick feeling in his gut. "It's too late. We're over."

"Do you really believe that or is it just fear talking?"

JT had no answer.

After a moment, Logan said, "I know you and your dad have issues, but he is your father. Do you want to meet with me and hear what I have to say?"

"No. I don't owe him anything."

"Have it your way. Take care, JT." And then he hung up, leaving JT wondering if he was really as done with everything as he thought.

CHAPTER ELEVEN

THE BLACK TOWN car her grandfather had sent to meet her at LaGuardia Airport stopped in front of the building that held Fontaine Resorts and Hotels' corporate headquarters in New York. Without waiting for the driver to open her door, Violet slipped from the back of the vehicle and crossed the sidewalk to the entrance.

Her heart was racing as she passed through security and ascended the elevator to the executive offices on the twentieth floor. She'd been here several times in the last five years, but those had been social visits with her grandfather. Most of her meetings with Fontaine's top executives happened in Las Vegas via video conference.

"You can go right in, Ms. Fontaine," her grandfather's assistant told her. "He's expecting you."

"Hello, Grandfather." By the time Violet crossed the enormous executive office, her grandfather had circled the desk. She walked straight into his arms and hugged him tight.

"My dear Violet." He squeezed back and released her. "You sounded upset on the phone. What's happened?"

"I've done so many things wrong I don't know where to begin."

"Start anywhere. I'll try to keep up." He drew her to the

leather couch occupying one side of his office and surveyed her face for a long moment before calling to his assistant. "Jean, can you get Violet a cup of tea?" He settled her on the sofa as if she was a fine piece of porcelain and added, "Something soothing."

Three minutes later Violet cradled a china cup of herbal tea and let the warmth seep into her skin. "Thank you," she murmured. "I'm afraid I'm a bit of a mess these days."

"Why don't you tell me what happened."

"As you know, I married JT Stone so that I could vote the shares of stock Tiberius left to me." Violet could tell her grandfather was making an effort not to offer his opinion on her rash action. "It started out as a business deal."

"And then you fell in love."

Violet nodded. "He's very guarded and has a hard time trusting because of the way his father has always treated him. But I really thought in time I could get through."

"And now you don't believe you can."

"Scarlett gave me some files that she inherited from Tiberius. Apparently there was an entire storage unit filled with thousands of files dating back fifty years. He had one for each of us—" she paused "—even you."

Henry smiled wryly. "I suppose when I entered your life, Tiberius wanted to make sure I wouldn't cause you harm. I rather liked his protective streak. Made me glad that you had someone looking out for you while you were growing up."

Something his own son had failed to do. It went unspoken, but Violet sensed Henry Fontaine was deeply disappointed that Ross had behaved with so little honor.

"When Scarlett started looking through the files, she discovered one on JT and his father. As I've already told you, Tiberius was making a move to take his family's company back from Preston. I think he wanted JT as his partner, but wanted to make sure his nephew wasn't like Preston."

"And JT found out about the file?"

"Scarlett had given it to me. I should have shown it to JT

right away but so much happened so fast and I forgot about it. Instead he found out I had it and accused me of using the information to trick him into getting married. Only Scarlett didn't give it to me until after JT and I got married and I never read it." The words tumbled out of her, each sentence coming faster until she ran out of breath.

"I'm sorry things are difficult between you," her grandfather said. "What can I do to help?"

"JT is losing Titanium. Preston is selling it to punish JT for going up against him. I don't think JT cares. He was planning on striking out on his own before I found out Tiberius had left me his stock. But that was before we got married. When Titanium is sold, he's going to leave Las Vegas."

"I'm still not sure how I can help," Henry said gently.

"I'd hoped you'd be able to find out who had shown an interest in Titanium and somehow interfere with the sale. I need some time. The longer JT sticks around, the more chance I have to save my marriage."

"And if he is still determined to go?"

"I belong with him. Wherever that is."

Her grandfather's expression registered surprise at her passionate declaration, but he didn't hesitate before asking, "Are you sure that's what you want to do?"

"Of course." She needed her grandfather to understand why this was important to her. "I love him and whether he believes it or not, he needs me."

"You know what's at stake if you leave Fontaine Chic."

"Any chance to run Fontaine Resorts and Hotels." Violet gave him a sad smile. "In the last year I've stopped seeing myself in the CEO job. Harper is the one you should choose. She's trained all her life to take over. You won't find anyone more dedicated or driven."

"I must say, I'm surprised."

Violet didn't pretend to wonder what he meant. "I'm not giving up because I feel I'm not capable or because I'm not performing well, but because I recognize the depth of commitment the position requires and I'm reluctant to make those sacrifices."

"I value your honesty, and you're right about the job requiring all your time and energy. Since starting the company I've lost my wife and my son and I've had to face that neither relationship was as good as I wished they'd been."

Nodding because her throat was too tight to allow words, Violet smiled at her grandfather. "Thank you for understanding. I was worried that after you gave me such an amazing opportunity, you'd be disappointed in my decision."

"You are an intelligent, compassionate woman with a creative, enthusiastic business presence. From the first you've been an asset to the Fontaine team. And I couldn't be more proud to call you my granddaughter. I've had my concerns that your heart might lie in Las Vegas and that you would eventually decide you wished to stay there, instead of coming here to assume the role of CEO. But now I see that what you truly love, you commit to, and I want you to understand that whatever happens with JT, you will always be a Fontaine."

His words were a warm embrace and Violet smiled gratefully. "Thank you."

She couldn't help but contrast JT's family experiences with her own. If she'd faced nothing but a string of ridicule and rejection from those who were supposed to love her, would she still wake up each morning feeling optimistic? Would she be able to create a safe haven that supported her and gave her a place to hide from all the negative words and actions that came at her?

"What are your plans for the rest of the day?" her grandfather asked.

"I thought I would do a little shopping for Scarlett's bridal shower and then head back to the apartment."

"I'll make some calls to see what I can find out about Titanium and meet you there at six. I'd like to take you to dinner. There's a restaurant I'd like your opinion on. I thought perhaps we could discuss the opportunity to open a new restaurant in Fontaine Richesse with the chef."

"Grandfather, I don't know," Violet said with a laugh. "The last chef you found has made Harper's life hell. I'm not sure the food is worth the drama."

"I had no idea she was having trouble."

And maybe Violet shouldn't have spilled the truth. "It's their personalities. Ashton is creative and spontaneous. And even more of a perfectionist than Harper, if you can believe it. He's had input on everything from the font on the menu to the décor and is forever changing things in his obsessive search for better or more spectacular. I'm starting to wonder if they'll ever get the restaurant open."

"Is that why the opening has been postponed two times? She told me there was a problem with the fixtures being delayed."

"Because he changed his mind on what he wanted at the last minute and new things had to be ordered." Violet put a hand on her grandfather's arm. "Please don't tell her I mentioned this. She'd kill me if she knew I'd said anything."

"Ross's neglect made her think she had to prove her worth. Even after his death the need for acceptance drives her hard." Henry's eyes darkened with sadness. "I'll figure out a way to speak with her without letting her know you and I discussed it."

As Violet kissed her grandfather on the cheek, her phone buzzed. Her stomach in knots, she exited his office. She'd been waiting for this call for the last three weeks. What she'd put in motion might not solve her problem with JT, but it was the best way she knew to convince him she had no intention of letting him go without a fight.

JT stepped off the plane he'd chartered to Miami and headed in the direction of the Porsche 911 Cabriolet waiting by the hangar. His cousin Brent leaned his six-foot-two-inch frame against the sports car, arms crossed, looking relaxed and amused at JT's surprise.

"What the hell are you doing here?" JT demanded, enfolding his cousin in a hearty hug, shocked by the strength of his emotion.

Brent looked equally caught off guard, but recovered quickly and gave JT a toothy grin. "Thought you could use a little moral support tomorrow."

"You have no idea."

"Violet couldn't come?"

"She…" What excuse could he give for his wife not being at his side, lending her support, at such a crucial time? He owed Brent the truth. "We're over."

"No way. You two are crazy about each other." Brent's confused dismay added punch to JT's self-doubt. "What happened?"

"It's a long story and better told over drinks." JT circled the car and opened the passenger door. "I've got a suite at the Marriott."

Brent slid his long frame behind the wheel. "You're not staying at Cobalt?" It was the premier Stone Properties hotel in downtown Miami where the stockholders' meeting would take place the next day.

JT grimaced. "That's another story better told with alcohol."

"Sounds like it's going to be a long evening." Brent started the car.

The explanations began when the two men settled into a booth at the hotel's bar. JT figured he'd start with what happened with his father and work his way into the more painful story.

Brent didn't look surprised when JT recounted how Preston had informed him that Titanium was going to be sold. "It's the only property without any significant debt," Brent reflected. "He needs the capital to make the balloon payments coming due."

"Despite how hard I fought to get my father out," JT said, for the first time voicing what had dawned on him several days earlier, "I'm not really sorry to be leaving Stone Properties."

"Really? The last time we talked you were determined to take over. It's your legacy."

JT shook his head. "A tainted one. My father ruined so many lives in order to take over the company. How can I sit in the CEO's chair and not be haunted by what he did to my uncle and countless others?"

"So, you're giving up?"

"I'm moving on." JT offered his cousin a wry smile. "Feel like buying thirty percent of Stone Properties?"

"You own forty-eight percent."

"Eighteen percent of that is Violet's."

"But if you two are divorced, she can no longer vote the shares."

"True." JT's focus sharpened. "Are you telling me you're interested?"

"With restructuring, the company could be made solid once more. I thought you'd want to be the one to do that."

"And now that you know I'm not?"

"I will."

The idea that his cousin wanted to take over Stone Properties gave JT a great deal of satisfaction, but there was still the problem of not having enough shares to remove Preston as chairman of the board. He refrained from bringing it up. The mood at the table had brightened considerably and JT wasn't about to kick sand on the fire.

After several more drinks over which Brent spelled out his plan to fix Stone Properties, JT's cousin grew somber.

"Are you drunk enough to tell me what went wrong between you and Violet?"

"No." JT offered an unhappy smile. "But I'll tell you anyway."

He then explained about Tiberius's files and how Violet had been in possession of one on JT. "She played me."

"How do you figure?"

"Every dirty little secret I have was in that file." All except one. The worst one.

And no one would ever know what happened the day his

mother died. How he could have been the one to save her if he hadn't disobeyed her.

"She knew exactly how to make me…" JT stopped. He'd been about to say *make me fall in love with her*. Because that's exactly what had happened. Suddenly he felt ill.

"Make you what?" Brent prompted.

"Make me trust her."

"She seemed pretty trustworthy to me," his cousin said. "Loyal, too."

"She is." JT was aware he wasn't thinking straight. "I mean she seems trustworthy." In fact she had been. Violet hadn't done a single thing to hurt him. Quite the opposite. She'd supported him.

JT dropped his head into his hands. "Oh, hell."

"I'm guessing you just realized you messed up."

So what if she'd had a file on him. So what if she'd memorized the damned thing. The fact that he refused to let her in, to open up his past so she could understand why he retreated the way he did, hadn't left her much choice. Given her open nature, it must have been stressful for her to come up against his defenses day after day. Sure, he'd let her in a little, but that could only have given her hope that he'd share more.

But how could he let her in when what lay hidden was so ugly? He was selfish and filled with bitter anger. His childhood scars made it impossible for anyone to love him, even Violet. So he'd pushed her away.

"I don't feel like drinking anymore," JT said, besieged by the need to retreat and regroup. His nerves were raw and exposed. If he went into the stockholders' meeting like this tomorrow, his father would eat him alive. "I'm heading back to my room."

"Sure." Brent regarded him with concern. "Are you sure you're okay?"

"No, but after some aspirin, a shower and a few hours' sleep, I might be able to get through tomorrow." What happened after that was anyone's guess.

* * *

Her grandfather's Gulfstream enabled Violet to arrive in Miami an hour before the shareholders' meeting was set to start. JT wasn't expecting her and she wasn't sure what sort of reception she'd receive. With each mile of road that passed beneath the town car's tires, her anxiety grew until she ran out of time to worry. She'd arrived at Cobalt.

The Stone Properties' flagship hotel was a towering thirty-story structure that overlooked the bright blue waters of Biscayne Bay. Everything about the lush landscaping bordering the circular driveway and the glassed entrance to the lobby was staged to impress. But as Violet exited the town car and headed inside, she noted a dozen tiny flaws in the way the staff conducted themselves and spied the dust lingering in the decorative moldings. At a quick glance everything appeared to be functioning, but Violet's trained eye recognized mismanagement.

Crossing the two-story foyer, Violet made her way to the conference room where the annual meeting was taking place. She picked up her pace when she saw the doors had already closed. If she'd hoped to slip in unobtrusively, she'd underestimated the number of stockholders who would be attending.

There were less than a dozen people scattered throughout the chairs that faced a raised dais with a podium in the middle. Seven pairs of eyes shifted in her direction, but she only cared about a particular pair of hard blue ones.

Simmering with ill-concealed annoyance, JT sat beside his cousin, Brent, half way up on the far side of the room. He didn't look happy to see her, but she hoped that would change when he understood why she was here. She took a seat in the back of the room while Preston ran through the day's agenda. As stockholder meetings went it was fairly routine. They would vote to accept the company's financials as well as several amendments to the bylaws. The agenda had been sent out months ago so no one really needed the review, but clearly Preston Rhodes enjoyed hearing himself speak.

While Preston spoke about the success of the company under his leadership and the direction he was taking Stone Properties in the future, Violet watched JT. He sat like a statue, his expression tight and unreadable. If things had gone differently, she'd be sitting beside him, offering him silent support. Her heart ached at the distance between them.

At long last, the explanation of what they were voting on wound down and they were invited to mark their ballots and bring them up to the ballot box. An external auditor would then count the votes while the shareholders enjoyed a specially prepared lunch. Everyone in the room knew it was all being done to satisfy the bylaws. Preston had control over the majority of the shares. What he wanted was what he would get.

Violet lingered in the back while JT voted, hoping to catch him as he left. A muscle jumped in his jaw as he approached.

"I thought maybe you'd mail in your vote." His gaze searched her face for a second before he leaned forward and kissed her cheek.

The fleeting contact caused a hiccup in Violet's pulse. She wanted so badly to wrap her arms around him and tell him everything would be all right, but he had his guard up.

"I wanted to be here for you."

"That's nice." JT's features softened for a moment, but then his father's laugh reverberated around the rapidly emptying room and JT's expression became like stone once more.

Violet watched her husband with a sinking heart. For a second she thought he might tell her he missed her. It was what she'd flown halfway across the country hoping to hear. What a fool she'd been to think their reunion would be joyful and romantic. "I'd better go vote."

"Of course."

JT's gaze clung to Violet's slender form as she walked away. He told himself to go after her. To beg her to love him. Wasn't her appearance here today proof that she wasn't ready to give up on him? But was it fair to take and take from her and give back nothing in return?

"JT, I was hoping I'd get to see you." A stocky man of average height clapped JT on his shoulder. "Sorry about not being able to swing my vote your way, but your father has been running this company successfully for a lot of years."

Clive Ringwald was the owner of a string of auto parts stores in the Midwest and married to JT's mother's cousin. An affable man, he was firmly in Preston's camp, believing whatever half-truths or outright lies he was told.

"I understand," he told Clive, but his attention was fixed on Violet.

She'd dropped her ballot in the box and handed some paperwork to the auditor. With a last glance his way, she slipped out the room's second door.

Watching the door close behind her, JT felt his entire world shatter. What the hell was he doing standing here letting Clive prattle on? He loved Violet. He didn't care if she'd read his file and knew every shameful thing about him. She'd known who he was and married him anyway. And here he was, acting like such a stubborn fool when he should be fighting for the woman who'd transformed his life.

Cutting off Clive with a brusque apology, JT moved to intercept Violet in the hallway, but she'd already vanished. Figuring she was heading to the restaurant where lunch was being served, JT raced down the hall to the escalator that led to the ground floor. As he rode it down, he caught a glimpse of her passing through the front doors. He was so intent on catching up to her that he didn't notice Brent waiting for him at the bottom of the escalator until his cousin stepped in front of him.

"The FBI's here." Brent's gaze was troubled. "They're taking your father in. Do you know what the hell is going on?"

JT immediately thought of George Barnes and a reporter in L.A. who might have some information on a man by the name of Preston Rhodes. "I think I do. Where are they?"

Before Brent could answer, his father appeared, flanked by two men in suits. In dazed silence JT watched the trio approach. They'd handcuffed Preston, but there was no question that JT's father was not cowed by the treatment.

"Do you know who I am?" Preston snarled.

The man to the left smirked. "Actually, that's what we'd like to chat with you about."

Preston caught sight of JT and his lips curled in disdain. "I suppose this is your doing."

JT shook his head. "I wish it was." And to his surprise he meant it. "Seems as if all your bad choices have finally caught up with you."

"Tell my assistant to call my lawyer," he snapped before he was out of range.

"You're not really going to do that, are you?" Brent inquired.

"Nope." JT glanced at his cousin. "Can I get a rain check on that drink? I need to catch my wife before she leaves."

"No problem. Give me a call later."

But before taking more than a step, once again, JT was prevented from going after Violet. This time it was the auditor who stopped him.

"Excuse me, but was that Mr. Rhodes I just saw leave?"

"It was."

"But I have the results of the election."

"The stockholders are having lunch in the dining room. Perhaps you'd like to tell them what happened." JT turned to go.

"Before you leave, Mr. Stone, you should know that your father was voted off the board."

JT spun around and stared at the auditor, wondering if he'd heard correctly. Then, JT realized he was grinning like an idiot. "Explain it to him." He indicated Brent. "I have more important things to take care of."

CHAPTER TWELVE

VIOLET WAS UNPACKING the last of her personal items from her suite at Fontaine Chic when her husband strode through the bedroom door. She glanced up as his presence filled the master suite and made the very air crackle with energy.

"Hello, husband," she said, her tone matter of fact. "Was your trip successful?"

"You know damned well it was." He tugged his tie loose and shrugged out of his suit jacket. When he looked as if he planned to drop both articles on a nearby chair, Violet moved to take them from him. A gentle tug-of-war ensued between them. "I don't need rescuing," he murmured a second before giving her the win.

"Not anymore," she responded, her voice equally soft.

It was going to be all right, she realized as she hung up his jacket and tie. He hadn't demanded to know what she was doing in his house. He'd simply accepted her presence. Her anxiety quieted.

She came out of the closet and found her husband had stripped off his shirt and was working on his shoes. Her mouth went dry as she took in all his chiseled perfection. Had it only been a week since they'd last made love? The severe ache in her loins made it seem like a whole lot longer.

His socks landed in a pile next to his shirt as he commented, "The FBI hauled my father in for questioning." JT slipped off his pants. Clad only in his boxer briefs, he carried his discarded clothes into the closet. "Any idea what that was about?"

"You didn't stick around to find out?"

"I was too busy chasing after my wife to care." He reappeared in fully naked glory and stood with his arms crossed, staring at her. "Perhaps you can enlighten me."

It was difficult for her to concentrate with her husband's flawless physique artlessly displayed for her perusal. Did he really intend to stand there like that and have a serious discussion? Her blood heated as she took in the rise and dip of his muscular arms and the flawless definition of his rock hard abs.

"Perhaps you'd like to shower first and then we can talk?" Violet suggested, hoping he'd take the hint that it was a conversation better conducted without distractions.

"Actually, I'd like to hear what you have to say first."

Damn him. Well, two could play at this game. She reached behind her and took ahold of her dress's zipper. His expression didn't change as she unfastened her dress, but when it pooled at her feet, she caught a minute widening of his eyes.

"Charity Rimes finally returned our call a few days ago," she said, unfastening her bra and letting it fall to the ground. She shimmied out of her underwear before continuing. "After Tiberius had contacted her, she'd been intrigued about his theory that George Barnes had taken Preston Rhodes's identity and tracked down George's high school yearbook."

The entire time she was speaking, JT kept his gaze fixed on hers, and off her naked form. He appeared utterly intent on what she was saying, but there was one part of his anatomy with a mind of its own. To provoke it further, Violet reached up and freed the pins holding her hair in a loose topknot. It cascaded around her shoulders, the strands tickling her sensitive nipples and turning them into hard buds. JT's Adam's apple bobbed.

"When she emailed me a copy of the photo from his graduation, it was obvious that your father is not Preston Rhodes."

"So you called the FBI?"

"No, Scarlett suggested we bring the issue to Logan. He had a buddy in the FBI."

Violet bent down and picked up her dress. As she straightened she thought she heard a strange noise emanating from JT's throat, but when she glanced his way, nothing revealed itself on his face, although his erection had surged higher.

"He called me a few days ago." JT's voice was tight and husky. "I didn't want to hear what he had to say."

"I thought you should know what we intended to do and would take it better from him."

"I was so damned mad at you."

Violet flinched at the intensity of his tone. "I know."

Needing a moment to regroup, she turned and walked to a nearby chair, putting her clothes on it. She felt more than heard JT come up behind her, and when he spoke next, he was mere feet away.

"You had a file on me. I felt betrayed."

"I know," she repeated without turning around. Rehashing their fight would not move them past her poor judgment or his interpretation of what she'd done. "I was a little surprised the FBI moved as fast as they did. I thought for certain they would investigate longer." When his hands gripped her shoulders, there was tension in his fingers. Alarmed, Violet hurried to explain her motivation. "I know he's your father, but he certainly had no right to be in charge of your family's business."

"I don't need rescuing." JT repeated his earlier declaration and turned her to face him. "Not by you. Not by anyone."

Her temper flared. "That's your whole problem," she said, hitting him with all her pent-up frustration. "You think you're doing fine on your own, that this isolated little world you've built for yourself can keep your heart safe." She put both hands on his chest and shoved hard. He stumbled back a step, his expression reflecting surprise at her fierceness, and she stalked after him. "Well, you're wrong." She wagged her finger a scant inch from his nose and he retreated a few more steps. "You need me." She prowled after him, all her heartache and worry rising to a boiling point. "Admit it. Damn you. Admit it."

JT stopped retreating and stood staring down at her face. His fingertips brushed her cheek and came away damp. Violet didn't even realize she was crying.

"I don't just need you," JT said, bending down and lifting her onto his shoulder in a fireman's carry.

He dumped her on the bed and pounced on her. Violet gasped; his rough handling had disrupted the efficient working of her lungs. Or maybe she couldn't breathe because of the way he was staring at her: as if she was the most amazing sight he'd ever seen.

"I don't just need you," JT repeated, his tone tender. "I can't live without you. And I swear I'll do whatever it takes to make sure I never have to."

And then he was kissing her passionately, reverently, without holding back any emotion. Violet's joy knew no bounds as she realized that he'd stopped running from her. He might not have let go of the pain that kept him isolated, but he was ready to let her help him heal.

Her tongue met every greedy thrust of his, devouring just as fervently as she was devoured. With her fingers fisted in his hair, she threw back her head and moaned as his teeth nipped at her throat and he investigated the level of her arousal. Her hips bucked as he slid one finger inside her, then two.

Heat built beneath her skin as his mouth latched onto one of her nipples. The firm tug sent a spear of longing straight down to her core. She twisted beneath him, pinned to the mattress by his weight, but managing to communicate her hunger.

"Now," she commanded breathlessly. "Don't make me wait any longer."

He used his knees to spread her thighs wide, opening her for his possession. "It's been hell for me as well."

And then he was thrusting inside her in one long, measured surge that nearly made her black out, such was her pleasure.

"Yes," she murmured, smiling as his lips claimed hers once more.

He retreated at a deliberate pace, letting her savor the friction of their joining before plunging fully inside her once more. Their union couldn't be measured by the pleasure he brought her body, but by the way her heart swelled to almost bursting.

"I love you," she told him, meeting his gaze as they danced together, hips moving in ancient rhythm.

JT laced his fingers with hers and set their hands on the pillow beside her head. Without breaking his steady stroke into her body, he kissed her gently on the lips before murmuring, "You're my everything."

His confession caused her body to spasm. Her orgasm rolled over her in slow waves of ever-increasing pleasure that slowly faded. When she opened her eyes, she found JT watching her. Her lips curved at the wonder in his expression. He began to move against her powerfully, chasing his own finish. In seconds his body shuddered as his climax claimed him. He let her watch every emotion play across his face.

Breathing harshly, JT collapsed on his stomach beside her on the bed. He peered at her from beneath his long lashes, a wryness in his expression making him look younger than his thirty years. Or, Violet corrected, he looked exactly the age he was and she'd grown accustomed to how stress and unhappiness had made him seem older.

She rolled over on her side and cupped her hands beneath her cheek. "I'm here to stay."

"I assumed that when I saw all the packing boxes in the hall."

"And by here I mean wherever you are." Her lips firmed. "I fully intend to fight dirty if that's what it takes to save our marriage."

"There's nothing to save." He lifted one hand to forestall her heated rebuttal. "Let me finish. I simply mean that I was wrong to push you away and that I'm fully committed to spending the rest of my life with you."

Violet let him see her delight. "Good. I think you made a wise choice."

"So do I." JT rolled onto his side until their noses were an inch apart. His heart rate had returned to its regular resting pace, but every third beat or so it skipped a little as he realized just how happy he was.

"Feel like telling me how the shareholder vote worked out?"

Why did he get the sense that she already knew?

"Strangely enough, it came out in our favor."

"Really?" She did a lousy job of sounding surprised. "How is that possible?"

"From what Brent was able to gather after I left, Casey didn't vote his shares."

"That's odd. Any idea what happened?"

JT decided Violet's poker face was improving, but he knew her well enough to pick up on the trace of amusement in her eyes.

"I don't know if you remember but he was in the midst of a nasty divorce."

"I seem to recall something about that."

Now JT knew she'd been up to something because she'd been the one to point that out to him in the first place. "He let his wife have his four percent of Stone Properties stock in the settlement."

"You don't say." Violet looked suitably fascinated. "But if his ex-wife had the shares, she wouldn't be able to vote them because she was no longer family."

"True." JT let the rest of his explanation hang in the air, but Violet didn't press him to continue. And why would she? JT suspected she already knew how it ended. "Without Casey's four percent, my father and I controlled an equal number of shares."

"So how did we win?"

"That's an excellent question. Perhaps you'd like to explain to me."

"Me?" She sounded innocent, but a smug smile tugged at her lips. "Why would you think I had anything to do with it?"

"Because I've met the ex-Mrs. Casey Stone and she's greedy and beautiful, but not particularly bright. I don't understand why she wanted the shares at all."

"Well..." Violet drew out the word, reveling in the telling of her tale. "It seems that a year ago Casey had bought a big, beautiful love nest for his new amore and hadn't declared it as part of the divorce settlement. So, I let Brittany know and suggested that she might want to ask for the Stone Property shares and let Casey have the house."

"And he went for that? The shares had to be worth more or that was one hell of a house."

"He was in a hurry to remarry, and he stood to lose big because he hadn't disclosed the house." Violet shook her head. "Brittany was thrilled to sell me the stock. After all, I'd done her a good turn. And in the end, I think she received more than Casey intended for her to have."

"You own the four percent?"

"I do."

"This wasn't something you managed overnight, was it?" JT didn't wait for her to answer. "After I told you it wasn't worth pursuing, you went behind my back, didn't you?"

"You refused to let me help."

"And now I see I was wrong." As much as he hated admitting that, Violet's delight took the sting away.

"Good. Maybe now you'll start listening to my advice."

"Yes, oh wise one."

JT put his arms around her and softly nuzzled the side of her neck. She smelled like fresh-cut grass and summer sunshine, both favorite scents from his time on the farm in Kentucky.

Lulled by the steady beat of her heart against his, JT felt the door to his most guarded secrets crack open.

"I don't know how to thank you," he told her, strangely at peace now that he was on the verge of telling her about the worst moment of his life.

"You don't have to thank me. I'm your wife. I'll always have your back."

"Then you should know what you're letting yourself in for."

"You don't think I do?" Violet's breath fell against his skin in a soothing cadence. "I didn't read your file, but I know that you're more troubled than the average person by mistakes you've made and that you carry childhood hurts that may never heal."

"I'm more troubled because the mistakes I've made aren't forgivable."

"That's impossible for me to believe."

He never stopped being astonished by her faith in him, but she needed to know everything. "The day my mother died…"

"JT." She cupped his cheek, offering comfort, and drew her thumb across his lips, silencing him. "You don't have to tell me."

"But I do. You were right about my needing to let go of the past. I can't do that if I continue to let fear hold me captive. I need you to know what happened with my mother." He pressed a kiss into her palm and closed his eyes. "I was the reason she died."

Violet's body jerked in reaction to his words, but instead of pushing him away, she moved even closer as if she wanted to slide under his skin and share the burden with him.

"That morning, she confronted me about using her credit card without asking and charging five hundred dollars' worth of video games. She didn't care that I'd bought the games, but the fact that I'd lied about it when she caught me made her angrier than I'd ever seen her. She'd found the games in my room and while I watched she threw them away. Then she told me I wasn't allowed to go on a weekend trip with my friends to

Universal Studios Orlando. We were supposed to leave from school that afternoon. I don't remember ever being that mad."

JT sucked in an unsteady breath as memories of that morning washed over him. They were crystal-clear and razor-sharp as if the fight had happened yesterday, not eighteen years earlier.

"I can see why she grounded you and I understand why you were upset, but I don't see how it's your fault that she died. She overdosed. You had nothing to do with that."

"I upset her. I told her I hated her and that I understood why Dad couldn't stand to be around her."

JT shook his head, but there was no denying what he'd done. For a moment he couldn't breathe. His throat had tightened past the point of pain. He'd never told anyone the role he'd played in his mother's death. He needed to claw through years of self-loathing to let it out. It felt as if his insides were shredded.

When he continued, his voice was thick with anguish. "Then I grabbed my backpack and acted like I was leaving for school, but I snuck back to my room and packed what I would need for the weekend."

"You went anyway?"

"I figured she'd be so out of it by the middle of the afternoon, she'd never realize that I wasn't home until I was long gone. By five that evening she was dead. No one found her until the next morning when the housekeeper showed up."

"You were twelve," Violet said. "Your mother was a troubled woman who retreated into drugs and alcohol to cope with an abusive husband. How can you think you were to blame?"

"I overheard someone talking at her funeral. I realized that if I'd come home after school like I was supposed to, I could have found her still alive and called 911."

A tear slid down his cheek. Before he could lift his hand to sweep the dampness away, Violet cupped his face in a fierce grip.

"JT, your mother was an addict. She could have overdosed at any time. You were not responsible for her illness."

He heaved an unsteady breath. Part of him recognized that she was right, and he sensed her love and support would help him forgive himself.

"I love you," he told her, speaking the words out loud for the first time.

Tears filled her eyes, but her smile was brighter than the sun. She wrapped her arms around his neck and hugged him hard. "I can't tell you how much I've needed to hear you say that."

"It's taken me a long time to understand what I was feeling," he murmured into her hair. "Before you came along, the emotions I was most familiar with were dark ones."

"All that is behind us now," she said crisply, her optimism revving up. She leaned back and regarded him, her eyes determined. "Starting today, we have an abundance of new adventures awaiting us. Starting with house-hunting in Miami. I spoke with Grandfather about acquiring some property downtown and building a Fontaine property."

"About that." JT hadn't expected her to be so enthusiastic about leaving Las Vegas for Miami and was worried that his news might not be what she wanted to hear. "We're not going to Miami."

"Why not? Now that your father has lost his chairmanship and is probably going to face jail time, the company is yours."

"Here's the thing. The night before the annual meeting, Brent and I had a long chat about the future of Stone Properties. We came to the conclusion that it would be better served with him at the helm."

"But…but…" she sputtered, "it was your grandfather who started Stone Properties."

"And with Brent running things it goes back into family hands."

She cocked her head and regarded him. "What are you planning to do?"

"What I told you I was going to do before the shareholders' meeting. Get out."

"I see." But it was obvious she didn't. "So, where are we going?"

He soothed her worries with a smile and the stroke of his palm along her arm. "Nowhere. Neither one of us is leaving Las Vegas. In fact, I've decided to sell my shares of Stone Properties and buy Titanium."

Her smile was blinding. "I think that's a wonderful idea. But are you sure you want to settle for one property when you could be in charge of a dozen?"

"With Brent at the helm, Stone Properties will be in good hands. And I'm not really a sit-in-an-office-and-do-nothing-but-read-reports-and-make-policies kind of guy. I like the pulse of Las Vegas and have decided whatever else I do, here's where my headquarters will be."

Violet frowned. "That's all well and good, but what happens if I win Grandfather's contest and take over Fontaine Resorts and Hotels? I'll have to move to New York City. What becomes of us then?"

JT had never considered that possibility. It wasn't that he lacked faith in Violet's abilities to do the job or her grandfather's shortsightedness in not recognizing her talents, but she'd always seemed as much a part of Las Vegas as the strip itself.

"I guess I'll have to rethink my plans."

Her eyes softened. "You'd do that for me?"

"Did you not hear me when I said I can't live without you?"

She snuggled closer and kissed his lips. "Then you'll be happy to know that we'll be living together in Las Vegas. I spoke with Grandfather and bowed out of the CEO race."

"Why did you do that?"

"Because I made you my priority. Whatever you want to do, wherever you want to go, I intend to be by your side supporting you."

"I feel the same way."

She laughed. "Then I guess we're pretty lucky that we both

love Las Vegas so much because this is where we're going to raise our children and grow old together."

Her vision of their future was so much better than any he'd ever dreamed of. Gone were the shadows that had kept him from believing he deserved to be happy. Violet's love had banished every one.

JT's arms tightened around her. "I can't imagine anything better than that."

* * * * *

Unlocking Her Boss's Heart

Christy McKellen

Formerly a video and radio producer, **Christy McKellen** now spends her time writing fun, impassioned and emotive romance with an undercurrent of sensual tension. When she's not writing, she can be found enjoying life with her husband and three children, walking for pleasure and researching other people's deepest secrets and desires.

Christy loves to hear from readers. You can get ahold of her at christymckellen.com.

Books by Christy McKellen

Harlequin Forever

Unlocking Her Boss's Heart
is Christy McKellen's first Harlequin Forever title.

Harlequin Kiss

Holiday with a Stranger
Lessons in Rule-Breaking
Fired by Her Fling

Visit the Author Profile page at
millsandboon.com.au for
more titles.

Dear Reader,

I've always loved the story of *Beauty and the Beast*, so I was really interested in using the disfigured hero trope in a modern-day retelling. Only in this story I wanted our hero, Max, to have locked himself away from the outside world because of mental rather than physical scars.

And he's certainly been through some dark times when we first meet him.

But of course, in true fairy-tale style, the unexpected appearance of a woman—in this case our gutsy (but equally humbled) heroine Cara—forces him to work past his irascible nature and self-imposed solitude and reveal the kind, caring man that's been hiding underneath for the past eighteen months.

It was wonderful to see these two help each other overcome the trials they've been through as the story played out on the page, and regain their pride and sense of self, finally finding the peace they'd been desperately missing, to become whole again.

And it certainly is a roller-coaster ride for these two!

I hope you enjoy their journey, through all its exhilarating ups and painful downs, and find the same satisfaction that I did in their eventual liberation from shame and regret through self-healing and their binding love for each other.

With best wishes,

Christy

This one is for Babs and Phil,
the most generous, loving and supportive parents in the world. You've seen me through all my ups and downs (and there have been a few) and always picked me up, dusted me off and cheered me on.

I love you. I hope you know that.

CHAPTER ONE

CARA WINSTONE CLIMBED the smooth slate steps to the shiny black front door of the town house in South Kensington and tried hard not to be awed by its imposing elegance.

This place was exactly the sort of house she'd dreamed about living in during her naïve but hopeful youth. In her fantasies, the four-storey Victorian house would be alive with happy, mischievous children, whom she and her handsome husband would firmly but lovingly keep in line and laugh about in the evenings once they'd gone to bed. Each room would have a beautiful display of fresh seasonal flowers and light would pour in through the large picture windows, reflecting off the tasteful but comfortable furnishings.

Back in real life, her topsy-turvy one-bed flat in Islington was a million miles away from this grand goddess of a mansion.

Not that it was going to be her flat for much longer if she didn't make good on this opportunity today.

The triple espresso she'd had for breakfast lurched around in her stomach as she thought about how close she was to being evicted from the place she'd called home for the past six years by her greedy landlord. If she didn't find another job soon she was going to have to slink back to Cornwall, to the village that time forgot, and beg to share her parents' box room with the dogs until she got back on her feet.

She loved her parents dearly, but the thought of them all bumping elbows again in their tiny isolated house made her shudder. Especially after they'd been so excited when she'd called six months ago to tell them about landing her dream job as Executive Assistant to the CEO of one of the largest conglomerates in the country. Thanks to her mother's prodigious grapevine, word had quickly spread through both the family and her parents' local community and she'd been inundated with texts and emails of congratulations.

The thought of having to call them again now and explain why she'd been forced to hand in her notice after only three months made her queasy with shame. She couldn't do it. Not after the sacrifices they'd made in order to pay for her expensive private education, so she'd have the opportunities they'd never had. No, she owed them more than that.

But, with any luck, she'd never be forced to have that humiliating conversation because this chance today could be the ideal opportunity to get her feet back under the table. If she could secure this job, she was sure that everything else would fall into place.

Shifting the folder that contained her CV and the glowing references she'd accumulated over the years under her arm, she pressed the shiny brass bell next to the door and waited to be greeted by the owner of the house.

And waited.

Tapping her foot, she smoothed down her hair again, then straightened the skirt of her best suit, wanting to look her most professional and together self when the door finally swung open.

Except that it didn't.

Perhaps the occupier hadn't heard her ring.

Fighting the urge to chew on the nails she'd only just grown out, she rang again, for longer this time and was just about to give up and come back later when the door swung open to reveal a tall, shockingly handsome man with a long-limbed, powerful physique and the kind of self-possessed air that made her heart beat a little faster. His chocolate-brown hair looked as though it could do with a cut, but it fell across his forehead into his striking gold-shot hazel eyes in the most becoming manner. If she had to sum him up in one word it would be *dashing*—an old-fashioned-sounding term, but somehow it suited him down to the ground.

His disgruntled gaze dropped from her face to the folder under her arm.

'Yes?' he barked, his tone so fierce she took a pace backwards and nearly fell off the top step.

'Max Firebrace?' To her chagrin, her voice came out a little wobbly in the face of his unexpected hostility.

His frown deepened. 'I don't donate to charities at the door.'

Taking a deep breath, she plastered an assertive smile onto her face and said in her most patient voice, 'I'm not working for a charity. I'm here for the job.'

His antagonism seemed to crackle like a brooding lightning storm between them. 'What are you talking about? I'm not hiring for a job.'

Prickly heat rushed across her skin as she blinked at him in panicky confusion. 'Really? But my cousin Poppy said you needed a personal assistant because you're snowed under with work.'

He crossed his arms and shook his head as an expression of beleaguered understanding flashed across his face.

'I only told Poppy I'd look into hiring someone to get her off my back,' he said irritably.

She frowned at him in confusion, fighting the sinking feeling in her gut. 'So you don't need a PA?'

Closing his eyes, he rubbed a hand across his face and let out a short, sharp sigh. 'I'm very busy, yes, but I don't have time to even interview for a PA right now, let alone train them up, so if you'll excuse me—'

He made as if to shut the door, but before he could get it halfway closed she dashed forwards, throwing up both hands in a desperate attempt to stall him and dropping her folder onto the floor with a loud clatter. 'Wait! Please!'

A look of agitated surprise crossed his face at the cacophony, but at least he paused, then opened the door a precious few inches again.

Taking that as a sign from the gods of perseverance, Cara scooped up her folder from the floor, threw back her shoulders and launched into the sales pitch she'd been practising since Poppy's email had landed in her inbox last night, letting her know about this golden opportunity.

'I'm *very* good at what I do and I'm a quick learner—I have six years of experience as a PA so you won't need to show me much at all.' Her voice had taken on an embarrassing squeaky quality, but she soldiered on regardless.

'I'm excellent at working on my own initiative and I'm precise and thorough. You'll see when you hire me,' she said, forcing a confidence she didn't feel any more into her voice.

He continued to scowl at her, his hand still gripping the door as if he was seriously contemplating shutting it in her face, but she was not about to leave this doorstep without a fight. She'd had *enough* of feeling like a failure.

'Give me a chance to show you what I can do, free of charge, today, then if you like what you see I can start properly tomorrow.' Her forced smile was beginning to make her cheeks ache now.

His eyes narrowed as he appeared to consider her proposal.

After a few tense seconds of silence, where she thought her heart might beat its way out of her chest, he nodded towards the folder she was still clutching in her hand.

'Is that your CV?' he asked.

'Yes.' She handed it to him and watched with bated breath as he flipped through it.

'Okay,' he said finally, sighing hard and shoving the folder back towards her. 'Show me what you can do today, then if I'm satisfied I'll offer you a paid one-month trial period. After *that* I'll decide whether it's going to work out as a full-time position or not.'

'Done.' She stuck out a hand, which he looked at with a bemused expression, before enveloping it in his own large, warm one.

Relief, chased by an unnerving hot tingle, rushed through her as he squeezed her fingers, causing every nerve-ending on her body to spring to life.

'You'd better come in,' he said, dropping the handshake and turning his broad back on her to disappear into the house.

Judging by his abrupt manner, it seemed she had her work cut out if she was going to impress him. Still, she was up for the challenge—even if the man did make her stomach flip in the most disconcerting way.

Shaking off her nerves, she hurried inside after him, closing the heavy door behind her and swivelling back just in time to see him march into a doorway at the end of the hall.

And what a hall. It had more square footage than her entire flat put together. The high, pale cream walls were lined with abstract works of art on real canvases, not clip-framed prints like she had at her place, and the colourful mosaic-tiled floor ran for what must have been a good fifty metres before it joined the bottom of a wide oak staircase which led up to a similarly grand stairwell, where soft light flooded in through a huge stained-glass window.

Stopping by a marble-topped hall table, which, she noted, was sadly devoid of flowers, she took a deep calming breath before striding down the hallway to the room he'd vanished into.

Okay, she could do this. She could be impressive. Because she *was* impressive.

Right, Cara? *Right?*

The room she entered was just as spacious as the hall, but this time the walls were painted a soft duck-egg blue below the picture rail and a crisp, fresh white above it, which made the corniced ceiling feel as if it was a million miles above her and that she was very small indeed in comparison.

Max was standing in the middle of the polished parquet floor with a look of distracted impatience on his face. Despite her nerves, Cara couldn't help but be aware of how dauntingly charismatic he was. The man seemed to give off waves of pure sexual energy.

'My name's Cara, by the way,' she said, swallowing her apprehension and giving him a friendly smile.

He just nodded and held out a laptop. 'This is a spare. You can use it today. Once you've set it up, you can get started on scanning and filing those documents over there,' he said, pointing to a teetering pile of paper on a table by the window. 'There's the filing cabinet—' he swung his finger to point at it '—there's the scanner.' Another swing of his finger. 'The filing system should be self-explanatory,' he concluded with barely concealed agitation in his voice.

So he wasn't a people person then.

'Okay, thank you,' she said, taking the laptop from him and going to sit on a long, low sofa that was pushed up against the wall on the opposite side of the room to a large oak desk with a computer and huge monitor on top of it.

Tamping down on the nervous tension that had plagued her ever since she'd walked away from her last job, she booted up the laptop, opened the internet browser and set up her email account and a folder called 'Firebrace Management Solutions' in a remote file-saving app. Spotting a stack of business cards on the coffee table next to the sofa, she swiped one and programmed Max's mobile number into her phone, then added his email address to her contacts.

Throughout all this, he sat at his desk with his back to her, deeply absorbed in writing the document she must have stopped him from working on when she'd knocked on his door.

Okay. The first thing she was going to do was make them

both a hot drink, then she'd make a start on the mountain of paperwork to be digitally backed up and filed.

Not wanting to speak up and disturb him with questions at this point, she decided to do a bit of investigative work. Placing the laptop carefully onto the sofa, she stood up and made for the door, intent on searching out the kitchen.

He didn't stir from his computer screen as she walked past him.

Well, if nothing else, at least this was going to be a very different experience to her last job. By the end of her time there she could barely move without feeling a set of judging eyes burning into her.

The kitchen was in the room directly opposite and she stood for a moment to survey the lie of it. There was a big glass-topped table in the middle with six chairs pushed in around it and an expanse of cream-coloured marble work surface, which ran the length of two sides of the room. The whole place was sleek and new-looking, with not a thing out of place.

Opening up the dishwasher, she peered inside and saw one mug and one cereal bowl sitting in the rack. *Hmm.* So it was just Max living here? Unless his partner was away at the moment. Glancing round, she scanned the place for photographs, but there weren't any, not even one stuck to the enormous American fridge. In fact, this place was so devoid of personalised knick-knacks it could have been a kitchen in a show home.

Lifting the mug out of the dishwasher, she checked it for remnants of his last drink, noting from the smell that it was coffee, no sugar, and from the colour that he took it without milk. There was a technical-looking coffee maker on the counter which flummoxed her for a moment or two, but she soon figured out how to set it up and went about finding coffee grounds in the sparsely filled fridge and making them both a drink, adding plenty of milk to hers.

Walking back into the room, she saw that Max hadn't budged

a centimetre since she'd left and was still busy tapping away on the keyboard.

After placing his drink carefully onto the desk, which he acknowledged with a grunt, she took a look through the filing cabinet till she figured out which system he was using, then squared up to the mountain of paperwork on the sideboard, took a breath and dived in.

Well, she was certainly the most *determined* woman he'd met in a long time.

Max Firebrace watched Cara out of the corner of his eye as she manhandled the pile of documents over to the sofa and heard her put them down with a thump on the floor.

Glancing at the drink she'd brought him, he noticed she'd made him a black coffee without even asking what he wanted.

Huh. He wasn't expecting that. The PAs he'd had in the past had asked a lot of questions when they'd first started working with him, but Cara seemed content to use her initiative and just get on with things.

Perhaps this wasn't going to be as much of a trial as he'd assumed when he'd agreed to their bargain on the doorstep.

It was typical of Poppy to send someone over here without letting him know. His friend was a shrewd operator all right. She'd known he was blowing her off when he promised to get someone in to help him and had clearly taken it upon herself to make it happen anyway.

Irritation made his skin prickle.

He was busy, sure, but, as he'd told Poppy at the time, it wasn't anything he couldn't handle. He'd allow Cara to work her one-month trial period to placate his friend, but then he'd let her go. He wasn't ready to hire someone else full-time yet; there wasn't enough for her to do day-to-day, and he didn't need someone hanging around, distracting him.

Leaning back into the leather swivel chair that had practically become his home in the past few months, he rubbed the heels of his hands across his eyes before picking up the drink and taking a sip.

He'd been working more and more at the weekends now that his management consultancy was starting to grow some roots, and he was beginning to feel it. It had been a slog since he'd set up on his own, but he'd been glad of the distraction and it was finally starting to pay dividends. If things carried on in the same vein, at some point in the future he'd be in a position to rent an office, hire some employees and start expanding. *Then* he could relax a little and things would get back to a more even keel.

The thought buoyed him. After working for other people since graduating from university, he was enjoying having full control over who he worked for and when; it seemed to bring about a modicum of peace—something that had eluded him for the past eighteen months. Ever since Jemima had gone.

No, *died.*

He really needed to allow the word into his interior monologue now. No one else had wanted to say it at the time, so he'd become used to employing all the gentler euphemisms himself, but there was no point pretending it was anything else. She'd died, so suddenly and unexpectedly it had left him reeling for months, and he still wasn't used to living in this great big empty house without her. The house Jemima had inherited from her great-aunt. The home she'd wanted to fill with children—which he'd asked her to wait for—until *he* felt ready.

Pain twisted in his stomach as he thought about all that he'd lost—his beautiful, compassionate wife and their future family. Recently he'd been waking up at night in a cold sweat, reaching out to try and save a phantom child with Jemima's eyes from a fall, or a fire—the shock and anguish of it often staying with him for the rest of the following day.

No wonder he was tired.

A movement in the corner of his eye broke his train of thought and he turned to watch Cara as she opened up the filing cabinet to the right of him and began to deftly slide documents into the manila folders inside.

Now that he looked at her properly, he could see the family resemblance to Poppy. She had the same shiny coal-black hair as his friend, which cascaded over her slim shoulders, and a very short blunt-cut fringe above bright blue almond-shaped eyes.

She was pretty. Very pretty, in fact.

Not that he had any interest in her romantically. It was purely an observation.

Cara looked round and caught him watching her, her cheeks flushing in response to his scrutiny.

Feeling uncomfortable with the atmosphere he'd created by staring at her, he sat up straighter, crossing his arms and adopting a more businesslike posture. 'So, Cara, tell me about the last place you worked. Why did you leave?'

Her rosy cheeks seemed to pale under his direct gaze. Rocking back on her heels, she cleared her throat, her gaze skittering away from his to stare down at the papers in her hands, as if she was priming herself to give him an answer she thought he'd want to hear.

What was *that* about? The incongruity made him frown.

'Or were you fired?'

Her gaze snapped back to his. 'No, no, I left. At least, I opted for voluntary redundancy. The business I was working for took a big financial hit last year and, because I was the last in, it felt only right that I should be the first out. There were lots of people who worked there with families to support, whereas I'm only me—I mean I don't have anyone depending on me.'

Her voice had risen throughout that little monologue and the colour had returned to her cheeks to the point where she looked uncomfortably flushed. There was something not quite right about the way she'd delivered her answer, but he couldn't put his finger on what it was.

Perhaps she was just nervous? He knew he could come across

as fierce sometimes, though usually only when someone did something to displease him.

He didn't suffer fools gladly.

But she'd been fine whilst persuading him to give her a shot at the PA job.

'That's it? You took voluntary redundancy?'

She nodded and gave him a smile that didn't quite reach her eyes. 'That's it.'

'So why come begging for this job? Surely, with your six years of experience, you could snap up a senior position in another blue-chip firm and earn a lot more money.'

Crossing her arms, she pulled her posture up straighter, as if preparing to face off with him. 'I wouldn't say I *begged* you for this job—'

He widened his eyes, taken aback by the defensiveness in her tone.

Noting this, she sank back into her former posture and swept a conciliatory hand towards him. '—but I take your point. To be honest, I've been looking for a change of scene from the corporate workplace and when Poppy mailed me about this opportunity it seemed to fit with exactly what I was looking for. I like the idea of working in a small, dedicated team and being an intrinsic part of the growth of a new business. Poppy says you're brilliant at what you do and I like working for brilliant people.' She flashed him another smile, this time with a lot more warmth in it.

He narrowed his eyes and gave her an approving nod. 'Okay. Good answer. You're an excellent ambassador for yourself and that's a skill I rate highly.'

Her eyes seemed to take on an odd shine in the bright midmorning light, as if they'd welled up with tears.

Surely not.

Breaking eye contact, she looked down at the papers in her hand and blinked a couple of times, giving the floor a small nod. 'Well, that's good to hear.' When she looked back up, her eyes were clear again and the bravado in her expression made him wonder what was going on in her head.

Not that he should concern himself with such things.

An odd moment passed between them as their gazes caught and he became uncomfortably aware of the silence in the room. He'd been on his own in this house for longer than he wanted to think about, and having her here was evidently messing with his head. Which was exactly what he didn't need.

Cara looked away first, turning to open one of the lower filing cabinet drawers. After dropping the documents into it, she turned back to face him with a bright smile. 'Okay, well, it won't take me too much longer to finish this so I'll nip out in a bit and get us some lunch from the café a couple of streets away. When I walked past earlier there was an amazing smell of fresh bread wafting out of there, and they had a fantastic selection of deli meats and cheeses and some delicious-looking salads.'

Max's stomach rumbled as he pictured the scene she'd so artfully drawn in his mind. He was always too busy to go out and fetch lunch for himself, so ended up eating whatever he could forage from the kitchen, which usually wasn't much.

'Then, if you have a spare minute later on, you can give me access to your online diary,' Cara continued, not waiting for his response. 'I'll take a look through it and organise any transport and overnight stays you need booking.'

'Okay. That would be useful,' he said, giving her a nod. It would be great to have the small daily inconveniences taken care of so he could concentrate on getting this report knocked into shape today.

Hmm. Perhaps it would prove more advantageous than he'd thought to have her around for a while.

He'd have to make sure he fully reaped the benefit of her time here before letting her go.

CHAPTER TWO

SHE WAS A terrible liar.

The expression on Max's face had been sceptical at best when she'd reeled out the line about leaving her last job, but Cara thought she'd pulled it off. At least he hadn't told her to sling her hook.

Yet.

She got the impression he was the type of person who wouldn't tolerate any kind of emotional weakness—something she was particularly sensitive to after her last boyfriend, Ewan, left her three months ago because he was fed up with her 'moaning and mood swings'. So she was going to have to be careful not to let any more momentary wobbles show on her face. It was going to be happy, happy, joy, joy! from here on in.

After slipping the last document into the filing cabinet, taking care not to let him see how much her hands were still shaking, she grabbed her coat and bag and, after taking a great gulp of crisp city air into her lungs, went to the café to pick up some lunch for them both, leaving the door off the latch so she wouldn't have to disturb Max by ringing the bell on her return.

Inevitably, she bought a much bigger selection of deli wares than the two of them could possibly eat in one session, but she told herself that Max could finish off whatever remained for his supper. Judging by the emptiness of his cavernous fridge, he'd probably be glad of it later.

This made her wonder again about his personal situation. Poppy had told her very little in the email—which she'd sent in a rare five minutes off from her crazy-sounding filming schedule in the African desert. Cara didn't want to bother her cousin with those kinds of questions when she was so busy, so it was up to her to find out the answers herself. For purely professional reasons, of course. It would make her working life much easier if she knew whether she needed to take a partner's feelings into consideration when making bookings away from the office.

Surprisingly, Max didn't put up much resistance to being dragged away from his computer with the promise of lunch and came into the kitchen just as she'd finished laying out the last small pot of pimento-stuffed olives, which she hadn't been able to resist buying.

'Good timing,' she said as he sat down. 'That deli is incredible. I wasn't sure what you'd prefer so I got just about everything they had—hopefully, there'll be something you like—and there should be plenty left over for tomorrow, or this evening if you don't already have dinner plans.'

Good grief—could she jabber more?

Clearly, this had occurred to Max too because he raised his eyebrows, but didn't say a word.

Trying not to let his silence intimidate her, Cara passed him a plate, which he took with an abrupt nod of thanks, and she watched him load it up with food before tucking in.

'So, Max,' she said, taking a plate for herself and filling it with small triangular-cut sandwiches stuffed with soft cheese and prosciutto and a spoonful of fluffy couscous speckled with herbs and tiny pieces of red pepper. 'How do you know Poppy? She didn't tell me anything about you—other than that you're friends.'

He gave a small shrug. 'We met at university.'

Cara waited for him to elaborate.

He didn't. He just kept on eating.

Okay, so he wasn't the sort to offer up personal details about himself and liked to keep things super professional with colleagues, but perhaps she'd be able to get more out of him once they'd built up a rapport between them.

That was okay. It was early days yet. She could bide her time.

At least she had some company for lunch, even if he wasn't interested in talking much. She'd spent all her lunchtimes at her last place of work alone, either sitting in the local park or eating a sandwich at her desk, forcing the food past her constricted throat, trying not to care about being excluded from the raucous group of PAs who regularly lunched together. The Cobra Clique, she'd called them in her head.

Not to their faces.

Never to their faces.

Because, after making the mistake of assuming she'd be welcomed into their group when she'd first started working there—still riding on a wave of pride and excitement about landing such a coveted job—she'd soon realised that she'd stepped right into the middle of a viper's nest. Especially after the backlash began to snap its tail a couple of days into her first week.

Fighting the roll of nausea that always assaulted her when she thought about it, she took a large bite of sandwich and chewed hard, forcing herself to swallow, determined not to let what had happened bother her any more. They'd won and she was not going to let them keep on winning.

'It's a beautiful house you have, Max,' she said, to distract herself from the memories still determinedly circling her head. 'Have you been here long?'

His gaze shot to hers and she was alarmed to see him frown. 'Three years,' he said, with a clip of finality to his voice, as if wanting to make it clear he didn't want to discuss the subject any more.

Okay then.

From the atmosphere that now hummed between them, you'd

have thought she'd asked him how much cold hard cash he'd laid down for the place. Perhaps people did ask him that regularly and he was fed up with answering it. Or maybe he thought she'd ask for a bigger wage if she thought he was loaded.

Whatever the reason, his frostiness had now totally destroyed her appetite, so she was pushing the couscous around her plate when Max stood up, making her jump in her seat.

'Let me know how much I owe you for lunch and I'll get it out of petty cash before you leave,' he said, turning abruptly on the spot and heading over to the dishwasher to load his empty plate into it.

His movements were jerky and fast, as if he was really irritated about something now.

It couldn't be her, could it?

No.

Could it?

He must just be keen to get back to work.

As soon as he left the room, she let out the breath she'd been holding, feeling the tension in her neck muscles release a little.

The words *frying pan* and *fire* flitted through her head, but she dismissed them. If he was a friend of Poppy's he couldn't be that bad. She must have just caught him on a bad day. And, as her friend Sarah had pointed out after she'd cried on her shoulder about making a mess of her recent job interviews, she was bound to be prone to paranoia after her last experience.

Once she'd cleared up in the kitchen, Cara got straight back to work, using the link Max gave her to log in to his online diary and work through his travel requirements for the next month. His former ire seemed to have abated somewhat and their interaction from that point onwards was more relaxed, but still very professional. Blessedly, concentrating on the work soothed her and the headache that had started at the end of lunch began to lift as she worked methodically through her tasks.

Mid-afternoon, Max broke off from writing his document for a couple of minutes to outline some research he wanted her to do on a few businesses he was considering targeting. To her frustration, she had to throw every molecule of energy into making scrupulous notes in order to keep focused on the task in hand and not on the way Max's masculine scent made her senses reel and her skin heat with awareness every time he leaned closer to point something out on the computer they were huddled around.

That was something she was going to have to conquer if they continued to work together, which hopefully they would. She definitely couldn't afford a crush on her boss to get in the way of her recuperating future.

After finally being released from the duress of his unnerving presence, she spent the remainder of the day happily surfing the internet and collating the information into a handy crib sheet for him, revelling in the relief of getting back into a mindset she'd taken for granted until about six months ago, before her whole working life had been turned inside out.

At five-thirty she both printed out the document and emailed it to him, then gathered up her coat and bag, feeling as though she'd done her first good day's work in a long time.

Approaching his desk, she cleared her throat and laid the printout onto it, trying not to stare at the way his muscles moved beneath his slim-fitting shirt while she waited for him to finish what he was typing. Tearing her eyes away from his broad back, she took the opportunity to look at his hands instead, noting with a strange satisfaction that he wasn't wearing a wedding ring on his long, strong-looking fingers.

Okay, not married then. But surely he must have a girlfriend. She couldn't imagine someone as attractive as Max being single.

He stopped typing and swivelled round in his chair to face her, startling her out of her musings and triggering a strange throb, low in her body.

'You've done well today; I'm impressed,' he said, giving her a slow nod.

She couldn't stop her mouth from springing up into a full-on grin. It had been a long while since she'd been complimented on her work and it felt ridiculously good.

'Thank you—I've really enjoyed it.'

His raised eyebrow told her she'd been a bit over-effusive with that statement, but he unfolded his arms and dipped his head thoughtfully.

'If you're still interested, I'm willing to go ahead with the one-month trial.'

Her squeak of delight made him blink. 'I can't promise there'll be a full-time job at the end of it, though,' he added quickly.

She nodded. 'Okay, I understand.' She'd just have to make sure she'd made herself indispensable by the end of the month.

He then named a weekly wage that made her heart leap with excitement. With money like that she could afford to stay in London and keep on renting her flat.

'I'll see you here at nine tomorrow then,' he concluded, turning back to his computer screen.

'Great. Nine o'clock tomorrow,' she repeated, smiling at the back of his head and retreating out of the room.

She floated out of the house on a cloud of joy, desperate to get home so she could phone her landlord and tell him she was going to be able to make next month's rent so he didn't need to find a new tenant for her flat.

It was all going to be okay now; she could feel it.

Back in her flat, she dialled her landlord's number and he answered with a brusque, 'Yes.'

'Dominic—it's Cara Winstone. I'm calling with good news. I've just started at a new job so I'll be able to renew my lease on your property in Islington.'

There was a silence at the end of the phone, followed by a long sigh. 'Sorry, Cara, but I've already promised my nephew he can move in at the end of the week. I got the impression you wouldn't be able to afford the rent any more and I've kept it pitifully low for the last couple of years already. I can't afford to sub you any more.'

Fear and anger made her stomach sink and a suffocating heat race over her skin as she fully took in what he'd just said. He was such a liar. He'd been hiking the rent up year on year until she'd felt as if she was being totally fleeced, but she hadn't wanted the hassle of moving out of her comfortable little flat so she'd sucked it up. Until she wasn't able to any more.

'Can't you tell your nephew that your current tenant has changed her mind?' Even as she said it she knew what his answer was going to be.

'No. I can't. You had your chance to renew. I couldn't wait any longer and my nephew was having trouble finding somewhere suitable to live. It's a cut-throat rental market in London at the moment.'

That was something she was about to find out herself, she felt sure of it.

'Do you have anywhere else available to rent at the moment?' she asked, desperately grasping for some glimmer of a solution.

'No. Sorry.'

He didn't sound sorry, she noted with another sting of anger.

'You've got till the end of the week, then I want you out,' he continued. 'Make sure the place is in a good state when you leave or I'll have to withhold your damage deposit.' And, with that, he put the phone down on her.

It took a few minutes of hanging her head between her knees for the dizziness to abate and for her erratic heartbeat to return to normal.

Okay, this was just a setback. She could handle it.

Just because it would be hard to find a decent flat to rent in London at short notice didn't mean she wouldn't find somewhere else. She'd have to be proactive though and make sure to put all her feelers out, then respond quickly to any leads.

That could prove tricky now that she was working so closely with Max and she was going to have to be very careful not to mess up on the job, because it looked as though she was going to need things to work out there more than ever now.

The rest of the week flew by for Max, with Cara turning up exactly when she said she would and working diligently and efficiently through the tasks he gave her.

Whilst it was useful having her around to take care of some of the more mundane jobs that he'd been ignoring for far too long, he also found her presence was disrupting his ability to lose himself in his work, which he'd come to rely on in order to get through the fiercely busy days.

She was just so *jolly* all the time.

And she was making the place smell different. Every morning when he came downstairs for his breakfast he noticed her light floral perfume in the air. It was as though she was beginning to permeate the walls of his house and even the furniture with her scent.

It made him uncomfortable.

He knew he'd been rude during their first lunch together when Cara had asked him about the house and that he'd been unforthcoming about anything of a personal nature ever since—preferring to spend his lunchtimes in companionable silence—but he was concerned that any questions about himself would inevitably lead on to him having to talk about Jemima.

Work was supposed to be sanctuary from thinking about what had happened and he really didn't want to discuss it with Cara.

He also didn't want them to become too sociable because it would only make it harder for him to let her go after the promised month of employment.

Clearly she was very good at her job, so he had no concerns about her finding another position quickly after her time was up, but it might still prove awkward when it came down to saying no to full-time employment if they were on friendly terms. He suspected Cara's story about taking voluntary redundancy wasn't entirely based on truth and that she and Poppy had cooked up the story to play on his sympathy in order to get him to agree to take her on. While he was fine with allowing his errant friend to push him into a temporary arrangement to appease her mollycoddling nature, he wasn't going to allow her to bully him into keeping Cara on full-time.

He didn't need her.

After waking late on Friday morning and having to let an ebullient Cara in whilst still not yet ready to face the day, he had to rush his shower and hustle down to the kitchen with a pounding headache from not sleeping well the night before. Opening the fridge, he found that Cara had stocked it with all sorts of alien-looking food—things he would never have picked out himself. He knew he was bad at getting round to food shopping, but Cara's choices were clearly suggesting he wasn't looking after himself properly. There were superfoods galore in there.

He slammed the fridge door shut in disgust.

The damn woman was taking over the place.

Cara was in the hallway when he came out of the kitchen a few minutes later with a cup of coffee so strong he could have stood his spoon up in it. She waved a cheery hello, then gestured to a vase of brightly coloured flowers that she'd put onto the hall table, giving him a jaunty smile as if to say, *That's better, right?* which really set his teeth on edge. How was it possible for her to be so damn happy all the time? Did the woman live with her head permanently in the clouds?

They'd never had fresh flowers in the house when Jemima was alive because she'd suffered with bad hay fever from the pollen, and he was just about to tell Cara that when he caught himself and clamped his mouth shut. It wasn't a discussion he wanted to have this morning, with a head that felt as if it was about to explode. The very last thing he needed right now was Cara's fervent pity.

'I thought it would be nice to have a bit of colour in here,' she said brightly, oblivious to his displeasure. 'I walked past the most amazing florist's on my way over here and I just couldn't resist popping in. Flowers are so good for lifting your mood.'

'That's fine,' he said through gritted teeth, hoping she wasn't going to be this chipper all day. He didn't think his head could stand it.

'I'll just grab myself a cup of tea, then I'll be in,' she said.

Only managing to summon a grunt in response, he walked into the morning room that he'd turned into an office. He'd chosen it because it was away from the distractions of the street and in the odd moment of pause he found that staring out into the neatly laid garden soothed him. There was a particular brightly coloured bird that came back day after day and hopped about on the lawn, looking for worms, which captivated him. It wasn't there today, though.

After going through his ever-growing inbox and dealing with the quick and easy things, he opened up his diary to check what was going on that day. He had a conference call starting in ten minutes that would probably last till lunchtime, which meant he'd need to brief Cara now about what he wanted her to get on with.

Where was she, anyway?

She'd only been going to make herself a hot drink. Surely she must have done that by now?

Getting up from his chair with a sigh of irritation, he walked through to the kitchen to find her. The last thing he needed was to have to chase his PA down. It was going to be a demanding day which required some intense concentration and he needed her to be on the ball and ready to knuckle down.

She was leaning against the table with her back to the door when he walked into the kitchen, her head cocked to one side as if she was fascinated by something on the other side of the room.

He frowned at her back, wondering what in the heck could be so absorbing, until she spoke in a hushed tone and he realised she was on the phone.

'I don't know whether I'll be able to get away at lunchtime.

I have to fetch my boss's lunch and there's a ton of other stuff I have to wade through. His systems are a mess. Unfortunately, Max isn't the type you can ask for a favour either; he's not exactly approachable. I could make it over for about six o'clock, though,' she muttered into the phone.

The hairs rose on the back of his neck. She was making arrangements to see her friends on his time?

He cleared his throat loudly, acutely aware of the rough harshness of his tone in the quiet of the room.

Spinning around at the noise, Cara gave him a look of horror, plainly embarrassed to be caught out.

Definitely a personal call then.

Frustration rattled through him, heating his blood. How could he have been so gullible as to think it would be easy having her as an employee? Apparently she was going to be just as hard work to manage as all the other PAs he'd had.

'Are you sure you took redundancy at your last place? Or did they let you go for taking liberties on the job?' he said, unable to keep the angry disappointment out of his voice.

She swallowed hard and he found his gaze drawn to the long column of her throat, its smooth elegance distracting him for a second. Shaking off his momentary befuddlement, he snapped his gaze back to hers, annoyed with himself for losing concentration.

'I do not expect behaviour like this from someone with six years of experience as a personal assistant. This isn't the canteen where you waste time gossiping with your mates instead of doing the job you're being paid to do. Things like this make you look stupid and amateurish.'

She nodded jerkily but didn't say anything as her cheeks flushed with colour and a tight little frown appeared in the centre of her forehead.

Fighting a twist of unease, he took another step forwards and pointed a finger at her. 'You do not take personal phone calls on my time. Is that understood? Otherwise, you and I are going to have a problem, and problems are the last thing I need right now. I took a chance on you because you came recommended by Poppy. Do not make a fool out of my friend. Or out of me.'

'I'm sorry—it won't ever happen again. I promise,' she said, her voice barely above a whisper.

The look in her eyes disturbed him. It was such a change from her usual cheery countenance that it sat uncomfortably with him. In fact, to witness her reaction you'd have thought he'd just slapped her around the face, not given her a dressing-down.

'See that it doesn't,' he concluded with a curt nod, an unnerving throb beginning to beat in his throat.

As he walked back into his office, he found he couldn't wipe the haunted expression in her eyes from his mind, his pace faltering as he allowed himself to reflect fully on what had just happened.

Perhaps he'd been a bit too hard on her.

Running a hand over his tired eyes, he shook his head at himself. Who was he kidding—he'd definitely overreacted. For all he knew, it could have been a sick relative on the phone whom she needed to visit urgently.

The trouble was, he'd been so careful to keep her at arm's length and not to let any of his own personal details slip he'd totally failed to ask her anything about herself.

And he was tired. So tired it was making him cranky.

Swivelling on the spot, he went back out of the room to find her, not entirely sure what he was going to say, but knowing he should probably smooth things over between them. He needed her on his side today.

Walking back towards the kitchen, he met her as she was coming out, a cup of tea in her hand.

Instead of the look of sheepish upset he'd expected to see, she gave him a bright smile.

'I know you have a conference call in a couple of minutes, so if you can walk me through what I need to tackle today I'll get straight on it,' she said, her voice steady and true as if the past few minutes hadn't happened.

He stared at her in surprise, unnerved by the one hundred and eighty degree turn in her demeanour.

Had he imagined the look in her eyes that had disturbed him so much?

No, it had definitely been there; he was sure of it.

Still, at least this showed she wasn't one to hold grudges and let an atmosphere linger after being reprimanded. He appreciated that. He certainly couldn't work with someone who struggled to maintain a professional front when something didn't go their way.

But her level of nonchalance confused him, leaving him a little unsure of where they now stood with each other. Should he mention that he felt he'd been a bit hard on her? Or should he just leave it and sweep it under the carpet as she seemed keen to do?

What was the matter with him? This was ridiculous. He didn't have time for semantics today.

Giving her a firm nod, he turned around and walked back towards the office. 'Good, let's get started then.'

Determined to keep her hand from shaking and not slop hot tea all over herself, Cara followed Max back into the office, ready to be given instructions for the day.

She knew she couldn't afford to show any weakness right now.

Based on her experiences with Max so far, she was pretty damn sure if he thought she wasn't up to the job he'd fire her on the spot and then she'd be left with absolutely nothing.

That was not going to happen to her today.

She needed this job, with its excellent wage and the prospect of a good reference from a well-respected businessman, to be able to stay here in London. All she had to do was keep her head down and stick it out here with him until she found another permanent position somewhere else. She had CVs out at a couple more places and with any luck another opportunity might present itself soon. Until then she'd just have to make sure she didn't allow his blunt manner and sharp tongue to erode her delicate confidence any further.

The trouble was, she'd allowed herself to be lulled into a false sense of security on her first day here after Max's compliment about her being a good ambassador for herself, only for him to pull the rug out from under her regrouping confidence later with his moods and quick temper.

The very last thing she needed was to work with another bully.

Not that she could really blame him for being angry in this instance. It must have looked really bad, her taking a personal phone call at the beginning of the working day. The really frustrating thing was that she'd never done anything like that before in her life. She was a rule follower to the core and very strict with herself about not surfing the Net or making personal calls on her employer's time, even in a big office where those kinds of things could go unnoticed.

Putting her drink down carefully, she wheeled her chair nearer to Max's desk and prepared to take notes, keeping her chin up and a benign smile fixed firmly on her face.

His own professional manner seemingly restored, Max outlined what he wanted her to do throughout the day, which she jotted down in her notebook. Once he appeared to be satisfied that he'd covered everything he leaned back in his chair and studied her, the intensity of his gaze making the hairs stand up on her arms.

'Listen, Cara, I'm finishing early for the day today,' he said, surprising her with the warmth in his voice. 'I'm meeting a friend in town for an early dinner, so feel free to leave here at four o'clock.'

She blinked at him in shock before pulling herself together. 'That would be great. Thank you.'

There was an uncomfortable pause, where he continued to look at her, his brows drawn together and his lips set in a firm line. He opened his mouth, as if he was about to tell her what was on his mind, but was rudely interrupted by the alarm going off on his phone signalling it was time for his conference call.

To her frustration, he snapped straight back into work mode, turning back to his computer and dialling a number on his phone, launching straight into his business spiel as soon as the person on the other end of the line picked up.

Despite her residual nerves, Cara still experienced the familiar little frisson of exhilaration that swept through her whenever she heard him do that. He'd set up a small desk for her next to his the day after he'd offered her the trial, which meant there was no getting away from the sound of his voice with its smooth, reassuring intonation.

He really was a very impressive businessman, even if he was a bit of a bear to work for.

Forcing her mind away from thinking about how uplifting it would be to have someone as passionate and dedicated as Max for a boyfriend—especially after the demeaning experience of her last relationship—she fired up her laptop and started in on the work he'd given her to take care of today.

After a few minutes, her thoughts drifted back to the fateful phone call she'd taken earlier, before their confrontation, and she felt a twitch of nerves in her stomach. It had been a friend calling to let her know about a possible flat coming onto the rental market—which was why she'd broken her rule and answered the call. If she managed to get there early enough she might just be able to snag it, which was now a real possibility thanks to Max's sudden announcement about leaving work at four o'clock.

Come to think of it, she was a little surprised about him finishing early to meet a friend in town. He'd never done that before, always continuing to work as she packed up for the day and—she strongly suspected—on into the evening. That would certainly account for the dark circles under his eyes. And his irascible mood.

The man appeared to be a workaholic.

After an hour of working through some truly tedious data inputting, Cara got up to make them both a hot drink, aware that Max must be parched by now from having to talk almost continuously since he'd begun his call.

Returning with the drinks, she sat back down at her desk to see she had an email from the friend that had called her earlier about the flat for rent.

Hmm. That couldn't be a good sign; she'd already mailed the details through earlier.

With a sinking feeling, she opened it up and scanned the text, her previously restored mood slipping away.

The flat had already been let.

An irrational impulse to cry gripped her and she got up quickly and made for the bathroom before the tears came, desperate to hide her despondency from Max.

Staring into the mirror, she attempted to talk herself down from her gloom. Her friend Sarah had offered to put her up on her sofa for a few days, so she at least had somewhere to stay in the interim. The only trouble was, her friend lived in a tiny place that she shared with her party animal boyfriend and he wouldn't want her hanging around, playing gooseberry, for too long.

The mere idea of renting with strangers at the ripe old age of twenty-seven horrified her, so she was going to have to be prepared to lower her standards to be in with a chance of finding another one-bedroom flat that she could afford in central London.

That was okay; she could do that. Hopefully, something would come up soon and then she'd be able to make some positive changes and get fully back on her feet.

Surely it was time for things to start going her way now?

CHAPTER THREE

AFTER MAKING UP the excuse about seeing a friend on Friday night in order to let Cara leave early, Max decided that he might as well phone around to see if anyone was available for a pint after work and actually surprised himself by having an enjoyable night out with some friends that he hadn't seen for a while.

He'd spent the rest of the weekend working, only breaking to eat his way through the entire contents of the fridge that Cara had stocked for him. Despite his initial disdain at her choices, he found he actually rather enjoyed trying the things she'd bought. They certainly beat the mediocre takeaways he'd been living on for the past few months.

Perhaps it *was* useful for him to have someone else around the house for a while, as Poppy had suggested the last time they'd seen each other. He'd baulked at her proposal that he should get back out on the dating scene though—he definitely wasn't ready for that, and honestly couldn't imagine ever being ready.

He and Jemima had been a couple since meeting at the beginning of their first year at university, their initial connection so immediate and intense they'd missed lectures for three days running to stay in bed together. They'd moved in with each other directly after graduating, making a home for themselves first in Manchester, then in London. After spending so much of his youth being moved from city to city, school to school, by his bohemian mother—until he finally put his foot down and forced her to send him to boarding school—it had been a huge relief to finally feel in control of his own life. To belong somewhere, with someone who wouldn't ask him to give up the life and friends he'd painstakingly carved out for himself—just *one* more time.

Jemima had understood his need for stability and had put up with his aversion to change with sympathetic acceptance and generous bonhomie. His life had been comfortably settled and he'd been deeply content—until she'd died, leaving him marooned and devastated by grief.

The idea of finding someone he could love as much as Jem seemed ludicrous. No one could ever replace his wife and it wouldn't be fair to let them try.

No, he would be fine on his own; he had his business and his friends and that would be enough for him.

Walking past the flower arrangement that Cara had left on the hall table on his way to sort through yesterday's junk mail, he had a memory flash of the expression on her face when he'd bawled her out in the kitchen the other day.

His chest tightened uncomfortably at the memory.

He needed to stop beating himself up about that now. He'd made amends for what had happened, even if she hadn't seemed entirely back to her happy, bright-eyed self again by the time she'd left on Friday afternoon. But at least he hadn't needed to delve into the murky waters of how they were both *feeling* about what had happened. He'd had enough of that kind of thing after forcing himself through the interminable sessions with grief counsellors after Jemima's death; he certainly didn't need to put himself through that discomfort again for something as inconsequential as a spat with his employee.

Fortunately, Cara seemed as reluctant to talk about it all as he was.

Rubbing a hand over his face, he gave a snort of disbelief about where his thoughts had taken him. Again. Surely it wasn't normal to be spending his weekend thinking about his PA.

Hmm.

His initial concerns about her being an unwanted distraction seemed to be coming to fruition, which was a worry. Still, there were only a few more weeks left of the promised trial period, then he'd be free of her. Until then he was going to have to keep his head in the game, otherwise the business was going to suffer. And that wasn't something he was prepared to let happen.

Monday morning rushed around, bringing with it bright sunshine that flooded the house and warmed the still, cool air, lifting his spirits a little.

Max had just sat down at his desk with his first cup of coffee of the day when there was a ring on the doorbell.

Cara.

Swinging open the door to let her in, he was taken aback to see her looking as if she hadn't slept a wink all night. There were dark circles around her puffy eyes and her skin was pallid and dull-looking. It seemed to pain her to even raise a smile for him.

Was she hung-over?

His earlier positivity vanished, to be replaced by a feeling of disquiet.

'Did you have a good weekend?' he asked as she walked into the house and hung up her coat.

She gave him a wan smile. 'Not bad, thanks. It was certainly a busy one. I didn't get much sleep.'

Hmm. So she had been out partying, by the sound of it.

Despite his concerns, Cara appeared to work hard all day and he only caught her yawning once whilst making them both a strong cup of coffee in the kitchen, mid-afternoon.

At the end of the day, she waved her usual cheery goodbye, though there was less enthusiasm in her smile than she normally displayed at knocking-off time.

To his horror, she turned up in the same state the following day.

And the next.

In fact, on Thursday, when he opened the door, he could have sworn he caught the smell of alcohol on her as she dashed past him into the house. She certainly looked as though she could have been up drinking all night and plainly hadn't taken a shower that morning, her hair hanging greasy and limp in a severely pulled back ponytail.

Her work was beginning to suffer too, in increments. Each day he found he had to pick her up on more and more things she'd missed or got wrong, noticing that her once pristine fingernails were getting shorter and more ragged as time went on.

Clearly she was letting whatever was happening in her personal life get in the way of her work and that was unacceptable.

His previous feelings of magnanimity about having her around had all but vanished by Thursday afternoon and he was seriously considering having a word with her about her performance. The only reason he hadn't done so already was because he'd been so busy with back-to-back conference calls this week and in deference to Poppy he'd decided to give Cara the benefit of the doubt and put her slip-ups down to a couple of off days.

But he decided that enough was enough when he found her with her head propped on her arms, fast asleep, on the kitchen table when she was supposed to be making them both a hot drink.

Resentment bubbled up from his gut as he watched her peaceful form gently rise and fall as she slumbered on, totally oblivious to his incensed presence behind her. He'd been feeling guilty all weekend about how he'd spoken to her on Friday and here she was, only a few days later, turning up unfit for work.

His concern that her presence here would cause more harm than good had just been ratified.

'Wakey, wakey, Sleeping Beauty!' he said loudly, feeling a swell of angry satisfaction as she leapt up from the table and spun around to look at him, her face pink and creased on one side where it had rested against her arm.

'Oh! Whoa! Was I sleeping?' she mumbled, blinking hard.

Crossing his arms, he gave her a hard stare. 'Like a baby.'

She rubbed a hand across her eyes, smudging her make-up across her face. 'I'm so sorry—I only put my head down to rest for a moment while I was waiting for the kettle to boil and I must have drifted off.'

'Perhaps you should start going to bed at a more reasonable time then,' he ground out, his hands starting to shake as adrenaline kicked its way through his veins. 'I didn't hire you as a charity case, Cara. For the money I'm paying, I expected much more from you. You had me convinced you were up to the job in the first couple of days, but it's become clear over the last few that you're not.' He took a breath as he made peace with what he was about to say. 'I'm going to have to let you go. I can't carry someone who's going to get drunk every night and turn up unfit to work.'

Her eyes were wide now and she was mouthing at him as if her response had got stuck in her throat.

Shaking off the stab of conscience that had begun to poke him in the back, he pointed a finger at her. 'And you can hold the "It'll never happen again" routine,' he bit out. 'I'm not an idiot, though I feel like one for letting you take me in like this.'

To his surprise, instead of the tears he was readying himself for, her expression morphed into one of acute fury and she raised her own shaking finger back at him.

'I do not get drunk every night. For your information, I'm homeless at the moment and sleeping on a friend's couch, which doesn't work well for her insomniac boyfriend, who likes to party and play computer games late into the night and who came home drunk and spilled an entire can of beer over me while I was trying to sleep and who then hogged the bathroom this morning so I couldn't get in there for a shower.'

Her face had grown redder and redder throughout this speech

and all he could do was stand there and stare at her, paralysed by surprise as she jabbed her finger at him with rage flashing in her eyes.

'I've worked my butt off for you, taking your irascible moods on the chin and getting on with it, but I'm not going to let you treat me like some nonentity waster. I'm a real person with real feelings, Max. I tried to make this work—you have no idea how hard I've been trying—but I guess this is just life's way of telling me that I'm done here in London.' She threw up her hands and took a deep shaky breath. 'After all the work I put into building myself a career here that I was so proud of—'

Taking in the look of utter frustration on her face, he felt his anger begin to drain away, only to be replaced with an uncomfortable twist of shame.

She was right, of course—he had been really unfriendly and probably very difficult to work with, and she was clearly dealing with some testing personal circumstances, which he'd made sure to blithely ignore.

He frowned and sighed heavily, torn about what to do next. While he could do without any extra problems at the moment, he couldn't bring himself to turn her away now he knew what she was dealing with. Because, despite it all, he admired her for standing up for herself.

Cara willed her heart to stop pounding like a pneumatic drill as she waited to see what Max would say next.

Had she really just shouted at him like that?

It was so unlike her to let her anger get the better of her, but something inside her had snapped at the unfairness of it all and she hadn't been able to hold back.

After spending the past few days using every ounce of energy keeping up the fake smile and pretending she could cope with the punishing days with Max on so little sleep, she'd hit a wall.

Hard.

The mix of panic, frustration and chronic tiredness had released something inside her and in those moments after she'd let the words fly she had the strangest sensation of the ground shifting under her feet. She was painfully aware that she'd probably just thrown away any hope of keeping this job, but at the same time she was immensely proud of herself for not allowing him to dismiss her like that. As if she was worth nothing.

Because she *wasn't*.

She deserved to be treated with more respect and she'd learnt by now that she wasn't going to get that from Max by meekly taking the insults he so callously dished out.

At her last place of work, in a fug of naïve disbelief, she'd allowed those witches to strip her of her pride, but there was no way she was letting Max do that to her, too.

No matter what it cost her.

She could get another job—and she would, eventually—but she'd never be able to respect herself again if she didn't stand up to him now.

Her heart raced as she watched a range of expressions run across Max's face. The fact that he hadn't immediately repeated his dismissal gave her hope that there might be a slim chance he'd reverse his decision to fire her.

Moving her hands behind her back, she crossed her fingers for a miracle, feeling a bead of sweat run down her spine.

Sighing hard, Max ran a hand through the front of his hair, pushing it out of his eyes and looking at her with his usual expression of ill-concealed irritation.

'I'm guessing you became homeless on Friday, which is when the mistakes started to happen?' he asked finally.

She nodded, aware of the tension in her shoulders as she held her nerve. 'I spent all day on Sunday moving my furniture into storage. I've been staying with my friend Sarah and her boyfriend ever since.'

'But that can't carry on,' he said with finality to his voice.

Swallowing hard, she tipped up her chin. 'No. I know. I've tried to view so many places to rent in the last week, but they seem to go the second they're advertised. I can't get to them fast enough.'

He crossed his arms. 'And you have nowhere else to stay in London? No boyfriend? No family?'

Shaking her head, she straightened her posture, determined to hang on to her poise. She wouldn't look away, not now she'd been brave enough to take him on. If she was going to be fired, she was going down with her head held high. 'My parents live in Cornwall and none of my other friends in London have room to put me up.' She shifted uncomfortably on the spot and swallowed back the lingering hurt at the memory of her last disastrous relationship. 'I've been single for a few months now.'

He stared back at her, his eyes hooded and his brow drawn down.

A world of emotions rattled through her as she waited to hear his verdict.

'Okay. You can stay here until you find a flat to rent.'

She gawped at him, wondering whether her brain was playing tricks on her. 'I'm sorry—*what*?'

'I said—you can stay here,' he said slowly, enunciating every word. 'I have plenty of spare rooms. I'm on the top floor so you could have the whole middle floor to yourself.'

'Really?'

He bristled, rolling his eyes up to the ceiling and letting out a frustrated snort. 'Yes, really. I'm not just making this up to see your impression of a goldfish.'

She stared at him even harder. Had he just made a *joke*? That was definitely a first.

Unfolding his arms, he batted a hand through the air. 'I'm sure it won't take you long to find somewhere else and until then I need you turning up to work fully rested and back to your efficient, capable self.'

Her eyes were so wide now she felt sure she must look as if she was wearing a pair of those joke goggle-eye glasses.

He was admitting to her being good at her job too now? Wonders would never cease.

But she was allowing these revelations to distract her from the decision she needed to make. Could she really live in the same house as her boss? Even if it was only for a short time.

Right now, it didn't feel as though she had much of a choice. The thought of spending even one more night in Party Central made her heart sink. If she turned Max down on his offer, that was the only other viable option—save staying in a hotel she couldn't afford or renting a place a long way out and spending her life commuting in. Neither of them were appealing options.

But could she really live here with him? The mere idea of it made her insides flutter and it wasn't just because he was a bit of a difficult character. During the week and a half that she'd known him, she'd become increasingly jittery in his presence, feeling a tickle of excitement run up her spine every time she caught his scent in the air or even just watched him move around his territory like some kind of lean, mean, business machine. Not that he'd ever given her a reason to think she was in any kind of danger being there alone with him. Clearly, he had no interest in her romantically. If anything, she'd felt it had been the total opposite for him, as if he didn't think of her as a woman at all, only a phone-answering, data-sorting robot.

So she was pretty sure he didn't have an ulterior motive behind his suggestion that she should stay in his house.

Unfortunately.

Naughty, naughty Cara.

'Well, if you're sure it won't be too much of an inconvenience to you,' she said slowly.

'No. It's fine,' he answered curtly. 'We'll have to make sure to respect each other's privacy, but it's a big place so that shouldn't be a problem. All the rooms have locks on them, in case you're worried.'

Her pulse picked up as a host of X-rated images rushed through her head.

Slam a lid on that, you maniac.

'I'm not worried,' she squeaked.

He nodded.

'And your girlfriend won't mind me staying here?' she asked carefully.

'I don't have a girlfriend.'

'Or your w—?' she began to ask, just in case.

'I'm single,' he cut in with a curt snap to his voice.

Okay, so the subject of his relationships was out of bounds then.

She was surprised to hear that he wasn't attached in any way, though. Surely someone with his money, looks and smarts would have women lining up around the block for the pleasure of his company. Although, come to think of it, based on her run-ins with him so far, she could see how his acerbic temperament might be a problem for some people.

'Right, I may as well show you your room now,' Max said, snapping her out of her meandering thoughts. 'Clearly, you're not in a fit state to work this afternoon, so you may as well finish for the day.' He turned and walked out of the room, leaving her gaping at the empty space he'd left.

So that was it then—decision made.

'Oh! Okay.' She hustled to catch him up, feeling her joints complain as she moved. *Crikey.* She was tired. Her whole body ached from sleeping on a saggy sofa and performing on so little sleep for the past few days.

She followed him up the sweeping staircase to the next level and along the landing to the third door on the right.

Opening it up, he motioned for her to walk past him into the bedroom.

She tried not to breathe in his fresh, spicy scent as she did so, her nerves already shot from the rigours of the day.

It was, of course, the most beautifully appointed bedroom she'd ever been in.

Light flooded in through the large window, which was

framed by long French grey curtains in a heavy silk. The rest of the furnishing was simple and elegant, in a way Cara had never been able to achieve in her own flat. The pieces that had been chosen clearly had heritage and fitted perfectly with the large airy room. His interior designer must have cost a pretty penny.

Tears welled in her eyes as she took in the original ornate fireplace, which stood proudly opposite a beautiful king-sized iron-framed bed. Fighting the urge to collapse onto it in relief and bury herself in the soft, plump-looking duvet, she blinked hard, then turned to face Max, who was hanging back by the door with a distracted frown on his face.

'This is a beautiful room—thank you,' she said, acutely aware of the tremor in her voice.

Max's frown deepened, but he didn't comment on it. 'You're welcome. You should go over to your friend's house and get your things now, then you'll have time to settle in. We'll start over again tomorrow.'

'Okay, good idea.'

'I'll leave you to it then,' he said, turning to go.

'Max?'

He turned back. 'Yes?'

'I'm really grateful—for letting me stay here.'

'No problem,' he said, turning briskly on the spot and walking away, leaving her staring after him with her heart in her mouth.

Well, she certainly hadn't expected this when she'd woken up this morning reeking of stale beer.

Sinking down gratefully onto the bed, she finally allowed her tense muscles to relax, feeling the tiredness rush back, deep into her bones.

How was she ever going to be able to drag herself away from this beautiful room when she managed to find a place of her own to rent?

More to the point, was she really going to be able to live in the same house as Max without going totally insane?

Steeling herself to make the journey over to Sarah's house and pick up her things, she rocked herself up off the bed of her dreams and onto her feet and took a deep, resolute breath.

There was only one way to find out.

CHAPTER FOUR

IF SOMEONE HAD asked Max to explain exactly what had prompted him to suggest that Cara move in, he was pretty sure he'd have been stumped for an answer.

All he knew was that he couldn't let things go on the way they were. Judging by her outburst, she was clearly struggling to cope with all that life had thrown at her recently and it was no skin off his nose to let her stay for a few nights in one of the empty bedrooms.

He had enough of them, after all.

Also, as a good friend of her cousin's he felt a responsibility to make sure that Cara was okay whilst Poppy was away and unable to help her herself. He knew from experience that good friends were essential when life decided to throw its twisted cruelty your way, and he was acutely aware that it was the support and encouragement of his friends that had helped him find his way out of the darkness after Jemima died.

Watching Cara working hard the next day, he was glad she was still around. When she was on good form, she was an asset to the business and, truthfully, it had become comforting for him to have another person around—it stopped him from *thinking* so much in the resounding silence of the house.

They hadn't talked about what had happened again, which

was a relief. He just wanted everything to get back to the way it had been with the minimum of fuss. With that in mind, he was a little concerned about what it would be like having her around at the weekend. He'd probably end up working, like he always did, so he wasn't too worried about the daytime, but they'd need to make sure they gave each other enough space in the evenings so they didn't end up biting each other's heads off again.

With any luck, she'd be out a lot of the time anyway, flat-hunting or seeing friends.

At six o'clock he leant back in his chair and stretched his arms above his head, working the kinks out of his tight muscles.

'Time to finish for the day, Cara,' he said to the side of her head.

She glanced round at him, the expression in her eyes far away, as if she was in the middle of a thought.

'Um, okay. I'll just finish this.' She tapped on her keyboard for a few more seconds before closing the laptop with a flourish.

'Okay then. Bring on the weekend.' She flashed him a cheeky smile, which gave him pause.

'You're not thinking of bringing the party to this house, I hope.'

Quickly switching to a solemn expression, she gave a shake of her head. 'Of course not. That's not what I meant.'

'Hmm.'

The corner of her mouth twitched upwards. 'You seem to have a really skewed impression of me. I don't go in for heavy drinking and partying—it's really not my style.'

'Okay.' He held up both hands. 'Not that it's any of my business; you can stay out all night at the weekends, for all I care,' he said, aware of a strange plummeting sensation in his chest as images of what she might get up to out on the town flashed through his head.

Good God, man—you're not her keeper.

'As long as your work doesn't suffer,' he added quickly.

'Actually,' she said, slouching back in her seat and hooking her slender arm over the back of her chair, 'I was thinking about cooking you a meal tonight, to say thank you for letting me stay.'

He wasn't sure why, but the thought of that made him uncomfortable. Perhaps because it would blur the lines between employee and friend too much.

'That's kind, but I have plans tonight,' he lied, racking his brain to remember what his friend Dan had said about his availability this weekend. Even if he was busy he was sure he could rustle up a dinner invitation somewhere else, to let Cara off the hook without any bad feelings.

'And you don't need to thank me for letting you stay here. It's what any decent human being would have done.'

Her face seemed to fall a little and she drew her arm back in towards her body, sliding her hands between her knees so that her shoulders hunched inwards. 'Oh, okay, well, I'm just going to pop out and shop for my own dinner, so I'll see you shortly,' she said, ramping her smile back up again and wheeling her chair away from the desk with her feet.

'Actually, I'm heading out myself in a minute and I'll probably be back late, so I'll see you tomorrow.'

Her smile froze. 'Right. Well, have a good night.'

This was ridiculous. The last thing he'd wanted was for them both to feel awkward about living under the same roof.

He let out a long sigh and pushed his hair away from his face. 'Look, Cara, don't think you have to hang out with me while you're staying here. We don't need to be in each other's pockets the whole time. Feel free to do your own thing.'

Clearly he'd been a bit brusque because she recoiled a little. 'I understand,' she said, getting up and awkwardly pushing her chair back under her desk. 'Have a good night!' she said in that overly chirpy way she had, which he was beginning to learn meant he'd offended her.

Not waiting for his reply, she turned her back on him and walked straight out of the room, her shoulders stiff.

Great. This was exactly what he'd hoped to avoid.

He scrubbed a hand over his face. Maybe it had been a mistake to ask her to stay.

But he couldn't kick her out now.

All he could do was cross his fingers and hope she'd find herself another place to live soon.

To his surprise, he didn't see much of Cara over the next couple of days. She'd obviously taken his suggestion about giving each other space to heart and was avoiding being in the house with him as much as possible.

The extremity of her desertion grated on his nerves.

What was it that made it impossible for them to understand each other? They were very different in temperament, of course, which didn't help, but it was more than that. It was as if there was some kind of meaning-altering force field between them.

On Sunday, when the silence in the house got too much for him, he went out for a long walk around Hyde Park. He stopped at the café next to the water for lunch, something he and Jemima had done most Sundays, fighting against the painful undertow of nostalgia that dragged at him as he sat there alone. It was all so intensely familiar.

All except for the empty seat in front of him.

He snorted into his drink, disgusted with himself for being so pathetic. He should consider himself lucky. He was the one who got to have a future, unlike his big-hearted, selfless wife. The woman who everyone had loved. One of the few people, in his opinion, who had truly deserved a long and happy life.

Arriving home mid-afternoon, he walked in to find the undertones of Cara's perfume hanging in the air.

So she was back then.

Closing his eyes, he imagined he could actually sense her presence in the atmosphere, like a low hum of white noise.

Or was he being overly sensitive?

Probably.

From the moment she'd agreed to move in he'd experienced a strange undercurrent of apprehension and it seemed to be affecting his state of mind.

After stowing his shoes and coat in the cloakroom, he went into the living room to find that a large display of flowers had been placed on top of the grand piano. He bristled, remembering the way he'd felt the last time Cara had started to mess with his environment.

Sighing, he rubbed a hand through his hair, attempting to release the tension in his scalp. They were just flowers. He really needed to chill out or he was going to drive himself insane. Jemima would have laughed if she'd seen how strung-out he was over something so inconsequential. He could almost hear her teasing voice ringing in his ears.

A noise startled him and he whipped round to see Cara standing in the doorway to the room, dressed in worn jeans and a sloppy sweater, her face scrubbed of make-up and her bright blue eyes luminous in the soft afternoon light. To his overwrought brain, she seemed to radiate an ethereal kind of beauty, her long hair lying in soft, undulating waves around her face and her creamy skin radiant with health. He experienced a strangely intense moment of confusion, and he realised that somewhere in the depths of his screwed-up consciousness he'd half expected it to be Jemima standing there instead—which was why his, 'Hello,' came out more gruffly than he'd intended.

Her welcoming smile faltered and she glanced down at her fingernails and frowned, as if fighting an impulse to chew on them, but when she looked back up her smile was firmly back in place.

'Isn't it a beautiful day?' She tipped her head towards the piano behind him. 'I hope you don't mind, but the spring sunshine inspired me to put fresh flowers in most of the rooms—not your bedroom, of course; I didn't go in there,' she added quickly. 'The house seemed to be crying out for a bit of life and colour and I wanted to do something to say thank you for letting me stay, even though you said I didn't need to.'

'Sure. That's fine,' was all he could muster. For some reason his blood was flying through his veins and he felt so hot he thought he might spontaneously combust at any second.

'Oh, and I stripped and remade the bed in the room next to yours,' she added casually. 'It looked like the cleaners had missed it. I gave it a good vacuum, too; it was really dusty.'

The heat was swept away by a flood of icy panic. 'You *what*?'

The ferocity in his tone obviously alarmed her because she flinched and blinked hard.

But hurting Cara's feelings was the least of his worries right then.

Not waiting for her reply, he pushed past her and raced up the stairs, aware of his heart thumping painfully in his chest as he willed it not to be so.

Please don't let her have destroyed that room.

Reaching the landing on the top floor, he flung open the door and stared into the now immaculate bedroom, the stringent scent of cleaning fluid clogging his throat and making his stomach roll.

She'd stripped it bare.

Everything he'd been protecting from the past had been torn off or wiped away. The bed, as she'd said, now had fresh linen on it.

He heard her laboured breath behind him as she made it up to the landing and whipped round to face her.

'Where are the sheets from the bed, Cara?' he demanded, well past the point of being able to conceal his anger.

Her face was drained of all colour. 'What did I do wrong?'

'The *sheets*, Cara—where are the *sheets*?'

'I washed them,' she whispered, unable to meet his eyes. 'They're in the dryer.'

That was it then. Jemima's room was ruined.

Bitterness welled in his gut as he took in her wide-eyed bewilderment. The woman was a walking disaster area and she'd caused nothing but trouble since she got here.

A rage he couldn't contain made him pace towards her.

'Why do you have to meddle with everything? Hmm? What is it with you? This need to please all the time isn't natural. In fact it's downright pathetic. Just keep your hands off my personal stuff, okay? Is that really too much to ask?'

She seemed frozen to the spot as she stared at him with glassy eyes, her jaw clamped so tight he could see the muscle flickering under the pressure, but, instead of shouting back this time, she dragged in a sharp, painful-sounding breath before turning on the spot and walking out of the room.

He listened to her heavy footsteps on the stairs and then the slam of her bedroom door, wincing as the sound reverberated through his aching head. Staring down at the soulless bed, he allowed the heat of his bitterness and anger and shame to wash through him, leaving behind an icy numbness in its wake.

Then he closed his eyes, dropped his chin to his chest and sank down onto the last place he'd been truly happy.

Oh, God, please don't let this be happening to me. Again.

Cara wrapped her arms around her middle and pressed her forehead against the cool wall of her bedroom, waiting for the dizziness and nausea to subside so she could pack up her things and leave.

What was it with her? She seemed destined to put herself in a position of weakness, where the only option left to her was to give up and run away.

Which she really didn't want to do again.

But she had to protect herself. She couldn't be around someone so toxic—someone who clearly thought so little of her. Even Ewan hadn't been that cruel to her when he'd left her after she'd failed to live up to his exacting standards. She'd never seen a look of such pure disgust on anyone's face before. The mere memory of it made the dizziness worse.

There was no way she was staying in a place where she'd be liable to see that look again. She'd rather go home and admit to her parents that she'd failed and deal with their badly concealed disappointment than stay here with Max any longer.

She'd never met anyone with such a quick temper. What was his problem, anyway? He appeared to have everything here: the security of a beautiful house in one of the most sought-after areas of London, a thriving business, friends who invited him out for dinner, and he clearly had pots of cash to cushion his easy, comfortable life. In fact, the more she thought about it, the more incensed she became.

Who was he to speak to her like that? Sure, there had been a couple of little bumps in the road when she'd not exactly been at her best, but she'd worked above and beyond the call of duty for the rest of the time. And she'd been trying to do something nice for him in making the house look good—pretty much the only thing she could think of to offer as a thank you to a man who seemed to have everything. What had been so awful about that? She knew she could be a bit over the top in trying to please people sometimes, but this hadn't been a big thing. It was just an empty guest room that had been overlooked.

Wasn't it?

The extremity of his reaction niggled at her.

Surely just giving it a quick clean didn't deserve that angry reaction.

No.

He was a control freak bully and she needed to get away from him.

As soon as she was sure the dizziness had passed, she carefully packed up all her things and zipped them into her suitcase, fighting with all her might against the tight pressure in her throat and the itchy heat in her eyes.

She'd known this opportunity had to be too good to be true—the job, working with someone as impressive as Max and definitely being invited to stay in this amazing house.

But she wasn't going to skulk away. If she didn't face up to Max one last time with her head held high she'd regret it for the rest of her life. He wasn't going to run her out of here; she was going to leave in her time and on her terms.

Taking a deep breath, she rolled her shoulders back and fixed the bland look of calm she'd become so practised at onto her face.

Okay. Time for one last confrontation.

She found Max in the guest room where she'd left him, sitting on the bed with his head in his hands, his hunched shoulders stretching his T-shirt tight against his broad back.

As she walked into the room, he looked up at her with an expression of such torment on his face that it made her stop in her tracks.

What was going on? She'd expected him to still be angry, but instead he looked—*beaten.*

Did he regret what he'd said to her?

Giving herself a mental shake, she took another deliberate step towards him. It didn't matter; there wasn't anything he could say to make up for the cruelty of his last statement anyway. This wasn't the first time he'd treated her with such brutal disdain and she wasn't going to put up with it any longer.

Forcing back her shoulders, she took one final step closer to him, feeling her legs shaking with tension.

'This isn't going to work, Max. I can't live in a place where I'm constantly afraid of doing the wrong thing and making you angry. I don't know what I did that was so bad, or what's going on with you to make you react like that, but I'm not going to let you destroy what's left of my confidence. I'm not going to be a victim any more.' She took a deep, shuddering breath. 'So I'm leaving now. And that goes for the job, too.'

Her heart gave a lurch at the flash of contrition in his eyes, but she knew she had to be strong and walk away for her own good.

'Goodbye, Max, and good luck.'

As she turned to go, fighting against the tears that threatened to give her away, she thought she heard the bedsprings creak as if he'd stood up, but didn't turn round to find out.

She was halfway down the stairs when she heard Max's voice behind her. 'Wait, Cara!'

Spinning round, she held up a hand to stop him from coming any closer, intensely aware that, despite her anger with him, there was a small part of her that was desperate to hear him say something nice to her, to persuade her that he wasn't the monster he seemed to be. 'I can't walk on eggshells around you any more, Max; I don't think my heart will stand it.'

In any way, shape or form.

He slumped down onto the top step and put his elbows on his knees, his whole posture defeated. 'Don't go,' he said quietly.

'I have to.'

Looking up, he fixed her with a glassy stare. 'I know I've been a nightmare to be around recently—' He frowned and shook his head. 'It's not you, Cara—it's one hundred per cent me. Please, at least hear me out. I need to tell you what's going on so you don't leave thinking any of this is your fault.' He sighed and rubbed a hand through his hair. 'That's the last thing I want to happen.'

She paused. Even if she still chose to leave after hearing him out, at least she'd know *why* it hadn't worked and be able to make peace with her decision to walk away.

The silence stretched to breaking point between them. 'Okay,' she said.

He nodded. 'Thank you.' Getting up from the step, he gestured down the stairs. 'Let's go into the sitting room.'

Once there, she perched on the edge of the sofa and waited for him to take the chair opposite, but he surprised her by sitting next to her instead, sinking back into the cushions with a long guttural sigh which managed to touch every nerve-ending in her body.

'This is going to make me sound mentally unstable.'

She turned to frown at him. 'Oka-ay…' she said, failing to keep her apprehension out of her voice.

'That bed hasn't been changed since my wife, Jemima, died a year and a half ago.'

Hot horror slid through her, her skin prickling as if she were being stabbed with a thousand needles. 'But I thought you said—' She shook her suddenly fuzzy head. 'You never said—' Words, it seemed, had totally failed her. Everything she knew about him slipped sickeningly into place: the ever-fluctuating moods, the reluctance to talk about his personal life, his anger at her meddling with things in his house.

His *wife's* house.

Looking away, he stared at the wall opposite, sitting forward with clenched fists as if he was steeling himself to get it all out in the open.

'I couldn't bring myself to change it.' He paused and she saw his shoulders rise then fall as he took a deep breath. 'The bed, I mean. It still smelled faintly like her. I let her mother take all her clothes and other personal effects—what would I have done with them?—but the bed was mine. The last place we'd been together before I lost her—' he took another breath, pushing back his hunched shoulders '—before she died.'

'Oh, God, Max… I'm so, so sorry. I had no idea.'

He huffed out a dry laugh. 'How could you? I did everything I could to avoid talking to you about it.' He grimaced. 'Because, to be honest, I've done enough talking about it to last me a lifetime. I guess, in my twisted imagination, I thought if you didn't know, I could pretend it hadn't happened when you were around. Outside of work, you're the first normal, unconnected thing I've had in my life since I lost her and I guess I was hanging on to that.'

He turned to look at her again. 'I should have told you, Cara, especially after you moved in, but I couldn't find a way to bring it up without—' He paused and swallowed hard, the look in his eyes so wretched that, without thinking, she reached out and laid a hand on his bare forearm.

He frowned down at where their bodies connected and the air seemed to crackle around them.

Disconcerted by the heat of him beneath her fingertips, she withdrew her hand and laid it back on her lap.

'It's kind of you to consider me *normal*,' she said, flipping him a grin, hoping the levity might go some way to smoothing out the sudden weird tension between them.

He gave a gentle snort, as if to acknowledge her pathetic attempt at humour.

Why had she never recognised his behaviour as grief before? Now she knew to look for it, it was starkly discernible in the deep frown lines in his face and the haunted look in his eyes.

But she'd been so caught up in her own private universe of problems she hadn't even considered *why* Max seemed so bitter all the time.

She'd thought he had everything.

How wrong she'd been.

They sat in silence for a while, the only sound in the room the soothing *tick-tock* of the carriage clock on the mantelpiece, like a steady heartbeat in the chaos.

'How did she die?' Cara asked eventually. She was pretty sure he wouldn't be keen to revisit this conversation and she wanted to have all the information from this point onwards so she could avoid any future blunders.

The familiarity of the question seemed to rouse him. 'She had a subarachnoid haemorrhage—it's where a blood vessel in the brain bursts—' he added, when she frowned at him in confusion. 'On our one-year wedding anniversary. It happened totally out of the blue. I was late for our celebration dinner and I got a phone message saying she'd collapsed in the restaurant. By the time I got to the hospital she had such extensive brain damage she didn't even recognise me. She died two weeks later. I never got to say goodbye properly.' He snorted gently. 'The last thing I said to her before it happened was "Stop being such a nag; I won't be late," when I left her in bed that morning and went to work.'

Cara had to swallow past the tightness in her throat before she could speak. 'That's why you didn't want me to leave here with us on bad terms.' She put a hand back onto his arm and gave it an ineffectual rub, feeling completely out of her depth. 'Oh, Max, I'm so sorry. What a horrible thing to happen.'

He leant back against the cushions, breaking the contact of her touch, and stared up at the ceiling. 'I often wonder whether I would have noticed some signs if I'd paid more attention to her. If I hadn't been so caught up with work—'

She couldn't think of a single thing to say to make him feel better—though maybe there wasn't anything she could say. Sometimes you didn't need answers or solutions; you just needed someone to listen and agree with you about how cruel life could be.

He turned to look at her, his mouth drawn into a tight line.

'Look, Cara, I can see that you wanting to help comes from a good place. You're a kind and decent person—much more decent than I am.' He gave her a pained smile, which she returned. 'I've been on my own here for so long I've clearly become very selfish with my personal space.' He rubbed a hand across his brow. 'And this was Jemima's house—she was the one who chose how to decorate it and made it a home for us.' He turned to make full eye contact with her again, his expression apologetic. 'It's taking a bit of adjusting to, having someone else around. Despite evidence to the contrary, I really appreciate the thoughtful gestures you've made.'

His reference to her *gestures* only made the heavy feeling in her stomach worse.

'I'm really sorry, Max. I can totally understand why you'd find it hard to see me meddling with Jemima's things. I think I was so excited by the idea of living in such a beautiful house that I got a bit carried away. I forgot I was just a visitor here and that it's your home. That was selfish of *me*.'

He shook his head. 'I don't want you to feel like that. While you're here it's your home, too.'

She frowned and turned away to stare down at the floor, distracted for a moment by how scratty and out of place her old slippers looked against the rich cream-coloured wool carpet.

That was exactly the problem. It wasn't her home and it never would be. She didn't really *fit* here.

For some reason that made her feel more depressed than she had since the day she'd left her last job.

'Have you had any luck with finding a flat to rent?' he asked, breaking the silence that had fallen like a suffocating layer of dust between them.

'Not yet, but I have an appointment to view somewhere tomorrow and there are new places coming up all the time. I'll find something soon, I'm sure of it,' she said, plastering what must have been the worst fake smile she'd ever mustered onto her face.

He nodded slowly, but didn't say anything.

Twitching with discomfort now, she stood up. 'I should go.'

He frowned at her in confusion. 'What do you mean? Where are you going?'

'Back to Sarah's. I think that would be best.'

Standing up, too, he put out a hand as if to touch her, but stopped himself and shoved it into the back pocket of his jeans instead.

'Look, don't leave. I promise to be less of an ogre. I let my anger get the better of me, which was unfair.'

'I don't know, Max—' She couldn't stay here now. Could she?

Obviously seeing the hesitation on her face, he leant forward and waited until she made eye contact. 'I like having you around.' There was a teasing lightness in his expression that made her feel as if he was finally showing her the real Max.

The one who had been hiding inside layers of brusque aloofness and icy calm for the past few weeks.

Warmth pooled, deep in her body. 'Really? I feel like I've made nothing but a nuisance of myself since I got here.'

He gave another snort and the first proper smile she'd seen in a while. It made his whole face light up and the sight of it sent a rush of warm pleasure across her skin. 'It's certainly been *eventful* having you here.'

She couldn't help but return his grin, despite the feeling that she was somehow losing control of herself.

'Stay. Please.'

Her heart turned over at the expression on his face. It was something she'd never seen before. Against all the odds, he looked *hopeful*.

Despite a warning voice in the back of her head, she knew there was no way she could walk out of the door now that he'd laid himself bare. She could see that the extreme mood swings were coming from a place of deep pain and the very last thing he needed was to be left alone with just his tormenting memories for company in this big empty house.

It appeared as though they needed each other.

The levelling of the emotional stakes galvanised her.

'Okay,' she said, giving him a reassuring smile. 'I'll stay. On one condition.'

'And that is?'

'That you *talk* to me when you feel the gloom descending—like a *person*, not just an employee. And let me help if I can.' She crossed her arms and raised a challenging eyebrow.

He huffed out a laugh. 'And how do you propose to help?'

'I don't know. Perhaps I can jolly you out of your moods, if you give me the chance.'

'*Jolly*. That's a fitting word for you.'

'Yeah, well, someone has to raise the positivity levels in this house of doom.' She stilled, wondering whether she'd gone a step too far, but when she dared to peek at him he was smiling, albeit in a rather bemused way.

A sense of relief washed over her. The last thing she wanted to do was read the situation wrong now they'd had a breakthrough. In fact, she really ought to push for a treaty to make things crystal clear between them.

'Look, at the risk of micromanaging the situation, can we agree that from this point on you'll be totally straight with me, and in return I promise to be totally straight with you?'

He gave her a puzzled look. 'Why? Is there something you need to tell me?'

She considered admitting she'd lied about why she'd left her last job and dismissed it immediately. There was no point going over that right now; it had no relevance to this and it would make her sound totally pathetic compared to what he'd been through.

'No, no! Nothing! It was just a turn of phrase.'

He snorted gently, rolling his eyes upward, his mouth lifting at the corner. 'Okay then, Miss Fix-it, total honesty it is. You've got yourself a deal.'

CHAPTER FIVE

JUST AS MAX thought he'd had enough drama to last him a lifetime, things took another alarming turn, only this time it was the business that threatened to walk away from him.

Opening his email first thing on Monday morning, he found a missive from his longest standing and most profitable client, letting him know that they were considering taking their business elsewhere.

Cara walked in with their coffee just as he'd finished reading it and the concern on her face made it clear how rattled he must look.

'Max? What's wrong?'

'Our biggest client is threatening to terminate our contract with them.'

Her eyes grew larger. 'Why?'

'I'm guessing one of our competitors has been sniffing around, making eyes at them and I've been putting off going to the meetings they've been trying to arrange for a while now. I haven't had the time to give them the same level of attention as before, so their head's been turned.'

'Is it salvageable?'

'Yes. If I go up there today and show them exactly why they should stay with me.'

'Okay.' She moved swiftly over to her desk and opened up her internet browser, her nails rattling against her keyboard as she typed in an enquiry. 'There's a train to Manchester in forty minutes. You go and pack some stuff; I'll call a cab and book you a seat. You can speak to me from the train about anything that needs handling today.'

He sighed and rubbed a hand through his hair, feeling the tension mounting in his scalp. 'It's going to take more than an afternoon to get this sorted. I'll probably need to be up there for most of the week.'

'Then stay as long as you need.'

Shaking his head, he batted a hand towards his computer. 'I have that proposal to finish for the end of Thursday, not to mention the monstrous list of things to tackle for all the other clients this week.'

'Leave it with me. If you set me up with a folder of your previous proposals and give me the questions you need answering, I'll put some sections together for you, so you'll only need to check and edit them as we go. And don't worry about the other clients; I can handle the majority of enquiries and rearrange anything that isn't urgent for next week. I'll only contact you with the really important stuff.'

'Are you sure you can handle that? It's a lot to leave you with at such short notice.'

'I'll be fine.' She seemed so eager he didn't have the heart to argue.

In all honesty, it was going to be tough for him to let go of his tight grip on the business and trust that this would work out, but he knew he didn't have a choice—there was no way he was letting this contract slip through his fingers. He really couldn't afford to lose this firm's loyalty at this point in his business's infancy; it would make him look weak to competitors as well as potential new clients, and presenting a confident front was everything in this game.

'Okay.' He stood up and gathered his laptop and charger together before making for the door. 'Thanks, Cara. I'll get my stuff together and call you from the train.'

Turning back, he saw she was standing stiffly with her hands clasped in front of her, her eyes wide and her cheeks flushed.

Pausing for a moment, he wondered whether he was asking too much of her, but quickly dismissed it. She'd chosen to stay and she knew what she was getting herself into.

They were in it together now.

To his relief, Cara successfully held the fort back in London whilst he was away, routinely emailing him sections of completed work to be used in the business proposal that he wrote in the evenings in time to make the deadline. She seemed to have a real flair for picking out relevant information and had made an excellent job of copying his language style.

She also saved his hide by sending flowers and a card in his name to his mother for her birthday, which he was ashamed to discover he'd forgotten all about in his panic about losing the client.

Damaging the precarious cordiality that he and his mother had tentatively built up after working through their differences over the past few years would have been just as bad, and he was immensely grateful to Cara for her forethought and care.

She really was excellent at her job.

In fact, after receiving compliments from clients about how responsive and professional she'd been when they'd contacted her with enquiries and complications to be dealt with, he was beginning to realise that he'd actually been very fortunate to secure her services. He felt sure, if she wanted to, she could walk into a job with a much better salary with her eyes shut.

Which made him wonder again why she hadn't.

Whatever the reason, the idea of losing her excellent skill base now made him uneasy. Even though he'd been certain he'd want to let her go at the end of the trial month, he was now beginning to think that that would be a huge mistake.

He had some serious thinking to do.

If he was honest, he reflected on Thursday evening, sitting alone in the hotel's busy restaurant, having time and space away from Cara and the house had been a relief. He'd been glad of the opportunity to get his head together after their confrontation. She was the first person, outside his close circle of friends, that he'd talked to in any detail about what had happened to Jemima and it had changed the atmosphere between them. To Cara's credit, she hadn't trotted out platitudes to try and make him feel better and he was grateful to her for that, but he felt a little awkward about how much of himself he'd exposed.

Conversely, though, it also felt as though a weight that he'd not noticed carrying had been lifted from his shoulders. Not just because he'd finally told Cara about Jem—which he'd begun to feel weirdly seedy about, as if he was keeping a dirty secret from her—but also because it had got to the point where he'd become irrationally superstitious about clearing out the room, as though all his memories of Jemima would be wiped away if he touched it. Which, of course, they hadn't been—she was still firmly embedded there in his head and his heart. So, even though he'd been angry and upset with Cara at the time, in retrospect, it had been a healthy thing for that decision to be wrenched out of his hands.

It felt as though he'd taken a step further into the light.

Cara was out when he arrived back at Friday lunchtime, still buzzed with elation from keeping the client, so he went to unpack his bags upstairs, return a few phone calls and take a shower before coming back down.

Walking into the kitchen, he spotted her standing by the sink with her back to him, washing a mug. He stopped to watch her for a moment, smiling as he realised she was singing softly to herself, her slim hips swaying in time to the rhythm of the song. She had a beautiful voice, lyrical and sweet, and a strange, intense warmth wound through him as he stood there listening to her. It had been a long time since anyone had sung in this house and there was something so pure and uplifting about it a shiver ran down his spine, inexplicably chased by a deep pull of longing.

Though not for Cara, surely? But for a time when his life had fewer sharp edges. A simpler time. A happier one.

Shaking himself out of this unsettling observation, he moved quickly into the room so she wouldn't think he'd been standing there spying on her.

'Hi, Cara.'

She jumped and gasped, spinning round to face him, her hand pressed to her chest. She looked fresh and well rested, but there was a wary expression in her eyes.

'Max! I didn't hear you come in.'

'I was upstairs, taking a shower and returning some urgent calls. I got back about an hour ago.'

She nodded, her professional face quickly restored. 'How was Manchester?'

'Good. We got them back on board. How have things been here?'

'That's great! Things have been fine here. It's certainly been very quiet without you.'

By 'quiet' he suspected she actually meant less fraught with angry outbursts.

There was an uncomfortable silence while she fussed about with the tea towel, hooking it carefully over the handle of the cooker door and smoothing it until it lay perfectly straight.

Tearing his eyes away from the rather disconcerting sight of her stroking her hands slowly up and down the offending article, he walked over to where the kettle sat on the work surface and flicked it on to boil. He was unsettled to find that things still felt awkward between them when they were face to face—not that he should be surprised that they were. Their last non-work conversation had been a pretty heavy one, after all.

Evidently he needed to make more of an effort to be friendly now if he was going to be in with a chance of persuading her to stay after the month's trial was up.

The thought of going back to being alone in this house certainly wasn't a comforting one any more. If he was honest, it had been heartening to know that Cara would be here when he got back. Now that the black hole of Jemima's room had been destroyed and he'd fully opened the door to Cara, the loneliness he'd previously managed to keep at bay had walked right in.

Turning to face her again, he leant back against the counter and crossed his arms.

'I wanted to talk to you about the quality of the work you've been producing.'

Her face seemed to pale and he realised he could have phrased that better. He'd never been good at letting his colleagues know when he was pleased with their work—or Jemima when he was proud of something she'd achieved, he realised with a stab of pain—but after Cara had given it to him straight about how it affected her, he was determined to get better at it.

'What I mean is—I'm really impressed with the way you've handled the work here this week while I've been away,' he amended.

'Oh! Good. Thank you.' The pride in her wobbly smile made his breath catch.

He nodded and gave a little cough to release the peculiar tension in his throat, turning back to the counter to grab a mug for his drink and give them both a moment to regroup. There was a brightly coloured card propped up next to the mug tree and he picked it up as a distraction while he waited for the kettle to finish boiling and glanced at what was written inside.

'You didn't tell me it was your birthday,' he said, turning to face her again, feeling an unsettling mixture of surprise and dismay at her not mentioning something as important as that to him.

Colour rushed to her cheeks. 'Oh, sorry! I didn't mean to leave that lying around.' She walked over and took the card from his hand, leaning against the worktop next to him and enveloping him in her familiar floral scent. She tapped the corner of the card gently against her palm and he watched, hypnotised by the action. 'It was on Wednesday. As you were away I didn't think it was worth mentioning.' She looked up at him from under her lashes. 'Don't worry—I didn't have a wild house party here while you were away, only a couple of friends over for dinner and we made sure to tidy up afterwards.'

Fighting a strange disquiet, he flapped a dismissive hand at her. 'Cara, it's okay for you to keep some of your things in the communal areas and have friends over for your birthday, for God's sake. I don't expect the place to be pristine the whole time.'

'Still. I meant to put this up in my room with the others.'

Despite their pact to be more open with each other, it was evidently going to take a lot more time and effort to get her to relax around him.

Maybe he should present her with some kind of peace offering. In fact, thinking about it, her birthday could provide the perfect excuse.

He'd seen her reading an article about a new play in a magazine one lunchtime last week, and when he picked it up later he noticed she'd put a ring around the box office number, as if to remind herself to book tickets.

Aftcr dispatching hcr back to thc officc with a list of clicnts to chase up about invoices, he called the theatre, only to find the play had sold out weeks ago. Not prepared to be defeated that easily, he placed a call to his friend James, who was a long-time benefactor of the theatre.

'Hey, man, how are things?' his friend asked as soon as he picked up.

'Great. Business is booming. How about you?'

'Life's good. Penny's pregnant again,' James said with pleasure in his voice.

Max ignored the twinge of pain in his chest. 'That's great. Congratulations.'

'Thanks. Let's just hope this one's going to give us less trouble arriving into the world.'

'You're certainly owed an easy birth after the last time.'

'You could say that. Anyway, what can I do for you, my friend?'

'I wanted to get hold of tickets for that new play at the Apollo Theatre for tonight's performance. It's my PA's birthday and I wanted to treat her, but it's sold out. Can you help me with that?'

'Your PA, huh?' There was a twist of wryness in James's voice that shot a prickle straight up his spine.

'Yeah. My PA,' he repeated with added terseness born of discomfort.

His friend chuckled. 'No problem. I'll call and get them to put some tickets aside for you for the VIP box. I saw it last week—it's great—but it starts early, at five, so you'll need to get a move on.' There was a loaded pause. 'It's good to hear you're getting out again.'

Max bristled again. 'I go out.'

'But not with women. Not since Jemima passed away.'

He sighed, beginning to wish he hadn't called now. 'It's not a date. She's my *PA*.'

James chuckled again. 'Well, she's lucky to have you for an *employer*. These tickets are like gold dust.'

'Thanks, I owe you one,' Max said, fighting hard to keep the growl out of his voice. To his annoyance, he felt rattled by what his friend was insinuating. It wasn't stepping over the line to do something like this for Cara, was it?

'Don't worry about it,' James said.

Max wasn't sure for a moment whether he'd voiced his concerns out loud and James was answering that question or whether he was just talking about paying him back the favour.

'Thanks, James, I've got to go,' he muttered, wanting to end the call so he could walk around and loosen off this weird tension in his chest.

'No worries.'

Max put the phone down, wondering again whether this gesture was a step too far.

No. She'd worked hard for him, under some testing circumstances and he wanted her to know that he appreciated it. If he wanted to retain her services—and he was pretty sure now that he did—he was going to have to make sure she knew how much she was valued here so she didn't go looking for another job.

Cara was back at her desk, busily typing away on her laptop, when he walked into the room they used as an office. Leaning against the edge of her desk, he waited until she'd finished and turned to face him.

'I'm nearly done here,' she said, only holding eye contact for a moment before glancing back at her computer.

'Great, because a friend of mine just called to say he has two spare tickets to that new play at the Apollo and I was thinking I could take you as a thank you for holding the fort so effectively whilst I've been away. And for missing your birthday.'

She stared at him as if she thought she might have misheard. 'I'm sorry?'

He smiled at her baffled expression, feeling a kink of pleasure at her reaction. 'We'll need to leave in the next few minutes if we're going to make it into town in time to catch the beginning.' He stood up and she blinked in surprise.

'You and *me*? Right *now*?'

'Yes. You don't have other plans, do you?'

'Um, no.'

He nodded. 'Great.'

Gesturing up and down her body, she frowned, looking a little flustered. 'But I can't go dressed like this.'

He glanced at her jeans and T-shirt, trying not to let his eyes linger on the way they fitted her trim, slender body. 'You're going to have to change quickly then,' he said, pulling his mobile out of his pocket and dialling the number for the taxi.

Cara chattered away in the cab all the way there about how the play had been given rave reviews after its preview performance and how people were already paying crazy money on auction websites for re-sold tickets to see it. Her enthusiasm was contagious and, stepping out of the car, he was surprised to find he was actually looking forward to seeing it.

The theatre was a recently renovated grand art deco building slap-bang in the middle of Soho, a short stroll from the hectic retail circus of Oxford Street.

It had been a while since he'd made it into town on a Friday night and even longer since he'd been to see any kind of live show. When he and Jemima had moved to London they'd been full of enthusiasm about how they'd be living in the heart of the action and would be able to go out every other night to see the most cutting-edge performances and mind-expanding lectures. They were going to become paragons of good taste and spectacularly cultured to boot.

And then real life had taken over and they'd become increasingly buried under the weight of work stress and life tiredness as the years went by and had barely made it out to anything at all. It had been fine when they'd had each other for company, but he was aware that he needed to make more of an effort to get out and be sociable now he was on his own.

Not that he'd been a total recluse since Jem had died; he'd been out with friends—Poppy being his most regular pub partner—but he'd done it in a cocoon of grief, always feeling slightly detached from what was going on around him.

Doing this with Cara meant he was having to make an effort again. Which was a good thing. It felt healthy. Perhaps that was why he was feeling more upbeat than he had in a while—as if there was life beyond the narrow world he'd been living in for the past year and a half.

After paying the taxi driver, they jogged straight to the box office for their tickets, then through the empty lobby to the auditorium to find their seats in the VIP box, the usher giving them a pointed look as she closed the doors firmly behind them. It seemed they'd only just made it. This theory was borne out by the dimming of the lights and the grand swish of the curtain opening just as they folded themselves into their seats.

Max turned to find Cara with her mouth comically open and an expression that clearly said *I can't believe we've just casually nipped into the best seats in the house.* He flashed her a quick smile, enjoying her pleasure and the sense of satisfaction at doing something good here, before settling back into his plush red velvet chair, his heart beating heavily in his chest.

A waft of her perfume hit his nose as she reached up to adjust her ponytail, which made his heart beat even harder—perhaps from the sudden sensory overload. Taking a deep breath, he concentrated on bringing his breathing back to normal and focused on the action on stage, determined to put all other thoughts aside for the meantime and try to enjoy whatever this turned out to be.

Cara was immensely relieved when the play stood up to her enthusiastic anticipation. It would have been pretty embarrassing if it had been a real flop after all the fuss she'd made about it on the way there. Every time she heard Max chuckle at one of the jokes she experienced a warm flutter of pleasure in her stomach.

Max bringing her here to the theatre had thrown her for a complete loop. Even though he'd finally let her into his head last weekend, she'd expected him to go back to being distant with her again once he came back from Manchester. But instead he'd surprised her by complimenting her, then not only getting tickets to the hottest play in London, but bringing her here himself as a reward for working hard.

Dumbfounded was not the word.

Not that she was complaining.

Sneaking a glance at him, she thought she'd never seen him looking so relaxed. She could hardly believe he was the same man who had opened the door to her on the first day they'd met. He seemed larger now somehow, as if he'd straightened up and filled out in the time since she'd last seen him. That had to be all in her head, of course, but he certainly seemed more *real* now that she knew what drove his rage. In fact it was incredible how differently she felt now she knew what sort of horror he'd been through—losing someone he loved in such a senseless way.

No wonder he was so angry at the world.

Selfishly, it was a massive relief to know that none of his dark moods had been about her performance—apart from when she'd fallen asleep on the kitchen table during business hours, of course.

After he'd left for Manchester, she'd had a minor panic attack about how she was going to cope on her own, terrified of making a mistake that would impact negatively on the business, but, after giving herself a good talking-to in the mirror, she'd pulled it together and got on with the job in hand. And she'd been fine. More than fine. In fact she'd actually started to enjoy her job again as she relaxed into the role and reasserted her working practices.

Truth be told, before she'd started working for Max, she didn't know whether she'd be able to hold her nerve in a business environment any more. He'd been a hard taskmaster but she knew she'd benefited from that, discovering that she had the strength to stand up for herself when it counted. She'd been tested to her limits and she'd come through the other side and that, to her, had been her biggest achievement in a very long time.

She felt proud of herself again.

As the first half drew to a close she became increasingly conscious of the heat radiating from Max's powerful body and his arm that pressed up against hers as he leaned into the armrest. Her skin felt hot and prickly where it touched his, as if he was giving off an electric charge, and it was sending little currents of energy through the most disconcerting places in her body.

It seemed her crush on him had grown right along with her respect and she was agonisingly aware of how easy it would be to fall for him if she let herself.

Which she wasn't going to do. He was clearly still in love with his wife and there was no way she could compete with a ghost.

Only pain and heartache lay that way.

As soon as the curtain swished closed and the lights came on to signal the intermission she sprang up from her seat, eager to break their physical connection as soon as possible.

'Let's grab a drink,' Max said, leaning in close so she could hear him over the noise of audience chatter, his breath tickling the hairs around her ear.

'Good idea.' She was eager to move now to release the pent-up energy that was making her heart race.

Max gestured for her to go first, staying close behind her as they walked down the stairs towards the bar, his dominating presence like a looming shadow at her back.

They joined the rest of the audience at the bottom of the stairs and she pushed her way through the shouty crowd of people towards the shiny black-lacquered bar, which was already six people deep with waiting customers.

'Hmm, this could take a while,' she said to Max as they came to a stop at the outskirts of the throng.

'Don't worry, I'll get the drinks,' he said, walking around the perimeter of the group as if gauging the best place to make a start. 'Glass of wine?' he asked.

'Red please.'

'Okay, I'm going in,' he said, taking an audible breath and turning to the side to shoulder through a small gap between two groups of chatting people with their backs to each other.

Cara watched in fascinated awe as Max made it to the bar in record time, flipping a friendly smile as he sidled through the crowd and charming a group of women into letting him into a small gap at the counter next to them.

After making sure his newly made friends were served first, he placed his order with the barman and was back a few moments later, two glasses of red wine held aloft in a gesture of celebration.

'Wow, nice work,' Cara said, accepting a glass and trying not to grin like a loon. 'I've never seen anyone work a bar crowd like that before.'

Max shrugged and took a sip of wine, pinning a look of exaggerated nonchalance onto his face. 'I have hidden depths.'

She started to laugh, but it dried in her throat as she locked eyes with someone on the other side of the room.

Someone she thought she'd never see again.

Swallowing hard, she dragged her gaze back to Max and dredged up a smile, grasping for cool so she wouldn't have to explain her sudden change in mood.

But it was not to be. The man was too astute for his own good.

'Are you okay? You look like you've seen a ghost,' he said, his intelligent eyes flashing with concern.

Damn and blast. This was the last thing she wanted to have to deal with tonight.

'Fine,' she squeaked, her cheeks growing hot under the intensity of his gaze.

'Cara. I thought we'd agreed to be straight with each other from now on.'

Sighing, she nodded towards the other side of the bar. 'That guy over there is an old friend of mine.'

He frowned as she failed to keep the hurt out of her voice and she internally kicked herself for being so transparent.

'He can't be a very good friend if you're ignoring each other.'

She sighed and tapped at the floor with the toe of her shoe. 'It's complicated.'

He raised his eyebrows, waiting for her to go on.

After pausing for a moment, she decided there was no point in trying to gloss over it. 'The thing is—his fiancée has a problem with me.'

'Really? Why?'

'Because I'm female.'

He folded his arms. 'She's the jealous type, huh?'

'Yeah. And no matter how much Jack's tried to convince her that our friendship is purely platonic, she won't believe him. So I've been confined to the rubbish heap of Friends Lost and Passed Over.' She huffed out a sigh. 'I can't really blame him for making that choice, though. He loves her and I want him to be happy, and if that means we can't be friends any more then so be it.'

The look of bewildered outrage in Max's expression made the breath catch in her throat and she practically stopped breathing altogether as he reached out and stroked his hand down her arm in a show of solidarity, his touch sending tingles of pure pleasure through every nerve in her body.

Staring up into his handsome face, she wondered again what it would feel like to have someone like Max for a partner. To know that he was on her side and that he had her back, no matter what happened.

But she was kidding herself. He was never going to offer her the chance to find out. She was his employee and she'd do well to remember that.

Tearing her gaze away from him, she glanced back across the room to where the fiancée in question had now appeared by Jack's side. From a distance they appeared to be having a heated discussion about something, their heads close together as they gesticulated at each other. As she watched, they suddenly sprang apart and Jack turned to catch her eye again, already moving towards where she and Max were standing.

He was coming over.

Her body tensed with apprehension and she jumped in surprise as Max put his hand on her arm again, then increased his grip, as if readying himself to spirit her away from a painful confrontation.

'Cara! It's been ages,' Jack said as he came to a stop in front of her, looking just as boyishly handsome as ever, with his lop-sided grin and great mop of wavy blond hair.

'It has, Jack.'

'How are you?' he asked, looking a little shame-faced now, as well he should. They'd become good friends after meeting at their first jobs after university and had been close once, spending weekends at each other's houses and standing in as 'plus ones' at weddings and parties if either of them were single and in need of support.

There had been a time when she'd wondered whether they'd end up together, but as time had passed it became obvious that wasn't meant to be. He was a great guy, but the chemistry just wasn't there for her—or for him, it seemed. But seeing him here now reminded her just how much she missed his friendship. She could have really done with his support after Ewan sauntered away from their relationship in search of someone with less emotional baggage, but it had been at that point that his fiancée had issued her ultimatum, and Cara had well and truly been the loser in that contest.

Not that she blamed him for choosing Amber. She had to respect his loyalty to the woman he loved.

'I'm great, Jack, thanks. How are you—' she paused and flicked her gaze to his fiancée, who had now appeared at his side '—both?' Somehow she managed to dredge up a smile for the woman. 'Hi, Amber.'

'Hi, Cara, we're great, thanks,' Amber said, acerbity dripping from every word as she pointedly wrapped a possessive arm around Jack's waist. Turning to look at Max, she gave him a subtle, but telling, once-over.

'And who's this?'

'This is Max…' Cara took a breath, about to say *my boss*, when Max cut her off to lean in and shake hands with Amber.

'It's lovely to meet you, Amber,' he said in the same smooth tone she'd heard him use to appease clients.

It worked just as well on Amber because her cheeks flooded with colour and she actually fluttered her lashes at him. Turning back to Cara, she gave her a cool smile, her expression puzzled, as if she was trying to work out how she'd got her hands on someone as impressive as Max.

'Did Jack tell you—our wedding's on Sunday so this evening is our last hurrah before married life?' Amber's eyes twinkled with malice. 'Jack's firm is very well reputed in the City and people practically throw invitations at him every day,' she said, her tone breezy but her eyes hard, as though she was challenging Cara to beat her with something better than that.

Which, of course, she had no hope of doing.

Pushing away the thump of humiliation, Cara forced her mouth into the shape of a smile.

'That's wonderful—congratulations! I had no idea the wedding was so soon.'

Amber leaned in and gave her a pitying smile. 'We've kept it a small affair, which is why we couldn't send you an invitation, Cara.'

Max shifted next to her, pulling her a bit tighter against him in the process and surprising her again by rubbing her arm in support. She wondered whether he could feel how fast her pulse was racing through her body with him holding her so close.

'But we had two spaces open up this week,' Jack said suddenly and a little too loudly, as if he'd finally decided to step out of his fiancée's shadow and take control. 'My cousin and her husband have had to drop out to visit sick family abroad. If you're not busy you could come in their place.'

Judging by the look on Amber's face, she obviously hadn't had this in mind when she'd agreed to be dragged over here.

'It would be great if you could make it,' Jack pressed, his expression open, almost pleading now. It seemed that he genuinely wanted her to be there. Perhaps this was his way of making things up to her after cutting her out of his life so brutally. At least that was something.

But she couldn't say yes when the invitation was for both her and Max and she hated the idea of turning up and spending the day on her own amongst all those happy couples.

Before she could open her mouth to make up an excuse and turn them down, Max leaned in and said, 'Thank you—we'd love to come.'

She swivelled her head to gape at him, almost giving herself whiplash in the process, stunned to find a look of cool certainty on his face.

'Are you sure we're not busy?' she said pointedly, raising both eyebrows at him.

'I'm sure,' he replied with a firm nod.

Turning back to Jack, she gave him what must have been the weirdest-looking smile. 'Okay—er—' she swallowed '—then we'd love to come. Thanks.'

'That's great,' Jack said, giving her a look that both said *I'm sorry for everything* and *thank you*.

'We'd better go and get a drink before the performance starts again,' Amber said with steel in her voice, her patience clearly used up now.

'I'll text you with the details, Cara,' Jack said as Amber drew him away.

'Okay, see you on Sunday,' Cara said weakly to their disappearing figures.

As soon as they were out of earshot she turned to stare at Max, no doubt doing her impression of a goldfish again.

'He's a brave man,' was all Max said in reply.

'You realise they think we're a couple?'

He nodded, a fierce intensity in his eyes causing a delicious shiver to rush down her spine. 'I know, but I wanted to see the look on that awful woman's face when we said yes, and I have no problem pretending to be your partner if it's going to smooth the way back to a friendship with Jack for you.'

Max as her partner. Just the thought of it made her quiver right down to her toes.

'That's—' she searched for the right words '—game of you.'

'It'll be my pleasure.'

There was an odd moment where the noises around her seemed to get very loud in her ears. Tearing her gaze away from his, she gulped down the last of her wine and wrapped her hands around the glass in order to prevent herself from chewing on her nails.

Okay. Well, that happened.

Who knew that Max would turn out to be her knight in shining armour?

CHAPTER SIX

MAX HAD NO idea where this strange possessiveness towards Cara had sprung from, but he hadn't been about to let that awful woman, Amber, treat her with so little respect. She deserved more than that. Much more. And while she was working for him he was going to make sure she got it.

Which meant he was now going to be escorting her to a wedding—the kind of event he'd sworn to avoid after Jemima died. The thought of being back in a church, watching a couple with their whole lives ahead of them begin their journey together, made his stomach clench with unease.

One year—that was all he'd been allowed with his wife. One lousy year. It made him want to spit with rage at the world. Why her? Why them?

Still, at least he didn't know the happy couple and would be able to keep a low profile at the wedding, hiding his bitterness behind a bland smile. He didn't need to engage. He'd just be there to support Cara; that was all.

After the play finished they travelled home in silence, a stark contrast to their journey there, but he was glad of the quiet. Perversely, it felt as though he and Cara had grown closer during that short time, the confrontation and subsequent solidarity banding them together like teammates.

Which of course they were, he reminded himself as he opened the front door to his house and ushered her inside, at least when it came to the business.

Cara's phone beeped as she shrugged off her coat and she plucked it out of her handbag and read the message, her smile dropping by degrees as she scanned the text.

'Problem?' he asked, an uncomfortable sense of foreboding pricking at the edge of his mind. It had taken him a long time to be able to answer the phone without feeling the crush of anxiety he'd been plagued with after the call telling him his wife had collapsed and had been rushed into hospital.

He took a step closer to her, glad she was here to distract him from the lingering bad memories.

Glancing up, she gave him a sheepish look. 'It's a text from Jack with the details of the wedding.'

'Oh, right.' He stepped back, relief flowing through him, but Cara didn't appear to relax. Instead her grimace only deepened.

'Um. Apparently it's in Leicestershire. Which is a two and a half hour drive from here. So we'll need to stay overnight.' She wrinkled her nose, the apology clear on her face.

Great. Just what had he let himself in for here?

'No problem,' he forced himself to say, holding back the irritation he felt at the news. It wasn't Cara's fault and he was the one who had pushed for this to happen.

More fool him.

'Really? You don't mind?' she asked, relief clear in her tone.

'No, it's fine,' he lied, trying not to think about all the hours he'd have to spend away from his desk so he could make nice with a bunch of strangers.

'Great, then I'll book us a couple of rooms in the B&B that Jack suggested,' she said, her smile returning.

'You do that.' He gave her a firm nod and hid a yawn behind his hand. 'I'm heading off to bed,' he said, feeling the stress of the week finally catching up with him. 'See you in the morning, Cara. And Happy Birthday.'

* * *

Cara disappeared for most of the next day, apparently going to look at potential flats to rent, then retiring to bed early, citing exhaustion from the busy, but fruitless, day.

After the tension of Friday night, Max was glad of the respite and spent most of his time working through the backlog of emails he'd accumulated after his week away.

Sunday finally rolled around and he woke early, staring into the cool empty air next to him and experiencing the usual ache of hollowness in his chest, before pulling himself together and hoisting his carcass out of bed and straight into the shower.

The wedding was at midday so at least he had a couple of hours to psych himself up before they had to head over to the Leicestershire estate where it was being held.

The sun was out and glinting off the polished windows of the houses opposite when he pulled his curtains open, momentarily blinding him with its brightness. It was definitely a day for being outdoors.

He'd barely breathed fresh air in the past week, only moving between office and hotel, and the thought of feeling the warm sun on his skin spurred him into action. He pulled on his running gear, something he'd not done for over a year and a half, and went for a long run, welcoming the numbing pain as he worked his lethargic muscles hard, followed by the rewarding rush of serotonin as it chased its way through his veins. After a while it felt as though he was flying along the pavement, the worries and stresses of the past week pushed to the very back of his mind by the punishing exercise.

For the first time in a long while he felt as if he were truly awake.

Cara appeared to be up and about when he limped back into his kitchen for a long drink of water, his senses perking up as he breathed in the comforting smell of the coffee she'd been drinking, threaded with the flowery scent of her perfume.

Glancing up at the clock as he knocked back his second

glass of water, he was shocked to see it was already nearly nine o'clock, which meant he really ought to get a move on if he was going to be ready to leave for the wedding on time.

Turning back from loading his glass into the dishwasher, he was brought up short by the sight of Cara standing in the hallway just outside the kitchen door, watching him. She'd twisted her long hair up into some sort of complicated-looking hairstyle and her dark eyes sparkled with glittery make-up. The elegant silver strapless dress she wore fitted her body perfectly, moulding itself to her gentle curves and making her seem taller and—something else. More mature, perhaps? More sophisticated?

Whatever it was, she looked completely and utterly beautiful.

Realising he was standing there gawping at her like some crass teenage boy, he cleared his suddenly dry throat and dredged up a smile which he hoped didn't look as lascivious as it felt.

'Hey, you look like you're dressed for a wedding,' he said, cringing inside at how pathetic that sounded.

She smiled. 'And you don't. I hope you're not thinking of going like that because I'm pretty sure it didn't say "sports casual" on the invitation.' Her amused gaze raked up and down his body, her eyebrows rising at the sight of his sweat-soaked running gear.

He returned her grin, finding it strangely difficult to keep it natural-looking. His whole face felt as if he'd had his head stuck in the freezer. What was wrong with him? A bit of sunshine and a fancy dress and his mind was in a spin.

'I'd better go and take a shower; otherwise we're going to be late,' he said, already walking towards the door.

'Could you do me a favour before you go?' she asked, colour rising in her cheeks.

'Er…sure. As long as it's not going to cost me anything,' he joked, coming to a stop in front of her. In her heels she was nearly as tall as him, making it easier to directly meet her gaze. She had such amazing eyes: bright and clear with vitality and intellect. The make-up and hair made him think of Audrey Hepburn in *Breakfast at Tiffany's*.

'Could you do up the buttons on the back of my dress?' she asked, her voice sounding unusually breathy, as if it had taken a lot for her to ask for his help.

'Sure,' he said, waiting for her to turn around and present her back to him. His breath caught as he took in the long, elegant line of her spine as it disappeared into the base of her dress. There were three buttons that held the top half of it together, with a large piece cut out at the bottom, which would leave her creamy skin and the gentle swells of muscle at the base of her back exposed.

Heaven help him.

Hands feeling as if they'd been trapped in the freezer, too, he fiddled around with the buttons, feeling the warmth of her skin heat the tips of his fingers. Hot barbs of awareness tracked along his nerves and embedded themselves deep in his body and his breath came out in short ragged gasps, which he'd like to think was an after-effect of the hard exercise, but was more likely to be down to his close proximity to a woman's body, after his had been starved of attention for the past year and a half.

'There you go,' he said, snapping the final button into its hole with a sigh of relief. 'I'll be back down in fifteen.'

And with that he made his escape.

Wow. This felt weird, being at Jack's wedding—a friend she thought she'd never see again—with Max—her recalcitrant boss—as her escort. The whole world seemed to have flipped on its head. If someone had told her a week ago that this was going to happen she would have given them a polite smile whilst slowly backing away.

But here she was, swaying unsteadily in the only pair of high heels she owned, with Max at her side. The man who could give Hollywood's top leading men a run for their money in the charisma department.

There had been a moment in the kitchen, after he'd turned around and noticed her, when she thought she'd seen something in his eyes. Something that had never been there before. Something like desire.

And then when he'd helped her with her dress it had felt as though the air had crackled and jumped between them. The bloom of his breath on her neck had made her knees weak and her heart race. She could have sworn his voice had held a rougher undertone than she was used to hearing as he excused himself.

But she knew she was kidding herself if she thought she should read more than friendly interest into his actions.

They had Radio Four on for the entire journey up to Leicestershire, listening in rapt silence to a segment on finance, then chuckling along to a radio play. Cara was surprised by how easy it was to sit beside Max and how relaxed and drawn into their shared enjoyment of the programme she was. So much so, that it was to her great surprise that they pulled into the small car park of the church where the wedding was taking place, seemingly only a short time after leaving London.

The sunshine that had poured in through her bedroom window that morning had decided to stick around for the rest of the day, disposing of the insubstantial candyfloss clouds of the morning to reveal the most intensely blue sky she'd ever seen.

All around her, newly blooming spring flowers bopped their heads in time to the rhythm of the light spring breeze, their gaudy colours a striking counterpoint to the verdant green of the lawns surrounding them.

Taking a deep breath, she drew the sweet, fresh air deep into her lungs. This should mark a new beginning in her life, she decided. The start of the next chapter, where the foundations she'd laid in the past few weeks would hopefully prove strong enough to support her from this point onwards.

'It's nearly twelve o'clock; we should go in,' Max said with regret in his voice as he cast his gaze around their beautiful surroundings.

Attempting to keep her eyes up and off the tantalising view of his rear in the well-cut designer suit he'd chosen to wear today, she tripped into the church after him, shivering slightly at the change in temperature as they walked out of the sunshine and into the nave.

Most of the pews were already full, so they hung back for a moment to be directed to a seat by one of the ushers.

And that was when the day took a definite turn for the worse.

Her world seemed to spin on its axis, rolling her stomach along with it, as her former and current life lined up on a collision course. One of the PAs who had belonged to the Cobra Clique was standing down by the altar, her long blond hair slithering down her back as she threw her head back and laughed at something that the man standing next to her said.

Taking a deep breath, Cara willed herself not to panic, but her distress must have shown plainly on her face because Max turned to glance in the direction she was staring and said, 'Cara? What's wrong?'

'Ah…nothing.' She flapped a dismissive hand at him, feeling her cheeks flame with heat, and took a step backwards, hoping the stone pillar would shield her. But serendipity refused to smile as the woman turned towards them, catching her eye, her pupils flaring in recognition and her gaze moving, as if in slow motion, from Cara to Max and back again. And the look on her face plainly said she wasn't going to miss this golden opportunity to make more trouble for her.

Looking around her wildly, Cara's heart sank as she realised there was nowhere to run, nowhere to hide.

It was usually at this point in a film that the leading lady would pull the guy she was with towards her and kiss him hard to distract him from the oncoming danger, but she knew, as she stared with regret at Max's full, inviting mouth, that there was no way she could do that. He'd probably choke in shock, then fire her on the spot if she even attempted it. It wouldn't just put her job in jeopardy—it would blow it to smithereens.

There was only one thing left to do.

'Max, I need to tell you something.'

He frowned at her, his eyes darkening as he caught on to her worried tone.

'What's wrong?'

'I—er—'

'Cara?' He looked really alarmed now and she shook her head, trying to clear it. She needed to keep her cool or she'd end up looking even more of an idiot.

'I wasn't entirely straight with you about why I left my last job. Truth is—' she took a breath '—I didn't take redundancy.'

He blinked, then frowned. 'So you were fired?'

'No. I—'

'What did you do, Cara? What are you trying to tell me?' His voice held a tinge of the old Max now—the one who didn't suffer fools.

'Okay—' She closed her eyes and held up a hand. 'Look, just give me a minute and I'll explain. The thing is—' Locking her shaking hands together, she took a steadying breath. 'I was bullied by a gang of women there who made my life a living hell and I handed in my notice before my boss could fire me for incompetence as a result of it,' she said, mortified by the tremor in her voice.

When she opened her eyes to look at him, the expression of angry disbelief on his face made her want to melt into a puddle of shame.

'What?'

She swallowed past the tightness in her throat. 'I had no choice but to leave.'

He shook his head in confusion. 'Why didn't you tell me?'

Out of the corner of her eye she saw her nemesis approaching and felt every hair on her body stand to attention. The woman was only ten steps away, at most.

'And why are you telling me this now?' he pressed.

'Because one of the women is here at the wedding and she'll probably tell you a pack of lies to make me look bad. I didn't exactly leave graciously. There was a jug of cold coffee and some very white blouses involved.' She cringed at the desperation in her voice, but Max just turned to glare in the direction she'd been avoiding, then let out a sharp huff of breath.

'Come outside for a minute.'

Wrapping his hand around her arm, he propelled her back out through the doors of the church and down the steps, coming to a sudden halt under the looming shadow of the clock tower, where he released her. Crossing his arms, he looked down at her with an expression of such exasperation it made her quake in her stilettos.

'Why didn't you mention this to me before?' he asked, shoving back the hair that had fallen across his forehead during their short journey, only drawing more attention to his piercing gaze.

Sticking her chin in the air, she crossed her own arms, determined to stand up for herself. 'I really wanted to work with you and I thought you might not hire me if you knew the truth. It didn't exactly look good on my CV that I'd only stuck it out there for three months before admitting defeat.'

'So you thought you had to lie to me to get the job?'

She held up her hands in apology. 'I know I should have told you the truth, but I'd already messed up other job interviews because I was so nervous and ashamed of myself for being so weak.' She hugged her arms around her again. 'I didn't want you to think badly of me. Anyway, at the time you barely wanted to talk to me about the work I had to do, let alone anything of a personal nature, so I thought it best to keep it to myself.' She looked at him steadily, craving his understanding. 'You can be pretty intimidating, you know.'

She was saved from having to further explain herself by one of the ushers loudly asking the stragglers outside to please go into the church and take their seats because the bride had arrived.

From the look on Max's face she wasn't sure whether he was going to walk away and leave her standing there like a total lemon on her own or turn around and punch the wall. She didn't fancy watching either scenario play out.

To her surprise, he let out a long, frustrated sigh and looked towards the gaggle of people filing into the church.

'We can't talk about this now or we'll be walking in with the bridal party, and there's no way I'd pass for a bridesmaid,' he said stiffly.

She stared at him. 'You mean you're not going to leave?'

'No, I'm not going to leave,' he said crossly. 'We'll talk more about this after the ceremony.'

And with that he put his hand firmly against the middle of her back and ushered her inside.

Sliding into the polished wooden pew next to Max and surreptitiously wiping her damp palms on her dress, she glanced at him out of the corner of her eye. From the set of his shoulders she could tell he wasn't likely to let *this* go with a casual wave of his hand.

In fact she'd bet everything she had left that he was really going to fire her this time.

Frustration churned in her stomach. After all the progress she'd made in getting back on her feet, and persuading Max to finally trust her, was it really going to end like this?

Looking along the pews, she saw that her nemesis was sitting on the other side of the church, a wide smile on her face as she watched the ceremony unfold. At least that threat had been neutralised. There wasn't anything left that she could do to hurt her.

She hoped.

Rage unfurled within Cara at the unfairness of it all. Why did this woman get to enjoy herself when she had to sit here worrying about her future?

As she watched Amber make her stately way up the aisle towards a rather nervous-looking Jack, she could barely concentrate for wondering what Max was going to say to her once they were facing each other over their garlic mushrooms at the lunch afterwards. There was no way she was going to be able to force down a bite of food until they'd resolved this.

Oh, get a grip, Cara.

When she dared take a peek at him from the corner of her eye again, he seemed to be grimly staring straight ahead. Forcing herself to relax, she uncrossed her legs, then her arms and sat up straighter, determined not to appear anxious or pitiful. She knew what she had to do. There would be no gratuitous begging or bartering for a reprieve. She would hold her head high throughout it all and calmly state her case.

And until she had that opportunity she was going to damn well enjoy watching her friend get married.

Judging by her rigid posture and ashen complexion, Cara really didn't appear to be enjoying the ceremony, which only increased Max's discomfort at being there, too. Not that he blamed her in any way for it. He'd chosen to come here with her after all. Though, from the sound of it, she must be regretting bringing him along now.

Had he really been so unapproachable that she'd chosen to lie to his face instead of admitting to having a rough time at her last place of work?

He sighed inwardly.

She was absolutely right, though. Again. He could be intimidating. And he'd been at the peak of his remoteness when she'd first arrived on his doorstep and asked him for a job. He also knew that if she'd mentioned the personal issues that had been intrinsic to her leaving her last job when they'd first met it would have given him pause enough to turn her away. He hadn't wanted any kind of complication at that point.

But he was so glad now that he hadn't.

Somehow, in her innocent passive-aggressive way, she'd managed to push his buttons and, even though he'd fought it at the time, that was exactly what he'd needed.

She was what he'd needed.

After the ceremony finished they were immediately ushered out of the church and straight up the sweeping manicured driveway to the front of a grand Georgian house where an enormous canvas marquee had been set up next to the orangery.

A small affair, his foot.

As soon as they stepped inside they had toxic-coloured cocktails thrust upon them and were politely but firmly asked to make their way back outside again to the linen-draped tables on the terrace next to the house.

'This is like a military operation,' he muttered to Cara, who had walked quietly next to him since they'd left the church, her face pale and her expression serious. She gave him a weak smile, her eyes darting from side to side as if she was seriously contemplating making a run for it and scoping out the best means of escape.

He sighed. 'Come and sit down over here where it's quiet,' he said, looping his arm through hers and guiding her towards one of the empty tables nearest the house.

To his frustration she stiffened, then slipped out of his steadying grip and folded her arms across her chest instead, her shoulders rigid and her chin firmly up as they walked. Just as they picked their way over the last bit of gravelled path to reach the table she stumbled and on reflex he quickly moved in to catch her.

'Are you okay?' he asked, placing a hand on the exposed part of her back, feeling the heat of her body warm the palm of his hand and send an echoing sensation through his entire abdomen.

His touch seemed to undo something in her and she collapsed into the nearest chair and gave him such a fearful look his heart jumped into his throat.

'I'm sorry for lying to you, Max. Please don't fire me. If I lose this job I'll have to move back to Cornwall and I really, really don't want to leave London. It's my home and I love it. I can't imagine living anywhere else now. And I really like working for you.' Swallowing hard, she gave him a small quavering smile. 'I swear I will never lie to you again. Believe it or not, I usually have a rock-solid moral compass and if I hadn't felt backed into a corner I never would have twisted the truth. I was on the cusp of losing everything and I was desperate, Max. Totally. Desperate.' She punctuated each of the last words with a slap of her hand on the table.

'Cara, I'm not going to fire you.'

How could she think that he would? Good grief, had he done such a number on her that she'd think he'd be capable of something as heartless as that?

'You're not?' Her eyes shone in the reflected brightness thrown up by the white tablecloth and he looked away while she blinked back threatening tears.

'Of course not.' He shifted forward in his seat, closer to her. 'You well and truly proved your worth to the business last week.' He waited till she looked at him again. 'I have to admit, I'm hurt that you thought I'd fire you for admitting to being bullied.' He leaned back in his chair with a sigh. 'God, you must think I'm a real tool if you seriously believed I'd do something like that.'

'It's just—you can be a bit…fierce…sometimes. And I didn't want to show any weakness.' She visibly cringed as she said it, and his insides plummeted.

'Tell me more about what happened at your last job,' he said quietly, wanting to get things completely straight between them, but not wanting to spook her further in the process.

Her gaze slid away. 'It's not a happy tale, or something I'm particularly proud of.'

'No. I got that impression.'

'Okay, I'll tell you, but please don't judge me too harshly. Things like this always look so simple and manageable from a distance, but when you're in the thick of it, it's incredibly difficult to think straight without letting your emotions get in the way.'

He held up his hands, palms forward, and affected a non-judgemental expression.

She nodded and sat up straighter. 'I thought I'd hit the jackpot when I was offered that position. Ugh! What an idiot,' she said, her self-conscious grimace making him want to move closer to her, to draw her towards him and smooth out the kinks of her pain. But he couldn't do that. It wasn't his place.

So he just nodded and waited for her to continue.

'When I started as Executive Assistant to the CEO of LED Software I had no idea about the office politics that were going on there. But it didn't take me long to find out. Apparently one of the other PAs had expected to be a shoo-in for my job and was *very* unimpressed when they gave it to me. She made it her mission from my first day to make my life miserable. As one of the longest-standing members of staff—and a very, er, *strong* personality—she had the allegiance of all the other PAs and a lot of the other members of staff and they ganged up on me. At first I thought I was going mad. I'd make diary appointments for my boss with other high-ranking members of staff in the company, which their PAs would claim to have no knowledge of by the time I sent him along for the meeting. Or the notes I'd print out for an important phone call with the Executive Board would go missing from his desk right before it took place and he'd have to take it unbriefed.' She tapped her fingers on the table. 'That did not go down well. My boss was a very proud guy and he expected things to be perfect.'

'I can relate to that,' Max said, forcing compassion into his smile despite the tug of disquiet in his gut. He was just as guilty when it came to perfectionism.

But, instead of admonishing him, she smiled back.

'Lots of other little things like that happened,' she continued, rubbing a hand across her forehead, 'which made me look incompetent, but I couldn't prove that someone was interfering with my work and when I mentioned it to my boss he'd wave away my concerns and suggest I was slipping up on the job and blaming others to cover my back. I let the stress of it get to me and started making real mistakes, things I never would have let slip at the last place I worked. It rattled me, to the point where I started believing I wasn't cut out for the job. I wasn't sleeping properly with the stress of it and I ended up breaking down one day in front of my boss. And that—' she clicked her fingers '—was the end of our working relationship. He seemed to lose all respect for me after that and started giving the other PAs things that were my job to do.'

Max snorted in frustration. 'The guy sounds like an idiot.'

She gave him a wan smile. 'I was the idiot. I only found out what was really going on when I overheard a couple of the PAs laughing about it in the ladies' bathroom.'

Her eyes were dark with an expression he couldn't quite read now. Was it anger? Resentment? It certainly didn't look like self-pity.

'So you left,' he prompted.

She took a sip of her drink and he did the same, grimacing at the claggy sweetness of the cocktail.

'I had to,' she said. 'My professional reputation was at stake, not to mention my sanity. I couldn't afford to be fired; it would have looked awful on my CV. Not to mention how upset my parents would have been. They're desperate for me to have a successful career. They never had the opportunity to get a good education or well-paid job themselves so they scrimped and saved for years to put me through private school. It's a point of pride for my dad in particular. Apparently he never shuts up to his friends about me working with "the movers and shakers in the Big Smoke".' She shot him an embarrassed grimace.

He smiled. 'You're lucky—my mother couldn't give two hoots whether I'm successful or not. She's not what you'd call an engaged parent.'

Her brow furrowed in sympathy. 'And your father?'

'I never met him.' He leant back with a sigh. 'My mother fell pregnant with me when she was sixteen and still maintains that she doesn't know who he was. She was pretty wild in her youth and constantly moved us around the country. Barely a term at school would go by before she had us packing up and moving on. She couldn't bear to stay in the same place for long. Not that she's exactly settled now.'

Her gaze was sympathetic. 'That must have been tough when you were young.'

He shrugged. 'It was a bit. I never got to keep the friends I made for very long.'

He thought about how his unsettled youth had impacted on the way he liked to live now. He still didn't like change, even all these years later; it made him tetchy and short-tempered. Which was something Cara had got to know all about recently.

Keen to pull his mind away from his own shortcomings, he leaned forward in his seat and recaptured eye contact with her. 'So what happened when you handed in your notice?'

She started at the sudden flip in subject back to her and twisted the stem of her glass in her fingers, looking away from his gaze and focusing on the garish liquid as it swirled up towards the rim. 'My boss didn't even bat an eyelid, just tossed my letter of resignation onto his desk and went back to the email he was typing, which confirmed just how insignificant I was to him. I took a couple of weeks to get my head straight after that, but I needed another job. I've never earned enough to build up any savings and my landlord chose that moment to hoick my rent up. I sent my CV out everywhere and got a few interviews, but every one I attended was a washout. It was as if they could sense the cloud of failure that hung around me like a bad smell.'

'And that's when Poppy sent you to me.'

Wrinkling her nose, she gave him a rueful smile. 'I told her a bit about what had happened before she went off to shoot her latest project and she must have thought the two of us could help each other out because she emailed me to suggest I try you for a job. She made it sound as if you were desperate for help and it seemed like fate that I should work for you.'

'Desperate, huh?' He leant back in his seat and raised an eyebrow, feeling amusement tug at his mouth. That was textbook Poppy. 'Well, I have to admit it's been good for me, having you around. It's certainly kept me on my toes.'

'Yeah, there's never a dull moment when I'm around, huh?'

The air seemed to grow thick between them as their eyes met and he watched in arrested fascination as her cheeks flamed with colour.

Sliding her gaze away, she stared down at the table, clutching her glass, her chewed nails in plain view. He'd known it the whole time, of course, that she was fighting against some inner trauma, as her nerve and buoyancy deteriorated in the face of his brittle moods. Her increasingly ragged nails had been the indicator he'd been determined to ignore.

But not any more.

A string quartet suddenly started up on the terrace behind them and he winced as the sound assaulted his ears. He'd never liked the sound of violins and an instrument such as that should never be used to play soft rock covers. It was a crime against humanity.

'Come on, let's take a walk around the grounds and clear our heads,' he said, standing up and holding out his hand to help her up from the chair.

She looked at it with that little frown that always made something twist in his chest, before giving a firm nod and putting her hand in his.

CHAPTER SEVEN

A WALK WAS exactly what Cara needed to clear her head.

She couldn't quite believe she'd just spilled her guts to Max like that, but it was a massive relief to have it all out in the open, even if she did still feel shaky with the effort of holding herself together.

Of course, seeing the concern on his handsome face had only made her ridiculous crush on him deepen, and she was beginning to worry about how she was going to cope with seeing him every day, knowing that they'd never be anything more than colleagues or, at the very most, friends.

A twinkling light in the distance danced in her peripheral vision and she stopped and turned to see what it was, feeling her heels sink into the soft earth beneath her feet. Pulling her shoes off, she hooked her fingers into the straps before running to catch up with Max, who was now a few paces ahead of her, seemingly caught up in his own world, his head dipped as a frown played across his brow.

'Hey, do you fancy walking to that lake over there?' she asked him.

'Hmm?' His eyes looked unfocused, as if his thoughts were miles away. 'Yes, okay.'

The sudden detachment worried her. 'Is everything okay?'

Perhaps, now he'd had more time to reflect on what she'd told him, he was starting to regret getting involved in her messed up life.

She took a breath. 'Do you want to head back to London? I wouldn't blame you if you did.'

Turning to look her in the eye again, he blinked, as though casting away whatever was bothering him. 'No, no. I'm fine.' His gaze flicked towards the lake, then back to her again and he gave her a tense smile. 'Yeah, let's walk that way.'

It only took them a couple of minutes to get there, now that she was in bare feet, and they stopped at the lakeshore and looked out across the water to the dark, impenetrable-looking forest on the other side.

'It's a beautiful setting they've chosen,' Cara said, to fill the heavy silence that had fallen between them.

'Yes, it's lovely.' Max bent down and picked up a smooth flat stone, running his fingertips across its surface. 'This looks like a good skimmer.' He shrugged off his jacket and rolled up the sleeves of his shirt, revealing his muscular forearms.

Cara stared at them, her mouth drying at the sight. There was something so real, so virile about the image of his tanned skin, with its smattering of dark hair, in stark contrast to the crisp white cotton of his formal shirt. As if he was revealing the *man* inside the businessman.

Supressing a powerful desire to reach out and trace her fingers across the dips and swells of his muscles, she took a step away to give him plenty of room as he drew his elbow back and bent low, then flung the stone hard across the water.

A deep, satisfied chuckle rumbled from his chest as the stone bounced three times across the still surface, spinning out rings of gentle ripples in its wake, before sinking without a trace into the middle of the lake.

He turned to face her with a grin, his eyes alive with glee, and she couldn't help but smile back.

'Impressive.'

He blew on his fingers and pretended to polish them on his shirt. ‘I’m a natural. What can I say?’

Seeing his delight at the achievement, she had a strong desire to get in on the fun. Perhaps it would help distract her from thinking about how alone they were out here on the edge of the lake. ‘Does your natural talent stretch to teaching me how to do that?’

‘You’ve never skimmed a stone?’ He looked so over-the-top incredulous she couldn’t help but laugh.

‘Never.’

‘Didn’t you say your parents live in Cornwall? Surely there’s plenty of opportunities to be near water there.’

She snorted and took a step backwards, staring down at the muddy grass at their feet. ‘Yeah, if you live near the coast, which they don’t. I never learnt to drive when I was living there and my parents didn’t take me to the beach that much when I was young. My dad’s always suffered with a bad back from the heavy lifting he has to do at work, so he never got involved in anything of a physical nature. And my mum’s a real homebody. She’s suffered with agoraphobia for years.’

She heard him let out a low exhalation of breath and glanced up to find an expression of real sympathy in his eyes. ‘I’m sorry to hear that. That must have been hard for you as a kid,’ he said softly.

Shrugging one shoulder, she gave a nod to acknowledge his concern, remembering the feeling of being trapped inside four small walls when she was living at home, with nowhere to escape to. Going to school every day had actually been a welcome escape from it and as soon as she’d finished her studies she’d hightailed it to London.

‘Yeah, it was a bit. My parents are good people, though. They threw all their energy into raising me. And they made sure to let me know how loved I was.’ Which was the absolute truth, she realised with a sting of shame, because she’d distanced herself from them since leaving home in an attempt to leave her stultifying life there behind her. But she'd left them behind, too. They didn't deserve that. A visit was well overdue and she made a pact with herself to call them and arrange a date to see them as soon as she got back to London.

Max nodded, seemingly satisfied that she didn't need any more consoling, and broke eye contact to lean down and pick up another flat pebble.

She watched him weigh it in his palm, as if checking it was worth the effort of throwing it. Everything he did was measured and thorough like that, which was probably why he was such a successful businessman.

'Here, this looks like a good one. It's nice and flat with a decent weight to it so it'll fly and not sink immediately.' He turned it over in his hand. 'You need to get it to ride the air for a while before it comes down and maintain enough lift to jump.'

He held it out to her and she took it and looked at it with a frown. 'Is there a proper way to hold it?'

'I find the best way is to pinch it between my first finger and thumb. Like this.' He picked up another stone and demonstrated.

She copied the positioning in her own hand then gave him a confident nod, drew back her arm and threw it as hard as she could.

It landed in the lake with a *plop* and sank immediately.

'Darn it! What did I do wrong?' she asked, annoyed with herself for failing so badly.

'Don't worry; it can take a bit of practice to get your technique right. You need to get lower to the ground and swing your arm in a horizontal arc. When it feels like the stone could fly straight forward and parallel with the water, loosen the grip with your thumb and let it roll, snapping your finger forwards hard.'

'Huh. You make it sound so easy.'

He grinned and raised his eyebrows. 'Try again.'

Picking up a good-looking candidate, she positioned the stone between her finger and thumb and was just about to throw it when Max said, 'Stop!'

Glancing round at him with a grimace of frustration, she saw he was frowning and shaking his head.

'You need to swing your arm at a lower angle. Like this.'

Before she could react, he'd moved to stand directly behind her, putting his left hand on her hip and wrapping his right hand around the hand she was holding the stone in. Her heart nearly leapt out of her chest at the firmness of his touch and started hammering away, forcing the blood through her body at a much higher rate than was reasonable for such low-level exercise.

As he drew their arms backwards the movement made her shoulder press against the hard wall of his chest and she was mightily glad that he couldn't see her face at that precise moment. She was pretty sure it must look a real picture.

'Okay, on three we'll throw it together.' His mouth was so close to her ear she felt his breath tickle the downy little hairs on the outer whorl.

'One…two…three!'

They moved their linked hands in a sweeping arc, Cara feeling the power of Max's body push against her as the momentum of the move forced them forwards. She was so distracted by being engulfed in his arms she nearly didn't see the stone bounce a couple of times before it sank beneath the water.

'Woo-hoo!' Max shouted, releasing her to take a step back and raise his hand, waiting for her to give him a high five.

The sudden loss of his touch left her feeling strangely light and disorientated—but now was not the time to go to pieces. Mentally pulling herself together, she swung her hand up to meet his, their palms slapping loudly as they connected, then bent down straight away, pretending to search the ground for another missile.

'Who taught you to skim stones? A brother?' she asked casually, grimacing at the quaver in her voice, before grabbing another good-looking pebble and righting herself.

He'd stooped to pick up his own stone and glanced round at her as he straightened up. 'No. I'm an only child. I think once my mother realised how much hard work it was raising me she was determined not to have any more kids.' He raised a disparaging eyebrow then turned away to fling the stone across the lake, managing five bounces this time. He nodded with satisfaction. 'I used to mountain bike over to a nearby reservoir with a friend from boarding school at the weekends and we'd have competitions to see who could get their stone the furthest,' he said, already searching the ground for another likely skimmer, his movements surprisingly lithe considering the size of his powerful body.

A sudden need to get this right overwhelmed her.

She wasn't usually a superstitious person, but she imagined she could sense the power in this one simple challenge. If she got this stone to bounce by herself, maybe, just maybe, everything would be okay.

She was throwing this for her pride and the return of her strength. To prove to Max—but mostly to herself—that she was resilient and capable and—dare she even suggest it?—brave enough to try something new, even if there was a good chance she'd fail spectacularly and end up looking foolish again.

Harnessing the power of positive thought, she drew back her hand, took a second to centre herself, then flung the stone hard across the water, snapping her finger like he'd taught her and holding her breath as she watched it sail through the air.

It dropped low about fifteen feet out and for a second she thought she'd messed it up, but her spirits soared as she saw it bounce twice before disappearing.

Spinning round to make a celebratory face at Max, she was gratified to see him nod in exaggerated approval, a smile playing about his lips.

'Good job! You're a quick study; but then we already knew that about you.'

The compliment made her insides flare with warmth and she let out a laugh of delight, elation twisting through her as she saw him grin back.

Their gazes snagged and held, his pupils dilating till his eyes looked nearly black in the bright afternoon light.

A wave of electric heat spread through her at the sight of it, but the laughter died in her throat as he turned abruptly away and stared off towards the house instead, folding his arms so tightly against his chest she could make out the shape of his muscles under his shirt.

He cleared his throat. 'You know, this place is just like the venue where Jemima and I got married,' he said, so casually she wondered how much emotion he'd had to rein in, in order to say it.

Ugh. What a selfish dolt she was. Here she'd been worrying about what he thought of her and her tales of woe, when he was doing battle with his own demons.

It had occurred to her earlier that morning, as she'd struggled to do up her dress, that attending a wedding could be problematic for him, but she'd forgotten all about it after the incident in the kitchen, her thoughts distracted by the unnerving tension that had crackled between them ever since.

Or what she'd thought was tension.

Perhaps it had been apprehension on his part.

And then, when he'd mentioned how transient and lonely his youth had been over drinks earlier, it had brought it home to her why Jemima's death had hit him so hard. It sounded as if she'd been the person anchoring his life after years of feeling adrift and insecure. And this place reminded him of everything he'd lost.

No wonder he seemed so unsettled.

He'd still come here to help her out, though, despite his discomfort at being at this kind of event, which was a decent and kind thing for him to do and way beyond the call of duty as her boss. Her heart did a slow flip in her chest as she realised exactly what it must have cost him to agree to come.

'I'm sorry for dragging you here today. I didn't think about how hard it would be for you. After losing Jemima.'

He put his hand on her arm and waited for her to look at him before speaking. 'You have nothing to apologise for. *Nothing.* I wanted to come here to support you because you've done nothing but support me for the last few weeks. It's my turn to look after you today.' He was looking directly at her now and the fierce intensity in his eyes made a delicious shiver zip down her spine.

'Honestly, I thought it would be awful coming here,' he said, casting his gaze back towards the house again, 'but it's not been the trial I thought it'd be. In fact—' he ran a hand over his hair and let out a low breath '—it's been good for me to confront a situation like this. I've been missing out on so much life since Jem died and it's time I pulled my head out of the sand and faced the world again.'

Cara swallowed hard, ensnared in the emotion of the moment, her heart thudding against her chest and her breath rasping in her dry throat. Looking at Max now, she realised that the ever-present frown was nowhere to be seen for once. Instead, there was light in his eyes and something else…

They stood, frozen in the moment, as the gentle spring wind wrapped around them and the birds sang enthusiastically above their heads.

It would be so easy to push up onto tiptoe and slide her hands around his neck. To press her lips against his and feel the heat and masculine strength of him, to slide her tongue into his mouth and taste him. She ached to feel his breath against her skin and his hands in her hair, her whole body tingling with the sensory expectation of it.

She wanted to be the one to remind him what living could be like, if only he'd let her.

To her disappointment, Max broke eye contact with her and nodded towards the marquee behind them. 'We should probably get back before they send out a search party. We don't want to find ourselves in trouble for messing with Amber's schedule of events and being frogmarched to our seats,' he said lightly, though his voice sounded gruffer than normal.

Had he seen it in her face? The longing. She hoped not. The thought of her infatuation putting their fragile relationship under any more strain made her insides squirm.

Anyway, that tension-filled moment had probably been him thinking about Jemima again.

Not her.

They walked in silence back to the marquee, the bright sun pleasantly warm on the back of her neck and bare shoulders, but her insides icy cold.

Despite their little detour, they weren't the last to sit down. It was with a sigh of relief that Cara slumped into her seat and reached for the bottle of white wine on the table, more than ready to blot out the ache of disappointment that had been present ever since he'd suggested they give up their truancy from the festivities and head back into the fray.

It wasn't that she didn't want to be here exactly; it was just that it had been so much fun hanging out with him. Just the two of them together, like friends. Or something.

Knocking back half a glass of wine in one go, she refilled it before offering the bottle to Max.

He was looking at her with bemusement, one eyebrow raised. 'Thirsty?'

Heat flared across her cheeks. 'Just getting in the party mood,' she said, forcing a nonchalant smile. 'It looks like we have some catching up to do.'

The raucous chatter and laughter in the room suggested that people were already pretty tiddly on the cocktails they'd been served.

'Okay, well, I'm going to stick to water if I have to drive to the bed and breakfast place later. I think one of us should stay sober enough to find our way there at the end of the night. I don't fancy kipping in the car.'

She gave him an awkward grin as the thought of sleeping in such close proximity to him made more heat rush to her face.

Picking up her glass, she took another long sip of wine to cover her distress.

Oh, good grief. It was going to be a long night.

The meal was surprisingly tasty, considering how many people were being catered for, and Cara began to relax as the wine did its work. She quickly found herself in a conversation with the lady to her right, who turned out to be Amber's second cousin and an estate agent in Angel, about the dearth of affordable housing to rent in London. By the end of dessert, the woman had promised to give Cara first dibs on a lovely-sounding one-bedroom flat that was just about to come onto her books. And that proved to Cara, without a shadow of a doubt, that you just had to be in the right place at the right time to get lucky.

Turning to say this exact thing to Max, she was disturbed to find he'd finished his conversation with the man next to him and was frowning down at the tablecloth.

'Sorry for ignoring you,' she said, worried he was getting sucked down into dark thoughts again with all the celebrating going on around him.

He gave her a tense smile and pushed his chair away from the table. 'You weren't. I overheard your conversation about finding a flat; that's great news—you should definitely get her number and follow that up,' he said, standing and tapping the back of his chair. 'I'm going to find the bathrooms. I'll be back in a minute.'

She watched him stride away with a lump in her throat. Was he upset about the prospect of her moving out? She dismissed the notion immediately. No, he couldn't be. He must be craving his space again by now. Even though she'd loved living there, she knew it was time to move out. Especially now that her feelings for him had twisted themselves into something new. Something dangerous.

'That's a good one you've got there—very sexy,' Amber's second cousin muttered into her ear, pulling back to waggle her eyebrows suggestively, only making the lump in Cara's throat grow in size.

Unable to speak, she gave the woman what she hoped looked like a gracious smile.

'Hi, Cara.'

The voice behind her made her jump in her seat and she swivelled round, only to find herself staring into the eyes of the woman she'd been trying to avoid since spotting her in the church earlier.

Her meal rolled uncomfortably in her stomach.

'Hi, Lucy.'

Instead of the look of cool disdain Cara was expecting, she was surprised to see Lucy bite her lip, her expression wary.

'How are you?' Lucy asked falteringly, as if afraid to hear the answer.

'Fine, thank you.' Cara kept her voice deliberately neutral, just in case this was an opening gambit to get her to admit to something she really didn't want to say.

'Can I talk to you for a moment?'

Cara swallowed her anxiety and gestured towards the chair Max had vacated, wondering what on earth this woman could have to say to her. Whatever it was, it was better to get it over with now so she didn't spend the rest of the night looking over her shoulder. Straightening her back, she steeled herself to deal with anything she could throw at her.

Lucy sat on the edge of the seat, as close as she could get to Cara without touching her, and laid her hands on her lap before taking a deep breath. 'I wanted to come over and apologise as soon as I could so there wasn't any kind of atmosphere between us today.'

Cara stared at her. 'I'm sorry? Did you say *apologise*?'

Lucy crossed her legs, then uncrossed them again, her cheeks flooding with colour. 'Yes… I'm really sorry about the way you were treated at LED. I feel awful about it. I let Michelle bully me into taking her side—because I knew she'd turn on me, too, if I stood up for you—and I was pathetic enough to let her. I want you to know that I didn't do any of those awful things to you, but I didn't stop it either.' She shook her head and let out a low sigh. 'I feel awful about it, Cara, truly.'

At that moment Cara felt a pair of hands land lightly on her shoulders. Twisting her head round, she saw that Max had returned and was standing over her like some kind of dark guardian angel.

'Everything okay, Cara?' From the cool tone in his voice she suspected he'd be more than willing to step in and eject Lucy from her seat if she asked him to.

'Fine, thanks, Max. This is Lucy. She came over to apologise for her *unfriendliness* at the last place I worked.'

'Is that so?'

Cara couldn't see the expression on his face from that angle but, from the sound of his voice and the way Lucy seemed to shrink back in her chair, she guessed it wasn't a very friendly one.

Lucy cleared her throat awkwardly. 'Yes, I feel dreadful about the whole thing. It was horrible working there. In fact, I left the week after you did. I couldn't stand the smug look on Michelle's face any more. Although—' she leaned forward in a conspiratorial manner '—I heard from one of the other girls that she only lasted a month before he got rid of her. She couldn't hack it, apparently.' She snorted. 'That's karma in action, right there.' Clearly feeling she'd said her piece, Lucy stood up so that Max could have his chair back and took a small step away from them. 'Anyway, I'd better get back to my table; apparently there's coffee on the way and I'm desperate for some. Those cocktails were evil, weren't they?'

'Why are you here today?' Cara asked before she could turn and leave, intrigued by the coincidence.

'I'm Jack's—the groom's—new PA.'

Cara couldn't help but laugh at life's weird little twist. 'Really?'

'Yeah, he's a great boss, really lovely to work for.' She leant forward again and said in a quiet voice, 'I don't think Amber likes me very much, though; she didn't seem very pleased to see me here.'

'I wouldn't take that too personally,' Cara said, giving her a reassuring smile. 'She's an intensely protective person.' She put a hand on Lucy's arm. 'Thanks for being brave enough to come over and apologise, Lucy; I really appreciate the gesture.'

Lucy gave her one last smile, and Max a slightly terrified grimace, before retreating to her table.

Max sat back down in his chair, giving her an impressed nod. 'Nicely handled.'

Warm pleasure coursed through her as she took in the look of approval in his eyes. Feeling a little flustered by it, she picked up her glass of wine to take a big gulp, but judged the tilt badly and some escaped from the side of the rim and dribbled down her chin. Before she had time to react, Max whipped his napkin under her jaw and caught the rogue droplets with it, stopping them from splashing onto her dress.

'Smooth!' she said, laughing in surprise.

'I have moves,' he replied, his eyes twinkling and his mouth twitching into a warm smile.

A wave of heat engulfed her and her stomach did a full-on somersault.

Oh, no, what was *happening* to her?

Heart racing, she finally allowed the truth to filter through to her consciousness.

It was, of course, the very last thing she needed to happen.

She was falling in love with him.

CHAPTER EIGHT

AFTER THE MEAL and speeches, all the guests were encouraged to go through to the house, where a bar had been set up under the sweeping staircase in the hall and a DJ in the ballroom was playing ambient tunes in the hope of drawing the guests in there to sit around the tables that surrounded the dance floor.

Waiting at the bar to grab them both a caffeinated soft drink to give them some energy for the rest of the evening's events, Max allowed his thoughts to jump back over the day.

He'd had fun at the lake with Cara, which had taken him by surprise, because the last thing he'd expected when he'd got up that morning was that he would enjoy himself today.

But Cara had a way of finding the joy in things.

In fact, he'd been so caught up in the pleasure of showing her how to skim stones, he hadn't thought about what he was doing until his hand was on the soft curve of her hip and his body was pressed up close to hers, the familiar floral scent of her perfume in his nose and the heat of her warming his skin. He'd hidden his instinctive response to it well enough, he thought, using the excessive rush of adrenaline to hurl more stones across the water.

And then she'd been so delighted when she'd managed to skim that stone by herself he'd felt a mad urge to wrap his arms around her again in celebration and experience the moment with her.

But that time he'd managed to rein himself in, randomly talking about his own wedding to break the tension, only to feel a different kind of self-reproach when Cara assumed his indiscriminate jump to the subject was down to him feeling gloomy about his situation.

Which it really hadn't been.

Returning with the drinks to where he'd left Cara standing just inside the ballroom, he handed one to her and smiled when she received it with a grimace of relieved thanks. The main lights in the room were set low and a large glitter ball revolved slowly from the ceiling, scattering the floor and walls with shards of silver light. Max watched them dance over Cara's face in fascination, thinking that she looked like some kind of ethereal seraph, with her bright eyes and pale creamy skin against the glowing silver of her dress.

A strange elation twisted through him, triggering a lifting sensation throughout his whole body—as if all the things that had dragged him down in the past eighteen months were losing their weight and slowly drifting upwards. The sadness he'd expected to keep on hitting him throughout the day was still notably absent, and instead there was a weird sense of rightness about being here.

With her.

Catching her giving him a quizzical look, he was just about to ask if she wanted to take another walk outside so they could hear each other speak when Jack and Amber walked past them and onto the empty dance floor. Noticing their presence, the DJ cued up a new track as a surge of guests crowded into the room, evidently following the happy couple in to watch their first dance as husband and wife.

Max found himself jostled closer to Cara as the edges of the dance floor filled up and he instinctively put an arm around her to stop her from being shoved around, too. She turned to look at him, the expression in her eyes startled at first, but then sparking with understanding when he nodded towards a gap in the crowd a little along from them.

He guided them towards it, feeling her hips sway against his as they moved, and had to will his attention-starved body not to respond.

Once in the space, he let her go, relaxing his arm to his side, and could have sworn he saw her shoulders drop a little as if she'd been holding herself rigid.

Feeling a little disconcerted by her obvious discomfort at him touching her again, he watched the happy couple blindly as they twirled around the dance floor, going through the motions of the ballroom dance they'd plainly been practising for the past few months.

Had he overstepped the mark by manhandling her like that? He'd not meant to make her uncomfortable but they were supposed to be there as a couple, so it wasn't as though it wasn't within his remit to act that way around her.

Ugh. There was no point in beating himself up about it. He'd just have to be more careful about the way he touched her, or not, for the rest of the evening.

As soon as the dance finished, other couples joined the newlyweds on the dance floor and, spotting Cara, Jack broke away from Amber and made his way over to them.

'Cara, I'm so glad you made it!' he said, stooping down to pull her into a bear hug, making her squeal with laughter as he spun her around before placing her back down again.

Cara pulled away from him, her cheeks flushed, and rubbed his arm affectionately. 'Congratulations. And thank you for inviting us. It's a beautiful wedding.'

'I'm glad you're having a good time,' Jack replied, smiling into her eyes. 'Want to dance with me, for old times' sake?' he said, already taking her arm and leading her away from Max onto the dance floor. 'You don't mind if I steal her away for a minute, do you, Max?' he tossed over his shoulder, plainly not at all interested in Max's real opinion on the matter.

Not that Max *should* mind.

Watching Cara laugh at something that Jack whispered into her ear as he began to move her around the dance floor, Max was hit by an unreasonable surge of irritation and had to force himself to relax his arms and let them hang by his sides instead of balling them into tight fists. What the heck was going on with him today? How messed up was he to be jealous of a new groom, who was clearly infatuated with his wife, just because he was dancing with Cara? It must be because the guy seemed to have everything—a wife who loved him, a successful career with colleagues who respected him, Cara as a friend…

The track came to a close and a new, slower one started up. Before he could check himself, Max strode across to where Jack and Cara were just breaking apart.

'You don't mind if I cut in now, do you?' he said to Jack, intensely conscious that his words had come out as more of a statement than a question.

Jack's eyebrows rose infinitesimally at Max's less than gracious tone, but he smiled at Cara and swept a hand to encompass them both. 'Be my guest.' Leaning forward, he kissed Cara on the cheek before moving away from her. 'It's great to see you so happy. You know, you're actually glowing.' He slapped Max on the back. 'You're obviously good for her, Max. Look after her, okay? She's a good one,' he said. 'But watch your feet; she's a bit of a toe-stamper,' he added, ducking out of the way as Cara swiped a hand at him and walked off laughing.

Turning back, Cara fixed Max with an awkward smile, then leaned in to speak into his ear. 'Sorry about that. I didn't want to admit to the truth about us and break the mood.'

Max nodded, his shoulders suddenly stiff, surprised to find he was disappointed to hear her say that her glow was nothing to do with him.

Don't be ridiculous, you fool—how could it be?

His feelings must have shown on his face because she took a small step away from him and said, 'You don't really need to dance with me, but thanks for the gesture.'

He shrugged. 'It's no problem. You seemed to be enjoying yourself and I was anticipating Jack being commandeered at any second by Amber or another relative wanting his attention so I thought I'd jump in,' he replied, feeling the hairs that had escaped from her up-do tickle his nose as he leaned in close to her.

She looked at him for the longest moment, something flickering behind her eyes, before giving him a small nod and a smile. 'Okay then, I'd love to dance.'

Holding her as loosely as he could in his arms, he guided her around the dance floor, leading her in a basic waltz and finding pleasure in the way she responded to his lead, copying his movements with a real sense that she trusted him not to make a false step. His blood roared through his veins as his heart worked overtime to keep him cool in the accumulated heat of the bodies that surrounded them. Or was it the feeling of her in his arms that was doing that to him?

He felt her back shift against his palm and turned to see she was waving to Lucy, the woman who had come over to apologise to her at dinner.

A sense of admiration swept thorough him as he reflected on how well she'd handled that situation. When he'd returned to the table, after needing to take a breath of air and talk himself down from a strange feeling of despondency when he heard she was likely to find a new place to live soon, and seen them talking, he'd feared the worst. An intense urge to step in and protect her had grabbed him by the throat, making him move fast and put his hands on her, to let her know he had her back if she needed him.

She hadn't, though. In fact she'd shown real strength and finesse with her response. Another example of why she was so good at her job. And why he respected her so much as a person. Why he liked her—

Halting his thoughts right there, he guided her over to the side of the dance floor as the music changed into retro pop and drew away from her, feeling oddly bereft at the loss of her warm body so close to his own.

The room was spinning.

And it wasn't from the alcohol she'd consumed earlier or even the overwhelming heat and noise—it was because of Max. Being so close to him, feeling the strength of his will as he whirled her around the dance floor had sent her senses into a nosedive.

'Max, do you mind if we go outside for a minute? I need some air.'

The look her gave her was one of pure alarm. 'Are you all right?'

'I'm fine, just a bit hot,' she said, flapping a hand ineffectually in front of her face.

Giving her a curt nod, he motioned for her to walk out of the ballroom in front of him, shadowing her closely as she pushed her way through the crowd of people in the hallway and out into the blissfully cool evening air.

Slumping down onto a cold stone bench pushed up against the front of the house, she let out a deep sigh of relief as the fresh air pricked at her hot skin.

'I'm going to fetch you a drink of water,' Max said, standing over her, his face a picture of concern. 'Stay here.'

She watched him go, her stomach sinking with embarrassment, wondering how she was ever going to explain herself if she didn't manage to pull it together.

Putting her head in her hands, she breathed in the echo of Max's scent on her skin, its musky undertones making her heart trip over itself.

'Are you okay there?'

The deep voice made her start and she looked up to see one of the male guests looking down at her, his brow creased in worry. She seemed to remember Amber's second cousin pointing him out as Amber's youngest brother and the black sheep of the family. *Womaniser* was the word she'd used.

Sitting up straighter in her seat, she gave him a friendly but dispassionate smile. 'I'm fine, thanks, just a bit hot from dancing.'

Instead of nodding and walking away, he sat down next to her and held out his hand. 'I'm Frank, Amber's black sheep of a brother,' he said with a twinkle in his eye.

She couldn't help but laugh as she shook his hand. 'I'm Cara.'

'I don't know whether anyone's told you this today, Cara, but you look beautiful in that dress,' he said, his voice smooth like melted chocolate. He wanted her. She could see it in his face.

Cara was just about to open her mouth to politely brush him off when a shadow fell across them. Looking up, she saw that Max had returned with her glass of water and was standing over them with a strange look on his face.

'Here's your drink, Cara,' he said, handing it over and giving Frank a curt nod.

Frank must have seen something in Max's expression because he got up quickly and took a step away from them both. 'Okay, well, it looks like your boyfriend's got this, so I'll say good evening. Have a good one, Cara,' he said, flashing her a disappointed smile as he backed away, then turning on his heel to disappear into the dark garden.

'Sorry,' Max said gruffly, 'I didn't mean to scare him off.' He didn't look particularly sorry, though, she noted as he sat down next to her and laid his arm across the back of the bench. In fact, if anything, he seemed pleased that the guy had gone. Turning to look him directly in the eye, her stomach gave a flutter of nerves as something flickered in his eyes. Something fierce and disconcerting.

Telling herself she must be seeing things, she forced a composed smile onto her face. 'It's okay; he wasn't my type anyway.'

Not like you.

Pushing the rogue thought away, she took a long sip of the water he'd fetched to cover her nerves. What was she doing, letting herself imagine there was something developing between them?

'Thanks for the water. I didn't mean to worry you. I'm feeling better now I'm in the fresh air.'

Despite her claims, he was still looking at her with that strange expression in his eyes.

'Why are you single?' he asked suddenly, making her blink at him in surprise.

'Oh, you know…'

He frowned. 'It's not because I've been working you too hard, is it?'

'No, no!' She shook her head. 'It's through personal choice.'

His frown deepened, as if he didn't quite believe her.

She swallowed before expanding on her answer, linking her fingers tightly together around the glass. 'I decided to take a break from dating for a while. My last relationship was a bit of a disaster.'

He relaxed back against the bench. 'How so?'

'The whole fiasco at LED pretty much ruined it. After I started having trouble coping with what was going on at work I got a bit down and it made me withdraw into myself. My ex-boyfriend, Ewan, got fed up with me being so…er…*unresponsive*.' She cringed. 'That's why I've been trying so hard to stay positive. I know how it can get boring, having people around who feel sorry for themselves all the time.'

He ran his hand through his hair, letting out a long, low sigh.

Heat rushed through her as she realised how Max might have interpreted what she'd just said. 'I didn't mean… I wasn't talking about you.'

He snorted gently and flashed her a smile. 'I didn't think you were. I was frustrated on your behalf. I can't believe the guy was stupid enough to treat you like that.'

'Yeah, well, it's in the past now. To be honest, that relationship was always doomed to fail. He was a little too self-centred for my liking. He made it pretty obvious he thought I wasn't good enough for him.'

'Not good enough! That's the most ridiculous thing I ever heard,' he snapped out, the ferocity in his tone telling her he had a lot more he wanted to say on the matter, but for the sake of propriety was keeping it to himself.

She smiled at him, her heart rising to her throat. 'It's okay. It doesn't bother me any more.' And it really didn't, she realised with a sense of satisfaction. Her experiences since breaking up with Ewan had taught her that her real self-worth came from her own actions and achievements, not pleasing someone else.

Putting the empty glass onto the ground by the bench, she tried to hide a yawn of tiredness behind her hand. It had been a long and intense day.

'Do you want to get out of here?' Max asked quietly.

Clearly she hadn't been able to hide her exhaustion from him.

Looking at him with a smile of gratitude, she nodded her head. 'I wouldn't mind. I don't think I've got the energy for any more dancing.'

He stood up. 'Okay, I'll go and fetch the car.'

'I'll just pop back in and say goodbye to Jack and Amber and I'll meet you back here,' she said, gesturing to the pull-in place at the end of the sweeping driveway.

He nodded, before turning on his heel and heading off towards where they'd left the car parked by the estate's church.

She watched him disappear into the darkness, with his jacket slung over his arm and the white shirt stretched across his broad shoulders glowing in the moonlight, before he dipped out of sight.

After saying a hurried goodbye to the now rather inebriated newlyweds, she came out to find Max waiting for her in the car and jumped in gratefully, sinking back into the soft leather seat with a sigh. Now she knew that bed wasn't far away, she was desperate to escape to her room and finally be able to relax away from Max's unsettling presence.

It only took them five minutes to drive to the B&B she'd booked them into and as luck would have it there was a convenient parking space right outside the pretty thatched cottage.

'We're in the annexe at the back,' she said to Max as he hauled their overnight bags out of the boot. 'They gave me a key code to open the door so we won't need to disturb them.'

'Great,' Max said, hoisting the bags onto his back and following her down the path of the colourful country cottage garden towards the rear of the house. The air smelled sweetly of the honeysuckle that wound itself around a large wooden arch leading through to the back garden where their accommodation was housed, and Cara breathed it in with a great sense of pleasure. The place felt almost magical, shrouded as it was in the velvety darkness of the night.

Cara tapped the code into the keypad next to the small oak door that led directly into the annexe and flipped on the lights as soon as they were inside, illuminating a beautifully presented hallway with its simple country-style furniture and heritage-coloured décor. Two open bedroom doors stood opposite each other and there was a small bathroom at the back, which they would share.

'I hope this is okay. All the local hotels were fully booked and Jack said this was the place his cousin and her family were going to stay in, so the owners were pleased to swap the booking to us, considering it was such a last-minute cancellation.'

Max nodded, looking around at the layout, his expression neutral. 'It's great.'

The hallway was so small they were standing much closer to each other than Cara was entirely comfortable with. Max moved past her to drop his bag into one of the rooms and his musky scent hit her senses, making her whole body quiver with longing. The thought of him being just a few feet away from her was going to make it very difficult to sleep, despite how tired she was.

After dropping her bag into the other room, Max walked back into the hallway and stood in front of her, a small frown playing across his face. 'Are you feeling okay now?'

She smiled, the effort making her cheeks ache. 'I'm fine.' She took a nervous step backwards, and jumped a little as her back hit the wall behind her. 'Thank you so much for coming with me. I really appreciate it.'

He was looking at her with that fierce expression in his eyes again and a heavy, tingly heat slid from her throat, deep into her belly, sending electric currents of need to every nerve-ending in her body. For some reason she was finding it hard to breathe.

'It was my pleasure, Cara,' he said, his voice gruff as if he was having trouble with his own airways. 'You know, that guy you were talking to earlier was right. You do look beautiful in that dress.'

She stared at him, a disorientating mixture of excitement and confusion swirling around her head.

His gaze flicked away from hers for a second and when his eyes returned to hers the fierce look had gone and was replaced with a friendly twinkle. 'It occurred to me that you might have a bit of trouble getting out it—after needing my help to do it up this morning. Want me to undo the buttons for you?'

What was this?

Cara knew what she wanted it to be: for Max to want the same thing that she did—to alleviate this unbearable need to touch and kiss and hold him. To slide off all their clothes and lose themselves in each other's body.

To love him.

Did he want that, too?

Could he?

Her heart was beating so hard and fast, all she could hear and feel was the hot pulse of her blood through her body.

'That would be great. Thank you,' she managed to force past her dry throat.

She rotated on the spot until her back was to him, her whole body vibrating with tension as she felt his fingers graze her skin as he released each of the buttons in turn.

As soon as the last one popped free, she trapped the now loose dress against her body and turned to face him again, trying to summon an expression that wouldn't give her feelings away.

He looked at her for the longest time, his eyes wide and dark and his breathing shallow.

She watched him flick his tongue between his lips and something snapped inside her. Unable to stand the tension any longer, she rocked forward on her toes and tipped her head up, pressing her mouth to his. His lips were firm under hers and his scent enveloped her, wrapping round her senses, only adding to her violent pull of need to deepen the kiss.

Until she realised he wasn't kissing her back.

He hadn't moved away from her, but she could feel how tense he was under her touch. As if he was holding himself rigid.

She stilled, one hand anchoring herself against his broad shoulder, the other still holding her dress tightly against her body, and pulled away, eyes screwed shut, her stomach plummeting to her shoes at his lack of response.

What had she *done*?

When she dared open her eyes, he was looking at her with such an expression of torment that she had to close them again.

'I'm sorry. So, so sorry,' she whispered, her throat locking up and her face burning with mortification.

'Cara—' He sounded troubled. Aggrieved. Exasperated.

Stumbling away from him, her back hit the wall again and she felt her way blindly into her bedroom and slammed the door shut, leaning back on it as if it would keep out the horror of the past few seconds.

Which, of course, it wouldn't.

What must he think of her? All he'd done was offer to help her with her dress and she'd thrown herself at him. What had possessed her to do that when she knew he wasn't over losing his wife? How could she have thought he wanted anything more to develop between them?

She was a fool.

And she couldn't even blame it on alcohol because she'd been drinking soft drinks for the past couple of hours.

She jumped in fright as she felt Max knock on the door, the vibration of it echoing through her tightly strung body. She knew she had to face him. To apologise and try to find some way to make things right again.

Struggling to get her breathing under control, she stepped away from the door and opened it, forcing herself to look up into Max's face with as much cool confidence as she could muster.

Before he could say anything, she held up a hand. 'I really am sorry… I don't know what happened. It won't ever happen ag—'

But, before she could finish the sentence, he took a step towards her, the expression in his eyes wild and intense as he slid his hand into her hair, drawing her forward and pressing his lips against hers.

They stumbled into the room, off balance, as their mouths crashed together. Electric heat exploded deep within her and she heard him groan with pleasure when she pressed her body hard into his. She could feel the urgency in him as he pushed her back against the wall, his hard body trapping her there as he fervently explored her mouth with his own, his tongue sliding firmly against hers. Taking a step back, he pulled his shirt over his head in one swift movement and dropped it onto the floor next to them.

'Are you sure you want this, Cara?' he asked, his voice guttural and low as she feverishly ran her hands over the dips and swells of his chest in dazed wonder.

'Yes.'

She smiled as he exhaled in relief and brought his mouth

back down to hers, sliding his hands down to her thighs so he could pick her up and carry her over to the bed.

Then there was no more talking, just the feel of his solid body pressed hard against hers and the slide and twist of his muscles under his soft skin and—sensation—a riot of sensation that she sunk into and lost herself in. Her body had craved this for so long it was a sweet, beautiful relief to finally have what she wanted.

What she needed.

In those moments there was no past and no future; they were purely living for the moment.

And it was absolutely perfect.

CHAPTER NINE

MAX AWOKE FROM such a deep sleep it took him a while to realise that he wasn't in his own bed.

And that he wasn't alone.

Cara's warm body was pressed up against his back, her arm draped heavily over his hip and her head tucked in between his shoulder blades. He could feel her breath against his skin and hear her gentle exhalations.

Memories from the night they'd just spent together flitted through his head like a film on fast-forward, the intensity of them making his skin tingle and his blood pound through his body. It had been amazing. More than amazing. It had rocked his world.

It had felt so good holding her in his arms, feeling her respond so willingly to his demands and clearly enjoying making her own on him.

But, lying here now, he knew it had been a mistake.

It was too soon after losing his wife to be feeling like that. It felt wrong—somehow seedy and inappropriate. Greedy.

He'd had his shot at love and it wasn't right that he should get another one. Especially not so soon after losing Jemima. In the cold light of day it seemed tasteless somehow, as if he hadn't paid his dues.

He'd been in such a fog of need all day yesterday that he'd pushed all the rational arguments to the back of his head and just taken what he'd wanted, which had been totally unfair on Cara.

He wasn't ready to give himself over to a relationship again. And he knew that Cara would need more from him than he was able to give. She'd want the fairy tale, and he was no Prince Charming.

The worst thing was: he'd known that this was going to happen. From the moment he'd set eyes on her. He'd been attracted to her, even though he'd pretended to himself that he wasn't. And he'd only made things worse for himself by keeping her at arm's length. The more he'd told himself *no*, the more he'd wanted her. That was why he'd really thought it best to get rid of her quickly, before anything could happen between them. And then, once it became clear there was no hiding from the fact she was a positive force in his life, he'd pretended to himself that he wanted her to stay purely for her skills as a PA.

Idiot.

It had well and truly backfired on him.

This was precisely why he'd stopped himself from becoming friends with her at the beginning. He'd known it would guide them down a dangerous path.

His concerns hadn't stopped him from knocking on her door after she'd run away from him last night, though. Even after it had taken everything he'd had not to respond to that first kiss. But she'd looked so hurt, so devastatingly bereft that he'd found himself chasing after her to try and put it right. And, judging by her reaction when he'd been unable to hold back a second time and stop himself from kissing her, she'd been just as desperate as him for it to happen. In fact, the small, encouraging noises that had driven him wild made him think she'd wanted it for a while.

And, as his penance, he was now going to have to explain to her why it could never happen again.

Drawing away from her as gently as he could so as not to

wake her, he swung his legs out of bed and sat on the edge, putting his head in his hands, trying to figure out what to do next. He wasn't going to just leave her here in the middle of rural Leicestershire with no transport, but the thought of having to sit through the whole car journey home with her after explaining why last night had been a mistake filled him with dread.

He jumped as a slender arm snaked round his middle and Cara kissed down the length of his spine, before pulling herself up to sit behind him with her legs on either side of his body, her breasts pressing into his back.

'Good morning,' she said, her voice guttural with sleep.

Fighting to keep his body from responding to her, he put his hand on the arm that was wrapped around his middle and gently prised it away.

'Are you okay?' she asked, her tone sounding worried now.

'Fine.' He stood up and grabbed his trousers, pulling them on roughly before turning back to her.

She'd tugged the sheet around her and was looking up at him with such an expression of concern he nearly reached for her.

Steeling himself against the impulse, he shoved his hands in his pockets and looked at her with as much cool determination as he could muster.

'This was wrong, Cara. Us, doing this.'

'What?' Her eyes widened in confused surprise.

'I'm sorry. I shouldn't have let it happen. I got caught up in the moment, which was selfish of me.'

Her expression changed in an instant to one of panic. 'No.' She held out her hands beseechingly. 'Please don't be sorry about it. I wanted it to happen, too.'

He swallowed hard, tearing his eyes away from her worried gaze. 'I can't give you what you want long-term, Cara.'

Pulling the sheet tighter around her body, she frowned at him. 'You don't know what I want.'

He smiled sadly. 'Yes, I do. You want this to turn into something serious, but I don't. I'm happy with my life the way it is.'

'You're *happy*?' She looked incredulous.

He rubbed his hand over his face in irritation. 'Yes, Cara, I'm happy,' he said, but he felt the lie land heavily in his gut.

'But what we had last night—and all day yesterday—I didn't imagine it.' She shook her head as if trying to throw off any niggling doubts. 'It was so good. It felt right between us, Max. Surely you felt that, too.'

He looked at her steadily, already hating himself for what he was about to say. 'No. Sorry.' He scrubbed a hand through his hair. 'Look, I was feeling lonely and you happened to be there. I feel awful about it and I won't blame you for being angry.'

She didn't believe him; he could see it in her eyes.

'I understand why you're panicking,' she said, holding out her hands in a pleading gesture, 'because we've just changed the nature of our relationship and it's a scary thing, taking things a step further, especially after what happened to Jemima…'

'See, that's the thing, Cara. I've been through that once and I'm not prepared to put myself through something like that again.'

'But it was so random—'

'The type of illness isn't the point here. It's the idea of pouring all your love into one person, only to lose them in the blink of an eye. I can go through that again.'

'But you can't cut yourself off from the world, Max. It'll drive you insane.'

He took a pace forward and folded his arms across his chest. 'You want to know what really drives me insane—that my wife was lying there in hospital with the life draining out of her and there wasn't a thing I could do about it. Not one damn thing. I promised her I'd look after her through thick and thin. I failed, Cara.' His throat felt tight with emotion he didn't want to feel any more.

'You didn't fail.'

He rubbed a hand over his eyes, taking a deep breath to

loosen off the tension in his chest. 'I'm a fixer, Cara, but I couldn't fix that.'

'There wasn't anything you could have done.'

'I could have paid her more attention.'

'I'm sure she knew how much you loved her.'

And there was the rub. He did love Jemima. Too much to have room for anyone else in his heart.

'Yes, I think she did. But that doesn't change anything between you and me. I don't want this, Cara,' he said, waggling a finger between the two of them.

She stared at him in disbelief. 'So that's it? You've made up your mind and there's nothing I can do to change it?'

'Yes.'

Tipping up her chin, she looked him dead in the eye. 'Do you still want me to work for you?' she asked, her voice breaking with emotion.

Did he? His working life had been a lot less stressful since she'd been around, but what had just happened between them would make his personal life a lot more complicated. They were between a rock and a hard place. 'Yes. But I'll understand if it's too uncomfortable for you to stay.'

'So you'd let me just walk away?'

He sighed. 'If that's what you want.'

The look she gave him chilled him to the bone. 'You know, I don't believe for a second that Jemima would have wanted you to mourn her for the rest of your life. I think she'd have wanted you to be happy. You need to stop hiding behind her death and face the world again. Like you said you were going to yesterday. What happened to that, Max? Hmm? What happened to *you*? Jemima might not be alive any more, but *you* are and you need to stop punishing yourself for that and start living again.'

'I'm not ready—'

'You know, I love you, Max,' she broke in loudly, her eyes shining with tears.

He took a sharp intake of breath as the words cut through

him. No. He didn't want to hear that from her right now. She was trying to emotionally manipulate him into doing something he didn't want to do.

'How can you love me?' Anger made his voice shake. 'We barely know each other.'

'I know you, Max,' she said calmly, her voice rich with emotion.

'You might think you do because I've told you a few personal things about myself recently, but that doesn't mean you get who I am and what I want.'

'Do you know what you want? Because it seems to me you're stopping yourself from being happy on purpose. You enjoyed being with me yesterday, Max, I know it.'

'I did enjoy it, but not in the way you think. It was good to get out of the house and have some fun, but that's all it was, Cara, *fun*.'

She shook her head, her body visibly shaking now. 'I don't believe you.'

'Fine. Don't believe me. Keep living in your perfect little imaginary world where everything is jolly and works out for the best, but don't expect me to show up.'

She reacted as if his words had physically hurt her, jolting back and hugging her arms around herself. 'How can you say that to me?'

Guilt wrapped around him and squeezed hard. She was right; it was a low blow after what he'd already put her through, but he was being cruel to be kind. Sinking onto the edge of the bed, he held up a pacifying hand. 'You see, I'm messed up, Cara. It's too soon for me. I'm not ready for another serious relationship. Maybe I'll never be ready. And it's not fair to ask you to wait for me.'

Her shoulders stiffened, as if she was fighting to keep them from slumping. 'Okay. If that's the way you feel,' she clipped out.

'It is, Cara. I'm sorry.'

The look she gave him was one of such disappointed disdain he recoiled a little.

'Well, then, I guess it's time for me to leave.' She shuffled to the edge of the bed. 'I'm not going to stick around here and let you treat me like I mean nothing to you. I'm worth more than that, Max, and if you can't appreciate that, then that's your loss.' With the sheet still wrapped firmly around her, she stood up and faced him, her eyes dark with anger. 'You can give me a lift to the nearest train station and I'll make my own way back to London.' Turning away from him, she walked over to where her overnight bag sat on the floor.

'Cara, don't be ridiculous—' he started to say, his tone sounding so insincere he cringed inwardly.

Swivelling on the spot, she pointed a shaking finger at him. 'Don't you dare say I'm the one being ridiculous. I'm catching the train. Please go and get changed in your own room. I'll meet you by the car in fifteen minutes.'

'Cara—' He tried to protest, moving towards her, but it was useless. He had nothing left to say.

There was no way to make this better.

'Okay,' he said quietly.

He watched her grab her wash kit from her bag, his gut twisting with unease.

Turning back, she gave him a jerky nod and then, staring resolutely ahead, went to stride past him to the bathroom.

Acting on pure impulse, he put out a hand to stop her, wrapping his fingers around her arm to prevent her from going any further. He could feel her shaking under his grip and he rubbed her arm gently, trying to imbue how sorry he was through the power of his touch.

She put her hand over his and for a second he thought she was going to squeeze his hand with understanding, but instead she pulled his fingers away from her arm and, without giving him another look, walked away.

* * *

Cara waited until Max's car had pulled away from the train station before sinking onto the bench next to the ticket office and putting her head in her hands, finally letting the tears stream down her face.

She'd spent the whole car journey there—which had only taken about ten minutes but had felt like ten painful hours—holding her head high and fighting back the hot pressure in her throat and behind her eyes.

They hadn't uttered one word to each other since he'd started the engine and she was grateful for that, because she knew if she'd had to speak there was no way she'd be able to hold it together.

It seemed they'd come full circle, with him withdrawing so far into himself he might as well have been a machine and her not wanting to show him any weakness.

What a mess.

And she'd told him she loved him.

Her chest cramped hard at the memory. When the words left her mouth, she hadn't known what sort of reaction to expect; in fact she hadn't even known she was going to say them until they'd rolled off her tongue, but she was still shocked by the flare of anger she'd seen in his eyes.

He'd thought she was trying to manipulate him, when that had been the last thing on her mind at the time. She'd wanted him to know he was loved and there could be a future for them if he wanted it.

Thinking about it now, though, she realised she had been trying to shock him into action. To reach something deep inside him that he'd been fiercely protecting ever since Jemima had died. It wasn't surprising he'd reacted the way he had, though. She couldn't begin to imagine the pain of losing a spouse, but she understood the pain of losing someone you loved in the blink of an eye or, in this case, in the time it took to say three small words.

Fury and frustration swirled in her gut, her empty stomach on the edge of nausea. How could she have let herself fall for a man who was still grieving for his wife and had no space left in his heart for her?

Clearly she was a glutton for punishment. And, because of that, she'd now not only lost her heart, she'd lost her home and her job, as well.

Back in London three hours later, she let herself wearily into Max's house, her nerves prickling at the thought of him being there.

Part of her wanted to see him—some mad voice in the back of her head had been whispering about him changing his mind after having time to reflect on what she'd said—but the other, sane part told her she was being naïve.

Walking into the kitchen, she saw that a note had been left in the middle of the table with her name written on it in Max's neat handwriting.

Picking it up with a trembling hand, she read the words, her stomach twisting with pain and her sight blurring with tears as she took in the news that he'd gone to Ireland a couple of days early for his meeting there, to give them a bit of space.

He wasn't interested in giving them another chance.

It was over.

Slumping into the nearest chair, she willed herself not to cry again. There was no point; she wasn't going to solve anything by sitting here feeling sorry for herself.

She had to look after herself now.

Her life had no foundations any more; it was listing at a dangerous angle and at some point in the near future it could crash to the ground if she didn't do something drastic to shore it up.

She'd *so* wanted to belong here with him, but this house wasn't her home and Max wasn't her husband.

His heart belonged to someone else.

She hated the fact she was jealous of a ghost, and not just

because Jemima had been beautiful and talented, but because Max loved her with a fierceness she could barely comprehend.

How could she ever compete with that?

The stone-cold truth was: she couldn't.

And she couldn't stay here a moment longer either.

After carefully folding her clothes into her suitcase, she phoned Sarah to ask whether she could sleep on her couch again, just until she'd moved into the flat that Amber's cousin had promised to let to her.

'Sure, you'd be welcome to stay with us again,' Sarah said, after finally coaxing out the reason for her needing a place to escape to so soon after moving into Max's house. 'But you might want to try Anna. She's going to be away in the States for a couple of weeks from tomorrow and I bet she'd love you to housesit for her.'

One phone call to their friend Anna later and she had a new place to live for the next couple of weeks. So that was her accommodation sorted. Now it was just the small matter of finding a new job.

She'd received an email last week from one of the firms that she'd sent a job application to, offering her an interview, but hadn't had time to respond to it, being so busy keeping the business afloat while Max was in Manchester. After firing off an email accepting an interview for the Tuesday of that week, she turned her thoughts to her current job.

Even though she was angry and upset with Max, there was no way she was just going to abandon the business without finding someone to take over the role she'd carved out for herself. Max might not want her around, but he was still going to need a PA. The meeting he had with a large corporation in Ireland later this week was an exciting prospect and if he managed to land their business he was going to need to hire more staff, pronto.

So this week it looked as if she was going to be both interviewer and interviewee.

The thought of it both exhausted and saddened her.

But she'd made her bed when she'd shared hers with Max, and now she was going to have to lie in it.

CHAPTER TEN

MAX HAD THOUGHT he was okay with the decision to walk away from a relationship with Cara, but his subconscious seemed to have other ideas when he woke up in a cold sweat for the third day running after dreaming that Cara was locked in the house whilst it burnt to the ground and he couldn't find any way to get her out.

Even after he'd been up for a while and looked through his emails, he still couldn't get rid of the haunting image of Cara's face contorted with terror as the flames licked around her. Despite the rational part of his brain telling him it wasn't real, he couldn't shake the feeling that he'd failed her.

Because, of course, he had, he finally accepted, as he sat down to eat his breakfast in the hotel restaurant before his meeting. She'd laid herself bare for him, both figuratively and literally, and he'd abused her trust by treating her as if she meant nothing to him.

Which wasn't the case at all.

He sighed and rubbed a hand over his tired eyes. The last thing he should be doing right now was worrying about how he'd treated Cara when he was about to walk into one of the biggest corporations in Ireland and convince them to give him their business. This was exactly what he'd feared would happen when he'd first agreed to let her work for him—that the business might suffer. Though, to be fair to Cara, this mess was of his own making.

Feeling his phone vibrate, he lifted it out of his pocket and tapped on the icon to open his text messages. It was from Cara.

With his pulse thumping hard in his throat, he read what she'd written. It simply said:

Good luck today. I'll be thinking of you.

A heavy pressure built in his chest as he read the words through for a second time.

She was thinking about him.

Those few simple words undid something in him and a wave of pure anguish crashed through his body, stealing his breath and making his vision blur. Despite how he'd treated her, she was still looking out for him.

She wanted him to know that he wasn't alone.

That was so like Cara. She was such a good person: selfless and kind, but also brave and honourable. Jemima would have loved her.

Taking a deep breath, he mentally pulled himself together. Now was not the time to lose the plot. He had some serious business to attend to and he wasn't about to let all the work that he and Cara had put into making this opportunity happen go to waste.

Fourteen hours later Max flopped onto his hotel bed, totally exhausted after spending the whole day selling himself to the prospective clients, then taking them out for a celebratory dinner to mark their partnership when they signed on the dotted line to buy his company's services.

He'd done it; he'd closed the deal—and a very profitable deal it was, too—which meant he could now comfortably grow the business and hire a team of people to work for him.

His life was moving on.

A strong urge to call Cara and let her know he'd been successful had him sitting up and reaching for his phone, but he stopped himself from tapping on her name at the last second. He couldn't call her this late at night without it *meaning* something.

Frustration rattled through him, swiftly followed by such an intense wave of despondency it took his breath away. He needed to talk to someone. Right now.

Scrolling through his contacts, he found the name he wanted and pressed *call*, his hands twitching with impatience as he listened to the long drones of the dialling tone.

'Max? Is everything okay?' said a sleepy voice on the other end of the line.

'Hi, Poppy, sorry—I forgot it'd be so late where you are,' he lied.

'No problem,' his friend replied, her voice strained as if she was struggling to sit up in bed. 'What's up? Is everything okay?'

'Yes. Fine. Everything's fine. I won a pivotal contract for the business today so I'm really happy,' he said, acutely aware of how flat his voice sounded despite his best efforts to sound upbeat.

Apparently it didn't fool Poppy either. 'You don't *sound* really happy, Max. Are you sure there isn't something else bothering you?'

His friend was too astute for her own good. But then she'd seen him at his lowest after Jemima died and had taken many a late night call from him throughout that dark time. He hadn't called her in a while though, so it wasn't entirely surprising that she thought something was wrong now.

'Er—' He ran a hand through his hair and sighed, feeling exhaustion drag at him. 'No, I'm—' But he couldn't say it. He wasn't fine. In fact he was far from it.

A blast of rage came out of nowhere and he gripped his phone hard, fighting for control.

It was a losing battle.

'You did it on purpose, didn't you? Sent Cara to me so I'd fall in love with her,' he said angrily, blood pumping hard through his body, and he leapt up from the bed and started to pace the room.

His heart gave an extra hard thump as the stunned silence at the other end of the line penetrated through his anger, bringing home to him exactly what he'd just said.

'Are you in love with her?' Poppy asked quietly, as if not wanting to break the spell.

He slapped the wall hard, feeling a sick satisfaction at the sting of pain in the palm of his hand. 'Jemima's only been dead for a year and a half.'

'That has nothing to do with it, and it wasn't what I asked you.'

He sighed and slumped back down onto the bed, battling to deal with the disorientating mass of emotions swirling though his head. 'I don't know, Poppy,' he said finally. 'I don't know.'

'If you don't know, that probably means that you are but you're too pig-headed to admit it to yourself.'

He couldn't help but laugh. His friend knew him so well.

'Is she in love with you?' Poppy asked.

'She says she is.'

He could almost feel his friend smiling on the other end of the phone.

Damn her.

'Look, I've got to go,' he said, 'I've had a very long day and my flight back to London leaves at six o'clock in the morning,' he finished, not wanting to protract this uncomfortable conversation any longer. 'I'll call you tomorrow after I've had some sleep and got my head straight, okay?'

'Okay.' There was a pause. 'You deserve to be happy though, Max, you know that, don't you? It's what Jemima would have wanted.'

He cut the call and threw the phone onto the bed, staring sightlessly at the blank wall in front of him.

Did he deserve to be happy, after the way he'd acted? Was he worthy of a second chance?

There was only one person who could answer that question.

The house was quiet when he arrived home at eight-thirty the next morning. Eerily so.

Cara should have been up by now, having breakfast and getting ready for the day—if she was there.

His stomach sank with dread as he considered the possibility that she wasn't. That she'd taken him at his word and walked away. Not that he could blame her.

Racing up the stairs, he came to an abrupt halt in front of her open bedroom door and peered inside. It was immaculate. And empty. As if she'd never been there.

Uncomfortable heat swamped him as he made his way slowly back down to the kitchen. Perhaps she hadn't gone. Perhaps she'd had a tidying spree in her room, then gone out early to grab some breakfast or something.

But he knew that none of these guesses were right when he spotted her keys to the house and the company mobile he'd given her to use for all their communications sitting in the middle of the kitchen table.

The silence of the house seemed to press in on him, crushing his chest, and he slumped onto the nearest chair and put his head in his hands.

This was all wrong. *All* of it.

He didn't want to stay in this house any longer; it was like living in a tomb. Or a shrine. Whatever it was, it felt wrong for him to be here now. Memories of the life he'd had here with Jemima were holding him back, preventing him from moving on and finding happiness again. Deep down, he knew Jem wouldn't have wanted that for him. He certainly wouldn't have wanted her to mourn him for the rest of her life.

She'd want him to be happy.

Like he had been on Sunday night.

He was in love with Cara.

Groaning loudly into his hands, he shook his head, unable to believe what a total idiot he'd been.

Memories of Cara flashed through his mind: her generous smile and kind gestures. Her standing up to him when it mattered to her most. Telling him she loved him.

His heart swelled with emotion, sending his blood coursing through his body and making it sing in his ears.

So this was living. How he'd missed it.

A loud ring on the doorbell made him jump.

Cara.

It had to be Cara, arriving promptly at nine o'clock for work like she always did.

Please, let it be her.

Tension tightened his muscles as he paced towards the door and flung it open, ready to say what he needed to say to her now. To be honest with her. To let her know how much he loved her and wanted her in his life.

'Max Firebrace?'

Instead of Cara standing on his doorstep, there was a tall, red-haired woman in a suit giving him a broad smile.

'Yes. Who are you?' he said impatiently, not wanting to deal with anything but his need to speak to Cara right then.

She held out a hand. 'I'm Donna, your new PA.'

The air seemed to freeze around him. *'What?'*

The smile she gave him was one of tolerant fortitude. 'Cara said you might be surprised to see me because you've been in Ireland all week.'

'Cara sent you here?'

'Yes, she interviewed me yesterday and said I should start today.'

He stared at her, stunned. 'Where is Cara?'

Donna looked confused. 'Er… I don't know. I wasn't expecting her to be here. She said something about starting a new job for a firm in the City next week. We spent all of yesterday afternoon getting me up to speed with the things I need to do to fulfil the role and went through the systems you use here, so I assumed she'd already served her notice.'

So that was it then. He was too late to save the situation. She was gone.

'You'd better come in,' he muttered, frustration tugging hard at his insides.

'So will we be working here the whole time? It's a beautiful house,' Donna said brightly, looking around the hall.

'No. I'm going to rent an office soon,' he said distractedly, his voice rough with panic.

How was he going to find her? He didn't have any contact details for her friends or her personal mobile number; she'd always used the company one to call or text him. He could try Poppy, but she'd probably be out filming in the middle of the desert right now and wouldn't want to be disturbed with phone calls.

A thought suddenly occurred to him. 'Donna? Did Cara interview you here?'

'No. I went to her flat.' She frowned. 'Although, come to think of it, I don't think it was her place; she didn't know which cupboard the sugar for my drink was kept in.'

He paced towards her, startling her with a rather manic smile. 'Okay, Donna. Your first job as my PA is to give me the address where you met Cara.'

At first Cara thought that the loud banging was part of her dream, but she started awake as the noise thundered through the flat again, seeming to shake the walls. Whoever was knocking really wanted to get her attention.

Pulling her big towelling dressing gown on over her sleep shorts and vest top, she stumbled to the door, still half-asleep. Perhaps the postman had a delivery for one of the other flats and they weren't in to receive it.

But it wasn't the postman.

It was Max.

Her vision tilted as she stumbled against the door in surprise and she hung on to the handle for dear life in an attempt to stop herself from falling towards him.

'Max! How did you find me?' she croaked, her voice completely useless in the face of his shocking presence.

She'd told herself that giving them both some space to breathe was the best thing she could do. After leaving his house on Monday she'd tried to push him out of her mind in an attempt to get through the dark, lonely days without him, but always, in the back of her mind, was the hope that he'd think about what she'd said and maybe, at some point in the future, want to look her up again.

But she hadn't expected it to happen so soon.

'My new PA, Donna, gave me the address,' he said, raising an eyebrow in chastisement, though the sparkle in his eyes told her he wasn't seriously angry with her for going ahead and hiring someone to take her place without his approval.

Telling herself not to get too excited in case he was only popping round to drop off something she'd accidentally left at the house, she motioned for him to come inside and led him through to the kitchen diner, turning to lean against the counter for support.

'You did say you'd understand if I couldn't work with you any more. After what happened,' she said.

He came to a stop a few feet away from her and propped himself against the table. 'I did.'

She took a breath and tipped up her chin. 'I'm not made of stone, Max. As much as I'd like to sweep what happened on Sunday under the carpet, I can't do that. I'm sorry.'

Letting out a long sigh, he shifted against the table. 'Don't be sorry. It wasn't your fault. It was mine. I was the one who knocked on your door when you had the strength to walk away.'

She snorted gently. 'That wasn't strength; it was cowardice.'

'You're not a coward, Cara; you just have a strong sense of self-preservation. You should consider it a gift.'

She stared down at the floor, aware of the heat of her humiliation rising to her face, not wanting him to see how weak and out of control she was right now.

'So you start a new job next week?' he asked quietly.

Forcing herself to look at him again, she gave him the most assertive smile she could muster. 'Yes, at a place in the City. It's a good company and the people were very friendly when they showed me around.'

'I bet you could handle just about anything after having to work for me.' He smiled, but she couldn't return it this time. The muscles in her face wouldn't move. They seemed to be frozen in place.

Gosh, this was awkward.

'You've been good for my confidence.' She flapped a hand at him and added, 'Work-wise,' when he raised his eyebrows in dispute. 'You were great at letting me know when I'd done a good job.'

'Only because you were brave enough to point out how bad I was at it.'

She managed a smile this time, albeit a rather wonky one. 'Well, whatever. I really appreciated it.'

There was a tense silence where they both looked away, as if psyching themselves up to tackle the real issues.

'Look, I'm not here to ask you to come back and work for me again,' Max said finally, running a hand over his hair.

'Oh. Okay,' she whispered, fighting back the tears. She would not break down in front of him. She *wouldn't*.

He frowned, as if worried about the way she'd reacted, and sighed loudly. 'Argh! I'm so bad at this.' He moved towards her but stopped a couple of feet away, holding up his hands. 'I wanted to tell you that I think I've finally made peace with what happened to Jemima. Despite my best efforts to remain a reclusive, twisted misery guts, I think I'm going to be okay now.' He took another step towards her, giving her a tentative smile. 'Thanks to you.'

Forcing down the lump in her throat, she smiled back. 'That's good to hear, Max. Really good. I'm happy that you're happy. And I do understand why you don't want me to come back and work for you. It must have been hard having me hanging around your house so much.'

'I'm going to sell the house, Cara.'

She stared at him in shock, her heart racing. 'What? But—how can you stand to leave it? That beautiful house.'

'I don't care about the house. I care about us.' This time he walked right up to her, so close she could feel the heat radiating from his body, and looked her directly in the eye. 'I'm ready to live again and I want to do it with you.'

'You—?'

'Want *you*, Cara.' His voice shook with emotion and she could see now that he was trembling.

'But—? I thought you said—when did you…?' Her voice petered out as her brain shut down in shock.

He half smiled, half frowned. 'Clearly I need to explain some things.' He took her hand and led her gently over to the sofa in the living area, guiding her to sit down next to him, keeping his fingers tightly locked with hers and capturing her gaze before speaking.

'When we slept together I felt like I'd betrayed a promise to Jemima.' He swallowed hard. 'After what happened to her I thought I had no right to be happy and start again when she couldn't do that. I truly thought I'd never love someone else the way I loved her, but then I realised I didn't need to. The love I feel for you is different—just as strong, but a different flavour. Does that make sense?'

He waited for her to nod shakily before continuing. 'I don't want to replicate Jemima or the way it was with her. I want to experience it all afresh with you. I'll always love Jem because she was a big part of my life for many years, but I can compartmentalise that now as part of my past.' He squeezed her fingers hard. 'You're my future.'

'Really?' Her throat was so tense with emotion she could hardly form the word.

'Yes. I love you, Cara.'

And she knew from the look on his face that he meant every word. He'd never given up anything of an emotional nature lightly and she understood what a superhuman effort it must have taken for him to come here and say all that to her.

Reaching out a hand, she ran her fingers across his cheek, desperate to smooth away any fears he might have. 'I love you, too.'

He closed his eyes and breathed out hard in relief before opening them again, looking more at peace than she'd ever seen him before. Lifting his own hand, he slid his fingers into her hair and drew her towards him, pressing his mouth to hers and kissing her long and hard.

She felt it right down to her toes.

Drawing away for a moment, he touched his forehead to hers and whispered, 'You make me so happy.'

And then, once again, there was no more talking. Just passion and joy and excitement for their bright new future together.

EPILOGUE

One year later

THE HOUSE THEY'D chosen to buy together was just the sort of place Cara had dreamed of owning during her romantic but practical twenties. It wasn't as grand or impressive as the house in South Kensington, but it felt exactly right for the two of them. And perhaps for any future family that chose to come along.

Not that having children was on the cards *right* now. Max was focusing hard on maintaining the expansion of his Management Solutions business, which had been flying ever since the Irish company awarded him their contract, and Cara was happy in her new position as Executive Assistant to the CEO of the company she'd joined in the City. But they'd talked about the possibility of it happening in the near future and had both agreed it was something they wanted.

Life was good. And so was their relationship.

After worrying for the first few months that, despite his assurances to the contrary, Max might still be in the grip of grief and that they had some struggles ahead of them, her fears had been assuaged as their partnership flourished and grew into something so strong and authentic she could barely breathe with happiness some days.

Max's anger had faded but his fierceness remained, which she now experienced as both a protective and supportive force in her life. Being a party to his sad past had taught her to count her blessings, and she did. Every single day.

Arriving home late after enjoying a quick Friday night drink with her colleagues, she let herself into their golden-bricked Victorian town house—which they'd chosen for the views of Victoria Park and its close location to the thriving bustle and buzz of Columbia Road with its weekly flower market and kitschy independent furniture shops—and stopped dead in the doorway, staring down at the floor.

It was covered in flowers, of all colours and varieties. Frowning at them in bewilderment, she realised they were arranged into the shape of a sweeping arrow pointing towards the living room.

'Max? I'm home. What's going on? It looks like spring has exploded in our hallway!'

Tiptoeing carefully over the flowers so as not to crush too many of them, she made her way towards the living room and peered nervously through the doorway, her heart skittering at the mystery of it.

What she saw inside took her breath away.

Every surface was covered in vibrantly coloured bouquets of spring flowers, displayed in all manner of receptacles: from antique vases to the measuring jug she used to make her porridge in the mornings. Even the light fitting had a large cutting of honeysuckle spiralling down from it, its sweet fragrance permeating the air. It reminded her of their first night together after Jack's wedding. Which quickly led her to memories of all the wonderful nights that had come after it, where she'd lain in Max's arms, breathing in the scent of his skin, barely able to believe how loved and cherished she felt.

And she was loved, as Max constantly reminded her, and her support and love for him had enabled him to finally say goodbye to Jemima and the past that had kept him ensnared for so long.

She'd unlocked his heart.

She was the key, he'd told her as he carried her, giggling, over the threshold into their house six months ago.

She'd finally found her home.

Their home.

He was standing next to the rose-strewn piano in the bay, looking at her with the same expression of fierce love and desire that always made her blood rush with heat.

'Hello, beautiful, did you have a good night?' he asked, walking towards where she stood, his smile bringing a mesmerising twinkle to his eyes.

'I did, thank you.' She swept a hand around the room, unable to stop herself from blurting, 'Max, what is this?'

The reverent expression on his face made her heart leap into her throat. 'This is me asking you to marry me,' he said, dropping to one knee in front of her and taking her hand in his, smiling at her gasp of surprise.

'This time last year I thought I'd never want to be married again—that I didn't deserve to be happy—but meeting you changed all that. You saved me, Cara.' Reaching into his pocket, he withdrew a small black velvet-covered box and flipped it open to reveal a beautiful flower-shaped diamond ring.

'I love you, and I want to spend the rest of my life loving you.' His eyes were alive with passion and hope. 'So what do you say—will you marry me?'

Heart pounding and her whole body shaking with excitement, she dropped onto her knees in front of him and gazed into his face, hardly able to believe the intensity of the love she felt for him.

'Yes,' she said simply, smiling into his eyes, letting him know how much she loved him back. 'Yes. I will.'

* * * * *

column – it will put the city into focus. It is not surprising that this is one of the world's densest cities (15,230 inhabitants per sq kilometre). Packed in between the Collserola range of hills and the Mediterranean, and bordered by Montjuïc and the River Besòs, all the available space has been consumed.

Parks tend to be in rocky knolls where no building could have been erected, or created latterly in disused industrial spaces. Inevitably, the next round of developments are centred on the sea, with extensions to the port and reclamation of land by the Diagonal Mar already underway.

Making the most of it

Barcelona is everything you have ever heard about: Gaudí and the Sagrada Família, Modernisme and contemporary design, Olympic achievements, sophisticated nightlife, hardworking Catalans and Mediterranean laid-back quality of life. But it is a lot more besides.

Many people go to Barcelona for a short break and understandably want to cram in as much as possible. Plans are carefully laid to take in the many cultural delights of this varied city. But those who enjoy their visit most may be those who spare some time to sit in a square and watch the world go by; to poke their noses into little shops that sell nothing but cologne; to watch women watering the forests of plants on their balconies. In other words, those who try to see the city through the eyes of a resident.

***Right:** the rooftop of Casa Milà, La Pedrera*

HISTORICAL HIGHLIGHTS

***circa* 300 BC** The Carthaginians penetrate Catalonia. According to legend, Hamilcar Barca, father of Hannibal, occupied the city and called it Barcino.

264 BC After the First Punic War between Romans and Carthaginians, Romans capture Barcelona.

200 BC–AD 300 Barcelona flourishes economically, and a magnificent city centre develops around the forum on the hill called Mons Taber.

AD 476 The Visigoths enter eastern Spain, capture Barcelona and make it their Iberian capital.

***circa* 713** The Moors capture Barcelona but are usurped by the Franks in 801.

8th–9th centuries Wilfred the Hairy establishes the House of Barcelona, a dynasty that continues for 500 years.

988 Barcelona gains autonomy, laying the foundation for an independent Catalonia.

Above: *Teatre Grec on Montjuïc*

1137 Berenguer IV, Count of Barcelona, marries the heiress to the throne of Aragón. Barcelona becomes capital of Aragón and enjoys a period of great success.
1284–95 The Catalan–Aragón confederation extends its power as far as Naples. A number of splendid buildings are erected in Barcelona (the Barri Gòtic).
14th century Catalonia develops into one of the most formidable maritime nations in the Mediterranean region.
1359 The Corts Catalanes, a representative body of nobility, citizens and priests, is officially appointed. The Generalitat de Catalunya is set up to regulate financial and political matters.
1395 Annual competitions for poets and troubadors, called the Jocs Florals, are initiated.
1469 Ferdinand II of Aragón marries Queen Isabela I of Castile, thus uniting the two kingdoms.
1492 Under the Catholic Monarchs, Barcelona become less

important. Madrid becomes the national centre, Barcelona suffers economic decline. Trade with the American colonies goes via Atlantic ports.
1639 The Thirty Years' War with France: Catalans rise up against Philip IV, supported by the French king Louis XIII. Spanish troops are unable to recapture Barcelona until 1651.
1714 Barcelona sides with Habsburgs in the Spanish War of Succession. The Bourbon king Philip V takes the city on 11 September, abolishes the Corts Catalanes. This date *(La Diada)* is the national day of celebration in Catalonia.

Above: *Ramón Berenguer IV, Count of Barcelona*

1808 After Barcelona's inhabitants rebel against the French, Napoleonic troops destroy large parts of the city.
1814 onwards An economic boom occurs under Ferdinand VII. The industrial revolution has positive effects; Barcelona becomes Spain's leading technical development centre.
1848 The first rail connection between Barcelona and Mataró.
1854–56 To ease congestion and insanitary conditions, the citadel and the old city walls are razed.
1860 The building of the new city (Eixample), designed by Idelfons Cerdà, begins.
1888 Barcelona hosts first Universal Exposition on Montjuïc. Numerous *Modernista* buildings erected throughout the city.
1901–9 Anarchism results in general strikes in 1901–02, and the *Setemana Tràgica* (Tragic Week) in 1909, when widespread rioting in the city leads to the destruction of 70 religious institutions.
1914 The Mancomunitat, a Catalan provincial government, is set up; Barcelona recovers administrative power. Industry flourishes during World War I.
1923 The military dictatorship of Primo de Rivera (1923–30) suppresses Catalan freedoms.
1929 Second Universal Exposition held on Montjuïc. Numerous buildings, including the Poble Espanyol, are built.
1931 Catalonia granted statute of autonomy. Francesc Macià becomes president of the Generalitat de Catalunya.

***Above:** bullet holes in a church wall – aftermath of the Civil War*

1936–39 The Spanish Civil War is fought between Republicans and Nationalists. After bitter fighting, Barcelona falls to General Franco's troops. Catalan language and customs are forbidden. The statute of autonomy is revoked and the president of the Generalitat, Lluís Companys, is executed. Immigrants from southern Spain flock to Barcelona. The resulting uncontrolled building boom creates barren dormitory towns with consequent social problems.
1975 General Franco dies. A constitutional monarchy is set up with Juan Carlos as king. Catalan is recognised as an official language.
1978 Statute of Autonomy.
1980 Jordi Pujol, the leader of the conservative Convergència party, becomes the president of Catalonia.
1986 Barcelona is chosen as host for the 1992 Olympic Games. A massive building wave gets under way, presided over by Pasqual Maragall, the popular socialist city mayor .
1992 Olympic Games are held.
1994 The Gran Liceu theatre devastated by fire
1995 Port Vell development completed. The Contemporary Art Museum (MACBA) opens
1997 Pasqual Maragall resigns; succeeded by deputy, Joan Clos.
1999 The new National Theatre completed. Maragall challenges Pujol in the Generalitat elections but the status quo is retained.

***Above:** Port Vell was completed in 1995*

PEOPLE AND CULTURE

The Catalan Character

Catalans in general, and Barcelonans in particular, are well-known for their business acumen, their passion for work, and their economic ability. In Barcelona, 10 o'clock means 10 o'clock, not half past 11, which is bliss if you want to do some serious business. *Anem per feina* is a common expression, once pressed into service as an election slogan: "Let's get down to work."

Like Britain, Catalonia has been dubbed a nation of shopkeepers and, indeed, Barcelona has a staggering number of shops. This bourgeois city was built up through family enterprise and is now being promoted as one of the places to shop. The slogan that once graced the carrier bags of the famous Vinçon design store puts it in a nutshell: "I shop, therefore I am."

But like all good Mediterraneans, Barcelonans are a street people. All it takes is a few tables and chairs squeezed on to a postage stamp of pavement, and there they'll sit for hours over their drinks and *tapas*, apparently oblivious to the fumes, traffic noise and even the dust and din of building works. When it rains, the

Above: *sitting back for a shoe shine on La Rambla*

milling throngs leap into cars and taxis, causing the traffic to "collapse", as they put it, in a cacophony of honking horns. Fortunately, it doesn't rain too often.

The Catalans call these apparently contradictory facets of their character *el seny* and *la rauxa*. The former is a combination of prudence, profound common sense and sensible judgement; the latter a fit, impulse or emotional outburst: an attack of wildness.

Dance with a Difference

The Catalan sense of tradition is manifested in the intricate national dance, the *sardana*. No festival is complete without it and each Sunday at noon and Saturday evening it is danced in the cathedral square, accompanied by a band called the *cobla*.

As the music gradually gets going, a few people in the growing crowd will start to dance, sometimes just a group of four, forming a small circle, in the centre of which will be placed a bag of some kind. Soon others join in, making their own circles or joining existing ones, until the whole square is filled with dancers, linked hands raised high, solemnly counting the short sedate steps, which suddenly change to longer, bouncy ones. Real *aficionados* wear espadrilles tied with coloured ribbons, but most people dance in their ordinary shoes, be they Sunday best or the ubiquitous trainers.

Above: *traditional costumes from the south are worn at festivals*

The Language

Barcelonans, like all Catalans are fiercely proud of their separate national identity and history, and are quick to insist that Catalonia is not Spain. To an outsider, this difference is most obvious in the language. Spoken Catalan has a sharp, staccato quality that makes it sound very different from the more familiar Spanish, but the good news for the visitor concerned with street signs, restaurant menus and so on is that on paper it looks no more incomprehensible than Spanish, French or Italian.

Under Franco's dictatorship Catalan was banned entirely from public use, although it continued to be spoken in the home. But with the recovery of democracy Catalan was established alongside Castilian as the official language of the region by the Spanish Constitution of 1978 and the Statutes of Autonomy. The language was reinstated in all aspects of public life, government, education and the media. In 1990 the European Parliament passed a resolution recognising Catalan and its use in the European Union.

Above: *Sant Miquel del Port on the Plaça Barceloneta*

Now Catalan thrives in the arts and sciences, the media and advertising. It is used by rock bands and on the Internet, in schools and on the radio. The rationale behind the Generalitat's controversial linguistic policy is that if Catalan is not actively defended it will decay into a mere local patois; its detractors, however, allege narrow-minded nationalism. There is some alleged discrimination against non-Catalan speakers in the job market but for the most part the two languages happily co-exist. Courtesy rules, and very few Barcelonans will refuse to speak Castilian to non-Catalan speakers.

A Mixture of Cultures

Among the population there is a large number of citizens from southern Spain who flooded into Barcelona in the 1950s and 1960s in search of work. Co-existence has not always been easy, with ethnic, class and cultural differences coming into play: the Catalan middle classes tend to take a dim view of the ebullient non-Catalan working class, and vice versa.

Known by the derogatory nickname of *xarnegos* (originally meaning a child of a Catalan and a non-Catalan), these "other Barcelonans" form a distinctive group, living in the outlying neighbourhoods of the city, with their own extrovert, boisterous lifestyle.

Barcelona's *Feria de Abril* (April Fair), held near the city, is no longer a pale, homesick

Right: *wine and sunshine on Passeig del Born*

imitation of the Andalusian original but a big event in its own right that attracts nearly a million visitors. Many older immigrants do not speak Catalan but the second and third generations, Barcelona born and bred and educated under the post-Franco system, always do.

A Cosmopolitan City

A busy port since its origins and close to the Crusade routes from western Europe, Barcelona has always been something of a melting pot. In his memoir, *Homage to Catalonia*, George Orwell chronicled the ideologically boiling Barcelona of 1936, filled with young foreigners from all over the world who had come to defend democracy. In the 1960s, as the Spanish-language publishing capital, the city was home to writers and intellectuals such as Gabriel García Márquez and Mario Vargas Llosa. The 1970s saw a huge influx of South Americans fleeing the dictatorships in Argentina and Chile.

Since Spain's return to democracy, and especially since the break-up of the former eastern bloc and the formation of the EU, the foreign community has continued to grow. Irish pubs, Greek restaurants and Pakistani grocers abound. And Barcelona's popularity as a venue for trade fairs and international meetings make for an exciting cosmopolitan buzz.

***Above:** teeming alleyways in the Gothic Quarter*

The last official census (1996) gave 58,385 foreigners but this only includes holders of residence permits. The real figure may be three times as high. The British Consulate – where registration is not obligatory – reports roughly 4,000 British people registered in the city.

Football Fever

Barça, Barcelona Football Club, is more than a football team, it is one of Catalonia's great institutions: during the repressive Franco years the dice were always carefully loaded in favour of Real Madrid, and so Barça – "the army of Catalonia" – was the only possible outlet for the collective expression of Catalan national identity. A victory over Real Madrid was seen as a victory over central government

Now Barcelonans of all ages, classes, genders and persuasions unite to dance in the streets in wild celebration when Barça beats Madrid or wins some kind of cup or league. The red and gold of the Catalan colours combine with Barça's blue and maroon *(blau grana)* in a swirling mass down La Rambla. Corks pop and champagne sprays while fireworks fizz far into the night.

Above: *a flashing red or green cross indicates a chemist shop*

Festivals

The pre-Lent Carnival is a big event in Barcelona and one that everyone joins in. On Carnival Thursday, for example, it's business as usual at La Boquería market on La Rambla – albeit in fancy dress. A cardinal in full regalia blesses the shoppers trundling their carts in and out. Ballet dancers, black chest hair bristling from inside their pink tutus, cart crates of potatoes around. Plumed cavaliers slice ham and chorizo sausages, while Roman emperors weigh out oranges and Moorish princesses gut fish.

But this isn't the only colourful event in the city. In the old districts of Gràcia and Sants local people work tirelessly all year round on the elaborate preparations for their *festa major* (annual fête), held in mid-August. Entire streets are turned into theme parks, with prizes for the best. Each street or square organises its own non-stop progamme of events. Old men drag tables and chairs out for chess and dominoes tournaments; children enjoy puppet shows and hot chocolate parties; live salsa and rock bands play through the night. But during the day it's still business as usual: except you'll go shopping in Jurassic Park, a space station, or something out of the Arabian Nights.

The wild celebrations of the Mercè festival take some beating.The festivities last for a week, centred around 24 September, the day

Above: *sombre Semana Santa procession in the Gothic Quarter*

of Barcelona's patron saint. Giants and fantastical creatures parade around the city on stilts, the night sky blazes with fireworks, thousands dance to rock bands in sedate historic squares, and fire-breathing dragons chase reckless citizens through the streets.

Perhaps the most Barcelonan of the festivals is Sant Jordi's day, 23 April. Sant Jordi (St George) is the patron saint of Catalonia, and his feast day, which is also the anniversary of both Shakespeare's and Cervantes' death, is celebrated by giving gifts of books and roses. Bookshops set up stalls in the streets and squares and give a 10 percent discount. It's a field day, too, for journalists and chat-show hosts, with round-the-clock live TV coverage from La Rambla, including celebrity signings and interviews. Massive public collections of books for hospitals are organised.

The city's hawkers and panhandlers make a killing, too, selling roses in the metro stations and at traffic lights instead of cleaning windscreens or peddling strings of garlic.

***Above:** highly ornate floats are carried by unseen men during Easter*

In the evening, you'll see men hurrying home from work: whether dressed in suits and carrying briefcases, plugged into mobile phones or Walkmans, in tracksuits or jeans, each bears a single red rose beautifully wrapped in cellophane and tied with red and yellow ribbon. At night festivites are rounded off with discos and shows.

Architecture

In 1999, RIBA, the Royal Institute of British Architects, awarded their annual gold medal – probably the most prestigious architectural award in the world – not to an individual but, for the first time, to a city: Barcelona. After years of neglect, Barcelona had already embarked on an extensive urban design programme by the time it won the bid for the 1992 Olympic Games. The work this involved transformed the city. As well as the the Vila Olímpica itself – now a much sought-after place to live – the whole city coastline changed, with promenades and reclaimed beaches leading to the Olympic village. The port area of Barcelona has been opened up as a major shopping and leisure area, and the World Trade Centre has been constructed at the

Above: *Gaudí's stunning Sagrada Família*

end of La Rambla. In the period after the Olympics there has been a slowing down of building work, but the regeneration programme continues. The area around the run-down Plaça de les Glories has been renovated and is now the site of the Auditorí (Concert Hall) by Raphael Moneo, and Ricardo Bofill's Teatre Nacional, built like a neo-classical temple.

There has been some major international input: Japanese architect Arata Isozaki built the Palau Sant Jordi, a huge steel and glass indoor arena with a levitating roof, on Montjuïc hill; English architect Sir Norman Foster designed the Torre de Collserola, now an icon of the Barcelona skyline, and sometimes known as the Torre Foster; US architect Frank Gehry constructed the huge copper fish glittering on the sea front, while another American, Richard Meier, designed and built the city's new contemporary art museum (MACBA), which forms the side of a square, cleverly framing vistas from the surrounding streets with the sculptural elements on its facade.

Characterful Quarters

There is an extensive *"Posat Guapa"* ("Make it Beautiful") campaign in the Casc Antic, the Old Quarter, with an emphasis on restoring facades and houses. EU grants have been obtained for the purpose. Parks are still being laid out in peripheral areas, and so-

Above: *Vila Olímpica – a much sought-after area*

called urban spaces are beginning to regenerate the heart of the city.

This is not to forget all that had gone before: the Gothic Quarter has a distinctive character – dignified but somewhat dour. Some of the buildings are very fine, embodying the secular and religious splendour of their time, such as the Saló del Tinell with its enormous arches, in the Palau Reial Major; the Museu Marítim/Drasannes, where the galleons of the Armada were made; and the Església de Santa María del Mar, renowned for its elegance and serenity.

Then there is *Modernisme* (similar to Art Nouveau), exemplified by the works of Antoni Gaudí, Lluís Domènech i Montaner and Josep Puig i Cadafalch. In the 1850s, when an expansion, or "Eixample", was needed to relieve overcrowding, an enormous grid was laid out, intersected by avenues lined with trees, a radical project for its time. Some streets quickly became the sites for grand *Modernista* blocks, with glazed balconies and tiled and carved facades. Outstanding are those around the Passeig de Gràcia. Along with the well-known ones: Gaudí's La Pedrera and the three houses that make up the Illa de la Discòrdia, are numerous shops and restaurants in the same attractively sinuous style. And Gaudí's unfinished cathedral, La Sagrada Familía, is in a class all its own.

The Art Scene

A city that can claim both Picasso and Miró has a lot going for it. Actually, Pablo Picasso (1881–1973) only spent a few years here before moving on to Paris, and Joan Miró (1893–1983), born and

Above: *the Museu Picasso has an extensive collection of the artist's work*

bred in Barcelona, also came and went. Picasso was born in Málaga,and his family arrived in Barcelona in 1895, where his father became Painting Professor at the city's La Llotja School of Art. A department of this school can still be found in Carrer Avinyó, and it is said that a brothel in this street inspired Picasso's painting *Les Demoiselles D'Avignon* (1906–7). As a young man he inspired Barcelona's artistic circle that met at the Els Quatre Gats (The Four Cats) cafe – Picasso designed the menu cover for the cafe. It was here, on 1 February 1900, that Picasso exhibited for the first time. The Museu Picasso, in the 15th-century Aguilar palace, houses an extensive collection of his early work and paintings from his Blue Period.

Miró is everywhere in Barcelona. You only have to walk out of the airport to find one of his large ceramic murals. Then there's his ceramic pavement in La Rambla, the monumental *Woman and Bird* sculpture in the Parc de Joan Miró, and the ubiquitous La Caixa bank logo he designed. The magnificent permanent collection at the Fundació Miró on Montjuïc amply covers all his wide-ranging skills, from painting and drawing to theatre design, printmaking, tapestry, ceramics and bronze sculptures.

The building must be a candidate for any "Best Art Space" award

Right: *sculpture in the Fundació Miró*

and is testimony to the close understanding that Miró had with his friend Josep Lluís Sert, who designed both this and Miró's studio in Mallorca.

Antoni Tàpies (born 1923), still living and working in Barcelona, is probably Spain's best-known living artist. His work forms an artistic link between Miró's generation and the new work being produced by the Catalan art world. Tàpies knew Miró and revered his work; the latter's influence is clearly seen in Tàpies' early work, on view at the Fundació Tàpies.

STREET ART

Street art is prevalent in all areas of the city. Artist-poet Joan Brossa's bronze tribute to *Barcino* (the Roman name for Barcelona) is set in front of the cathedral.In the Passeig Picasso, Tàpies pays homage to his idol with a large glass cube containing planks, a piano and painted blankets. On the beach at Barceloneta is Rebecca Horn's reminder of the beach huts and restaurants that were torn down to make way for the waterfront development. Models of the huts, cast in bronze and lit like beacons from within, lie piled one on top of the other.

Also down by the port is Lichtenstein's *Head*, just in front of the main post office. This massive piece uses Gaudí's technique of setting broken pieces of ceramic into cement to impressive effect.

Above: *caricaturist busy at work on La Rambla*

Food

No one should visit Barcelona without making some attempt to get to know Catalan food. The experience would be incomplete, and any assesment of its people merely superficial. Eating is an important part of Catalan culture, something to be valued, taken seriously and enjoyed to the full, in true Catalan style.

The cooking of this region combines the natural products of the sea, plains and mountains in a style known as *mar i muntanya* (sea and mountain). It makes for strange sounding, though delicious marriages, such as *mandonguilles amb sèpia* (meatballs with cuttlefish), or *gambes amb pollastre* (prawns with chicken).

One of the most famous Catalan dishes is the most simple: the ubiquitous *pa amb tomàquet* (bread rubbed with fresh tomato, a trickle of virgin olive oil and a pinch of salt).

A few local specialities are: *arròs negre* (black rice, made with squid and its ink); *escalivada*, grilled peppers and aubergines dressed with oil; and *esqueixada*, salad of raw salt cod, onions and peppers. Fish *(peix)* and shellfish *(marisc)* should not be missed in Barcelona: the simplest and perhaps the best way is grilled; *suquet*, is a good seafood stew; *calamars farcits* are stuffed squid. For dessert *(postre)*, don't miss the famous *crema catalana*, a cinnamon-flavoured custard with a burnt caramel top.

Getting to know Catalan food is hardly a chore. With nearly 3,000 restaurants in Barcelona, choice is not a problem. People eat late: peak lunchtime is 2pm lingering on to 4pm or even later at week-

Right: *fresh fish from La Boqueria market on La Rambla*

ends, and dinner is usually eaten between 9 and 11pm. Lunch is the most economical meal, when nearly every restaurant has a *menú del día* (set menu), offering a choice of starters (soup, salad, or vegetables), a main course of meat or fish, a dessert and wine.

Although it's not originally a Catalan tradition, there are nevertheless many bars offering *tapes*, including a new wave of Basque bars and some Catalan ones which specialise in *torrades* (large slices of toast), with which you can make your own *pa amb tomàquet* and request different toppings.

There is also a new generation of chefs producing exciting results. As an increasingly cosmopolitan capital, the broad range of restaurants reflects the tastes and demands of its inhabitants. There are restaurants from other regions of Spain, particularly Galicia, as well as French, Italian, Greek, Lebanese, Mexican, Indian, Chinese and Japanese, and a growing number of improved vegetarian restaurants. There really is no excuse to resort to one of the fast-food outlets, insidiously taking root in some of the most historic streets and squares of the city – the latest sign of cultural colonisation.

Wine

There was a time when Spanish wine meant plonk and the only vintage to have any international acclaim was *Rioja*. Today, these misconceptions are buried in the past. Spain has many different regions producing a range of high-quality wines. One is Catalonia, which has nine of its own

Above: *instantly recognisable advertisment for a famous Spanish sherry*

regions officially classified as D.O. *(Denominació de Origen*, similar to the French *appelation contrôlée)*. The largest is Penedès where 100 companies produce 65 million litres of still wine annually. And that's not including the *cava*: this sparkling wine made by the *méthode champenoise*, is obligatory at fiestas and almost essential for Sunday lunch. Regarded as one of the world's great sparkling wines, cava is warmer and less acid than Champagne.

Markets

Barcelona has a huge number of markets from the famous La Boqueria food market and Els Encats flea market to a myriad smaller ones all over the city. While the trend in most parts of Europe is towards out-of-town hypermarkets, Barcelona's food markets are being renovated and rebuilt. Second-hand books are sold outside the Cathedral, rare stamps and coins in the Plaça Reial and paintings in the Plaça Sant Josep.

Nightlife

The most important thing to remember about Barcelona nightlife is that it means just that: in the clubs, nothing gets going until around 1am, then keeps going until about 4am. Those with real stamina go on to an "Afters" bar, until breakfast. This demanding schedule is usually followed from Thusday to Saturday, but there are those who are out to play any night of the week, and still get to work the next day.

Right: *the famous La Boqueria food market*

A–Z OF BARCELONA

L'Aquàrium

Set in Barcelona's disused wharf, which has been landscaped in the best tradition of the city's new urban spaces, the spectacular new aquarium is the largest in Europe and holds more than 5 million litres (1.1 million gallons) of water. Since opening in 1995 it has become the largest crowd-puller in Barcelona, beating the Sagrada Família into second place. *www.aquariumbcn.com*

L'Auditori

The Auditorium is Barcelona's grand new concert hall, the home of the city's resident orchestra, the Orquestra Simfònica de Barcelona (OBC). It comprises a large hall (2,500 seats) and a smaller room for chamber music and will eventually house the Music Museum and a conservatory. Together with the Teatre Nacional it is part of a high-profile, high-cost, cultural complex that opened in the late 1990s in the Plaça de les Glòries Catalanes. *www.auditori.com/*

Barceloneta

Above the Moll de la Barceloneta is a broad, landscaped, promenade with benches and palm trees, a favourite spot for roller-bladers. But it is the back streets of Barceloneta that are the destination of serious eaters. By cutting through these streets to the Passeig Marítim, you get to Platja Barceloneta. The promenade, wooden walkways, palms and designer showers are the stamp of the post-Olympic sea front. The six beaches are easily accessible by public transport, and both the sand and the water's surface are cleaned daily.

Many people fondly remember the *chiringuitos*, colourful restau-

Left: *the Aquàrium is the largest in Europe*

rants which were no more than huts on the beach here where you could eat good fish with your toes in the sand. They were swept away in the early 1990s under a cloud of controversy, but Barcelonans now derive obvious pleasure from these wide open beaches.

Barri Gòtic

The oldest part of the city, the Gothic Quarter or Barri Gòtic, is built around Mont Tàber (Taber Hill), a misnomer for what is little more than a mound in an otherwise flat city. This section of the Old Town is surrounded by the remains of Roman walls, within which little has changed for centuries. Layer upon layer of different architectural styles illustrate different periods of Barcelona's history, from remnants of the Roman city to contemporary architectural solutions. The Gothic period predominates, reflecting the glorious medieval period when Catalonia was at its height.

It is the centre of municipal administration and is home to the splendidly housed Catalan autonomous government, but it is also an area of narrow alleys hung with washing and trailing plants; of shady squares, dubious bars and tiny, specialist shops.

Cable cars

On the Moll de Barcelona jetty stands the 119-metre (390-ft) Torre de Jaume I, the link for the cross-harbour cable car, which comes from

***Above:** a cable car ride offers unrivalled views of the city*

Miramar, located on Montjüic, and completes its spectacular 1,292-metre (4,200-ft) journey at the tower on the other side of the harbour, the 78-metre (257-ft) Torre de Sant Sebastià. The cable car has hardly changed since its introduction in 1931.

Camp Nou

Football fans will inevitably be drawn to Barça's impressive Camp Nou stadium (part of a sports complex between the university campus and the Avinguda Diagonal). A 1990s extension made it the largest stadium in Europe with a seating capacity of 120,000. The club's on-site museum is the second most visited in the city. Getting to see a game shouldn't be too difficult, although tickets for a fixture against arch rivals Real Madrid are virtually impossible to find. *www.fcbarcelona.com/*

Casa de la Ciutat

The Ajuntament (Town Hall) presides over Barcelona from the Casa de la Ciutat, and the Generalitat (Autonomous Government) presides over Catalonia from the Palau de la Generalitat. The two buildings, both of Gothic origin, face each other across the Plaça Sant Jaume. This square was inaugurated in 1823 and is considered the

***Above:** flags flutter on the Casa de la Ciutat in Plaça Sant Jaume*

civic heart of the city. The oldest part of the Casa de la Ciutat is the Saló de Cent, created by Pere Llobet in 1373; the Gothic facade tucked down the side street, also called Ciutat, is the most delicate. This official building can be visited on major public holidays (such as Sant Jordi, 23 April) or at weekends by prior arrangement.

Cathedral

The candle-scented cathedral, begun in 1298, constantly buzzes with activity. The main area consists of three naves and an apse with an ambulatory beneath an octagonal dome. The oldest part is that of the Porta de Sant Ivo (St Ive's Door), where some Romanesque windows and archways can still be seen. Two 14th- and 15th-century towers rise at each end of the transept. The tomb of Santa Eulàlia, co-patron saint of Barcelona, behind the altar, is an important 14th-century work of art, executed in alabaster by a disciple of Giovanni Pisanol. The most outstanding altarpiece is the *Transfiguration*, designed by Bèrnat Martorell, in the chapel dedicated to Sant Salvador (1447). The 15th-century Capella del Santo Cristo de Lepanto is considered to be the finest example of Gothic art in the cathedral; it contains the crucifix borne in the Christian

Above: *Santa Eulàlia Cathedral*

flagship against the Ottomans in the battle of Lepanto (1571). The cloister is an atmospheric haven with a pretty fountain and a garden of elegant palms and perfumed magnolia trees. Thirteen geese are the sole residents, symbolising Santa Eulàlia's age when she died.

Centre de Cultura Contemporània de Barcelona

A former 18th-century hospice in El Raval district to the west of La Rambla has been transformed into the Centre de Cultura (CCCB), a series of exhibition spaces dedicated to the exploration of urban phenomena, through diverse cultural activities including dance, music, film, video and seminars. The complex – a wonderful renovation by prestigious architects Piñon and Vilaplana – rivals MACBA *(see page 40)* for its architectural interest. *www.cccb.org/*

Eixample

This is one of the most characteristic districts of Barcelona, with some of its most distinctive elements, such as the Sagrada Família and much of its famed *modernista* architecture. Eixample means "enlargement" and it stands as a symbol of the 19th-century boom that initiated the city's modern era; today it is the most populated district in the city. After the narrow, irregular streets of the Barri Gòtic, the Eixample feels like a new town. Its rigid, regular structure forms a repeated pattern from its southern boundary by Plaça d'Espanya to its

***Right:** worshippers light votive candles for Easter in the Cathedral*

northern limit leading up from Plaça de les Glòries. The traffic roars up and down in a well-structured one-way system. The Eixample is also a district of designer shops, sophisticated restaurants and smart galleries, interspersed with fast-food joints and *tapes* bars.

Fundació Joan Miró

Situated on Montjuïc hill *(see page 38)* the Fundació Joan Miró is an understated yet powerfully impressive gem. Designed by Josep Lluís Sert, eminent architect and friend of Miró, the gallery has been open since 1974. A Mediterranean luminosity floods the building and shows one of the largest collections in the world of Miró's work in its best light. It includes paintings, drawings, sculptures and tapestries as well as his complete graphic work. It also contains the mercury fountain designed by Alexander Calder for the Spanish Republic's pavilion in the 1937 Paris Exhibition. Contemporary exhibitions and concerts are held here. *www.fjmiro.es/*

Above: *the Fundació Joan Miró is a wonderful setting for his work*

Fundació Tàpies

In noisy Carrer Aragó in the Eixample district, is the Fundació Tàpies, housed in what is reputedly the first *modernista* building in Barcelona, designed in 1886 by architect Domènech i Montaner. From the opposite side of the street you get the full perspective, and pick out the chair in the airy Tàpies sculpture which crowns it, *Núvol i Cadira* (*Cloud and Chair*).

The interior spaces make a good setting for the large collection of work by Antoni Tàpies, who is considered to be Spain's greatest living artist. *www.fundacio-tapies.org*

Golondrinas

Take a trip around the harbour in one of the historic *Golondrinas* (Swallows) which, apart from a pause during the civil war, have been plying these waters since the 1888 Exposition. The ferries wait patiently in the Moll de Drassanes, the jetty opposite the Columbus monument. Half-hour trips take you out to the sea wall and back again, although you can disembark there and have a drink before catching a return boat. Be sure to choose one of the older, more elegant Golondrinas with names like *Mercedes, Lolita* and *Encarnación.*

As the ferry chugs through the working port you get a different perspective on the waterfront, seeing the enormity of the surrounding vessels and the battering they take in high seas.

Right: Golondrina *pleasure boats give you a different view of the city*

Gran Teatre del Liceu

Barcelona's opera house is the cathedral of *bel canto* in Spain and launch-pad for names such as Montserrat Caballé and Josep Carreras, who made his debut here. The original building, dating from 1861, was badly damaged by fire in 1994, but still peeks out of the enormous edifice within which it is enclosed.

Architect Ignasi de Solà Morales modernised the acoustics, lighting and stage, and doubled the theatre's overall size while keeping to the original, sumptuous style. The theatre reopened in October 1999. With its new technology and second stage, it now takes over a whole block in La Rambla dels Caputxins.

Illa de la Discòrdia

Close to the Passeig de Gràcia Metro is a trilogy of Catalan Modernista works known as the Illa de la Discòrdia (the Block of Discord), each of them striking in quite different ways. On the southern corner of the block is the Casa Lleó Morera. Situated three houses up is Casa Amatller, now the centre for the Modernisme Route (this is an option for visiting key buildings normally closed to the public by purchasing a multi-ticket). Next to it is the Casa Batlló, the facade covered in blue-green ceramic work, and the windows sensuously curved.

Unfortunately, none of them are open to the public but you can still enjoy the splendid facades, peeking in to see extraordinary ceramic work (Lleó Morera), stained-glass ceiling

Above: *Gran Teatre del Liceu, Barcelona's opera house*

and lamp details (Amatller), and amazing Gaudí touches (Batlló), which are also stunning at night.

The architect of the first, the Casa Lleó Morera, was Lluís Domènech i Montaner (1850–1923); he was the mentor of Josep Puig i Cadafalch (1867–1957), designer of the neighbouring, Dutch-gabled Casa Amatller, while Casa Batlló was the work of Antoni Gaudí *(see page 20)*. All were leading figures of the 19th-century Catalan Renaissance, the Renaixença.

La Boqueria (Market)

The city's most popular, colourful and famous market, the Mercat de la Boqueria, is also known as the Mercat de Sant Josep. The first stone was laid on St Joseph's day, 19 March 1840, to appease the saint whose convent in the same spot had been burnt down in the 1835 riots.

Here, discerning shoppers – restaurateurs early in the morning, housewives mid-morning and the men in charge of the paella on Saturdays – queue patiently for the best produce, bark their orders and refuse to be fobbed off with anything below par. The fishwives also holler, trying to seduce passers-by into the day's best catch.

It is a heady experience, and despite the frantic crowds, exceedingly heart-warming: there is something quintessentially Mediterranean about the noise, human warmth and the serious business of buying wonderfully fresh produce.

Right: *Gaudí's organic Casa Batlló*

La Pedrera

Situated on Passeig de Gràcia is one of the best-known buildings in Barcelona, Gaudí's Casa Milà, more often known as *La Pedrera* (The Quarry). This splendid building has been cleaned, refurbished and polished up by its present owners, the Caixa de Catalunya (a prominent bank with a foundation that supports the arts).

At the time of its construction in 1910 it was the subject of passionate debate between enthusiasts and denigrators. For many years it was left to fall apart, but UNESCO declared it a monument of world interest and the Caixa stepped in. This exceptional building has the Espai Gaudí, an exhibition of the architect's work, in the attic; a spectacular roof where the spooky chimneys have been dubbed the "witch scarers", and from where there's a wonderful view of the Sagrada Familía; and El Pis, one of the flats now open to the public and decorated as it would have been when the building was first occupied. Major temporary exhibitions are held on the first floor and are open to the public free of charge.

Above: *La Pedrera with its spooky chimneys*

Maremàgnum

In Port Vell you will find Maremàgnum, site of L'Aquàrium *(see page 27)* and the Imax cinema. Take heed of warning signs to mind your step at the start of the Rambla de Mar walkway, as the designers take no responsibility for sprained ankles. The undulating design fits in well with the maritime environment, and is a great concept for crossing the harbour, but the subtle "waves" and changes in level can catch you out.

Cross the swing bridge above the yachts to the Maremàgnum shopping and eating emporium, where you can shop until 11pm. A selection of bars and restaurants is dominated by fast food outlets but there are some old favourites, too. Despite the commercialisation, a few *tapes* in the spring sunshine while watching the maritime traffic or looking across the harbour at Barcelona's Gothic towers takes some beating. The place throbs at night with salsa music.

Monestir de Pedralbes

To the northwest of the city is the district of Pedralbes, a neighbourhood of exclusive apartment blocks, with verdant gardens, manicured lawns and swimming pools. Here you will find the welcoming old stones of the Monestir de Pedralbes, without doubt one of the most peaceful corners of the city. The monastery was founded in 1326 by Queen Elisenda de Montcada, widow (and fourth wife) of King Jaume II. She took the vows of the Order of St Clare, and today some 20 nuns are still in residence. The fine Gothic

Right: *for wraparound images, choose the Imax cinema in Maremàgnum*

architecture, most notably the unusual three-tiered cloister, evokes the spiritual side of monastic life, while the rooms that are open to the public provide an insight into the day-to-day life of the building's inhabitants. There are some remarkable 14th-century murals by Catalan painter, Ferrer Bassa.

Part of the complex houses the Col.lecció Thyssen-Bornemisza. Some 70 canvasses and a few sculptures from the medieval, Renaissance and Venetian baroque periods were selected for Barcelona from the main collection in Madrid, and include works by Canaletto, Velázquez and Tintoretto.

Montjuïc

The small hill of Montjuïc is only 213 metres (699 ft) high, but has an undeniable presence that is noticeable from most parts of the city: from along the waterfront it marks the end of the port, and from the Ronda Litoral it acts like a barrier between the inner residential area of the city and the industrial sprawl of the Zona Franca, the gateway to the south. From here you can see how densely packed a city Barcelona is.

A pre-Roman civilisation made a settlement on Montjuïc and the Romans built a temple to Jupiter here, which is thought to explain its name: Mons Iovis, which evolved into Montjuïc. In 1929 the hill was landscaped and used as the grounds of the Universal Exposition. More recently, it was seen by millions of people worldwide as it hosted the opening and closing ceremonies and core events of the 1992 Olympic Games.

***Above:** Monestir de Pedralbes, a peaceful enclave*

Today it is a large city park offering a wide range of cultural, leisure and sporting activities. It is a wonderful space for walking dogs and allowing children to run wild, or just for clearing the head and getting a bird's-eye view of Barcelona, especially its maritime area. Apart from the cable car that crosses the harbour, this is the only place where you can piece together the waterfront at a glance, and watch the comings and goings of the busy industrial port.

Montserrat

About 48 km (30 miles) west of Barcelona, but reached easily and spectacularly by train (and cable car) from Plaça d'Espany, is Catalonia's most important religious retreat, Montserrat. Looming 1,236 metres (4,055 ft) over the valley floor, it is the highest point of the Catalan lowlands, and visible from miles around. Groups of young people from all over Catalonia make overnight hikes at least once in their lives to watch the sunrise from its heights. "La Moreneta" (The Black Virgin), Catalonia's favourite saint, resides in the sanctuary of the Mare de Deu de Montserrat, next to the monastery.

The basilica is packed with works of art by a number of prominent painters and sculptors, including El Greco. Catalan poets have dedicated some of their most inspired verse to this site. Goethe is

Above: *a view of the Monastery at Montserrat*

said to have dreamed of Montserrat and Parsifal sought the Holy Grail here in Wagner's last opera. The monastery's *escolans*, the oldest boys' choir in Europe, sings twice a day.

Museu Barbier-Mueller d'Art Precolombí

Opposite the Picasso Museum in Carrer Montcada is the Museu Barbier-Mueller d'Art Precolombí, which has a prestigious and fascinating collection of pre-Columbian art, representing most styles of pre-Hispanic American civilisations. It was bequeathed to Barcelona by a Geneva museum. The gift shop has some beautiful contemporary Indian work, albeit at Western prices.

Museu d'Art Contemporani de Barcelona

The Plaça dels Angels in El Raval district opens up into the unexpected space dominated by the breathtaking Museu d'Art Contemporani de Barcelona (MACBA). Designed by US architect Richard Meier and opened in 1995, the building is dazzling against

Above: *Museu d'Art Contemporani, strikingly designed by Richard Meier*

the Mediterranean blue sky and gigantic within the context of the humble buildings nestling beyond.

The social and urban significance of the architecture in this once declining area have been almost more of a talking point than the collection inside, which comprises Catalan, Spanish and some international art, mostly from the second half of the 20th century. The museum also hosts temporary exhibitions. Its large forecourt has evolved into a popular public space for skate-boarding and football matches. Filipino families often gather here with picnic suppers on warm evenings: the square is a fascinating melting pot of local residents and cosmopolitan visitors. *www.macba.es*

Museu d'Art Modern

Set in the Parc de la Cuitadella *(see pages 53–4)* and sharing a building with the Catalan Parliament is the Museu d'Art Modern. It holds a large collection of Catalan paintings, drawings, sculpture and decorative art, including furniture from the 19th and early 20th centuries. It is an attractive collection, in which work by Ramón Casas (1866–1932), Santiago Rusiñol (1861–1931) and other Modernista artists successfully evokes the heady atmosphere of Barcelona at the turn of the 20th century.

Museu Frederic Marès

At the side of the Cathedral a tiny square, Sant Iu, leads into the lovely courtyard of the Museu Frederic Marès. This private collection, donated

Right: *Museu d'Art Modern, home of Catalan Modernista works*

by the sculptor, Marès, includes one of the most important displays of Spanish sculpture. The Museu Sentimental, on the upper floors, gives an insight into daily life in Barcelona from medieval times to the present. The summer cafe is even more enticing.

Museu de la Ciència

The excellent Science Museum in Teodor Roviralta, near the stop for the Tramvia Blau *(see page 65)*, is one of the few museums conveniently open on a Sunday afternoon. The whole approach is state-of-the-art, with plenty of hands-on exhibits and usually a fascinating temporary exhibition. There is plenty to do for all ages, including 3–6-year-olds in the "Clik dels Nens", a space to play and learn created by high-profile designer Javier Mariscal. Funded by the affluent Fundació La Caixa, the cultural foundation of the savings bank, no expense has been spared, and the large red brick Modernista building has been well converted and equipped.

Above: *Museu Frederic Marès' shady courtyard*

Museu de Zoologia

The Zoological Museum is set in the Parc de la Ciutadella in a building designed by Domènech i Montaner called the Castell dels Tres Dragons (Castle of the Three Dragons). It was intended to be the restaurant of the 1888 World Exposition, although it never opened as such. However, it was one of the first *Modernista* projects in Barcelona and the architect's studio for years. The museum's collections of zoological specimens and impressive skeletons are well-housed amid the 19th-century marble and polished floors.

Behind is the beautiful Hivernacle, an elegant greenhouse bursting with tropical plants, which has been restored to include a restaurant. Jazz and classical concerts are held on summer evenings.

Like its neighbour, the Museu de Geologia, the Zoological Museum is pleasingly old fashioned, a different breed from the new generation, state-of-the-art museums.

Museu d'Història de Catalunya

Part of Barcelona's once-busy working quays now shelter the Marina Port Vell, where some of the most exclusive motor and sailing yachts in the Mediterranean overwinter or pass through. In 1992 the former warehouse complex, the Magatzem General de Comerç (1878) by Elias Rogent, was transformed into the Palau de Mar. This is a handsome building, very well renovated, and part of it now houses the fascinating History of Catalonia Museum. True to its name, it elucidates Catalan history but also serves as a generic history museum with various bits of technical wizardry and plenty of inter-

Above: *the Museu de Zoologia, housed in the Castle of the Three Dragons*

active spaces – try walking in a suit of armour, or building a Roman arch – which kids of all ages love.

Museu Marítim

A pleasing museum that appeals to all ages and gives a vivid sense of Catalonia's seafaring past, the Maritime Museum is housed in the magnificent, 13th-century Gothic shipyards at the foot of La Rambla – a fine and rare example of civil architecture from that period. There is something quite breathtaking about the lines and structure of the building, which as art critic Robert Hughes says in his book *Barcelona* is "perhaps the most stirring ancient industrial space of any kind that has survived from the Middle Ages: a masterpiece of civil engineering".

The collection includes real fishing boats from the Catalan coast, as well as models of vessels from all ages. Also on display is a modern Olympic winner. The highlight is the *son et lumière* show known as "La Gran Aventura del Mar" (The Great Sea Adventure), which charts Catalonia's maritime history and includes a tour around the full-scale replica of the Barcelona-built 16th-century galley in which Don Juan of Austria led the Christian fleet to defeat the Turks in the Battle of Lepanto in 1571.

Above: *a masted ship in the Museu Marítim*

Museu Nacional d'Art de Catalunya

Since 1934 the imposing Palau Nacional on Montjuïc has housed the Museu Nacional d'Art de Catalunya (MNAC), which has the most important Romanesque art collection in the world, including murals peeled off the walls of tiny churches in the Pyrenees in the province of Lleida and brought down by donkey. There is also a good Gothic collection and a small selection of Renaissance and baroque art.

The interior, partly remodelled by Italian architect Gae Aulenti, is being renovated to house other collections,and eventually, the plan is to encompass the whole range of Catalan art under one roof.

Museu Picasso

The Picasso Museum at Carrer Montcada 15–23 in La Ribera district opened in 1963 and now occupies five palaces: Palau Berenguer d'Aguilar, Baró de Castellet, Meca, Casa Mauri and Finestres. The latter two, opened in October 1999, are for temporary exhibitions; the main entrance is through the 15th-century Aguilar palace. Its beautiful courtyard, with a surrounding first-floor gallery and pointed archways resting on slender columns, was designed by Marc Safont, best known for the inner patio of the Generalitat building.

The museum has the most complete collection of Picasso's early works, including sketches in school books and a masterly portrait of his mother done when he was only 16. The Blue Period (1901–4) is also well represented. It is an absorbing

Right: *graceful statue outside the Museu Nacional d'Art de Catalunya*

collection although there's only a limited selection of Picasso's later works, apart from the fascinating studies of *Las Meninas* dating from the 1950s.

National Theatre

Long awaited, much discussed and finally opened in the late 1990s is the cultural complex that includes the Teatre Nacional de Catalunya (TNC) – the National Theatre – and L'Auditori *(see page 27)*. The theatre is in the unmistakable neoclassical style of Ricardo Bofil, Barcelona's best-known modern architect. Its three stages cope with a varied programme, mainly in Catalan, of classic and experimental theatre and dance.

Olympic Port

The strikingly designed Port Olímpic, close to the Olympic Village *(see page 48)*, is a pleasant place to walk. The quayside is lined with

***Above:** an air of bustle at the Vila Olímpica*

bars and restaurants, many with entrances on the promenade above, and with new ones spreading out along the beach. Inevitably, a tacky element has crept in – the overpowering smell of fried fish and the ubiquitous Andean flutes detract from the glamorous yachts in the port. But there are some great places to eat and sitting outside one of them with the sea sparkling a few feet away, is sheer pleasure.

Wander beneath Frank Gehry's awesome fish and imagine the heady view from the exclusive rooms in the Hotel Arts that towers above. Down at ground level, what was once an exclusive shopping area is now the home of the Barcelona Casino.

At the end of the Moll de Gregal, jutting out to sea, is the municipal sailing school, offering courses to the public.

Olympic Stadium

The Estadi Olímpic, to give its Catalan name, is on Montjuïc hill, nowhere near the Olympic village and port. It was built for the 1929 Universal Exposition, to a design by Pere Domènech. Its opening football match was a victory for the Catalan side against Bolton Wanderers – a little known fact. It remained open until the Mediterranean Games in 1955, then fell into disrepair. Extensive works for the 1992 Olympics involved lowering the arena by 11 metres (36 ft) to create the extra seating needed for 55,000 spectators. Most of the track events and the opening and closing ceremonies were held here. You can relive the excitement of Barcelona's glory in the Galeria Olímpica, an exhibition space at the rear of the stadium.

Right: *the Telecom Tower at the Olympic Stadium*

Below and west of the stadium stretches the immense Olympic Terrace, lined with pillars. In the middle of the main terrace is a lawn through which flows an artificial stream; on the left is a small forest of identical sculptures.

The terrace drops down to a second level in the middle distance, and then to a third – the Plaça d'Europa – a circular colonnaded area built on top of a massive water tank containing 60,000 cubic metres of drinking water for the city. The whole has the atmosphere of a re-created Roman forum.

Olympic Village

The Vila Olímpica is unmistakable, distinctive by virtue of its two skyscrapers and the copper fish sculpture (*Pez y Esfera* by Frank Gehry) rippling in the sun. A new park just before the Hospital del Mar does justice to the Modernista Watertower (1905) by Jose Domènech i Estapà, virtually the only original industrial building left standing in this area. The formerly gloomy hospital underwent a metamorphosis for the Olympics, when it played an important role, treating the athletes; it is now more reminiscent of an international airport than a major public hospital.

It is worth taking time to go inland a block or two, to see the architectural feats of the Olympic village. Built on land formerly occupied by 19th-century ramshackle warehouses and tumbledown factories, the flats accommodated athletes in 1992 and since then have been sold for high prices. It was a major undertaking, and a

Above: *skyscrapers at the Olympic Village*

vital part of Barcelona's wider plan of improving the infrastructure. In order to assimilate the village into the city, the major railway lines into Estació de França, the international train terminus, had to be buried below ground.

Palau de la Generalitat

Facing the Casa de la Ciutat *(see pages 29–30)* across the Plaça Sant Jaume, the Palau de la Generalitat is the seat of the autonomous government that presides over Catalonia. Of Gothic origin, this splendid building can be visited on key public holidays or at weekends by prior arrangement. The Pati dels Tarongers (a 16th-century courtyard full of orange trees) is perhaps the most famous part of the Palau and the scene of many official photographs.

Palau de la Música Catalana

This extravaganza of a concert hall, designed by leading *Modernista* architect Domènech i Montaner in 1908, should not be missed.

Above: *seat of the Catalan government – Palau de la Generalitat*

The Palau de la Música Catalana has been declared a World Heritage building by UNESCO, and is the only concert hall in Europe to be naturally lit. After a lifetime crammed into the side of a church (it was built on the site of the former cloister), this bold, colourful building decorated with tiles and mosaics, stained glass and statuary, is emerging in all its splendour.

The old church has been demolished and there are bold new plans by Barcelona architect Oscar Tusquets for a new underground rehearsal space and a spacious patio for open-air concerts.

Don't miss the chance to see inside the Palau de la Música: visitors can't wander around alone but you can take a guided tour (the building is also included on the Modernisme Route multi-ticket). Perhaps the best way to appreciate the place is to attend one of the concerts in its busy classical season, or a jazz concert during the International Jazz Festival.

Palau del Lloctinent

In the fine medieval square called the Plaça del Rei, located in the Barri Gòtic, is the Palau del Lloctinent. When the kingdoms of Catalonia and Aragón were joined with that of Castile, Carlos V created the office of Deputy *(Lloctinent)* for the court's representative, and this palace, the official residence, was built in 1549 by Antoni Carbonell. The facade is Catalan-Gothic but the inner courtyard is one of the few extant examples of Renaissance architecture left in the city. Today the palace is the headquarters of the Arxiu de la Corona d'Aragó (Archive of the Crown of Aragon).

Above: *the fine Renaissance tower at the Palau Reial Major*

Palau Reial Major

At one end of the Plaça del Rei is the Palau Reial Major, with vast vaulted ceilings, 13th-century triple-recess windows and 14th-century rose windows. The silhouette of the box-shaped Renaissance tower of Rei Martí is an outstanding feature of the palace. Built like a dovecote, it has fine views down over the royal complex.

The main room of the palace, the great Saló del Tinell (begun in 1359) was later converted to a baroque church, and recovered its original appearance after restoration work during and after the civil war. During the 15th century this was where the Inquisition held court. Legend has it that the walls of the tribunal cannot bear a lie to be told and that, when this occurred, the ceiling stones would move. Today, the salon functions as an exhibition area.

Palau Sant Jordi

One of the Olympic installations most in the public eye today is the Palau Sant Jordi (St George's Palace), an indoor stadium designed by Japanese architect, Arata Isozaki. The ultra-modern

***Above:** tourists gather in the Plaça del Rei*

design in sleek steel and glass can seat 15,000, with not a pillar in sight. Since the Olympics, the Palau has proved popular for concerts and exhibitions as well as sporting events.

Parc d'Atraccions

The Parc d'Atraccions funfair has a wonderful retro air and is not exhaustingly large or terrifying – a real old-fashioned fairground. Some of its attractions date back to 1901 when the funicular first reached the summit of Tibidabo, and some are from renovations that took place in 1986. There is a miniature train, a hall of mirrors, and a much-loved rotating plane, dating from 1928, as well as bumper cars, big dippers, carousels, fast food in all its forms, and all the usual fun of the fair.

There is also a delightful little museum in the park, the Museu d'Autòmats, which has a collection of fascinating mechanical toys and slot machines built during the first half of the 20th century.

The whole complex is open from Easter to December, but the times change according to daylight hours and whether it is peak season. The tram and funicular that bring you here run in conjunction with the opening times.

***Above:** all the fun of the Parc d'Atraccions fair*

Parc de Collserola

The Parc de Collserola is a green belt measuring 17 by 6 km (11 by 4 miles), which is literally on the city's doorstep. Its 8,000 hectares (20,000 acres) of vegetation border on the Ronda de Dalt ring road, and spread over the Collserola range of hills to Sant Cugat and beyond.

This easily accessible area – reached from the centre via the efficient and frequent FGC train service from Plaça de Catalunya – is a bonus to city living. It is best known for its highest peak, Tibidabo (512 metres/1,664 ft) and its distinctive skyline, with the Sagrat Cor church and the Torre de Collserola communications tower, which forms a backdrop to Barcelona. But it is a lot more besides.

There are endless activities on offer from horse riding to nature trails, picnic spots, restaurants and *merenderos* – open-air restaurants where you can barbecue your own food, which are extremely popular with local people on summer weekends.

Parc de la Ciutadella

Located between the Old Town and the new Vila Olímpica, on the eastern side of Mercat del Born, just across Passeig de Picasso, is the City Park, Barcelona's oldest and most visited park and one of the most attractive in Barcelona. It is easy (and therapeutic) to while away half a day here, simply walking in the fresh air among the greenery, or enjoying some of the activities on offer.

Interesting buildings remain from its military past, and from its

Right: *boating in the Parc de la Ciutadella*

glorious time as the 1888 World Exposition showground, but the best thing about it is its refreshing tranquillity.

This is a real city park, where young skateboarders vie for space with old men playing *petanca*, and toddlers inadvertently wander on to the pieces of cardboard where retired couples play card games. You can hire bicycles made for six and rowing boats on the lake. On Sundays, families parade in their best outfits before heading for lunch. Constantly tended by municipal gardeners, Parc de la Ciutadella is verdant, scented and shady, a soothing place to walk in all seasons.

Here you'll find the Museum of Modern Art and the Zoological Museum, and behind the latter, the Hivernacle greenhouse *(see pages 41 and 43*).

Follow signs to the Cascada, the monumental fountain and artificial lake designed in 1875. Gaudí worked on this project as a young architectural student. Something of a landmark and meeting place, its esplanade is often used for concerts, shows or fairs.

Above: *Parc de la Ciutadella – Barcelona's oldest park*

Parc Güell

One of the city's star attractions, the Parc Güell owes its magnetic attraction to the fact it was designed by Antoni Gaudí and it is one of the best examples of *Modernisme* in the city.

It was originally intended to emulate an English garden city on the estate of Gaudí's patron, the wealthy industrialist, Eusebi Güell, encompassing 60 building plots, but only five buildings were completed: the two pavilions flanking the entrance, both designed by Gaudí, and three others inside the park, one of which is today the Casa-Museu Gaudí, where the architect lived from 1906 until his death 20 years later. Some of his furniture, drawings and projects are housed here.

In creating Parc Güell, Gaudí used shapes that harmonised with the landscape. Always aware of the struggle between man and nature, he built a complex garden of staircases, zoomorphic sculptures, sinuous ramps and viaducts. The most important single element of the park is a two-tiered plaza, at 86 by 40 metres (280 by 130 ft).

The lower part of the plaza, made up of a series of columns in the form of a *sala hipóstila*, was designed to be the housing estate's market-place. The upper portion is an open area with grand views over the city, surrounded by an undulating bench of mosaics, whose detailing is largely the work of Josep Maria Jujol.

Recently restored, this ceramic serpentine seat is

***Right:** the Modernista Parc Güell was designed by Gaudí*

quite spectacular and, like the park itself, should not be missed. Built between 1900 and 1914, it has been declared a monument of world interest by UNESCO.

Parc Joan Miró

On the extreme left of the Eixample district you will find one of the first parks to be created in the 1980s as part of the design for a new Barcelona. Covering four blocks above Plaça d'Espanya where Diputació and Aragó meet Tarragona, the Parc Joan Miró is also known as the Parc de l'Escorxador because it was the location of the municipal slaughterhouse until 1979. It is a great area for kids to run wild. The 22-metre (70-ft) Miró statue, *Dona i Ocell (Woman and Bird)*, is striking in its simple setting on a small island in the middle of a pool in the park. One of Miró's last works, it was unveiled in 1983, just a few months before he died.

Plaça de Catalunya

The Plaça de Catalunya is not very picturesque but it is a pivotal point, acting as a logistical centre for the city's transport. Here you'll find the Metro; the FGC trains (the Ferrocarrils de la Generalitat de Catalunya, which run to areas outside the city); RENFE (national) trains; public and privately run buses, including one for the airport; tourist coaches and taxis. The main tourist office is also here.

This plaça is the centre of the city in a wider sense: in the middle of the square are

Above: *Miró's* Woman and Bird *in the Parc Joan Miró*

paving stones arranged into the shape of a star which, they say, marks the centre of the capital of Catalonia. Pigeons flock here to be fed by children and old ladies. Tacky stalls hawk plastic toys and caramelised nuts. Families wander around aimlessly, lovers meet beneath the gushing fountains or under the shady trees and predatory youths lurk, with an eye on handbags and cameras. On the newly paved and urbanised outer rim, men gather to play chess beneath the monument to a much-loved Catalan leader, Macià, designed by contemporary sculptor, Subirachs.

Plaça d'Espanya

One of Barcelona's most imposing squares, the Plaça d'Espanya is a large, noisy junction at the southern end of the city with good metro and bus connections; it is also one of the best approaches to Montjuïc *(see page 38)*. The monumental statue in the centre was commissioned for the 1929 Universal Exposition.

Turning your back on the roundabout, past the twin Venetian-style towers that formed the main entrance to the Universal Exposition of

Above: *Plaça de Catalunya is the centre of Barcelona*

1929, you will be faced with a sweeping vista up to the Palau Nacional, the enormous, overbearing building at the top of the steps that houses the Museu Nacional d'Art de Catalunya *(see page 45)*.

Plaça Reial

Reached through an arcaded passageway from La Ramba is Plaça Reial, a real Barcelona landmark and one of the most handsome yet decadent of its squares. Recent attempts to clean it up have done little to change its character, so tourists eating on restaurant terraces still jostle with junkies and there is usually a police presence.

Restaurants and bars predominate, including some new ones that are both stylish and economical. The well-established Jamboree jazz club is here, along with its sister club Tarantos, for flamenco, and other good places for dancing. The buzz never lets up, day or night.

On Sunday, stamp and coin collectors gather around the Font de Les Tres Gràcies and the two lovely *fanals* (street lamps) designed by Antoni Gaudí. Inspired by the French urban designs of the Napoleonic period, this is the only one of many squares planned in Barcelona during the 19th century that was built entirely according to its original plan. Its uniform, arcaded buildings were constructed on the plot where the Capuchin Convent once stood.

Above: *outdoor cafes in the decadent Plaça Reial*

Poble Espanyol

In the northwest corner of Montjuïc is the Poble Espanyol (Spanish Village), built for the 1929 World Exposition. The village is pure kitsch, but it provides numerous diversions, from a *tablao* where you can watch flamenco dancing, to demonstrations of glass-making, and "The Barcelona Experience", an audio-visual show. Teenagers flock here for the night scene and retired people arrive in busloads. The village is one of the most popular venues in Barcelona, welcoming more visitors each year than even the Sagrada Família, the Aquarium or the major museums.

It was built as a showpiece for regional architecture, handicrafts, and cultural and gastronomic styles from all over Spain. It has a Plaza Mayor, typical of many squares you might find in the country, where popular fiestas take place. The square is seen at its best when it stages jazz and rock concerts during the Grec summer festival.

Javier Mariscal, one of Barcelona's most popular designers – it was Mariscal who was responsible for the Olympic mascot – put the Poble Espanyol into the limelight in the early 1990s by creating a trendy bar within the village's stage-set gateway, the Torres de Ávila. It was briefly fashionable but it's now a dance club, open only at weekends. *www.poble-espanyol.com*

Right: *Barcelona's 1929 World Exposition Spanish Village*

Port Vell

Beneath the towering Columbus Monument at the foot of La Rambla, the *Golondrinas* (ferries, *see page 33*) mark a divide between the industrial port and the leisure areas encompassed in the ever-busy Port Vell, the old port. A walkway and footbridge leads across the water to the large commercial complex in the middle of the harbour. Alternatively, you can continue on the mainland along the Moll de la Fusta, a promenade built in the 1980s on the site of the old wooden cargo sheds. Studded with palm trees and dance bars, it was designed to minimise the noise of an increasingly traffic-saturated highway with surrounding recreational zones.

La Rambla

There are five different parts of this broad, leafy parade that leads from Plaça de Catalunya to the sea, and all have different names, but are known simply as La Rambla. This is one of the most famous boulevards in Europe, and one of the distinguishing features of Barcelona.

***Above:** a new look for the Old Port (Port Vell)*

This kaleidoscopic avenue throbs day and night, exerting a magnetism which attracts both visitors and locals, and which never fails to entertain.

The best advice is to plunge in, go with the flow and enjoy the constant weird and wonderful activity all around you. Linger at newspaper stands, let yourself be carried past lottery ticket booths, shoe shiners, cheap *pensiones*, human statues, tourists in shorts and locals in sharp suits. Stop for a coffee – more expensive at the outdoor tables, but the entertainment value makes it worthwhile. Let your senses be assailed by the squawking of caged birds, the perfumed air of the flower stalls, the chatter of the gossips and the shrieks of the lads delivering fruit to the market. Don't miss a thing, especially the ubiquitous pickpockets who prey on the crowds.

El Raval

Enclosed by Ronda Sant Antoni and Ronda Sant Pau, in the 1930s El Raval was one of the most densely populated urban areas in the world. Although it seems harsh and run-down in places, some of the most interesting cultural activities in the city now take place here. In its medieval past the area was heavily populated by religious institutions; with the advent of industrialisation in the late 18th century the emphasis switched to factories, and dense urbanisation began.

Relics of the religious past still stand out in today's bustling Raval: considered the oldest church in Barcelona, Sant Pau del Camp is a fine example of Romanesque architecture, quite rare in the city. The present building is 12th century but it incorporates elements

Right: *a bird's-eye view of La Rambla*

of an earlier church built in 912. Trendy second-hand clothes shops (unusual in Barcelona) are another new thread in this multicoloured fabric. Riera Baixa, a short pedestrian street, has some wacky shops and an outdoor market on Saturday.

Some old bars in the lower part of El Raval are popular haunts at night. Founded in 1820, the Marsella still serves absinthe (to be taken with caution) and is one of the most atmospheric, with its marble tables and local characters.

For a different perspective on the city, don't miss the view from the Sala de Mirador in the Centre de Cultura Contemporània.

La Ribera

The *barri* of La Ribera is loosely defined as that part of the Old Town which is separated from the Barri Gòtic by Via Laietana. There is a very beaten track to the door of its star museum, the Museu Picasso *(see page 45)*, but the area has many other charms that should not be overlooked. From the present-day rag trade to medieval merchants' houses, from new social and urban developments to the most beautiful church in Barcelona, from contemporary artists' studios to carpenters' workshops: like so many of the city's *barris*, La Ribera is a richly woven texture of contrasts.

Sagrada Família

The Sagrada Família, Gaudi's celebrated temple, is the symbol of Barcelona for many, and the reason the name Gaudí spread around

Above: *12th-century Sant Pau del Camp in El Raval district*

the world. Here, in the centre of this bustling, ordinary neighbourhood is a staggering sight, visited by more than 1 million people a year.

The enormously ambitious undertaking, begun in 1883, became Gaudí's main project for the rest of his life. At the time of his death in 1926, only the crypt, apse and part of the Nacimiento façade and one tower had been completed. Many people believe the temple should be left as an unfinished monument to its famous creator. Yet such is Barcelona's commitment to the Sagrada Família that work has continued on its construction for more than 70 years after his death, apart from a break during the Civil War years.

The Sagrada Família has three facades: the *Pasión* (Passion), the *Nacimiento* (Nativity) and the *Gloria* (Glory). The first two, with their soaring mosaic-topped towers, are closest to completion.

The restoration and continuation of the sculptures on the *Nacimiento* facade is being undertaken by a Japanese sculptor, Etsuro Sotoo, in a spirit that is remarkably faithful to Gaudí's original work.

Those on the *Pasión* facade, designed by local artist Josep M. Subirachs, have aroused less enthusiasm. The *Gloria* facade, which was originally planned as the principal entranceway and is orientated towards the midday sun, is slowly beginning to take form.

***Right:** soaring turrets of the Sagrada Família*

Sagrat Cor

The Sacred Heart church on the summit of Tibidabo is a great wedding-cake of a building and is, in fact, a very popular place for weddings. Begun at the start of the 20th century but not finished until the 1950s, its best-known feature is the huge bronze figure of Christ, with arms outstretched, that crowns the central tower. A lift takes you to the top of the tower, from where the view is stunning.

Santa María del Mar

The best-loved church in the city, situated in the Passeig del Born. A towering Gothic building, Santa María has a beautiful stained-glass rose window.

Tibidabo

Tibidabo, at 512 metres/1,664 ft, is the most visible summit of the Parc de Collserola *(see page 53)*. An FGC train goes to Avinguda Tibidabo station from Plaça de Catalunya. From here you can experience Barcelona's last tram service, the Tramvia Blau.The tram stops at the Plaça del Funicular, where you can catch the funicular to the summit to visit the funfair, the Sagrat Cor church or enjoy the view.

Torre de Calatrava

One landmark among the Olympic installations on Montjuïc that caused ructions when built, not least with the architects who created

Above: *the huge bronze figure of Christ on the Sagrat Cor*

the whole Olympic Ring, was this great white communications tower (188 metres/616 ft) designed by Spanish architect Santiago Calatrava, known for his elegant bridges. Despite opposition, the Telefònica tower went ahead, and the result is quite stunning.

Torre de Collserola

Also known as the Torre Foster, after its architect, Sir Norman Foster, who designed it for the 1992 Olympics, this striking communications tower is impressive from a distance and even more awesome up close, with giant stays anchoring it to the hillside. A transparent lift will take you up for a panoramic view 560 metres (1,837 ft) above sea level.

Tramvia Blau

The Tramvia Blau, the last surviving tram in the city, rattles up Avinguda Tibidabo, an avenue of beautiful *Modernista* houses that winds up the hill. This open-sided blue wooden tram has been plying the route to the base of the Tibidabo funicular since 1901 and is hugely popular with residents and visitors alike.

Zoo

The Parc Zoologic, to give it its full name, is in the Parc de la Ciutadella. Founded in 1892, it remains as popular as ever. A dolphin show is one of its highlights; another is Floquet de Neu, or Snowflake, the only albino gorilla in captivity, although now getting so old that he can't be counted on to last much longer.

Right: *view from Tibidabo*

ESSENTIAL INFORMATION

The Place

Area: 99 sq km (38 sq miles).

Situation: Approximately 42°N, 2°E on the same latitude as New York City and Peking. Barcelona is situated on the Mediterranean roughly 150 km (95 miles) south of the Pyrenees.

Population: 1.6 million; 2.9 million in the greater metropolitan area. Forty percent of the population is from other parts of Spain.

Currency: The euro replaced the peseta in January 2002.

Electricity: 220 volts, two-pin plug.

Weights and measures: metric.

Languages: Catalan and Spanish (Castilian).

Religion: Predominantly Roman Catholic, though there is a strong anti-clerical tradition.

Highest point: Mt Tibidabo, 516m (1,700 ft).

Time zone: One hour ahead of GMT in winter, 2 hours in summer.

International Dialling Code for Spain: 34.

The Climate

Average temperatures are 54°F (10°C) in winter and 75°F (25°C) in summer. December and January are coldest; November and February/March are rainy; spring and autumn are mild and sunny; July and August are humid. There are 2,500 hours of sunlight a year.

Government

The Autonomous Region of Catalonia is governed by the *Generalitat* in Barcelona, opposite which is the *Ajuntament* (Town Hall), where the mayor and the city council preside. For more than two

***Left:** Barcelona street scene*

decades (after free elections), the *Generalitat* has been governed by the conservative Convergencia i Unió under Jordi Pujol, and the Town Hall has been socialist, now under Mayor Joan Clos.

Economy

Catalonia, and in particular Barcelona, is of outstanding economic importance to the Spanish state. It has 25 percent of the nation's industry, and supplies nearly 20 percent of the GDP. The economy of Catalonia has a greater turnover than Portugal or Ireland. Foreign investment has increased in recent years, a reflection of confidence in Catalonia as a progressive and dynamic region.

Public Holidays

1 January *New Year's Day*; **6 January** *Reis Mags*; **March/April** *Good Friday*; **March/ April** *Easter Monday*; **1 May** *Festa del Treball*; **end of May** *Whitsun*; **24 June** *Sant Joan*; **15 August** *Assumpció*; **11 September** *Diada*; **24 September** *La Mercè*, the patron saint of Barcelona; **12 October** *Hispanitat/Pilar*; **1 November** *Tots Sants*; **6 December** *Día de la Constitució*; **8 December** *Immaculada Concepció*; **25–26 December** *Christmas*

Tourist Information

ABROAD

For information about Barcelona before leaving home, contact your nearest Spanish Tourist Office or look on the web: *www.barcelonaturisme.com* or *www.bcn.es*

***Above:** bars abound in Catalonia's capital*

Canada 2 Bloor Street West, 34th Floor, Toronto, Ontario, M4W 3E2, tel: 416-961 3131, fax: 416-961 1992.

United Kingdom, 22–23 Manchester Square, London W1M 5AP, tel: 020-7486 8077 or 0900-166 9920 (for brochures), fax: 020-7486 8034, *www.tourspain.es*

United States, 666 Fifth Avenue, New York, NY 10103, tel: 212-265 8822, fax: 212-265 8864.

IN SPAIN

Plaça de Catalunya, tel: 93-304 3135. Open daily 9am–9pm.

City Hall, Plaça Sant Jaume. Open Mon–Sat 10am–8pm; Sun 10am–2pm.

Sants Station, open daily 8am–8pm (summer). Rest of year: Mon–Fri 8am–8pm, weekends/holidays 8am–2pm.

El Prat Airport, tel: 93 478 4704. Mon–Sat 9.30am–8.30pm, Sun 9.30am–3pm.

Tourist Information Centre for Catalonia, Palau Robert, Passeig

***Above:** bullfighting is less popular now, but still retains a following*

de Gràcia 107, tel: 93 238 4000; *www.gencat.es/probert*. Mon–Fri 10am–7pm Sat 10am–2.30pm.

In addition to the above, information booths are situated in **Plaça Catalunya**, the **Port** and the **Sagrada Família**. Open daily 9am–9pm.

Business Hours

Offices: 9am–2pm and 4–8pm. Most **official authorities**: 8am–2pm. Companies in the **outer industrial zones** tend to close at 6pm. From mid-June to mid-September many businesses practise *horas intensivas* from 8am–3pm in order to avoid the hottest part of the day.

Getting There

By Air

Iberia (tel: 902 400 500), the national carrier; **British Airways** (tel: 0845 7733377), and other major airlines all have frequent flights to Barcelona. Various companies compete over cheap deals, especially off-season, and there are numerous charter flights available.

The airport is 12 km (7 miles) south of the city and there are regular buses and trains into the city centre.

Useful websites include *www.go-fly.com*; *www.easyjet.com*; *www.buzzaway.com*; *www.britishmidland.com*

By Train

An international service, the **Talgo**, a high-speed, comfortable train, runs daily from Paris, Milan, Zurich and Geneva. All other inter-

Above: *traffic in the city can be confusing*

national connections involve a change at the French border, in Port Bou on entering Spain and Cerbère when leaving. These trains have fewer facilities, so travel prepared.

The Talgo terminates in the Estació de França (Av. Marquès de l'Argentera, near Parc de la Ciutadella); other trains go to Estació de Sants, Barcelona's central station, in Plaça Països Catalans.

BY BUS

The international bus companies Julià, Via (Eurolines) and Linebús run a regular service all over Europe, linking up with the national bus companies in each country. Buses arrive and depart either from Estació d'Autobusos Sants (tel: 93 490 4000), or Barcelona Nord (tel: 93 265 6508).

BY CAR

Barcelona is 160 km (100 miles) or 1½ hour's drive from La Jonquera on the French border and can be reached easily along the A7 motorway (autopista, toll payable) and then, nearer Barcelona, the A19. The toll cost from the border to the city is approximately 1,500 ptas. Petrol prices are similar to those in Britain. The ringroads *(cinturones)*

Above: *the Talgo terminates in the Estació de França*

surrounding the city can be very confusing for first arrivals; you are strongly advised to study a road map carefully beforehand. A car in Barcelona can be a liability. If you do decide to drive, look for an underground car park when you get there.

Entry Regulations

Passports are required for all nationalities entering Spain. Carry a photocopy with you around the city. If your passport is lost or stolen, report the fact immediately to the National Police.

Visas are needed by non-EU nationals, unless their country has a reciprocal arrangement with Spain.

Health

Barcelona is a modern European city and there are no special health risks to be aware of. An unaccustomed diet, too much alocohol or too much sun are the cause of most tourist complaints. The water is safe to drink but tastes rather unpleasant – most people drink bottled water.

Residents of EU countries are entitled to receive state medical treatment in Spain if they present an E111, but fees have to be paid then reclaimed later. In the UK you get this form from any post office.

Private health insurance is highly advisable. In an emergency go to the *Urgencias* department at one of the main hospitals – your hotel will tell you which is the nearest. Chemists *(farmacias)* are

Above: *flying the flag for Catalonia*

very helpful and able to sell many medicines that would need a prescription in the UK – a good first stop if you have a minor complaint.

Money

Bank opening hours vary, but as a general rule are 8.30am–2pm Monday to Friday, and 8.30am–1pm on Saturday between 1 October and 31 May. Most banks have ATMs operating 24 hours a day, where money can be withdrawn by credit card.

There are numerous currency exchange offices in the centre, particularly La Rambla and in the Plaça Catalunya Information Centre, which advertises its commission rates outside. Credit cards are widely accepted in shops and restaurants, but check in advance.

Media

El País is the most respected Spanish paper internationally. *La Vanguardia* is the traditional newspaper of Barcelona and has good coverage of local news and events. International newspapers can be found on the newsstands on La Rambla and Passeig de Gràcia, and in several bookshops. The main fashion magazines, such as *Vogue*, *Marie Claire* and *Elle* publish a Spanish edition.

Guia del Ocio is a useful weekly listings magazine for Barcelona. *Metropolitan*, Barcelona's first monthly magazine in English, carries useful listings. It is distributed free at bookshops, bars and cinemas. You can check out their website on *www.showcom/ metropolitan*.

Right: *there are plenty of places to change currency in Barcelona*

The principal television channels are TVE1 and TVE2 (state-owned); TV3 and Canal 33, the autonomous Catalan channels. Private channels include Antena 3 (general programming), Tele 5 (daytime soaps, etc) and Canal Plus (mostly films, but for subscribers only). Satellite programmes are obtainable in many of the larger hotels. News bulletins in various languages are on TVE and TV3 from July to September. Check the daily press for details.

Security and Crime

Take care, as you would in any large city. Loosely swinging handbags and ostentatious cameras are easily snatched by the desperate. Barcelona is not a den of iniquity: with due care and common sense, you can avoid dangerous situations. Carry enough money for the day, leaving the rest in the safe deposit box at your hotel.

At airports, railway and bus stations don't leave luggage unattended. Never leave anything valuable in a car, especially radios, even in a crowded street.

There are three main types of police:

Policia Municipal, tel: 092 – city police, known as *Guardia Urbana*, have a blue-and-white checked band around their caps and on their vehicles. Responsible for traffic, civilian care and security.

Policia Nacional, tel: 091 – state police, wear navy-blue uniforms. Responsible for law and order and civilian security.

***Above:** night-time fun*

Mossos d'Esquadra – autonomous police of Catalonia, in navy-blue and red. Mostly responsible for the *Generalitat* buildings.

In case of theft, assault or loss, you should first contact the Policia Nacional to make a statement (*denuncia* – vital if you want to claim on an insurance policy or seek further help from the City Police or your consulate. The main police station is at Via Laietana, 49.

The City Police has a special scheme for tourists, at La Rambla 43 (tel: 93 301 90 60, 7am–noon, 7am–2am in summer), offering legal advice, medical help, provision of temporary documents and a telephone line for the speedy cancellation of credit cards, etc.

Emergency Numbers

Fire Brigade tel: 080; **Ambulance** tel: 061; **Road accidents** tel: 93 352 6161; **Policia Nacional** tel: 091; **Policia Municipal** tel: 092

Accommodation

Barcelona has more than 400 hotels, offering a wide range of accommodation from the humble *pensión* to 5-star luxury. But the city has become an increasingly desirable tourist and business destination, especially since the high-profile opening of the Trade Centre on

Right: *keeping law and order during the Holy Week festivities*

the waterfront, and it's advisable to book accommodation well in advance of a visit. Most places will ask for your credit card number when you book.

You will find more availability and better prices in the hottest months, July and August, than in September and October (high season). Take care when choosing a *pensión*: it could have all the charms and comforts of staying with a local family or it could be rather squalid and next door to the local brothel.

Websites

www.aboutbarcelona.com provides general information on tourist events and articles on current exhibitions, hotels, maps, weather, etc. The site also lists things to do in surrounding cities.

www.barcelona-on-line.es/eng a crisp, clean site providing information for everything from restaurants to flamenco, and information on tourist services and entertainment.

www.barcelonanews.com daily online English newspaper covering current affairs in Barcelona.

Get by in Catalan

Good morning Bon dia
Good afternoon/evening Bona tarda
Good night Bona nit
How are you? Com està vostè?
Very well thank you, and you? Molt bé, gràcies i vostè?

Above: *striking facade of the Plaza Hotel*

Goodbye, see you again Adéu, a reveure
See you later Fins després
See you tomorrow Fins demà
What's your name? Com us diu?
My name is… Em dic…
Pleased to meet you Molt de gust
Do you have any rooms? Per favor tenen habitacions lliures?
I'd like an external/internal/ double room Voldria una habitaci exterior/interior/doble
…for one/two persons …per a una persona/dues persones
I want a room with a bath Vull una habitació amb bany
I have a room reserved in the name of… Tinc reservada una habitació a nom de…
How much is it? Quin és el preu?
It's expensive Es car
Could I see the room? Podria veure l'habitació?
At what time do you serve…? A quina hora es pot…?
Breakfast/lunch/dinner esmorzar/dinar/sopar

Above: *bright and brash window display*

How do you say that in Catalan? Com es diu això en català?
Speak a little more slowly, please Parleu una mica més a poc, si us plau
How do I get to...? Per a anar a...?
Is it far/near? Es lluny/a prop?
Where's the nearest motor mechanic? On és el pròxim taller de reparació?
Can I change this traveller's cheque? Pot canviar-me aquest xec de viatge?

Where can I find a dentist? On puc trobar un dentista?
This tooth is hurting Em fa mal aquesta dent
Don't take it out. If possible give me something for it until I get home No me l'extregui. Si és possible doni'm un remei fins que torni a casa
Please call a doctor Cridi un metge, per favor
Where does it hurt? On li fa mal?
I have a bad cold Estic molt refredat
I want to make a phone call to... Vull telefonar a...
It's engaged La línea está ocupada
I am... I'd like to speak to Mr... Sóc... voldria parlar amb el senyor...
What time will he be back? A quina hora tornarà?
Tell him to call me at this number Digui-li que truqui al número...
I'll be in town until Saturday Seré a la ciutat fins dissabte

Above: *in the mood for dancing – in Plaça Catalunya*